"In *A Thread So Fine*, Susan Welch has writt[en] history and love. The Malone sisters remind[ed me of an era] ago — when a woman's autonomy and self-realization often came at a price. Shannon and Eliza grabbed hold of my heart and carried it with them until the final, satisfying pages."

—**TARA CONKLIN,** *NEW YORK TIMES* BESTSELLING AUTHOR OF *THE LAST ROMANTICS*

"*A Thread So Fine* is a psychologically acute family story about the interwoven bond between two sisters, Eliza and Shannon, weaving an invisible thread running through their lives from 1946-1965. In *A Thread So Fine* the complexity, darkness and opacity of a family emerges... In this page-turner the reader sees not only what goes on around the characters and to them, but what goes on inside them... This gripping first novel announces the arrival of a strong, distinct and fully evolved new voice."

—**DIANA PAUL,** AUTHOR OF *THINGS UNSAID*

"*A Thread So Fine* deftly captures the complications of sisterhood in a way that is both intimate and relatable. This is a compelling family saga that explores the contradictions of the mid-1900s, a period when appearances did not reflect the often-fraught reality of women's lives."

—**ELISE HOOPER,** AUTHOR OF *LEARNING TO SEE*

"As romances, politics, and trauma arise for each sister, patterns of the past threaten to overwhelm and separate their connections: "Eliza pulled the receiver away from her face and brought it to her chest, her mind reeling. Again, Fa was asking her to bury her needs in the shadow of Shannon's trauma. Again, pushed aside by Shannon's neediness."Can the ties that bind prove changeable rather than breakable? Some things never change, and readers who undertake the journey of this evolving relationship between two sisters from childhood to adulthood will find that A Thread So Fine lassos the heart with stories of close connections tested by life's progression. Readers of women's fiction who especially enjoy stories of sister relationships will relish this engrossing saga of change and survival."

—**DIANE DONOVAN,** SENIOR REVIEWER, *MIDWEST BOOK REVIEW*

"There are so many issues in this beautifully written book: unwed mothers, veterans with PTSD, violence against women, a broken family, women's ambitions, and adoption. Welch makes her readers ache for these two sisters and their unnecessary separation for so many years. This is one of those rare novels that forces you to sit for a few minutes after you've finished reading it until you are ready to return to the real world."

—**MARY ANN GROSSMANN**, *TWIN CITIES PIONEER PRESS*

"Ms. Welch was herself adopted and this journey provided the impetus for her to write this wonderful book. I fell in love with the characters and their separate journeys. If you are searching for a wonderful summer read this may be the book for you."

—**MICHELLE KAYE MALSBURY**, BOOKPLEASURES.COM

"A Thread So Fine is one of the most memorable and inspiring historical fictions I've ever read. It exceeded all my expectations. My first impression was that this is an adorable story about two sisters, but it's a haunting tale with a rich story-line about a family torn apart by secrets with two incredibly powerful women at its core. The relationship between the two sisters was consuming for me. I ached at their estrangement and rooted for their reconciliation. Susan Welch portrays a family drama mirroring her own experience and fully mastering the genre."

—**LAURA BACH,** ONLINEBOOKCLUB.ORG

"In skillful, straightforward prose, Welch sets her character-driven narrative against the backdrop of postwar societal changes. Along the way, she implicitly contrasts the more traditional St. Paul society with the nascent progressive movements in Ithaca. The addictive melodrama weaves a tale of secrets, misunderstandings, resentments, and squandered opportunities for reconciliation that keep the sisters apart for almost two decades... An engaging and poignant historical novel."

—*KIRKUS REVIEWS*

"A touching story about family; A Thread So Fine will captivate and enlighten you...Susan Welch is a very talented writer; the story flows well and her attention to detail is fascinating. This book teaches you that not every family is perfect, and when things go wrong, you must take care of yourself."

—**REEDSY DISCOVERY**

"The prose possesses a sophistication with a certain air of wistfulness for a time long past. The dialogue doesn't suffer from any pretensions, and nothing feels too dated. The story hits a high note for originality, and the conflict between close families and the war between truth and lies ripping at the inner structure of family is very moving."

—**THE BOOKLIFE PRIZE**

NOTE TO READERS

This is a work of historical fiction. Some of Shannon's experiences are based on my mother's stories about her many months as a quarantined TB patient in St. Paul, Minnesota in the mid-1940's when she was nineteen years old. While many sites in the novel are real, others are fictitious. Milner Hospital is an imagined representation of hospital facilities such as the one where my mother lived as a patient, and was treated with surgeries such as those described. The St. Paul Catholic Infants Home, cruelly nicknamed 'Watermelon Hill,' was real, but opened in 1954 in St. Paul, Minnesota. I'm told it is also the place I called 'home' for the first days of my life in the fall of 1962.

A THREAD SO FINE

a novel

BY SUSAN WELCH

"… *You must lay your forefinger, the same that wore the ring, upon the thread, and follow the thread to wherever it leads you…. But, remember, it may seem to you a very round-about way indeed, and you must not doubt the thread. Of one thing you may be sure, that while you hold it, I hold it too.'*

The Princess and the Goblin, George MacDonald, 1871

PART ONE

1

St. Paul, Minnesota – August 1946

n the middle of a Charleston twist, one of the open-toed pumps Shannon had borrowed from Eliza snapped its heel. She slipped and plunged into the belly of a foot-tapping gentleman who watched from the dance-floor sidelines, the very image of Sir Winston Churchill. Grateful for the soft landing, she hoped that perhaps only a few people noticed. She straightened up, lightheaded, cheeks flushing with embarrassment as laughter erupted around her. Had her sister been nearby, Shannon wouldn't have minded and both would have laughed along. Anyone would find the scene funny, like a slapstick skit from Laurel and Hardy— she, the skinny, hapless klutz.

The College of St. Thomas's gilded ballroom reverberated to the swing beat of Glenn Miller, and the air, like the grand chandeliers above, shimmered with a lightness not felt, she supposed, since the Roaring Twenties. Shannon bent down to remove the traitorous shoes, irked that this morning's clandestine raid on her sister's wardrobe now required a confession. The man, probably a professor or dean like her father, smiled while using his fingertips to straighten his bow tie. With a generous wink, he took Shannon by the elbow and escorted her to a chair by the arched windows. Then, still chuckling, he delivered a cup of water from a nearby table and returned to his place as a spectator.

The band kicked up the tempo with *I've Got a Gal in Kalamazoo*. Shannon tucked a wavy strand of hair behind her ear and inhaled deeply. For a moment, the mingled, bitter fragrances of newly stained wood, freshly painted walls and polished floors stayed with her. She shifted impatiently in her chair, watching as dancers paired off and turned rowdy with fancy lifts and swooping drops. With Eliza, Shannon would've gladly stayed. The two would have danced the Lindy Hop barefoot, showing off moves they'd practiced all summer in the backyard—step, step, triple-step-twirl; step, step, triple-step-dip! Repeat, repeat, repeat, until they fell to the grass, exhausted, legs wobbling, arms aching, teasing each other, and laughing until their bellies hurt as when they were little girls. Instead, pumps in one hand, broken heel in the other, she left.

Night had fallen and white globes set like small moons atop slender poles illuminated the campus sidewalk. An opened pack of Lucky Strikes on the wide steps of the college chapel caught her attention, and with no one to stop her, she sat down beside it. She pulled out one cigarette, rolled it between her thumb and fingers, and inhaled its earthy scent. She looked about; seeing no one, she smiled and dropped her elbow to her knee while gesturing with her hand and imagining herself as Greta Garbo in the film *Mata Hari*.

If Shannon had been with her sister, they'd have walked arm-in-arm straight through campus across the street and into the house they'd lived in since birth, chatting like two birds on a wire, and Shannon would never have met the boy with a tilted grin and a mess of curly black hair who showed up in front of her while the unlit cigarette still hung between her fingers.

"Nice move in there. I liked your quick recovery." He sat beside her, his trousers almost touching the tulle skirt of her summer gown; still grinning, he raised his brow in a practiced shortcut to affection.

She smiled back, forcing away shyness to look right at him. "I can teach it to you if you want. It took me years to learn, though." She held her gaze steady, secretly recalling the game she used to play with her brother, Ed: who could stare longest without blinking.

He reciprocated, inched himself closer, and told Shannon that she had pretty eyes, especially in the light of a full moon. She looked down, unable to manage a poised response, and laughed instead, the same timid giggle she'd disliked in herself since childhood. She felt heat rise to her cheeks and said his were pretty too. Big and chestnut brown with long, thick lashes, they were the nicest eyes on a boy she'd ever seen.

He leaned back and took a brass lighter from his pocket. In a swift motion, his thumb flipped open the top and spun the striker wheel down to ignite the wick, which shone a halo of flickering light onto their faces. She brought the cigarette to her lips, wondering if he saw her hand tremble, and reminded herself to exhale as if she were whistling silently up to the sky, just like she'd seen in the movies.

She inhaled the bitter smoke and a set of sharp coughs followed. She sputtered, her eyes watering enough for a single, embarrassing tear to form. She wiped it away with a laugh. Her throat burned as if she'd swallowed hot sand, and she wished she'd not taken the puff at all, and then wished she hadn't laughed. She passed the cigarette to the boy, grateful he didn't laugh too, though she caught his slight smile as he put his arm on her shoulder. He patted her back—not in a firm, functional way as to help her regain a steady breath, but lightly, as if to say, *"There, there, child; you'll be all right."* After taking a single short drag, he dropped the cigarette and smashed the glowing end into the step with his shoe.

He leaned toward Shannon as if suddenly wanting to share a secret. His cheek grazed hers and lingered there, a musky fragrance of chocolate and cinnamon mixing with words as he whispered in her ear, "You're a sweet gal. Come visit me sometime. Southeast corner of Marshall and Fairview." He put the lighter in his back pocket and loped off to join his friends. Halfway across the lawn, he turned to look at her—or at least she thought he did—and she realized she didn't even know his name.

⌒◯

THE NEXT MORNING AS CHURCH bells tolled nine, Shannon stepped away from her bedroom window and the mounted square of rag-paper on which she'd penciled an outline of the red-brick chapel across the street. She cocked her head to the side and ran a hand through untidy hair, surprised at how her scalp, moist and hot with perspiration from the humid August air, bristled with sensitivity as if needles tipped her fingers. Glancing at the broken heel on her dresser, her cheeks flushed again as she imagined the boy from last night watching her careen into the man on the dance floor. She would never be as comfortable as Eliza around boys. With few exceptions, they made her feel out of sorts, and, aside from last night's little encounter, she'd rather not think about them at all.

Only if she saw this boy again would she tell her sister about her interrupted walk home after the dance-floor incident. She knew better than to tell Eliza about even one try at a cigarette—it would be just like telling Mother—but Shannon could imagine describing how the boy had moved close, his cheek brushing hers, how he'd whispered in her ear, and how her nostrils had filled with the spicy-sweetness of his skin. Even as she relived the moment, uncertainty picked at her thoughts—had he been flirting with her or did she just want it to be so?

Absent-mindedly exploring a tender bump in the crook of her neck, she leaned against the window's dark frame. For three days now streams of young men—mostly G.I.s in olive drabs—had been milling about campus like so many ants in a colony. Finally home, the soldier boys, as her father called them, poured back into daily life seeking more jobs than existed. Many, like Ed, had accepted the government's offer for free education instead. Distracted from her sketch, she watched from her upstairs perch as they strayed from sidewalks onto summer-browned grass and branched off in pairs toward the military surplus huts positioned in two rows on the field facing the Malone home. From the comfortable distance of her room, she searched their faces as best she could, ignoring the unlikely odds of recognizing a particular boy—especially one she had met only once and at night—amidst the campus activities of Orientation Week.

She returned to the watercolor, which, if it turned out, would be a long-promised birthday gift for Eliza. One leg of her easel—a clever French portable device from her grandparents who had traveled to Paris between the First and Second Wars—met the wall inches under the windowsill. A late-morning ray of sunlight pierced the glass rinsing jar, and captured by a brush's metal ring, reflected back into the pink water, illuminating it as if it were electrified. Shannon imagined crimson and pink poppies—a jarful of glorious, translucent petals bursting from spindly, opaque stems.

She crossed the room for a fresh perspective on the glowing water with stem-like brushes, the open window, her white paint-box dotted with vibrant colors, and the easel itself, all part of her composition. Hesitating near the door, she peered into the darkened hallway where the burgundy wool runner cascaded down the steps to the kitchen at the back of the house. She closed her eyes and wished for familial sounds—Mother working at the sink; Fa in his office preparing his satchel for work on campus; Ed cleaning eggs from the backyard hens. Eliza, who would normally be quietly moving about earlier than Shannon on a summer morning, remained at the lake house after deciding at the last minute to forgo the dance and help Grandma Edith in her garden.

An image of the boy resurfaced, and Shannon told herself she wouldn't be so timid if she met him again. What harm would there be in strolling through campus together one afternoon? ... If she found him. She looked at her diary where she'd written down the cross-streets he'd whispered in her ear and, despite nagging ambivalence, a new thrill traveled from her wrist to her neck, causing her to blush again.

All was quiet, she and the house, and the unwanted silence overcame her suddenly, like a tiny earthquake. A sharp kernel of air caught in her throat, provoking an unexpected cough that reminded her of the horrible cigarette. She returned to her easel and looked out again to the cream-colored masonry of the new Science Building and to the chapel's wide, stone steps where she'd met the boy last night. A couple sat so close that their thighs touched, and they laughed as they tried to calm their child, who danced about while pulling at his infant sister as if she were a doll. The young mother coaxed her little boy to relent, caressing him and whispering—perhaps promises of treats for good behavior.

Shannon only half-smiled.

2

August 1946

Nell caught her husband's frown as he read from the front page that due to the summer's polio epidemic this year's State Fair would be canceled. "Can you imagine? It's unprecedented. A dozen confirmed cases in West Minneapolis last month. Four children hospitalized from St. Louis Park alone."

On most Sunday mornings, after the family returned from Mass at the St. Thomas Aquinas Chapel on campus, Cecil settled his large, lean body into his chair at the head of the dining table and read aloud the best bits of news from the weekend edition Pioneer Press while Nell and the girls prepared a breakfast of hot buns and ham. But on this particular Sunday, the day of Nell's late summer picnic to celebrate the girls' high school graduation, Edmund's safe return, and Cecil's recent promotion to Dean, they had postponed the ritual until they'd found a site in Minnehaha Falls Park and unpacked the car. Only then did Cecil sit on the wooden picnic bench, unroll the newspaper from the delivery boy's tubular fold and remove the first section, running his hand over it to flatten creases.

"I'm glad they didn't cancel last night's dance. I didn't say so to Shannon, but I was pleased that she went on her own," Nell said. She unpacked the last baking dish from the picnic basket and glanced about. Here on the fields above the river, people still gathered. They hovered around tables laid out with summer meals, played tag football or croquet, or strolled along paths connecting one picnic site to another.

Sticky air hung around the tables and across the nearby bluffs above dense brush hiding the creek below. Distant church bells marked three o'clock. The lunch of salads and a summer casserole enjoyed and over, Nell settled in a portable picnic chair, took out her knitting needles and yarn, and laid the lavender skein on her lap. She buried her fingers in its cool threads and hesitated. Her eyes met Eliza's, and they exchanged a smile as her daughter cleared half the table for her grandparents so they could play Canasta. Nell pulled the two crossed needles from their nest of wool, set her forefingers at the ready, and commenced the ancient motion of yarn over tip, tip over yarn. Her entire body relaxed, and her thoughts wandered.

Eliza, her youngest who excelled at almost everything, looked happy. She had grown tall early like Nell—three inches short of six feet, fully curved at seventeen, and blessed with a confident ease and intelligence that intensified her youthful beauty—the kind of beauty Nell believed would turn to elegance with age and experience. Nell had known about her suitor, David Whitaker, for several months. She wondered what Cecil thought as they'd not much discussed the young man's interest in Eliza. David's grandpa, rooted in the Whitaker's modest lumber fortune, had been a state senator; his aunt served as the Chief Nurse of the local American Red Cross, and David's father and uncle had established a growing pharmacy business in St. Paul. He was a solid young man from a prestigious family, a varsity athlete, and one of St. Thomas's brightest freshman students. But still, Nell worried. Eliza was too young for love and commitment. Surely, Eliza would not want that. Not yet. She and Shannon both, unlike Nell at that age, had opportunities just beginning to unfold. Of her three children, Nell trusted Eliza most to make sound decisions—as she had done when she came to Minneapolis as a young runaway and eventually met Cecil.

Nell was not one to coddle children—even her own. But in recent years, she'd found many satisfying occasions to nurture both girls toward womanhood, although Shannon often rankled her nerves and caused her to worry. Sighing, she put her knitting down and strained to see Shannon, who'd earlier ventured beyond the bluff's edge to the river below.

"Eliza, find your sister and tell her to come back, please," Nell said. "I saw her go down toward the bluff, though I told her not to. She's too old for climbing through trees with that easel in tow. She can join the card game."

"All right, Mother," As Eliza spoke, she walked around the cloth-lined tables to take her cardigan from the back of a picnic chair, her bobbed hair blowing about her face as a warm wind passed through the nearby trees. "Did you see the skies over there?" She pointed to the west.

"Cecil, what do you make of it?" Nell rested her hands on the ball of yarn in her lap and looked to where black clouds formed a menacing layer beneath the gray ones. They hovered above a greenish aura that stretched upward from the nearby tree-line and blended into the darkening sky.

"Looks like tornado weather to me, Nell. Came in from nowhere," Cecil looked to Ed, who sat at a metal fold-out table practicing blackjack poker. "What do you reckon, Son? Do we have time for another slice of pie before the rain starts?" As Cecil spoke, a strong gust lifted a corner of the red-checkered tablecloth, tipping a vase of multi-colored phlox brought from his parents' garden.

A surge of cool wind rushed through the muggy air. Nell rubbed her bare forearms and looked to the sky once more. "No, I think not. Let's pack up before it's too late." She stood quickly. Her cotton dress snagged on the aluminum armrest, and the flimsy chair fell backward, tumbling a short distance with the wind. She ignored it and watched Eliza as she headed toward the river path. She'd lose sight of her before long. She stood petrified—skein of wool in her hands, the two needles fallen to the grass at her feet. Eliza disappeared down the rough, granite stairway surrounded by bushes that led to the dirt path and the sandy creek-side below. Nell's shoulders tightened; she held her breath and wondered whether Shannon had gone as far as the big river—Eliza would not find her easily if she had.

She held still, listening and looking toward the creek as a faint siren sounded far to the west. Something unpleasant, a remnant fear, grazed her thoughts like an acrid ribbon of smoke. A memory followed of lightning and explosive thunder shaking the plywood siding of a familiar hovel where the frightened child Nellie hid:

"Where the hell is thah lil bitch? Mary, where ehz she? Gaahdammit. I'll whup her ahss." Her father, tall and strong as an ox, had been an angry man. She recalled his boozy face bent with rage as he circled the room. A slurring, wicked dervish, he knocked into the table where Ma sat frozen in fear for Nellie, the child who crouched—eyes wide and alert, her breath suspended—in a crevice behind the tub in the far corner of the room.

"My God, Thomas, she's only seven!" Ma said.

From her hiding place, the little girl saw his beefy arm strike out, and his wrist make contact with her mother's cheek. She heard Ma gasp as the blow knocked her to the floor. A person never forgets such terror. She memorizes her fears and carries them well beyond childhood, the same fiends hiding in the thunder-crashes of summer storms, ready to strike with a vengeance.

Now in sight once again, Eliza bounded up the path carrying Shannon's easel. She smiled and waved broadly to Nell, an assurance that her older daughter followed close behind. Relieved, Nell exhaled and pulled the yarn to her chest before turning to clear the table of lunch and desserts.

Cecil and the children loved storms—lightning and thunder thrilled them, but not her. For Nell, unbridled forces of nature terrified her in ways her family could not understand. She paused, closed her eyes, and crossed herself in the Holy Trinity, praying for their safekeeping. Neither her husband nor her children had ever felt the fear she had—that of being alone in a clapboard house, howling wind menacing through thin walls, carrying rain mixed with dust that bit the skin and drove nails out of wood. They'd never been abandoned for days at a time, left to protect two younger siblings from thunderous storms and greater, more sinister threats.

Eliza bit her lower lip and studied her mother's profile from the backseat of Grandpa Theo's Cadillac. From where she sat between Ed and Shannon, she could see Mother's white-knuckled grip on the seat, her other hand clutching the back of her neck, her eyes wide open and alert. The car, a deluxe sedan, felt suddenly puny as surges of broad wind shoved and pulled at it until they'd crossed the Ford Parkway Bridge to return home.

Minutes later, after Fa had parked in the alley and they'd

unloaded the car, the storm crashed through the Merriam Park neighborhood where stately homes on oversized lots stood amidst giant elms and maples. Eliza stood in the enclosed back porch off the kitchen gripping Fa's large, smooth hand. Distant cracks of lightning and sheets of rain mixed with gusty winds barreled by and faded like the long rumble of a freight train.

"Where's Shannon, 'Lyza?" Fa cocked his head, his bushy brows arching over pale-blue eyes.

Eliza let go of Fa's hand and grabbed his wrist instead, the mesmerizing trance of the storm abruptly broken.

"She's downstairs with Mother, isn't she?"

Fa's jaw clenched; his sizable frame swung from side to side as he left the porch and ran into the house. Eliza heard him yell down the kitchen stairs to the basement, "Nell, Shannon down there?"

She didn't hear Mother's response, only Fa, his voice carrying above the noise of the storm, telling her not to worry—he would find Shannon.

Ed pulled open the screen door, but lost his grip as he entered from the yard; the wind flung it hard against the siding before slamming it behind him. Eliza flinched as a pair of lightning bolts lit the eerie-green sky and raced toward earth, followed a few seconds later by a crack of nearby thunder, then a loud, slow crash. She pictured a limb, probably a big one, of a nearby tree shearing and falling.

"Do you know where Shann is, Ed?" Fa called out as he crossed the kitchen to join them. "Mother is beside herself."

"She's all right," Ed said, shaking his head like a wet dog so that Eliza took a step back. "She came out in the coop to help me, making sure all the hens got in. One kept refusing ... I told her to hurry it up."

A siren interrupted them with a long, dissonant wail. Before it ended, Fa rushed through the door and ran to Shannon, who was half way across the yard, and pulled her inside. "We'd better all get downstairs with Mother. Who knows where the twister could be heading."

In the basement, Eliza went to Nell, who sat on an old loveseat by the boiler and took the place beside her. "It's almost over, Mother; the siren is off and the wind's all but stopped."

She noticed Shannon keeping her distance from them both; a good instinct, given the scare she'd caused.

When the late-afternoon light returned to the sky, Mother packed a basket with leftovers from the picnic and instructed Eliza to walk to Mrs. Sawyer's. "Be sure to let her know she can come and stay with us, Eliza," Mother said. "I hate to think of Gertie all alone after a day like this one."

Shannon, avoiding Mother after being reprimanded, snuck from the house unseen and joined Eliza on the front steps. Ed, Fa, and the Malone children's longtime friend, Harvey Bligh, gathered on the street with a group of neighbors around the fallen limb—almost as big as the trunk itself—that had smashed Dr. Prudholm's car. Humidity lingered, but the sky had cleared and a few sparrows could be seen nervously poking in and out of nearby bushes as if somehow at fault for the weather.

"Don't touch any downed wires, Shannon," Eliza said as they walked across campus and north on Cretin Avenue. "And be careful where you step, as there could be sharp things anywhere."

"I can see, Eliza," Shannon said with a cool edge as she twisted a loose strand of hair before tucking it away.

"Maybe, but common sense is not your strong suit."

"If you are referring to my argument with Mother, you can stop right now. I hate it when you do that." Shannon came to a halt, turned to face Eliza, narrowed her eyes, and continued, "I lack judgment; I'm irrational; I'm impulsive; that's all I ever hear from Mother. I don't need to hear it from you, too." She cleared her throat, and Eliza took the opportunity to take a tube of lipstick from her dress pocket. "Really, Eliza. Make-up? Now?"

"Well, Shannon," Eliza said as she lightly applied the color to her lips, "Mother does have a point. And lipstick is always appropriate. Want some?"

She smiled when Shannon nodded. Her sister was predictable, though not in a way that bothered her. Shannon craved Mother's approval, much more than she ever had. Although she supposed she'd never thought it missing—approval from any adult had always come easily. How often had Eliza wished she could intervene and overwhelm Shannon with the security she craved but never got from the very same mother? She'd imagined as a little girl that maybe a guardian angel could cast a spell over them, and she used to pray for such a divine intervention. But as she grew older, she gave up the notion. Instead, she considered herself Shannon's earthly protectress, and she admitted the sentiment sometimes turned to a feeling of superiority even as she struggled to avoid it.

Shannon returned the lipstick, and Eliza used a leaf from the ground to wipe the top of the pale pink tube. Wind had scattered branches and leaves everywhere, but the storm seemed to have been no worse here than in Merriam Park. She glanced sideways at Shannon, who still carried a wounded look.

"I'm sorry, Shann; forget I said that. You have plenty of sense; it's just not common." Eliza grabbed Shannon's hand and squeezed it. "It's nice to be out after a storm, isn't it?" As she spoke, they turned the corner onto Temple Court, and both girls stopped short.

"I had no idea—" Shannon shuddered and struggled to find words to continue.

"It's terrible," Eliza said, putting her arm around Shannon, who, though older, was much shorter and slighter. As Grandpa Theo liked to say, she was an Irish pixie-queen of a girl, while Eliza was a Nordic Valkyrie. She brought her other hand to her chin and pulled herself closer to Shannon. "I hope no one was hurt. Look at the Borchardts'; half of their roof is missing."

In the middle of the block, a telephone pole had snapped in half; the top part lay down on the street with wires dangling on both sides. Neighbors had barricaded it with sawhorses and benches. More than a dozen people milled about, dazed and grim as they surveyed the damage or gathered the debris littering yards, roofs, and sidewalks. Children clung close to their parents, wide-eyed and quiet.

Mrs. Sawyer, a compact woman with gray, pin-curled hair, sat perched on the edge of a wooden lawn chair. She wore a plaid frock, thick nylon stockings, and practical shoes. Eliza couldn't be sure whether the two men who lingered on the porch were coming or going, but most likely they were checking on the house for safety.

"Hello, Mrs. Sawyer." She nodded to the elderly woman she and Shannon had known forever as she crossed the lawn, avoiding clusters of debris and fallen branches. "Mother wanted us to check on you, but we had no idea the storm hit so hard here."

"So kind of you girls to come," Mrs. Sawyer said as Eliza bent to kiss her on the cheek. Shannon followed a step behind. "You can let Nellie know I'm fine; though it caused quite a scare. Come sit down for a moment." She patted the seat of an empty chair to her left and shook her head. "I wanted to get some air while the men check things out."

"We brought you some snacks from our picnic today. We left Minnehaha in time to get home before the rain started," Eliza said as she sat.

Shannon unfolded a red metal chair and sat down. "Are you sure you'll be all right tonight, Mrs. Sawyer?" she asked. "We have a darling guest room."

"I'll be fine. Would you girls like to stay for some lemonade?" She nodded in the direction of a small, square table, upon which sat a glass pitcher glistening with condensation. "We should enjoy it before the ice melts—or it'll be that much wasted sugar." Mrs. Sawyer gripped the aluminum armrest and shifted forward to leave her chair.

"Yes, thanks," Eliza said. "But please don't get up; I can serve it."

Branches and leaves covered the lawns—more modest than those in Merriam Park—as well as the pavement and narrow sidewalks running between them. A mess of unrelated items lay scattered like shrapnel across the neighboring lawns—one twisted bicycle wheel with several missing spokes, a metal grate, a large plastic tub. Eliza found it otherworldly—like Alice having tea with the Mad Hatter—that they sipped lemonade and visited in the midst of the upheaval.

"I hightailed it to the basement once the siren started," Mrs. Sawyer said. "I actually thought for a moment we were back to the War. Mr. Sawyer would have loved that storm. Except for the twister, of course. As loud as a locomotive. A real fright." She gestured to the end of the block fifty yards away, where the Borchardt house singled out for the tornado's worst destruction lay in partial ruins, the upstairs exposed like a ransacked dollhouse with boards and roof material piled knee-deep in chaotic pyramids in the front yard. "Look how close it came. Thank the Lord they're not home. Gone for the whole month of August. Won't they be devastated …? Oh my." Mrs. Sawyer shook her head and continued, "If Mr. Sawyer were here, my Lord, he'd have every able man on this block over there already."

Eliza remembered Mrs. Sawyer's late husband. Like Fa, he'd been a deacon at the campus church, well-known for his deep, booming voice in the pulpit that seemed out of step with his small stature and otherwise soft-spoken manner. The polio diagnosis had come as a swift blow the day after Easter Sunday last spring. He'd died less than three weeks later.

"You must miss him something terrible," Eliza said. "I hope the storm didn't frighten you too badly."

"I do miss him. But I'm quite all right, thank the Lord." She crossed herself, then kissed her thumb and forefinger as if holding a rosary. "How is your mother?" she asked after a pause. "I'll bet you girls didn't know how we first met Nellie and your father. On the day of a storm like this one. Oh, years ago now. Not quite as bad as today, mind you … but plenty of wind and rain, I remember."

"I thought they knew you from church, or from campus," Shannon said.

"Yes, indeed, but another chapter came first. We met your folks years before, in '23 or maybe '24. A summer of terrible storms—the year they built your house. So few houses around here back then, not like today. Ours was the first on this block, built in 1918, right before Mississippi Boulevard started going up with those magnificent homes. Your mother, God bless her, got confused out there in the rain—pouring cats and dogs; thunder and lightning … like today—Mr. Sawyer found her wandering about on Otis. He said he'd watched her cross the park, said she'd been frantic … searching for her children…." Mrs. Sawyer paused, squinting hard at no one in particular.

Eliza glanced over at Shannon.

Mrs. Sawyer noticed their silent exchange and continued, "No, that can't be right. Edmund came later, in '25, didn't he? Well, in any case, she'd wandered off, distraught and lost, beside herself, and he brought her here. She calmed down fine. After the storm, Mr. Sawyer walked her back to that big, new house your grandpa built for them. We thought it must belong to some rich, uppity couple. But not Cecil and Nell; no such thing. They're the salt of the earth, those two."

"She must have been thinking of someone else, don't you think, Eliza?" Shannon asked as they neared home.

Eliza slowed her pace and turned to look at Shannon, who'd fallen a few steps behind. "I can't imagine Mother would be frantic about anything." She waited for Shannon to join her. "She might have exaggerated—or maybe Mr. Sawyer found someone else out there in the rain. I think Mrs. Sawyer is older than Grandma Edith; she must be well over seventy. Memory starts to fade, you know."

"Mother may have been pregnant with Ed; maybe that's what confused her," Shannon said. "Did you know aphids are born pregnant? Grandma Edith told me that today."

Eliza shook her head, bristling at the thought of being tied down by pregnancy, now or ever. *Mother was just twenty when she carried Ed. Three years older than I am now.* She replaced the image of herself as a housewife with the more exciting idea of Orientation Day at St. Catherine's, scheduled for this Tuesday, a date she'd been looking forward to all summer.

"Eliza, there's David," Shannon said, as they turned the corner onto Cleveland Avenue. "It looks like he's talking with Ed and Fa."

"I can see what he's doing, Shann." Eliza winked at her and acted as if she hadn't noticed David as she headed toward the front steps of home with Shannon a step behind. She saw David watching her and heard him excuse himself from the conversation. Before she arrived at the door, he came up beside her and rested his bicycle on the edge of the porch.

"Hi, Eliza, Shannon, I came to check on you. I heard on the shortwave these blocks got hit hard."

"We're fine, David, thank you. Kind of you to think of us, though," Eliza said.

"How about you and I walk down to the river bluff? Oh," he turned to Shannon, "if you don't mind."

Acts of thoughtfulness such as this deference to Shannon had charmed Eliza even more than his good looks. "Maybe for a moment," she said. "Let me tell Fa we're going. I shouldn't stay out for long."

The Mississippi River ran to the west of the stately houses built on the edge of St. Thomas campus. David and Eliza crossed the boulevard and walked along the pathway leading into the park. Heavy winds, if not the twister itself, had passed through here as well, stripping smaller branches from trees.

"Did the thunder scare you, Eliza?"

"No, I wouldn't say so," she replied. "We've always loved storms in our family. Everyone except Mother. She'd rather we all stay in the basement from beginning to end."

"You don't scare easily, do you?"

"Oh, I don't know. Plenty of things make me afraid." She thought about this, and the image she'd conjured moments ago—a vision of herself surrounded by a gaggle of children and a round belly as heavy as a medicine ball—surfaced first. Of course, children didn't scare her; she feared being trapped here in St. Paul, married before she had a chance to … do what? She looked away from David toward the river as he reached out to take her hand. He led her to the edge of the stone wall around the obelisk in the center of the park.

"Things now … or in the past? Or in the future?"

"I guess I'm afraid of the usual: death, bad grades, spider bites, disappointing people … but I think I'm mostly excited about things. I can't wait to start classes next month. And you?"

"I feel the same," David said. "I want to help Pop with the pharmacies when I graduate. He plans to have three or four locations by then. I know it doesn't rank with the likes of Malone Steelworks, but it'll be plenty for me. Now with my cousin Pat back from the Pacific, we can really go to town."

She had an urge to step away from him, but instead took his

hand and led him to the nearby railing, where together they looked down the bluff to the turbulent river. Gifted in math and science, clean-cut and good-looking, he was also the most compassionate boy she knew. Harvey, their Cupid, had told her how David Whitaker, his best friend since second grade, had stuck up for him, even defending him once from a gang of older boys. David was "the real McCoy." But she wished he hadn't mentioned Grandpa Theo's business. The comment made her uncomfortable. Speaking of their family's wealth had been taboo growing up, especially with Fa. Plus, she didn't want to think so far into the future—at least not about things like building businesses, or putting down roots, or starting a family, if that's where his intentions fell.

"As long as you're not scared of me, we should be fine," David joked, ending the brief silence between them. "I like you, Eliza," he paused, "really, really like you, I should say."

Her eyebrows arched—an involuntary reflex she hoped he hadn't noticed. It wasn't as if she knew where she wanted to be, or what she wanted to achieve, but her life would be more than getting a degree and a marriage license. She didn't like being hemmed in—even by David Whitaker.

"I know you're only seventeen, but in some ways you act older than me," he continued. "Eliza, would you ... ya know ..." He searched for the next words.

She couldn't deny it; she did feel older than her classmates and friends—and David as well, although the opposite was often true. She held his gaze, buoyed by a light confidence.

"Would I ... dance a jig?" she teased. "No, probably not. Shannon's better at jigs than I am. But I can do the Can-Can!"

"Would you ... ya know, be my girl?" he blurted out as if he might lose courage.

What could it hurt, Eliza thought, to accept? It wasn't marriage, after all, just a boyfriend. Her first. "Hmmm," she demurred, tapping her forefinger on her cheek. "Does the title come with any special privileges? Free cough syrup? A discount on corn removal pads?"

"Very funny." David rallied and grabbed her around the waist, pulling her close.

An unexpected spark of pleasure ignited where his hand rested on her hip, sending a rush through her body like the long, slow brush of a feather. The gentle squeeze of his hand left her breathless. She tried but couldn't turn away from him. He held his face close to hers, and for a moment, her constant companions of reason and good sense faded into a mesmerizing joy. Everything changed. She wanted only for David to kiss her. His face flushed almost imperceptibly as he closed his eyes. When he opened them, she recognized the same emotion—she thought it joy—which overwhelmed her as well. He put two fingers under her chin, making her feel like a child, and somehow, the tables were turned.

David used his thumb to stroke her dimple once before tilting her chin and tipping his head to the side. He pulled her in. She put her hand on his chest, not as a barrier, but as an invitation. She saw his lips parting; he pushed gently closer, a hint of sweet, citrusy air followed as he exhaled. Just like the movies, she thought, her eyes closing as if on cue. His lips, at first dry and cool, turned supple and sweet like his breath. She wanted more. She leaned closer and slipped her hand from his chest, down to his side, to his waist. Later that night, Eliza reckoned her first kiss had lasted only five seconds, though it felt at the time like an eternity.

"Nicest kiss I've ever had," David murmured, his face inches from hers.

She smiled wryly, thrilled but wrestling with doubt. She was crazy about David, but going steady? What would Mother and Fa say? Was she allowing it to move too quickly? Her mind couldn't resist a flashing series of scenes: boyfriend, wedding, babies, working at the pharmacy. What about college? A career? Travel? She hadn't yet considered she might not be able to have both: a conventional boyfriend, husband, family, and also satisfy her yearning to participate in the bigger world, wherever it may take her. Fa and Mother both expected she could and would do whatever she put her mind to, and, unlike Shannon and most girls she knew, she had plenty she wanted to do on her own. Eliza suspected she hadn't yet discovered the interests that would most ignite the passions of her mind and direct her future. She knew her thinking might be considered unusual, but surely life—at least her life—should, above all else, be an intellectual journey, a journey of personal growth. Could she take that journey with someone like David? With any boy? She stopped herself from going further. She was smitten by David, and he with her. For right now, that felt good enough.

"I'll be working at the pharmacy all week. Do you think you could meet me for lunch one day?"

"Shannon and I are going to St. Kate's for registration and a campus tour Tuesday. Of course, we don't need it. Fa taught classes there for years during the War. We could leave the tour part early," Eliza said, knowing Shannon would be pleased with the invitation to join them. "We could meet you at the pharmacy afterward."

"It'd be swell. Pat will be there too. He came back to work last week. Poor guy. Ma says his nightmares are fierce, and he got a stomach bug over there he can't get rid of. He's tired all the time."

"Do you see him lots?"

"Yes, but it's not like before. We used to go hunting with Uncle Royce, and you couldn't shut him up when it came to nature. He knew the names of every living creature, especially the small ones: frogs, butterflies, even beetles." David squeezed Eliza's hand. "Now, he can't seem to find his stride. In one way, he's fine: talks to us for a while, smiles and laughs, then his face darkens and his eyes glaze over, and before you know it, he excuses himself and leaves. If he didn't look the same, I'd hardly recognize him as the same guy." David shoved his free hand into his pocket and kicked at the gravel. He tilted his head in the direction of the Malone home, put his arm around Eliza's waist to guide her to the pathway, and continued, "I miss the old Pat, but Ma tells me it'll take some time."

"It'll be nice to meet him, I'm sure," Eliza said softly. What had she been worried about a moment before? Why would she not be excited to be his girl? David was the sweetest, most considerate boy she'd ever known.

They stood together, holding hands on the porch. Eliza could hear Mother and Fa talking with Ed in the parlor behind the closed screen door.

"You haven't given me a real answer yet, Eliza," David said, holding her gaze.

"I'm honored to be your girl, David," she whispered to be heard by him alone. She stood on her tiptoes and pecked him on his cheek, putting to rest the small remaining voice of doubt.

Once upstairs, Eliza stopped by the open door of the room she and Shannon had shared as young girls and peeked in to see Shannon sleeping. She cleared her throat in her sleep, her breathing shallow as she rolled over to face the wall.

Tomorrow she would share with Shannon every detail of her walk in the park with David and try to explain the new territory she'd entered, more impulsive than planned, more head-over-heels than logical.

3

August 1946

Forty-eight hours after the storm, electrical power had not yet been restored to the homes on their street. A note in Mother's loopy script had been placed on the corner of the new Formica table, which fit against the kitchen wall between two stairwells—one leading to the second floor and another leading downstairs to the basement. Shannon filled a glass with tap water before sitting down alone to her daily breakfast of bread and jam.

Girls,

We don't yet have working electricity—no telephone either. Edmund is on campus, helping with clean-up. I am at the chapel, then to Garden Club. Will be home by 1 or so.

I'd like one or both of you to run errands with me this afternoon—maybe two o'clock?

Please clean the chandelier before you leave the house.

M

Without leaving her chair, Shannon leaned toward the portico behind her, tipping back the two front legs so they left the floor, and called upstairs. "Eliza? Aren't you up yet?" Her throat caught and a painful cough took her by surprise.

"Damn this damned summer cold," she muttered to herself, while looking around, expecting someone to admonish her either for mistreating the new furniture, cursing, or possibly both.

Eliza was less than a year younger than Shannon; her Irish twin, relatives liked to say, winking year after year across the family dinner table. Although Shannon couldn't imagine why, she sensed Mother approved of, and even secretly relished, the recurring comment.

"Yes, difficult—although I can't imagine it any other way." Pause. Sigh. "Just ten months and twenty-seven days between them." Mother would sigh again and shake her head as if she'd had nothing to do with the matter.

Only the color of their eyes had set them apart as children when they'd looked similar enough to be mistaken as twins. Eliza's eyes were pools of silvery blue rimmed with a thin smoky halo, bright with a confidence Shannon admired but occasionally scorned. Her striking eyes framed by dark, long lashes made Eliza not simply pretty but beautiful, while Shannon's mono-color blue ones did nothing to distinguish her. Hers were like most other eyes in the Malone family for that matter, probably like a good portion of the entire population of Irish-Americans.

Shannon did not begrudge Eliza her beauty or her precociousness. She considered herself to be plenty talented in ways different from Eliza, but she worried about her shortcomings. A certain kind of trouble, mostly harmless, followed her—and she felt too easily reminded of it.

On a summer day years ago as a child playing make-believe behind the garden shack near the alley, Shannon discovered a slow mouse, which she trapped in a corner and caught barehanded. Delighted, she remained crouched, and, cradling it in her palm, stroked its silky, gray back with her forefinger.

"'Lyza, come see what I've got. It's adorable."

But her mother, not Eliza, had come out of nowhere and bellowed, "Drop it. Right now, Lady Godiva."

She smiled now at the mysterious reference Mother made when upset about something either she or Eliza had done. When Shannon finally discovered Lady Godiva's story, the comparison to a beautiful, headstrong noblewoman venturing naked through the cobbled streets of England centuries ago in defense of the poor pleased her. A woman! But at the time, the shock of Mother's disapproving bark and the painful pinch as she lifted her up by the tip of her ear had crashed through Shannon's happiness and dissolved it. Even now she could recall the hot sting in her flesh as she released the little rodent and fought back tears by squeezing her eyes shut until they hurt more than Mother's angry grip.

That same year the headmistress of St. Joseph's primary school for girls suggested that Eliza, six years old and "smart as a whip", be moved up a grade. Mother and Fa had agreed, hoping her presence might help settle Shannon and focus her academic performance. Shannon admitted it did both.

She heard the water running in the upstairs bathroom. A moment later, Eliza appeared, skipping down the stairwell's last three steps. Shannon pushed Mother's note across the table. "Is there enough time? If not, you can explain that for once you slept late, not me."

"We'll need to be at St. Catherine's by ten o'clock for registration. I said we'd meet David by eleven-thirty. If we start now, we can manage it."

Shannon smiled when Eliza's face brightened at the mention of his name.

"You want to join us, right?" Eliza turned to the sink as if she didn't need to witness the obvious answer.

Shannon looked longingly at the electric fan, unplugged on the floor. The August heat had crept into the house and dizzied her when she stood. She hesitated and leaned both hands on the table edge for support. Eliza didn't notice; she'd finished an equally small breakfast and followed her to the dining room where Shannon had gathered the necessary items: two large enameled bowls, several towels, vinegar and warm water. Shannon covered the midsection of the walnut dining-room table with a single wide sheet of cheesecloth and poured equal parts of each liquid into the matching bowls.

"Why don't you take the crystals down, 'Lyza, and I'll dip them?"

"Let's open the curtains to see if the sun will make prisms. It's called refraction, Snell's Law," Eliza said when they'd finished, and Shannon bit back a retort—as if they'd not completed the same high school science course two months ago!

Eliza drew back the gauze curtains, and the sun struck the oval-shaped crystals, sending multi-colored shafts of light shimmering above the wainscoting on the white dining room wall. The girls sat at the corner of the table with the bowls and towels in front of them, transfixed by the display they'd seen dozens of times before.

As a child, Shannon had believed—and had convinced Eliza—that the crystal drops held the same magic they'd discovered in Fa's storybook worlds.

Fa had been Associate Professor at St. Thomas, where he'd taught nineteenth century English literature. He'd had a special affinity for children's authors. Characters from the fantastical stories of writers like Edith Nesbit, George MacDonald, Kenneth Grahame, JRR Tolkien, Lewis Carroll—the list went on and on—had grown as familiar to the three Malone children as real cousins and neighbors.

"I'm not sure about St. Catherine's, Eliza," Shannon said. "I'm nearly petrified about starting classes there. Sometimes, I get almost physically sick when I think about it." She watched as one crystal took a slow, final turn and cast a flickering shaft of refracted light on the wall. "I think I'd rather take a few art classes now and start at St. Kate's next year."

"For goodness sake, Shannon, you're only taking four courses. It'll be far easier than high school. And I'll help, though I don't believe you'll need me. You did plenty well at St. Joe's. Why would you worry?"

Shannon's thoughts had been jumbled lately by a physical weakness she attributed to a mounting dread of yet higher academic expectations. Or perhaps it arose from her discomfort around boys and dating, which she'd begun to see as an unavoidable gateway to a family of her own. Four days later she had still not mustered the courage to visit the chocolate-cinnamon boy. Her uncertainty seemed even more shameful knowing that Fa had made his way to the position of Dean of Academic Affairs at St. Thomas and that Mother had worked to earn her way through the U of M before she had turned twenty. That her parents had met, courted, married and given birth to Ed before Mother completed her degree unnerved Shannon all the more. Why did it all seem insurmountable to her?

"You're coming with me today. Don't you even think about ditching. You'll be fine. You'll see." Eliza smiled, grabbed her by both hands and pulled her up. "You should be grateful Mother and Fa don't expect us to marry and mindlessly procreate—at least before we finish our studies. I don't care if I ever wed unless it's to a man who's smarter than I am."

Eliza put the rags under her arm and used both hands to carry the bowl of water into the kitchen. "Let's get this mess cleaned and go. We'll have time to stop at Woolworth's on the way. They've got bunches of new patterns in."

"Why can't you use two regular words, like 'have babies,' instead of one fancy one, Eliza?" Shannon said, sighing, as she removed the remaining items from the table and followed Eliza. "And what's wrong with getting married and having a family?"

"Nothing," Eliza said. "I'm just happy I have a say in the matter."

Shannon sometimes wished she could feel the confidence Eliza felt, to interact with the world as Eliza did, to have the world embrace her as it embraced her sister.

SHANNON SLIPPED IN THE FRONT door, she hoped unnoticed, as the grandfather clock struck noon. She spied a sliver of Mother's back as she knelt in front of the bottom compartment of the ice-box and placed a large covered bowl inside. The new electric refrigerator wasn't much good today. How had people managed before ice-boxes? she wondered as she removed her shoes. She imagined herself two inches tall and invisible, sneaking by Mother and taking a nap in its cool racks, finally able to rid herself of the gnawing discomfort that had distracted her for several days.

"Shannon?" Mother called from the kitchen.

"Yes, Mother?"

"Please come and help me a bit. I've got ham soup from Saturday—we can eat it cold tonight. We should finish what we have from the picnic too. If the electricity doesn't return by tomorrow, we'll have a problem."

Shannon finished drying the blue-ceramic bowls and sat down at the kitchen table with a seed of hope that maybe Mother had spent her anger elsewhere, or had released it like any good Catholic should during her Confession yesterday.

"Where is Eliza, dear?" Mother asked, handing Shannon a bowl of radishes for slicing.

"She's having lunch with David Whitaker."

"Yes, and you came back early?"

"I was ready to come home. The registration line stretched outside, and the room was so hot I thought I'd die. David's cousin Patrick showed up at the pharmacy afterward. You've heard about him, haven't you?"

Shannon avoided mentioning that despite oppressive midday heat, she'd gone several blocks out of her way, hoping to meet the boy who'd grazed her cheek with his and whispered in her ear. At the intersection of Marshall and Fairview, she'd taken her time watching from across the street as he—the mop of hair unmistakably his—filled a customer's tank at the corner gas station. A girl, blond and pretty, and maybe a few years older than Shannon, had leaned against the pump stand. Shannon had watched as she playfully gathered her full mane and placed it so it fell over her right breast, while her other hand rested on her hip. The boy abandoned the pump-handle, leaving it to fill the tank, and leaned against the same stand so close to the girl that Shannon could no longer see a space between them.

Heart sinking, Shannon watched the girl tilt her head and laugh as she stroked the boy's cheek with the palm of her hand; she watched as he brushed the girl's hair aside and inched closer as if to whisper a secret. Shannon's cheeks reddened, the thought of secrets suddenly repulsive. She quickened her pace, almost running to the next bus stop at the end of the block but not quite able to find the energy to do so. Her chest constricted with foreboding like a hot, moist sponge being twisted and wrung, and her legs threatened to buckle. She slowed to a stop, leaned over and put both palms on her knees while trying to catch her breath.

During the last fifty feet of her walk to the bus stop, Shannon saw pricks of light—tiny stars swimming in a puddle of darkness above, even though the sun shone brightly. She suddenly felt not quite right about this boy—not quite right that the flirtation might have amounted to something true, something like what Eliza had with David. But in the absence of confidence one way or the other, her heart held onto its idyllic moonlit-campus vignette. Just in case.

Shannon's attention came back to the kitchen when Mother responded, "Yes. I read about his return last week. Was he polite?"

The act of recalling David's cousin and describing him to Mother made her images of the boy at the gas station fade. "Patrick is absolutely dashing. He looks like Gregory Peck, only more dark and handsome."

Mother chuckled. "I hardly think that's possible, Shannon." She wiped her hands on the cheesecloth towel and joined her at the table. "His parents must be relieved to have him home."

"Well, he's a grown man; he's twenty-five. He barely acknowledged me—I think he was impressed with Eliza, though. She came off cool as a cucumber. She pretended she hadn't heard about him being MIA. Patrick didn't want to talk about it anyway. I don't think he wanted to talk at all."

"Eliza has the good sense to realize some stories are better left untold. I'm sure he saw some horrible things ... missing for two years ..." Mother looked over her glasses at Shannon across the kitchen table. "Also, Shannon, you know Edmund's hens would survive just fine out there in the coop, storm or not. Even if not, you should have come in here with us when you were called. Bad enough your dress is full of stains from holding wet birds. The hem is fallen too." Mother sighed. "Honestly, Shannon, you're nearly an adult. Time you start acting like one."

"Mother, please don't be angry. The lightning was magnificent; even Fa said so." She rested her cheek on her folded arms. "I'm tired, and I think I'm coming down with something. Swear to God, I almost blacked out on the bus."

"Watch your language, dear." Her mother's tone softened: "I think it must be the pollen. Happens to you every year come August. If you aren't feeling better in a few days, we'll see if Dr. Johnston has something to help, although I doubt it. Rest half an hour now, then we'll go."

Nell sighed, picked up her knitting and kept her eyes on Shannon as she took unsteady steps up the kitchen stairs to her room. The thought struck her that her daughter, small and slight at eighteen, was three years older than she'd been when, in her fifteenth year, she'd run away while her widowed father and young siblings Abel and Jessica slept.

Shannon in no way reminded her of her younger self. Instead, Shannon's lack of guile brought memories of Ma. Nell mostly remembered her own mother as a pale, ghostly woman who lay dying under a thin sheet of muslin in the corner of her grandmother's modest home in the rocky farmland of eastern Oklahoma. But she could still recall a faded image of the younger mother who'd taught her to read storybooks and maps of foreign countries, to figure numbers on the palm of her hand, and to dance to the unaccompanied music of her clear, soprano voice. Memories of that infrequent happiness came to her only as dreamlike bits of light that floated above her and disappeared, as fragile and iridescent as soap bubbles.

At age eight, Nell had assisted the birthing of Ma's twins in the corner of their two-room shack, an hour's walk from Grandma's homestead. She could not forget the local midwife, a red-faced bundle of a woman the likes of a fairy tale witch who thrust bloodied towels at her small body as if she were trying to shove Nell away for good. While Grandma held Ma's hand, Nell had done as she was told, partly horrified by the blood and moans of her mother, but also entranced by the midwife, whose skill emanated from each motion as the two babies—soon to be motherless—made their painful journey out and into the world.

Months after her eleventh birthday, when the twins turned three, Grandma had pulled Nellie close and told her, "There'll come a time when yea'll see the chance to leave that mean bastard of a man, and yea'll need to act with courage. Yea may never see me again, but yea'll know yea have every right to find yer own way—to be who yea want, to find what's important to yea."

Soon thereafter, Pa packed their few belongings on the old mule-cart. He and his children left with enough food for a fortnight and without saying goodbye to Grandma or anyone else. After years of moving north, one town at a time, of anticipating the nightly tirades of a drunken widower, of suffering his vicious blows, and of stealing food from strangers' gardens to feed her mother's babies, Nell had taken the chance to flee that Grandma had predicted.

Now, Nell lost herself in her knitting.

Later, another storm brewed across the Minnesota skies south of campus, and gray clouds slowed the afternoon pace. Nell stepped outside to take measure of the darkening skies and wondered whether the rain and wind would be as unrelenting, as frightening, as they'd been two days ago. When had they seen such a dramatic August?

WHEN ELIZA HAD RETURNED FROM her lunch with David, she'd

spotted Mother in the kitchen knitting as if in a trance. She left before being noticed and walked alone back to the park, not intending to recreate Sunday night's scene with David. Or maybe it was her intention—but what was wrong with that? She closed her eyes and leaned back against the railing where she and David had kissed two nights ago. An unsettling image of Patrick Whitaker darkened her memory. She didn't know what to think of his older cousin who'd joined them earlier in the day at the soda fountain in the front of the pharmacy. He and David looked remarkably alike, though Patrick looked every bit the six years older, and more serious. His smoky gray eyes gave him a broody intensity absent in David. When Patrick smiled, a short, hairline scar caused his lip to curl awkwardly to one side, making Eliza feel self-conscious, as if he could sense her strange and frightening urge to reach out and touch it.

David had stepped behind the counter to help a customer, and Eliza had caught herself, seconds too late, staring at Patrick's profile. He'd turned his head to look at her and then spun slowly on the stool until his knee touched hers. While he watched the flame of his lighter flicker on the tip of his cigarette, he'd asked her if she'd ever smoked one.

"No, I have not," Eliza had replied. "I find them dirty, and Mother says they can't possibly be good for one's health."

Recalling the exchange, she wished she'd ignored him. Instead she'd given him cause to deem her prim. Immature. Exactly the person she didn't want to be.

"Hah!" Patrick had said, still looking at the glowing tip as if fueling it with his stare. "Mother knows best, then." He'd switched his focus from the cigarette to Eliza, and his steely gaze, somehow distant and close all at once, had caused her heart to pound. "Well, I'm going to smoke one now. I guess I won't ask you to join me, princess." He'd lifted his chin, curved his lips into a rueful smile so the scar pulled at his lip, then had taken a prolonged drag of smoke and with slow deliberation swiveled back to face the soda fountain.

The brief exchange agitated the memory of an otherwise lovely visit with David, wedging itself in like a sliver. Eliza ran her fingertips over the fraternity pin David had fastened on her blouse and returned to the walkway, heading for home.

IN HER BEDROOM, VERTIGO OVERCAME Shannon. She reached for a bedpost and sat at the foot of her bed. As she'd left the kitchen, she'd caught, or maybe imagined, a concerned look and hoped Mother's anger had vanished. Storms strengthened Shannon. Blizzards, lightning, thunder, driving rain; events such as these brought the people she loved together. A pity the elements sometimes caused so much damage. Right now in the calm of a hazy summer afternoon, surrounded by the hand-stitched, lavender coverlets and matching curtains she and Eliza had sewn as young girls, her row of treasured Dionne Quintuplet dolls looking down at her from the shelf above, a prickly heat pulsed through her, like a wave of tiny shards pulsing under her skin and in her teeth and eyes.

Shannon fell into a nap. She awoke minutes, or maybe hours later, in a fit of coughs. In search of a handkerchief, she sat up and reached to open the drawer of her nightstand. Her vision blurred. Her neck ached. Another cough came and another. Not yet trusting herself to stand, she gripped the folded cloth and shut the drawer.

Looking up, she caught a glimpse of her face—flushed and hot—in the small mirror sitting atop the embroidered blotter on her bedside table and recoiled as she recognized the bright red droplets on her lips as blood.

Like a series of heavy doors shutting one after the other,

Shannon's mind retreated. She stood, regained balance, and stepped into the hallway. She needed to get Mother. Now. Mother or Eliza. Now, Now! Cold in her fingers and heat in her scalp confused her. She imagined herself disconnected from her legs and feet, though they followed her wish and took her to the top of the kitchen stairwell, a safer course than the open stairs leading down to the foyer. Once there, she considered in hazy fragments returning to her room. But her knees buckled, her body crumpled to the floor, and she tumbled down step after step until the curved walls stopped her limp and unconscious body.

4

August 1946

Shannon regained consciousness at the base of the staircase, and the kitchen came into focus along with Mother, who, in a series of hushed, insistent phrases, instructed her to lie still: "Don't move," she murmured, then, "Stay still, Shannon," followed by, "Doctor is coming. Fa will be here soon."

Shannon tried to order events in her mind. She could only recall waking hot with fever and on the verge of collapse. She didn't recognize the tremble of Mother's hand, and she recoiled as Mother pressed a cold, moist towel to her aching left eyebrow. Mother responded by relaxing her palms so that they once again became steady and warm against Shannon's skin.

Her mother formed questions in a quiet tone as strange to Shannon as her shaking hands had been: Could she breathe properly? Did she feel pain anywhere else? Was her vision blurred? All the while, she gently prodded each limb of Shannon's upper body to check for broken bones.

Mother's kindness, like that of an angel, surprised Shannon. She had a fleeting thought, which she'd not been able to recall either a moment later, or ever again: had she died on her way down the stairs? Had an eternity passed and she now resided in heaven, well on the other side of mortal life?

The screen door in the kitchen swung shut, and Dr. Johnston's familiar voice called out, "Hello." He arrived quickly at Mother's side and repeated the physical checklist of Shannon's limbs.

Mother stepped back and stayed silent, a clenched fist pressed to her lips. Shannon could hear her breathing and see the white of Mother's knuckles. She imagined the layer of smooth skin covering them to be as warm and soft as her palms had been, and she yearned to feel her gentle, capable hand pressing into her fevered skin again instead of Dr. Johnston's clammy fingers. She tried to suppress a cough, then another.

Dr. Johnston took a pillow from Mother and inserted it under Shannon's upper back. "No broken bones, just the gash above her eyebrow," he said as he bandaged the cut. "But that cough, Shannon." He pulled out his stethoscope, and his face drew tight, his bushy, graying eyebrows crowding around the bridge of his nose. "Let's take a look. How long has that been going on? A few weeks, I'd bet."

After being given an injection to relax her muscles and an oral dose of a green liquid to bring down the fever, Shannon heard murmurs between Mother and Dr. Johnston. She thought she heard a third voice—maybe Fa's, maybe Ed's. Though she tried to concentrate, the fragments floated away before she could put them together.

She recoiled weakly at a prick on her finger and again at a cotton swab wiping the inside of her cheek, both which she supposed would be used to diagnose something, though she didn't know what. Fear gave way to an inviting drowsiness followed by a dreamless slumber.

A FULL NIGHT HAD PASSED since Shannon's fall, and Nell's sleep had not returned. Her eyes remained closed, her body heavy with drowsiness, but she lay awake listening for faint but familiar footsteps in the hallway.

"Sorry, Nell. I went back downstairs to read on the couch," Cecil said, his voice low and, to her ear, gravelly and strained. The mattress sagged as he sat on the edge opposite Nell, who lay on her side facing him. "Before I knew it, I'd nodded off. I checked on Shannon. She's fast asleep. The basement's so cool; I put the extra blanket on her." A few seconds passed and, with a small note of guilt, he added, "Can't help thinking about tomorrow's meeting with the president."

Nell saw the shadowy profile of his face in the mirror across the darkened room. "It's all right, Ceece. You're right to be preoccupied with the new school year. Dean of Academic Affairs …" She paused, then said in a whisper, "And now, Shannon."

He came to bed and drew close to her. She put the palm of her hand on his chest and rubbed in a slow, circular motion—a simple act of marital language, intimate and comforting to both.

After two decades of marriage, Nell still felt Cecil's attraction, as primal as when they'd first made love. She often saw his cheeks flush red when she loosened her hair and brushed it around her shoulders, or when she caught him looking at her reflection in her dressing mirror. Nell complied, always, as she did now. With slow-moving hands under the bedsheet, she inched her cotton nightgown up to her hips. As he positioned himself behind her, the full length of their bodies touching, she relaxed her pelvic muscles, placed one hand on his bare thigh, fingertips of her other hand guiding him, his arousal as erect and firm, as hungry and insistent as it had been on their wedding night. Fair or not, she did not share his physical desire as she had in their early years. Nell's heart had never released Cecil from his part in her anguish at the death of Baby Theodore, nor had she yet overcome the fear of conceiving and losing another child.

Often, in the moments after Cecil fell away satisfied and lulled toward sleep, un-beckoned memories of her blue-eyed baby, cherubic with a billowy mass of curly red hair, surfaced and still stung four years after his death. "All suffering is relative," she had told herself again and again, as she had stood like a pillar of salt beside the casket of her youngest child, who didn't survive to see his second winter.

For a dozen weeks after she had discovered Baby Theodore, ash-gray with death already stiffening him in his crib, she had walked from one place to another as if the devil floated beside her coaxing her to the edge of insanity. When she lay down to rest, her head echoed with cries, distorted, strident, amplified, from her own unendurable childhood. She took them to be the demons and dead souls of a hell she absolutely believed in.

Cecil had suffered their unspeakable loss as much as she had, Nell thought as she lay in bed, but in those first weeks and months she'd been unable to console—or be consoled. She had trusted, quite mistakenly, that God had forgiven her with the birth of Theodore as proof, and she had opened her heart to the baby in a way she had not sixteen years before with Edmund, nor with Shannon and Eliza thereafter. The shameful secret of leaving her twin siblings, Abel and Jessie, in the sole care of her widower father had burrowed inside and damaged her. Nell approached bonding with her three older children distrustfully, and over time.

Nell pushed the memories away, and edged toward Cecil so he would hold her, his large, muscled body enveloping hers, making her feel safe as only he could. Nell's nights had been restless and peppered with anxiety for two years until the War had ended and her eldest had finally returned home just weeks ago. On the day of his deployment, she'd predicted God hadn't finished punishing her and that Edmund, her uncomplicated, good-natured boy with a strong physical likeness to Cecil's father (thankfully not her own), would be killed in some far-off land, wounded, terrified, alone in his final moments.

Now, she conjured a vision of another smaller child, eyes locked forever with fear, but lifeless. Her heart fluttered and a dark thought struck her, and the fleeting safety of Cecil's embrace fell away. It wasn't Edmund whom God had set His sights on, but Shannon, the child whom she knew felt her affection least of all.

⁓

SHANNON AWOKE, BACK IN HER bedroom, to find Eliza sitting by her side with a moist, cold towel in her hands. She placed it on Shannon's forehead, the back of her other hand stroking Shannon's cheek. Eliza's hands, Shannon held a dreamy and fragmented thought, *Eliza's perfect hands.... I should paint them. A new watercolor ... they are more familiar to me than anyone's. Even my own.*

"The electricity's back," Eliza said. "Are you?"

Shannon smiled thinly. "How long have I been sleeping? Wasn't I in the basement?"

"Yes, you were, for a whole night. You slept almost twenty-four hours, you lazy head. I came home from lunch with David yesterday and found you napping. Next thing we know, you're at the bottom of the stairs in a heap. I see what you mean you're not ready for college ..." Eliza, her eyes downcast, did not convince

Shannon in her small talk.

"What's the matter, Eliza?" she asked, unable to suppress a note of alarm.

"Not sure ..." she said, her eyes still diverted. "I told Mother and Fa I'd tell them as soon as you awoke. I'll be back in a moment." Eliza went to the top of the stairwell and called down, a surprise to Shannon since yelling in the house topped the list of Mother's pet peeves.

"Edmund will be here soon, Shannon; he went to get Mother some supplies," said Fa, who had come into the bedroom. "How do you feel, darling?"

"I feel ... all right," said Shannon. "Why is everyone here?" She could not catch up; she bit her lower lip to stop it quivering. She saw Eliza and Mother exchanging furtive glances; her sister grabbed her hand, while her mother sat on the bed beside her.

"Shannon, Dr. Johnston says you almost certainly have tuberculosis," Mother said in a quickened, matter-of-fact voice that only frightened her more. She looked at Shannon and held her attention as if to hypnotize her, the way Ed hypnotized his hens in the backyard. "In a few hours, an ambulance will take us—you, me and Fa—to the hospital ..." Mother's voice buckled. Shannon watched her strained eyes as she paused to regain her composure. "... where you will stay for quite a while. Fa and I will visit you as much as they allow."

Eliza squeezed Shannon's hand as if doing so could stop the tears forming in her downcast eyes, her face contorting though she tried to control it. Shannon felt a knot in her chest and her sore throat constricted, making it difficult to swallow. Eliza managed a reluctant smile but did not speak again. A welcome breeze passed through the room, and Shannon looked to the opened window. She felt removed, as if seeing herself and her family from afar, maybe from another world.

Eliza could not shake from her mind Shannon's changed expression when she'd heard Mother say tuberculosis. The word itself sounded vulgar, menacing as it crossed her sister's face like a dark stain, clouding her eyes and draining color from her cheeks. Sitting at the kitchen table, Mother across from her, Fa and Ed on each side, all three leaning forward over their teacups, each sounding as if the grim reaper sat at the table with them, Eliza tried focusing on her hands resting on her lap, but even so, struggled to follow their conversation. Such lack of concentration was foreign to Eliza and this, too, frightened her.

"After Shannon goes … to the ward …" Mother's strained voice hesitated. Her words faded in and out, but Eliza heard her say, "… we will have the bedrooms sanitized. Fa and I are leaving now for Lake Minnetonka; Grandma and Grandpa need to know, and telephoning won't do. We'll bring them back here to see Shannon before she leaves." Mother seemed about to cry, something Eliza had seen her do only once--on a day she could not bear to think about, especially now.

Her parents exchanged a brief, sorrowful glance and Fa continued for her. "If you must go upstairs, then be quick. Shannon is …"

"We'll go with her in the ambulance to get her registered," Mother finished when Fa fell silent, "and you'll bring Grandma and Grandpa back to the lake house. Best if you and Edmund stay with them for a few days."

Eliza turned her attention to Ed. He reached his hands across the table and looked at Mother as if to give her courage. She had never seen Ed act with this kind of compassion, and she felt a prick of physical pain that their lives had already begun to shift, that a private natural disaster worse than the twister whose damage they'd so gratefully avoided just days ago had forced itself upon them.

~~○~~

Eliza slipped back into Shannon's bedroom, the one they had first shared as a nursery sixteen years ago. Electricity had returned and the family's two largest fans had appeared—one on the dresser facing at an angle blowing air out the window, and the other, newer one at the foot of Shannon's bed, oscillating indifferently on the slow setting. Eliza relaxed with the constancy of the curved, metal paddles circulating in their round cages. The whirling sound reminded her of cicadas that had once, years ago, descended upon St. Paul in the heat of summer, an infinite number of harmless creatures, large and unbeautiful, making a brilliant staccato chorus high in the branches of elm trees where they mated.

"If we capture enough of them," Shannon had said, "we can see exactly how they make their sounds."

But Eliza had not let her. "They'll die, Shann. And it would be our fault. Bugs won't do in a box what they need to do in a tree. It's not their instinct."

Now the sun had moved beyond its midday peak. Eliza absorbed the familiarity of the two fans' production as if they might be a source of cleansing and spiritual strength. If only the current of air could blow things back to rightness. Back to how life had been before the storm. She looked at Shannon's pale hands clasped together and pressed between her cheek and pillow. Though she hadn't noticed before, Shannon's face appeared drawn. Eliza wondered how she'd overlooked the disappearance of its healthful glow— the pink color of cooked rhubarb, as Grandpa Theo would say to tease their vanity. Until today.

"Shann?" she whispered. "Shann, are you awake?"

Shannon opened her eyes soberly as Eliza sat nearby on the floor with her legs tucked under her.

"I am, Eliza. I'm afraid to sleep. I'm so very tired, but I'm scared I'll wake up and be gone." She closed her eyes again and a tear fell, like a punctuation mark, on the pillow. Eliza, a stickler for verbal clarity, didn't know precisely what Shannon meant but found that, in this case, she didn't want to ask. Shannon being gone for quarantine was one thing—but her being truly gone? Unthinkable.

"Aren't you afraid of getting sick?" Shannon asked.

"If I am not sick now, I doubt I am going to be in the next hour. And if I already have it, well, so be it." Eliza said. "Please don't be afraid, Shann. Please. Come now, I'll lie down with you for a moment."

Eliza propped her own two pillows against her sister's headboard and rested her weight on her left shoulder, putting her body above Shannon's; she pressed her chin to the top of Shannon's fevered head and reached over for her sister's hand, damp and tense, which she held until it relaxed in her grasp as Shannon fell asleep.

5

AUGUST 1946

A week passed with Shannon lying in a pale green hospital room big enough only for an infirmary cot and a chair. Strictly issued orders for nothing but rest came regularly through older, disinterested nurses. No reading, no laughing, no excessive chatting (a silly rule, she thought, since no one could visit her anyway), no moving about unless the doctors deemed it necessary. Coughing, vomiting, drowsing medications and sheer exhaustion kept Shannon from defiance; she could barely stay awake.

She had no issue with this first, private place she occupied at Milner Hospital. She felt grateful for its smallness. About the size of the kitchen pantry at home, in her few moments of consciousness the room could at least be imagined as cozy. Mother had brought a few items— a bedside clock, her silver crucifix and rosary, her quilt from Grandma Edith and a lovely wax violet in a tiny pink vase from Eliza.

At her bedside, while still too weak to walk but less feverish, Shannon met Dr. Johnston, Mother, and Fa. For the first time, the doctor who brought her into this world confirmed the diagnosis: advanced pulmonary tuberculosis. "Shannon, I won't sugarcoat it. You are a very ill young lady. With rest and treatment, you have a chance of recovery. But it will take many months"—he hesitated and looked away from Shannon to where Fa stood with his arm around Mother's shoulders—"and perhaps, surgeries. There are no guarantees."

Moments later, a nurse pushed Shannon in a wheelchair down a series of halls and then through a long, narrow ramp leading to the floor below. Without speaking a word, she stopped to check in at the workstation, looked at a chart on the counter and resumed the course through the door across the hall marked QUARANTINE.

Now in a cavernous room bigger than her high school refectory and just as uninviting, Shannon looked around and felt the eyes upon her of a dozen or more women with varying degrees of the deadly infection.

Once transferred to a larger bed at the far end of the sterile, overly-bright room, Shannon looked toward the small window in the one door facing the main corridor and the nurses' station. If she'd had the strength to bolt out of bed and run, Shannon thought, she'd do it now. Instead, exhaustion was giving way to anxiety. She needed to relax the passages of her throat and stop the nauseous waves teasing at her chest.

"One. White pillow. Two. White sheets. Three. White ceiling. Four. White shoe. Five. White … White window frames. Six.

White stools. Seven …" She tried to avoid the strange, pale faces following hers as she searched for another white, cream, or even light yellow item to inventory.

She looked again at the not-white door, just as Mother walked in with the nurse who'd wakened Shannon that morning.

"Are you counting your whites, Shannon?" Mother asked in a kind, modulated voice Shannon thought she'd never heard before.

Disturbed that Mother somehow knew of her private ritual, Shannon responded with a weak nod. Not that Shannon cared to think about this right now—because seeing Mother pleased her—but did she also know how it began, or when? Or how much Shannon had depended on it for a sense of emotional safety, hundreds or maybe thousands of times as a very little girl?

In her earliest memory she sat on the smooth stump of an elm tree. She had been four years old. "One. White posts. Two. White sleeping dog, well, sort of yellow. Three. White dog bowl. Very white." She held her mama teddy bear—Eliza had been given a similar papa one—while playing her very own counting-colors game. It'd been late in the day, near dusk; she'd heard crickets chirping, a sound she loved. She'd looked around to see if any of her adults—Grandpa Theo, Grammy Edie, Mother, Fa—were near, as she knew they had been seconds ago. No. Not even Eliza or Ed.

She pulled at the hem of her little mama bear's dress, then at the perfect lace hem of her own. Had everyone disappeared from the yard? Her bottom lip pushed out, and her eyes stung. Shannon resisted the tears; babies cried, not her. But the thought struck her hard—hard enough to create a hollow pit in her stomach—if she were truly alone, perhaps she wouldn't exist at all.

"One. White post. Two. White-yellow dog …" Still sitting on the stump, she counted whites again as if the action were already an old, soothing ritual from the time before, when she'd felt safe and not invisible.

The gray metallic bed frames, trays, and chairs, and the shiny green and black tiled floors of the hospital room had terrified her at first. They conspired to bring Shannon back to a place and time where the unique tools of surviving childhood once again became vivid and useful. But now she could see Mother, and Fa must be close by. Her heartbeat slowed; she relaxed her shoulders and stopped counting. Her chest, though aching with infection, expanded enough to invite calm, and her nausea receded. Mother took her hand, and Shannon closed her eyes to sleep, listening again for crickets.

~

THEY DROVE UNDER FAMILIAR CANOPIES of gigantic maples and elms, marshlands, and open fields before hugging the water's edge and finally reaching the gates marking the long driveway to her grandparents' home, a plaster and beam mansion overlooking a large bay in the south end of Lake Minnetonka.

Eliza, who shared her grandmother's love of gardening, sensed that adjusting to the lake-country society of Wayzata had come easy for Fa's mother Edith, a slight, unassuming Swedish grandma out of a Hans Christian Anderson fairy tale, who wore privilege and wealth like an old, favored housecoat. She, herself, had designed the flower and vegetable gardens that surrounded the wide steps of the large verandah. A few native red maples had survived Grandpa's drastic clearing and were scattered around the lawns like gigantic misplaced sentinels.

Eliza passed the time as she'd always done at the lake house, reading and swimming and reading again, except now it felt dull without Shannon's company, and she constantly awaited news from the hospital. Grandpa Theo spent little time at home. He traveled back and forth to his manufacturing plant near Duluth, even as he claimed to be retired from day to day management.

Grandma Edith kept busy in the kitchen and gardens, and Ed did his best to be a ready companion. If friends were nearby, she didn't care; socializing didn't interest her.

Ed walked down the dock to where Eliza sat dangling her feet in the cool, clear water while watching the minnows gather around the bread balls she'd dropped as if throwing pennies in a fountain for good luck. "'Lyza, I'm leaving tomorrow morning for campus," he said.

"Et tu, Brutus?" She couldn't help but pity herself. She handed him the bag of bread and leaned back far enough to rest her elbows on the dock's rough wood planks. The very act of thinking, which had always been a friend to her, seemed now an enemy. As new thoughts surfaced—tuberculosis, college, womanhood, Shannon—and turned dark, she rejected them by standing or sitting or turning away and then forcing her mind elsewhere. By staying close to Ed these last few days, she'd managed to function almost normally again.

"One more week until your classes start, right?"

"One week is forever, Ed," Eliza said. "Besides, what'll happen then? It feels all wrong to go on with college classes while she's in there."

"Shannon is right where she should be. It's the best thing for her. You know it's true."

Eliza couldn't help thinking it came too easy for Ed to compartmentalize Shannon's uncertain fate into a convenient platitude. She considered a rebuttal: what about the TB? People died from tuberculosis, and Shannon's diagnosis could hardly be any worse. How could Ed be so undisturbed? But instead of saying anything, she dropped her head and kicked at the minnows circling her toes in the water. She bit her lip, surprised to feel the sting of tears again.

She saw, gratefully, that Ed didn't seem to notice. In her current mood she'd snap at him if he had, and she would regret it.

He continued unaware, "Roger Scofield's family is hosting an end-of-summer dance at the Lake Club this Saturday. How 'bout I ask David to come back here with me Saturday morning? We can spend the day together and go to the dance."

"That'd be lovely, Ed. It would. Only, I don't know if I'm up for a dance right now." Unwilling to admit it to Ed, just hearing David's name brightened her. Spending time with him here at her favorite place on Earth would be wonderful—if she could break from her dark mood.

"I'm sure David doesn't care if you go to the party or not. And it'll do you good, Eliza. Did I tell you he'll be in my dorm this year? Right down the hall."

Edmund put down his bag of bait from the pantry and opened the wooden dock box Fa and Grandpa had built years ago. He found an old pole with its line and tackle intact, set a live worm on the hook, and cast the line fifteen feet out.

Her feet still dangling in the water below, Eliza stayed to watch the bobber float toward them as he reeled it in. She looked toward the house where the late afternoon sun threw bright shafts of light on the large windows of the second floor. Grandma Edith—her floppy, straw hat tied neatly under her chin and large sunglasses obscuring her eyes—leaned forward on her knees as she weeded the flower gardens that trailed from the house to the shore. Eliza closed her eyes and conjured the playful ghosts of her childhood running up the slope to bring a younger Grandma gifts from the lake. As a child, Shannon had been more resilient in the face of Ed's outdoor games, his dares and misadventures, more curious about his backyard menagerie of fowls and orphaned dogs or cats, and more willing to be an accomplice in his unsanctioned experiments. Eliza had preferred to stay clean, safe, and on the good side of adults; in those days she'd cast Ed in the lot of immature, trouble-seeking, and misguided boys. What did she care if Shannon wanted to invite trouble and dirt, especially when a library of Fa's childhood books awaited her upstairs?

She tried to identify what had changed about Ed, because despite her initial doubts, she considered him a different, better person since his return from the War. No longer boisterous in the way that used to drive her mad, his presence, at least for now, comforted her. She wondered if he felt different since his return. She couldn't shake the thought that although he was easier to be around, something about Ed had never been, nor ever would be, clear to Eliza. When they were young, Grandpa Theo would tease him, saying, "Boy, if you stand for nothing, you fall for everything." Fair or not, lack of conviction had since been a moral failing she ascribed to Ed.

"Why do you suppose Fa spent so little time here with us in the summers?" Eliza asked, missing her father, and suddenly remembering how she and Shannon celebrated his rare arrival by chasing his car down the long driveway and jumping into his arms when he emerged laughing, ready to play with his girls.

"I suppose it's because he liked to work, plus he didn't always see eye to eye with Grandpa, you know."

"No, I didn't know. Why do you say that?"

"Not sure why—it's just so. I always saw them as opposites. Fa is a devout intellectual, and Grandpa is more of a wheeler-dealer, self-made type."

"It's too harsh to call Grandpa those things," Eliza said. She thought of Grandpa Theo as a modern-day Ulysses, slaying monsters and weathering storms cast at him by angry gods. "You make him sound like a common hustler."

"What do I know, 'Lyza? I think Grandpa's spot on. I hope to work with him once I get my engineering degree. Stainless is the future as far as I can tell. Malone Steelwork's on the cutting edge, you know."

How simple it is for Ed, Eliza thought. Even fifteen months in the middle of the South Pacific had not shaken his optimism.

Ed was neither a good student nor athlete, but with his large eyes that won forgiveness easily, his tanned face and curly blond hair, girls flocked to him. His uncomplicated nature, despite what she might have thought about it, made people want to do things for and with Ed. Much more like Grandpa Theo than Fa. Difficult to reconcile, but true.

Eliza curled up on a lounge chair and took her stationery pad from her bag. The afternoon sun had mellowed. High time, she thought, to write to Shannon. Perhaps it would shake her from her dismal brooding.

September 4th, 1946

Dear Shannon,

Edmund and I are stuck in Wayzata, which simply isn't fun without you—the lake is cold, the fish are gray and grouchy, and all we do is help Grandma with chores. (I hope that makes you feel better, darling sister!) I know Mother is visiting you as much as they allow; she and Fa were here over the weekend and told us everything.

Shannon, I hope you understand—I couldn't write until now because I was sick with worry and not very pleasant to be around. Everyone has been very kind to me, which somehow made me feel more miserable. But I feel now that you will be fine. Fa says you are being so brave and that the scar from the gash above your eye is nearly disappeared so you don't look like a pirate anymore!

I want to hear about everything—your routine, your roommates, the gossip! I know very well you don't care for writing letters, Shannon, but really, you must. We can save them all and show them to our grandchildren someday. Can't you see them now, clamoring around your rocking chair? (I'm kidding about that ... you'll be jumping on the bed with them!) "Granny, did you stay in a hospital THAT long?"

Fa says your fever had subsided, and that you have more energy now than you have had since the terrible 'D' (for Diagnosis) day. Mother says while the women are in their thirties or older, you're befriending them all and that you behave much better with them than you do with her. She says there is one woman in particular, Betty, who you find easy to talk with. I can't imagine what it all must be like. I can't wait to meet them—especially Betty—but in the meantime, please write me.

Your loving sister,
Eliza

6

SEPTEMBER 1946

liza's spirits recovered by her first morning on campus at St. Catherine's, and at times she believed Shannon might be all right without her constant worry. She walked from Our Lady of Victory Chapel to Derham Hall as if she were Queen of the campus or Dean of something (like Fa); it didn't matter what. She was charmed by everything: the vast, well-groomed lawns leading down to the fish pond; the geranium and begonia gardens scattered around campus; the students—all women—walking and chatting between buildings, all marked by the quarter-hour chimes resounding from the chapel bell tower. Their message, "You belong here. Always."

"Eliza Malone?"

Eliza smiled at seeing a familiar face and waved, feeling like she'd been here at this very place in the heart of St. Kate's for years.

"Jody? Did you start classes yesterday? I didn't know you were here."

Jody Remminger was an only child who'd grown up in a Cape-Cod-style home on Lake Minnetonka, three properties down from her grandparents'. A frequent visitor to the lake house, she had charmed Eliza and Shannon as little girls; she knew every hiding place and could recount every intrigue in the tightly knit community of homes around the prestigious bay.

"I thought about U of M, but it's too big. I'd heard you planned to postpone at least a semester—due to Shannon, you know."

"I changed my mind," Eliza said. "I'm glad I did in any case. No sense wallowing around at home with nothing to do. Besides, Mother and Fa insisted."

"How is Shannon? Mother said she'll need surgery, maybe more than one. Is that right?"

Eliza stepped back and pursed her lips, masking her distaste for the question. Mother had not seen Mrs. Remminger in years, and aside from annual holiday dances at the lake, she and Shannon had seen Jody very infrequently. "We don't know yet. She's doing quite well, though. I'll be going to visit her next week. I can't wait to see her."

"You're going to visit? Aren't you frightened? A room full of sick women?" Jody caught herself. "Though I do suppose they keep it very clean. And she's your sister, after all."

"Are you finished with classes today?" Annoyance edged Eliza's voice despite an attempt to hide it. Was this type of gall regarding Shannon's illness something she would regularly encounter?

Jody shook her head. "One more. My calculus class starts in a half hour. Mother of Grace Hall."

"We must be in the same one. I'll see you later. I'm heading to the bookstore now," Eliza said, leaving it there.

~⌒

"Shannon, finally, I get to see you. One more day and I would have gone mad," Eliza said when she was close enough to Shannon's bed to not disturb her neighbors.

She struggled to reconcile the solemnity of the large, rectangular room so unlike the vision she'd created in an effort to calm her anxiety. Eliza wanted to believe the TB ward would be like a college classroom before the professor enters, buzzing with laughter and chattering women, a place where Shannon would feel safe.

"Is it always like this?" she asked.

"Not really, we're just resting now," Shannon replied. "In the mornings, all of us Catholics pray together, afterward we chat a while, while the nurses do medications—everyone loves that, of course." She rolled her eyes and smirked. "When breakfast comes, we're pretty much all dressed up with nowhere to go, so to speak. Then we have medical hour where we each get our treatments and measurements and what not. It's not all bad. I think we're tired by this time of day, and the nurses insist on plenty of quiet anyway."

Mother and Fa had described the room to Eliza in such detail that she'd expected familiarity. Instead, she was taken aback by the sickly sheen of the pale-green walls and austere metal structures, and more so by the fact that Shannon had managed to adapt.

"Thanks for the letters, Eliza. They're swell. I'll start writing back, I promise, I will," Shannon said. "Have you found a dress pattern for the Harvest Ball?"

"Mother says I can buy a ready-to-wear. I'm so busy with class work. I can't imagine sewing. I wish I could pack you in my purse and take you shopping with me. I'm trying to decide which color." She waited a moment. "It doesn't bother you for me to go on and on, does it?"

"Of course not, 'Lyza. I need to know all about it, before, during and after. But I want you to meet Betty. She was working the women's dresses floor at Dayton's, living on her own downtown and dating a darling man who's working in Sioux Falls, right up to the day she couldn't get out of bed. She's the next youngest after me. She's wonderful, and I'd be a mess if she weren't here."

If Eliza hadn't known otherwise, she would've thought Betty was not a patient, but a visitor to the TB Ward. The woman, several years older than Shannon and nearly as tall as Eliza, wore pale-blue capris and white oxfords, and she'd piled her mane of red hair on top of her head in a loose twist, kept in place with a black elastic band.

"Nice to meet you," Eliza said, fending off an impulse of insecurity brought on by a combination of Shannon's gush and Betty's confident manner. "Is your family from here?"

"My, yes. I'm the fifth of ten. Pops is in the hospital, too. He's down the hall recovering from an acute attack of the hiccups—true story! Poor Ma doesn't know which way is up."

A large, red porcelain piggy bank sat on Betty's nightstand with a sign taped to the front that read, Betty-B's New York Dream Trip Fund. Below it was a sketch of a young woman with wavy red hair standing in front of the Statue of Liberty and waving a flag with a big 'M' for Minnesota.

"Oh, that," Betty said, when Eliza asked. "Mom and Pops have a laundry shop, and they have a matching piggy bank there asking for donations. It's mostly for fun. They know how much I want an adventure."

"Don't forget, Betty, I'm coming with you," Shannon said, looking sideways at her sister with an air of triumph Eliza knew was intended for her.

7

November 1946

I n the four months Shannon had been in the ward, she had embroidered dozens of autumn-themed tea towels, holiday napkins with holly leaves and snowflakes, and pudgy little boy and girl figures. It would come as no surprise if the combined needle and thread output of the twelve women in the TB Ward was enough to supply all of France—Versailles, Alsace, and, of course, Paris, and a few other places she'd add to her list if she ever did get out of here. Embroidery was a poor substitute for worldly adventures, very poor indeed. She put down the last in a set of six towels stitched with white snowflakes and dancing snowmen, and swore aloud to never take up a needle again.

"That's what they all say," Betty said. "There's always a new napkin waiting for idle hands around here. I'm going to sneak out for a smoke, Shannon. Bud's waiting for me there. When I get back, I'll brush and braid your hair if you feel well enough."

"Say goodbye to him for me. He was so kind to bring the candied oranges."

"His mother makes more of those nasty peels than we do stitches. I'll tell him, though. He sure is sweet."

"Don't let him know how you feel about his mother's cooking if you know what's good for you. Not yet anyway."

"I've got more sense than that. By this time next year, I'll have a diamond ring on my finger; I'll wager money on it."

"That's all fine and good. But don't think I'm not holding you to our promise."

"Come hell or high water, Shannon, we are going to New York City for New Year's Eve, 1947. I promise," Betty said, her smile replaced with frank sincerity.

Friendships ran deep between women in the ward. Ed had once written in a letter from Manila saying that in a strange way, the war had made him better, and despite the horrors on the front, he cherished the uplifting comradery with his mates. Shannon now understood. During her first terrifying weeks in the intake ward, instructed to stay inactive, thoughts of death teased at her mind so that she'd prayed aloud for sleep to come. The day she transferred to the main ward, she feared loneliness amongst these strangers would drive her to insanity.

But her fear of emotional isolation was unfounded. Almost overnight, Shannon became part of the daily routine of the twelve women in the ward. They made light of the strange intimacy forced upon them, bound together in their quarantine. There was no gallows' humor about their shared disease, but plenty of joking and chatter that seemed at times as if they were school girls away at summer camp.

At first, Shannon chafed under strict orders for bed rest; she wasn't allowed to even sit up without permission. She learned through the women's stories that the sharp edge of desperation would lessen, and while fear remained and loss hid around every corner, a carefully woven fabric of friendship and unity would help her survive. As she came to appreciate years later, her experiences at Milner Hospital had provided valuable tools of resiliency unique to those who had suffered and survived together as she and these women had.

Not everyone was cured. Mary Lou Norman—Lu Lu as her husband called her—had died two weeks ago. A quiet, reserved black lady in her mid-thirties with caramel-brown eyes and freckles across her nose, she was an exotic beauty to the white girls in the ward. With an island accent left over from a childhood in Barbados, she spoke softly as though perhaps afraid to share a thought. But she sang with a resounding contralto voice, the likes of which Shannon had never heard before.

The many ills of TB pervaded all the ward's women, each privately measuring her place in the ever-changing pecking order. With Mary Lou gone, Shannon understood she was now the most seriously afflicted patient. The probability of her own untimely death frightened her, so to overcome the fear, she'd learned to narrow her thoughts to the past and the day at hand. Only rarely would she let them wander to the far-distant future—to the imagined days where she and Eliza would recount stories of their youth to their grandchildren.

~⌒

Eliza couldn't shake her yearning for life as it had been before the August storm in the days leading to Shannon's collapse. Before her sister's first procedure in October, Eliza had alternately paced around the house or holed up on Fa's office couch, sinking into internal monologues of the worst possible outcomes. This second time around felt almost as terrible.

Despite their usual restrictions regarding dates with boys, Mother and Fa encouraged her to accept David's invitation for dinner and a movie on Friday night before Christmas. The evening was to be a family celebration of his eighteenth birthday. It helped that dinner would include his parents, his sister, Jan, and according to the note from David, his older cousin, Patrick.

The holiday movie of the year, It's a Wonderful Life, disappointed Eliza, though the affable Jimmy Stewart was her favorite actor—that wouldn't change—and a movie couldn't go wrong with Donna Reed. But the many dark scenes unsettled her. Despite redemption in the end, the movie was too heavy-handed. Simply not merry enough. She much preferred last year's Christmas in Connecticut, a family film that made everyone laugh. Of course, last year had included Shannon as well.

"And by the way," she said, speaking mostly to David and Jan as Patrick drove them home, "why was the villain, Potter, allowed to get away with his theft? Did you think it was fair, Jan?"

"Do you kids mind if we stop at the pharmacy for a moment?" Patrick interrupted. "I think I left my house key there."

On the three occasions that Eliza had been in the company of David's cousin, she'd noticed he was sometimes abrupt and had the manner of appearing bored by conversation. Twice she found herself studying him, only to have him catch her staring, as he'd done the day at the pharmacy months ago. Maybe she imagined it, but his facial expressions seemed awkward, like an automaton following some internal, mechanical instruction. Yes, he was handsome, but he made her uncomfortable. The more she tried to peg why, the more uneasy she became. The awkwardness of those unfortunate moments felt obvious to her. Right now, she was grateful to be in the backseat next to David, who was holding her hand between both of his.

"That's fine, Pat. We can walk a bit—nice chance to see the holiday decorations," David said.

"It'll just take a moment," Patrick said. "Your parents won't mind, will they, Eliza?"

"Not at all. They might not be home, not yet anyway—though Ed might be."

"I doubt Ed'll be home," David said. "The dorms are still open, and I'll bet he's at the holiday party for the basketball team tonight. Would you like me to stay with you for a while?"

"No, David; I'll be fine. Besides, I don't think Mother and Fa would approve."

The holiday lights along Marshall Avenue glittered red and green, illuminating the street as if night had never arrived. Nativity vignettes, playful displays of top-hatted snowmen, and piles of outsized gifts around Christmas Trees adorned the storefronts—all more abundantly than in recent wartime years. Eliza and David held back, falling a few steps behind. Jan caught up to Patrick and looked back, giving them both a wink before saying, "I'll visit the pharmacy powder room, while we're at it."

David put his arm around Eliza's shoulder, and together they ducked into a shop portico near the pharmacy. He held her close and whispered into her ear, "You look beautiful, Eliza." Then he stepped back a little, still embracing her. "I especially loved your fuzzy sweater in the movie theater," he added, making light and smiling.

On an impulse, she took his hand, ungloved it and guided it under her coat, and under the white-angora sweater he'd given her for Christmas. She held his hand there between her cotton slip and the soft-knit garment, while holding his gaze, wordlessly inviting a kiss. One eyebrow rose in surprise, and he brought his lips to hers. She moved his hand to her breast, and a thrilling rush took her breath away.

FROM THE FRONT PORCH, ELIZA waved goodbye to Patrick, who'd dropped off David and Jan at their house on Summit Avenue before bringing her home. She unlocked the front door and entered the foyer, tired but elated, already anticipating her next date with David. She wanted to memorize their moment in the shop's alcove, her blush of happiness and the unexpected flash of desire. She smiled as she removed her overcoat, galoshes, and shoes.

Her happy mood dimmed as she envisioned the complicated surgery Shannon had endured hours ago. An unexpected fear rose in her chest as she walked into the cold parlor, its familiarity robbed by the silent darkness. She rushed across the dining room to the kitchen and turned on the lights. As quickly as the fear had come, it faded into a sense of solitary calm.

Fa's leather satchel sat on the kitchen table, and Eliza thought perhaps he was here after all. A note had fallen to the chair: Shannon had taken on a fever. Fa and Mother planned to stay at the hospital's family quarters for the night. She should call them there if she needed anything.

How few the occasions that she'd been home at night with no one else to keep her company. There had always been at least Shannon, and in recent weeks Mother had called on Ed to return from his campus dorm whenever she thought they'd be late or chose to stay overnight. Since late August, her grandparents had planned regular visits so Fa could stay on campus if he needed to in the evening, and Mother would not have to worry. But tonight, the house was empty. Eliza was at the base of the enclosed stairwell when a knock on the kitchen door startled her. Her back muscles tensed, and her skin prickled with a rush of adrenaline. She turned around to return to the sink, halfway to the door.

Another insistent knock came, followed by another. Eliza thought she saw someone standing on the porch between the kitchen and the yard, with his back to the screen door. A man? Was Ed locked out? The figure was too tall. Was it Patrick? The bright beam of a flashlight crossed the yard, and several of Ed's chickens squawked, ruffled by the commotion. She pressed the button to re-light the ceiling lamp, and peered at the grandfather clock that sat against the wall in the foyer. It was just after nine pm. She crossed the kitchen to the back door.

"Patrick Whitaker, is that you? Are you all right?" Eliza unlocked the door, confused. Why would he be here?

"I'm not all right. I need help. I've been right across the street. 'Lyza, I need to come in."

Only Shannon or Ed called her 'Lyza, and she neither appreciated nor understood the familiarity from this person she'd met but three times. "Patrick, what's the matter? Are you hurt? Was there an accident?" As she let him in, she tried to make sense of what was wrong, of why he was here, alone and in her kitchen at this hour.

"Yes, I'm hurt," he said, slurring his words. He turned to her and threw his jacket on the floor.

Eliza smelled alcohol, cigarettes, and sweat. Bewildered and disgusted, she tried to turn away.

"It's you, 'Lyza; it's you." He grabbed her wrist and wrenched it behind her back, shooting a blazing pain through to her shoulder, then he leaned in and placed his other hand on the wall, entrapping her. She felt the cold from outside emanate from his skin and the heat of his acrid breath on her face. "I'm sorry, princess." His malice bored through her, and he tried to press his stiff, swollen appendage into her thigh.

Fear erupted; hot bile rose from her abdomen and up her throat.

"Patrick, you need to leave," Eliza whispered, trying to step back as if the wall could absorb her. "You need to leave. Now. Ed will be home soon, and he'll …" Her voice disappeared, and her knees weakened. She saw her face in the kitchen mirror disfigured by fear. Confused, she crumpled onto the oak bench beneath it. She couldn't bear to look at Patrick, whose face reflected in the mirror was equally contorted by aggression and lust.

Looming above her, he gripped the doorknob and used his other hand to lock the bolt above it. Eliza saw his hands trembling and felt repulsed, suddenly nauseous, and unable to distinguish Patrick's hands from David's. In a second of cruel recollection, she felt again the warmth of David's palm and the blush of her cheek when he'd held her breast only an hour ago.

Patrick's left hand flew away from the door and reappeared holding a hunting knife that seemed to have come from nowhere. She opened her mouth to scream, but transfixed by the blade and the deadliness in his eyes, she couldn't find her voice.

"Please, no, Patrick. Please," she whispered. "I didn't mean to make you think …" Stop, she thought with a flash of lucidity and anger. After all, what had she done? For Patrick to equate a glance with something justifying an attack was madness. Is that what this was? She wanted to turn the tables and attack him, to tear at his face and pound his flesh. She would not let this happen. Defiant, she tried to stand, but Patrick grabbed her wrist again, twisted her around, and put his left elbow on her chest and the knife to her chin.

"Don't scream. I'll slit your throat. I've done it before. To gals over there, prettier than you. Get down on the floor, Eliza," he said, his voice husky as he pushed her down.

She recoiled at the sound of her name. Fear commanded her, and Eliza did as she was told. Time slowed; each movement Patrick made, each liquor-drenched breath, was deliberate. She felt the cool linoleum beneath the arm painfully pinned behind her back. He ripped at her skirt as his powerful thighs clenched hers. Paralyzed, she couldn't direct her free arm to move, not that it would've helped. His eyes, no longer calm but wild and distant, bore into hers. One hand reached up the back of her sweater and grabbed her neck in a pinch-hold. With his other hand, he put the knife in his back pocket before loosening his pants and shoving them to his knees.

Eliza froze—a wounded animal caught in a trap. Unable to move her body, she began to shake her head like a person possessed, hitting her head on the floor, unaware of pain as lucidity vanished into panic.

He forced himself into her in an awkward series of thrusts and fell on top of her. The growth on his unshaven face chafed her skin, and the hot odor of his sour, ashy breath gagged her. She didn't see the moist handkerchief, but as he held the sweet-smelling cloth over her mouth, she felt grateful for it. Toxic air stung her nostrils, making her dizzy, and she gulped like a person drowning, as he released the cloth from her mouth. Seeing confused images of Patrick and David, David and Patrick, she blacked out.

8

December 1946

Eliza felt the hard, cool floor under her cheek and the palm of her hand. She opened her eyes, a forest of metal legs only inches away—the kitchen table and chairs—confused her. She followed an urge to curl up like a caterpillar, but in trying to do so, she found she was lying on her stomach. She tried to lift her head but stopped. A sharp pain stabbed her forehead and sank into her neck, hurting as if she'd been struck with a hammer. Her skirt was bunched at her waist. Her wool knee-socks hung loose at her ankles and she felt stickiness between her legs. After seconds of searching for an explanation, her confusion dissolved into an abrupt and visceral memory. Her body froze as her earlier terror and the pain of having her arm awkwardly pinned behind her flooded into the present. Motionless, she used only her eyes and ears to search the room for signs he could be close by. How much time had passed? Her body ached and she began to tremble, but the house was quiet. Patrick Whitaker was gone.

She concentrated on the sound of the grandfather clock chiming hours in the foyer. She wondered if she'd missed one. Could it be just ten in the evening? Wasn't it after nine when she'd heard pounding at the door? Only forty-five minutes ago? Eliza felt exposed and chilled. She moved her legs in an effort to stand, not expecting the soreness in her thighs and back. She cried out as she recalled again what had happened. Struck anew with fear, she fought to hold back a wave of nausea as she crawled to the door and pulled down Fa's Adirondack coat from the nearby hook. She covered herself, leaned into the corner between the boot bench and the wall, and cried in small, quiet whimpers.

Her head throbbed if she turned too quickly, so she remained still, worked to suspend thought, and prayed for her parents' return. She nodded off for a quarter hour and awoke with a start, remembering the note from Fa. It was not yet midnight, and they'd not be home until morning.

Using the boot bench to steady herself, she stood and found her legs weakened but no longer shaking. She wrapped the coat around her shoulders and took awkward steps, the stiffness in her thighs and buttocks diminishing with each one. She walked to the sink, moistened a rag with cold running water, washed between her legs, and got to her knees to scrub spots of congealed blood from the floor. She paused, blinked hard, and bit her bottom lip. Her mind struggled to force back the violent memory as she scrubbed the linoleum tile until any remnant of the attack had gone.

Job done, she sat motionless on the floor with the scrub brush in hand. She felt as if she'd been placed on a razor-thin layer of ice over a dark and sinister lake, protected only by her ability to focus on the frozen surface within her limited view. She was afraid to leave the kitchen, worried that if she did, she'd leave an essential part of herself there forever. Instead, she narrowed her world to what she could see, put on the kettle for a cup of tea, and made a plate of bread and jam—every action an effort to maintain control. She heard a familiar mechanism click in the grandfather clock, indicating it was about to chime.

She felt relief in the mundanity of the clock's function and forced herself to remember each detail of the day Fa had brought it home, as if by doing so she could guide herself away from the present. It had been Mother's birthday. Fall had come late; the grass was still green but covered with brown pods from the two honey locust trees framing the sidewalk. The new grandfather clock had chimed once, and Eliza remembered Mother's gasp as she brought her hands to her cheeks.

"Cecil, it's … It looks just like my grandmother's. How could you've known?" Mother had approached the clock and touched it gently. She'd caressed the darkened grain of the nineteenth-century Irish masterpiece and gazed at its large, round face encased in polished mahogany and decorated with carved laurels.

Grandpa Theo had twisted the silver acorn knob and opened the curved door, revealing the fulcrum and weights. He'd also taken a key from his pocket and unlocked the glass door to the face.

It was the most beautiful piece of furniture Eliza had ever seen. She'd watched as Grandma Edith helped Grandpa Theo adjust the chimes, and it'd occurred to Eliza that her mother had been a daughter to someone else, though she knew nothing of that part of her mother's life.

"Tell us about your mother, Mother. You never have. Did she die?" Eliza had asked.

Mother looked at Grandma Edith and Grandpa and then

at the clock. She hesitated as if she might let the question go unanswered, but then replied, "Yes, she died quite a long time ago. Long before you children came along. She was a—" Mother averted her eyes, pursed her lips into a slight smile, and nodded her head as if communicating with a spirit, but she said nothing to complete her thought. She turned to Eliza, who'd put Baby Theodore in the crib kept in the foyer and was gently rocking it.

The memory turned dark as Eliza recalled touching a pimple on the baby's neck. The skin around it had felt rough and hot, but her thoughts had dwelled on the grandmother she'd never met and ghosts in the room, and she'd said nothing. She'd felt competent, like a trusted surrogate when Mother said, "Why don't you take him upstairs, Eliza, and get him ready for bed? I'll come in a moment to help. Then we'll all have hot cocoa and toast."

The following morning, Baby Theodore had awakened, wailing as if possessed, with a spiked fever and thick cough. He'd died before sunset. Eliza remembered retreating under blankets on the armchair with Shannon, next to the clock, taking comfort in its chimes, scrutinizing and memorizing its crafted details, while Mother and Fa seemed to fade away, consumed with their grief. She no longer felt like Mother's trusted aide, but rather like a bewildered child unable to grasp the unbearable loss.

She directed her mind back to her mother, who'd been unable to share the slightest bit of her own childhood. Who had been her mother's mother? What had that woman looked like? How had she died? According to Mother, she herself could not remember since her mother had died before she was ten.

How little I know. This thought lodged in Eliza's mind and terrified her again as she sat in the kitchen in the earliest hours of the morning, waiting for time to pass.

"Eliza, did you shower last night?" Mother asked the following morning as she opened the bedroom door, looking fatigued from a long day and night at Shannon's bedside. "I found this button on the bathroom floor. It must be from your skirt. Make sure you mend it before you lose it."

For a long moment, Eliza couldn't speak, afraid her voice would be altered and somehow Mother would divine what had happened. "Yes, Mother, I did," she said eventually. "I don't feel well today. I might stay in bed for a few hours, all right?"

"Eliza, please don't tell me you're coming down with something. You must take care of yourself, dear. You mustn't work too hard at school or skimp on sleep. It's too frightening to think that you or Edmund might get ill as well."

"I'm fine, Mother. I stayed up reading last night. I was worried about Shannon and couldn't sleep. If you leave the button, I'll sew it on later." Forming each word was a challenge, as if she'd forgotten the English language, and this time Eliza was sure her voice was deeper, sharper, in a way that Mother would certainly perceive.

But her mother went on as if nothing had changed: "Shannon had a difficult time," she said while refolding a pair of Fa's undershirts from the laundry basket. "The surgery went fine, but she reacted poorly to the pain medication later in the day. Dizziness mostly. A touch of fever. The nurses let Fa and I stay with her until near dawn." She finished folding the shirts and looked at Eliza with a hint of concern, as if her words had caused Eliza harm. "But she's better now, dear."

"Thank God, Mother. I was so worried."

"The doctors don't want any visitors until she's back in the ward." Mother looked out to the backyard and cocked her head, seeming to reconsider before saying, "Then you might go, if you're feeling well yourself. Poor Shannon—she'll need you to be strong, Eliza."

9

JANUARY 1947

Shannon touched her nightshirt and let her finger trail over the outline of a puffy scar that began beside her left breast and continued under her arm and across her shoulder blade. She pulled at a tie string at the neck of her loose hospital gown so she could see and touch the stitched wound, a tender and hideous purple-red bruise, where the thread met the skin and pulled the two sides together so the wound resembled a pair of long, ugly fish lips. She took her hand-mirror from her dresser to inspect it now that the bandage had been removed. The cut formed a crescent beside her breast; together, the scar and nipple resembled a misshapen, oversized eye, a grotesque image from

Shelly's Frankenstein. The boy who smelled like chocolate and cinnamon surely wouldn't find this eye very pretty. Shannon grimaced, relieved she'd not tried again to find him, and relieved they'd never had a chance to share a kiss. But the relief came with a wave of anxious shame so potent it threatened to take her breath away. She was three months from her nineteenth birthday. What man would ever find her anything but repulsive, when she couldn't stand to look at herself? And more scars would come. The mirror fell from her hand, and she did not try to stop it as it slipped off the bed to the floor. She didn't care if she ever looked in a mirror again.

"Letter for you, Miss Malone." A nurse Shannon hadn't seen before retrieved the mirror, returned it to the dresser, and thumbed through a wire basket held above her hip. With her free hand, she removed one of several colorful holiday envelopes and handed it to Shannon. Grateful as she was to receive it, the letter was from Harvey—not, as she'd hoped, from Eliza.

Shannon sank her shoulders into the pillows, straightened the collar of her white nightshirt and adjusted the baby-blue scarf the nurse had suggested, a gift from Harvey and Gloria that matched her eyes. The arcane skill of primping in bed was a useless one, she thought, one she couldn't wait to abandon. After this small, exhausting effort, she relaxed, comfortable enough to read Harvey's letter. But disturbing thoughts of the boy-who-smelled-like-chocolate lingered and morphed to equally disturbing thoughts of Eliza that needed to be reconciled first. She took from the stack of letters by her drawer the most recent one, which Mother had delivered on Christmas Day. Maybe she'd missed something in the wording that would explain why Eliza had not written since then to cheer her through the awful surgery and to share every detail of her weekend date with David.

December 23rd, 1947

Dearest Shannon;

I hope you are well, darling sister. You must be spending your days and nights resting. I wish so much I could be there when you awake from surgery on Friday. I'll go to the lake house tomorrow morning (Tuesday) with Ed to spend Christmas Eve and Day with Grandma and Grandpa. They are trying to be cheerful; you know how Grandma loves this time of year. She's made oodles of pepperkaker already (still your favorite, I hope)—enough to string five trees—and she's expecting help with more. It's funny how Grandma acts as Irish as the rest of us until Christmas, and only then does she reveal her true Swedish roots! Everybody wants to be Irish, I suppose.

As you probably know, classes at St. Kate's ended on Friday. I absolutely love each one, as I've already told you, but I've been feeling the winter blues.... It's nothing a few days near the lake won't cure. Grandma called to say the ice is already strong enough for skating, but I think I'll wait for you—even if it's next year. I want to place all of my energy in good thoughts for Friday, Shannon. I'll be with you in spirit, darling!

Things with David are wonderful, though we don't see each other all that much. He invited me to see the new Donna Reed and Jimmy Stewart Christmas movie with Jan (do you remember his sister?) and his cousin, Patrick, when I return Friday. Mother says I should go since she and Fa will be with you. It's not fair you and the others in the ward can't see new movies. Don't worry, Shannon, I'll tell you all about it!

David's been busy with classes and the pharmacy. I'm hoping Mother and Fa will allow him to study with me on Saturday afternoons next semester. We'll see. They're not keen on unchaperoned visits, and if he comes over to the house during the week, he can only stay for a short while before going to work. So, for the time being, I think Ed sees him more than I do.

Mother says I can visit you again after New Year. I know your recovery from surgery will be speedy; you'll keep thinking positive thoughts, won't you?

Merry Christmas - Your loving sister,
Eliza

P.S. I'm sorry I've only written once this week. I'll write more in January; you're off the hook until your darned lungs recover (though it wouldn't hurt you to dictate a letter to someone for me…. How about asking Betty?)
P.p.s I hope you enjoy the pepperkaker and 'Windswept.' The novel was Fa's recommendation, so it must be good. I'll find another copy at the library, so we can read it together in the New Year.

P.p.p.s Do you remember I told you that Jody R. is in my calculus class? It's been fun seeing so much of her this semester—she is as lively as ever, if not a little bit crass (I would say it only to you). She'll be at the lake for Christmas as well. Her parents invited some of the Wayzata servicemen for Christmas punch and caroling tomorrow. Her mother asked if I'd help. It'll be swell, I'm sure—especially if it snows!

Shannon held onto the letter with both hands, squeezed her eyes shut, and cried as quietly as she could so as not to attract attention. Reading letters from Eliza was the most bittersweet medicine—she knew her so well. Right now, she wanted to laugh as well as cry, touched by Eliza's equal measures of nurture and intuition, and, of course, bossiness. If Eliza were here, she would probably take her to task for crying and smiling at the same time, then quickly make up for it by squeezing Shannon's shoulder in apology for being dismissive. It was as if Eliza knew she was just like Mother sometimes, as if she knew and she struggled to moderate her inherited tendencies toward harshness.

How long had it been since Eliza had written? Shannon struggled to concentrate on a single thought, a reminder that she was only a week out of surgery.

During her first month at Milner Hospital, she'd hardly been able to sit up without her head spinning and her vision clouding. The infection had traveled throughout her left lung. Doctors warned of the risk that it could spread to other organs. Dismal as it was, she'd been strictly limited to bed rest.

By late September, she'd been well enough to remain awake for five or six hours a day. Around then, surgeons had collapsed her left lung, and, like a pricked balloon, it was flat, defunct. Doctors hoped a non-working lung would heal more quickly—at least that was how she understood it.

Breathing was painful, as if a vice had entrapped her chest, and too much movement brought on fierce, unrelenting headaches and dizziness that led to nausea and a persistent itchiness in her legs and arms.

October and November had passed quickly enough; her energy and appetite both stabilized, but more worries surfaced from results of tests taken in early December. X-rays confirmed that not only did bacteria remain stubborn in her left lung; it had also entered her bloodstream and infected her uterus. Another more serious approach was needed. She would have to endure three separate surgeries--all in quick succession-- to remove eight ribs, permanently collapsing the tubercular cavities thereby making room for the diseased lung to repair.

And, if she survived those surgeries, she'd need another to

remove her reproductive organs unless by some miracle the infection cleared.

She narrowed her thoughts, trying to focus on the image of a calendar, in which Monday, December 23rd was separated from today, January 3rd, by only ten days. No, eleven. The calendar faded, and Shannon remembered that after surgery, she'd spent at least three days in a different place, another private room like the one to which she'd first been assigned. So, it hadn't been that long, after all. And Mother, who'd often hand-delivered Eliza's letters, had not been able to visit because of a yeast infection. *When was that?* Just a few days ago, surely. She'd seen Mother and Fa since surgery, hadn't she? And she was certain Ed had come since Christmas. So maybe nothing was wrong, maybe she was only imagining that Eliza wasn't with her in the same way now as she had been before.

Shannon's mood lightened. She recalled Eliza's letter had ended with news of Jody Remminger, their 'summer friend' from the lake. Her body relaxed and she replayed a long, vivid childhood memory, the kind of recollection that, when stumbled upon in everyday thoughts and then revisited in each available detail, could make time pass for Shannon as sweetly as reading a familiar scene from a beloved book.

Jody had been a delightful, magical creature to Shannon when the sisters first met her ten years ago. She'd been the very image of Princess Irene, the girl protagonist in George MacDonald's series *The Princess and the Goblin*. At the urging of all three Malone children, Fa had been reading the second book aloud in the evenings after dinner using his full suite of character voices.

"Just like the Princess," Shannon had whispered to Eliza, when Mother introduced her. *"Her face was fair and pretty, with eyes like two bits of night sky, each with a star dissolved in the blue ..."*

Such writing! Shannon had memorized many of the best passages, and this was one of them. Even Mother had turned sentimental with the loveliness of the images.

The girls had agreed that Jody had many of Princess Irene's best attributes. She was, of course, very privileged, but inquisitive, strong, adventurous, and impulsive, which sometimes got her into trouble. Shannon and Eliza told Jody the story in great detail as they floated for hours on the lake in Grandpa's small rowboat. From that day forward in the summer of 1936, and for several years thereafter, the girls, and occasionally Ed, transformed themselves into its cast of characters: Princess Irene, her grandmother, the humble coal miner's son Curdie, and the despicable, hideous, toeless goblin king.

"I have a grand idea," Eliza had said when the girls helped Grandma Edith prepare lunch one day in the summer of her tenth year. "A surprise birthday party for Fa in the garden!"

"We'll have cake and punch and play games like bean-bag toss and follow-the-leader," Shannon had said, in step with Eliza's thinking. "We'll string lanterns around the patio and paint gigantic butterflies and have a dance."

"May I come?" Jody asked.

"Of course," Eliza said, trying to sound as ladylike as Mother. "You have to help us."

"Jody, it'll be so much fun if you can," Shannon said. "You must ask your parents to come as well. I'm sure Ed will like the idea."

"I do," said Ed, who'd come in as they chatted. "Tomorrow's Monday; how much time do we have to prepare?"

"Plenty of time," Grandma said. "My boy's birthday isn't for another four weeks, mid-August, and I think a surprise party sounds grand."

"What do you mean, your boy, Grandma?" Shannon asked.

"She means Fa is her little boy, Shannon," Eliza said with the familiar bossy tone Shannon both liked and disliked. "But we want to be in charge of the whole party, Grandma," Eliza continued.

"Invitations, decorations, food; we won't need much help at all. You've got to promise to keep it a secret from Mother and Fa."

"Why from Mother?" Shannon asked.

"Because she'll tell Fa, silly. That's what wives and husbands do. They tell each other everything."

Fa had joined them for the first and the last of the seven weeks they spent at the lake that summer, as well as some weekends in between. He was working on a book of his own, an academic manuscript requiring long hours of research. He liked to say he needed to be close to the library so he could hear the books calling him to task—otherwise, he'd be tempted to lounge by the lake with his girls all day long.

It was, of course, Eliza's idea to highlight the celebration with a theater performance of *The Princess and the Goblin*. Shannon thought it obvious that Jody should play Princess Irene; but Eliza, at her imperious best, thought otherwise. Ed had no interest in any role but the horrible goblin king, which left Jody to be Curdie, and Shannon, the ageless grandmother.

With Grandpa's help in gathering construction materials, the four children spent the next two weeks making a stage that rested against the large French doors leading out to the terrace. The set was not, as Shannon remembered, perfect by any measure. It was big, with a few stage props they'd painted on plywood: sinister caves on the side of a dark mountain, a cottage window from the outside, and a bedroom fireplace—the effect was magical.

Eyes closed, Shannon now replayed scenes from that summer evening. Colored lanterns bejeweling the lake house decks for Fa's birthday party mixed with images from their play. She dreamed about the shimmering ball of string Princess Irene's mysterious grandmother had spun for her in the days before her misadventure. She dreamed she was a spectator, watching herself as an eight-year-old playing the enchanted grandmother who tied one end of the silvery thread—so fine as to be almost invisible—

to an opal ring, a useful gift to guide her beloved granddaughter back home from whatever evils might befall her as she wandered from the kingdom.

A clacking sound, like tap-dancing in a distant room, distracted her from the stage, and she looked about, trying to see the cause of the interruption. She awoke to see Mother sitting beside her, knitting intently, but looking surprisingly placid, given the frantic speed of her purling and looping. Slowing her pace but not stopping, she looked over her glasses at Shannon.

"Shannon, would you like a bath this afternoon?" A full bathing in bed was limited to once a week, though Shannon never understood why. The patients had plenty of time for more. She much preferred Mother's confident, methodical scrubbing to the unpredictable styles of the various nurses. Moreover, the ward was kept cool for healing purposes, and Shannon often felt an unpleasant chill in the sheets when a nurse administered her baths. Mother had a way of proceeding, one section at a time, using perfectly tepid water and lots of drying towels, which minimized discomfort. Although light snow was falling outside, nurses had cracked open the windows in the center of the wall behind Shannon.

"Yes, but maybe just my legs, Mother. They feel like lead today, though I'm doing my ankle exercises all the time."

Mother left to find two oval metal bowls—one for soapy water and one for clear—and several washcloths. When she returned, she rolled up her sleeves and placed a folded larger cloth near Shannon's head for drying. "Has Dr. Paul been in to see you today? Your next surgery has been scheduled for six weeks from now."

Shannon shook her head. Dr. Paul had not visited yet. Seeing him—especially with Eliza so far away—was another consideration, like a sinister cave in the offing, to dread.

Nurses, patients, and visitors in the women's ward, even doctors, all perked up whenever Harvey Bligh came around. Two days after New Year, he arrived with his usual assorted bounty; this time it was holiday cookies, new Harper's Bazaar magazines, bright-colored nail polishes, and green-glass bottles of cola. He'd drawn plump, oversized, bright-red lips on the white cotton mask all visitors were encouraged to wear. A flock of less-sick women gathered around him, reviewing the magazines, admiring the colored polishes he'd brought, and appreciating his willingness to look ridiculous, none more so than Shannon.

"What a ham you are, Harvey," Shannon said later as he recounted New Year's Eve with his father and Uncle John, a Jesuit priest.

"Sure, they're a barrel of laughs. I'll never forgive my brothers for taking Pop's car and leaving me alone with those two geezers. Their idea of a good time is debating whether the eighth station of the cross is Women Weeping over Jesus or Jesus Falls the Third Time."

"Harvey! You'll go to purgatory for that! And stop! You're making me laugh, and I'm not supposed to do that yet."

"I'm not too worried about purgatory, but I don't want to make you too happy now, do I? I'll stop. I'll tell you one more thing, though. My mother would've never forgotten the stations. She might have been born Jewish, but she knew Catholicism better than anyone. I guess it's true of most converts." Harvey picked up the embroidery rings Shannon had set down earlier that day and made a stitch. "May I?" he asked, though he'd already begun. "You missed a bunch of stitches."

Shannon raised her eyebrow.

"What?" Harvey said sharply. "My mother taught me."

"Really? When?"

"When I was nine years old." He sighed. "I wish she were here."

"I wish that, too, Harvey."

"The holidays are torture. Boiled ham and potatoes, for one thing. The two foods Pop doesn't ruin. I do know how to boil cranberries, which does help."

"At least you have Matthew and John at home. Thank God the war ended. Now families can get back to normal."

"Any chance for our 'normal' died with Mother, I think," Harvey said, then, not one to be down for long, he asked, "Have you gotten letters from Gloria? Her mother says, 'No' to a visit, but she asks about you every time I see her."

"Yes, I've gotten some swell letters from her. I love the scarf you two found. Look how well it contrasts with the white sheets!"

"You don't hold it against her, do you?"

"No, of course not; but it does make me feel like a leper, I suppose."

"Or like Jennifer Jones in Song of Bernadette, maybe? Remember the scene where she's praying and the townspeople are convinced she's the Virgin Mary?" Harvey said with his eyes rolled to heaven and his hands clasped in prayer as if he were the Academy-Award-winning actress.

"God, Harvey, how could you say that to me? You remember how the film ended?" Shannon's shoulders heaved up and down while she tried not to laugh. She couldn't afford to disturb the stitches in her chest, but Harvey in prayer with the two big red lips was too much. "Honestly, you're going to kill me right here and now." She lay back with a smile, closed her eyes, and held her hand out for Harvey's. "I love you, Harvey. Thank you for not being too careful with me."

"Life is too precious for that, Shannon. You're going to make it." He leaned over and kissed Shannon on the forehead with the two plump lips he'd drawn on his mask, leaving a red smear on her skin. "And we're going to be great friends for a very long time."

"What have you heard from Eliza? Anything?" she asked.

Harvey looked taken aback by the question and hesitated as if he couldn't decide amongst several available answers. His eyebrows arching, possibly in resignation, he looked away from Shannon and let the words run together in a long, fast sentence: "I saw David at the pharmacy a few days ago. He looked like hell. Said Eliza broke up with him." He paused to look at Shannon as if gauging her inevitable shock. "I figured you already knew..."

10

January 1947

liza was, at first, surprised to find her secret so easy to keep. Ed had taken refuge on campus, and Fa, habitually inclined to compartmentalize his life, spent long hours in his campus office or at the library. Mother did her best to keep her volunteer commitments at the chapel because, Eliza knew, cleaning, especially at church, brought her comfort and hope—two useful guideposts of Catholic faithfulness.

She could immerse herself in preparation for the next semester at school. She could busy herself with errands for Mother. But she could not write a letter to Shannon. Not yet. She could not under any circumstance see David. She'd left a note for him last week at the pharmacy indicating that she'd spend New Year's Eve and the remainder of winter break at the lake house with Grandma and Grandpa. If Ed told him otherwise, she would have to deal with it later. For now, she knew that seeing David and facing the horror of that night, or worse, risking an encounter with her attacker, would make her fall apart.

Eliza entered University of Minnesota's student library reverently, like a holy pilgrim. She sat alone at a long, wooden table in the back of the second-floor study area and let the feelings of tranquility wash over her. As long as she could be here or somewhere like it, as long as she could do this and stay clear of her darker thoughts and fears, she would be fine.

She walked among the shelves of classic English literature and searched for books listed on the syllabus for her upcoming advanced literature course. She found all four and took them to the table, where she reviewed the editions and confirmed their availability for being checked out. After an hour immersed in study, Eliza felt satisfied and was ready to leave, knowing full well she would return very soon. She copied the Dewey decimal catalog numbers for each and gathered her belongings, ready to cross campus and take the city bus home before dark.

As she waited in the check-out line near the library's main entrance, Eliza's attention turned to a poster in the center display window:

– MRS. FRANCES PERKINS –
SECRETARY OF LABOR 1932-1945
FIRST WOMAN CABINET MEMBER IN US HISTORY
PROFESSOR OF INDUSTRIAL AND LABOR RELATIONS
CORNELL UNIVERSITY, ITHACA, NY
Speaking at U of M Founders Hall
11 am – Saturday, February 22nd
Free admission for students and alumni

$1 General Admission
WOMEN AND DISCRIMINATION
– IN THE MODERN WORKPLACE –

It hadn't occurred to Eliza that a woman could've held such an important position as Secretary in the Federal Government. She wondered what Mrs. Perkins taught in her classes; surely some of her students were women. She couldn't imagine why not, and the thought excited her. She jotted down the details of the lecture, relieved it was scheduled for a Saturday morning. To be outside after dark was impossible.

~⌒~

LYING TO SHANNON FOR THE first time would be difficult. Before sitting down next to the hospital bed, Eliza repeated to herself several times the story she'd fabricated about her break-up with David. Two weeks had passed since Shannon's surgery, and a note of get-well wishes from David's family sat next to a bowl of blooming narcissus bulbs—even this remote reference to the horrible night was enough to cause a pit of dread in her chest.

"What?" After listening to Eliza's story, Shannon tried to bolt upright, but the effort failed, and she lay back down. "Why would he say such a thing? Things were so nice between you. You said yourself after the Harvest Ball you couldn't imagine a nicer fellow than David." She sighed. "Do Mother and Fa know? Mother'll be disappointed. She likes David, thinks he's good for you. She told me so."

"I don't want to talk about it, Shannon. I told you. He's not interested in taking things further right now, and I'm not either. School's keeping me busy enough; I'd rather focus on that."

Shannon eyed Eliza with suspicion as if her illness might give her special powers to pry hidden truths. The tactic may have worked in the past, but Eliza knew her sister would not discover much this time. By necessity, the truth was buried deeply, and no one, not even Shannon, could persuade her to reveal it.

"But I'll tell you what, Shannon," she said. "Spring classes start next week at St. Kate's, and I can hardly wait. I've been looking at the class offerings at U of M for next year. I might ask Fa if he thinks it'd be a good idea to transfer. They have so much more to offer."

"Fa wants me to audit a class while I'm here," Shannon said. "I don't know. I don't have your passion for all that."

"I think he wants you to keep your mind busy. No harm in trying."

"How about if you read some of *Windswept* aloud, to get me going on it."

"Yes," Eliza said, "like we used to do. What was the last book I read to you? Must be years ago."

"'Lyza," Shannon interjected, "I'm having the next surgery in two weeks. Has Mother told you? She tried to schedule it then, the day after the Feast of St. Blaise. She'll probably have every priest in the city come to give me the blessing of the throat."

"Will you be ready? Yes, Mother did tell me. And don't tease her about St. Blaise. Extra blessings can't hurt, anyway."

"I've never felt like I did after the surgery; as if I were an old, old lady. My body hurt like it'd been run over by a truck. Funny, though, after a few days I could feel the healing begin inside, like mending from the inside out."

Eliza understood Shannon's description, but in her case, there was no such productive internal mending. Instead, Eliza feared Patrick as if he were a supernatural villain who resided within and could threaten her at any moment if she let her guard down. She had ways to trick her mind, to fend off the serpentine imaginings of danger, but it was not, she knew, any form of real healing. She fought an unexpected urge to tell Shannon all that had happened at home the night of her first surgery. She felt a flash of self-pity, but admonished herself just as quickly. Shannon had been through far worse in the past five months, not to mention all she had to bear still ahead. She took Shannon's hand and squeezed it.

"You'll be strong enough to survive another couple of truck collisions, won't you?" she asked.

Mother had her hat and coat on when she strode into the ward. While the familiar, purposeful clicking of Mother's heels sounded almost cheerful as she crossed the room, Eliza noted a tired sagging in her eyes and jawline.

"Of course she'll do well," Mother said. "The doctors all said she may look like a sparrow, but her heart's as strong as a horse's." She turned her attention to Eliza. "We should leave in a few moments, dear. I'd like to be home by three o'clock. Edmund is joining us for dinner with a new friend, Olivia O'Rourke. I think you girls know her."

"Could I stay for another hour, Mother? I promised I'd get Shannon going on this new book."

Mother nodded and pulled up a chair alongside the girls. "We'll stay for a little while longer, then. I haven't heard you read aloud for some time, Eliza." She took off her coat and smiled, her tired contentment palpable, no doubt for the simple pleasure of seeing her two girls together. Eliza read from the beginning, introducing the three Malone women to the fictional Philip Marston clan and their post-Civil War family saga.

~⌒⊃

Eliza fell back asleep after her alarm rang. She missed the bus she'd intended to catch, but was still among the first to arrive at Founders Hall for the lecture. By ten thirty in the morning, the hall was three quarters full. Eliza took a seat in the center of the front row.

In the weeks since she'd first seen the announcement, Eliza had visited the library twice to find what she could in newspapers and magazines on both the career of Mrs. Frances Perkins and the topic of discrimination against women in the workplace. She was smitten. Multiple new worlds of curiosity and potential unfolded before her with each new article she found. True, she'd been taken off track: first, by the horrible week, then by the week of Shannon's second surgery. All went well, though no one would confirm whether or not the procedure would result in a cure. God and time would tell.

The University Dean of Labor Studies called Mrs. Perkins to the podium and introduced her as one of the great policy thinkers and humanitarians of the day. She spoke without notes for forty minutes in an impassioned monologue about the nature of discrimination in America, the history of the laws surrounding fairness in the workplace, and the inevitable weave of immigration, poverty, and women's rights. Eliza leaned forward, at once enthralled with the speaker herself and the content of her discourse. She welcomed every word of Mrs. Perkins' speech as an invitation to dive deeper into her own new understanding of labor and women's rights. At the end of her presentation Mrs. Perkins made closing comments and took several questions before nodding a final thank you to the audience. Eliza, jolted from her thrall, rose to join others who stood to applaud.

"Oh, my—Someone …!" She heard the woman next to her shout. A thought flashed through her mind that her neighbor was either very distressed or shocked by something Eliza hadn't seen. But at the same time her body slackened and both knees buckled. The room swirled and went black as she fell.

Eliza came to and focused on the man with thinning hair and a neat mustache who knelt next to her, his tie hovering above her chest. "Dear? What is your name? Young lady?" He reached over to find her wrist and take her pulse.

Imagining he was trying to pin her down, Eliza screamed and pulled away from him into the legs of a bystander. She crossed one arm around her chest and buried her face in the other.

"Young lady. Please, calm yourself. You fainted, and now you are awake. My name is Dr. Pugh." The man spoke matter-of-factly and looked into Eliza's eyes. He made a motion to dismiss the few strangers who'd gathered around.

Her fear receded, and in a rush of recognition Eliza took account of where she was: in the lecture hall. Safe. She'd just heard Mrs. Perkins speak. This had nothing to do with what had happened before.

"Take a moment to relax, and we'll sit here together until I'm sure you're well enough to go home. Have you fainted before today?" he asked.

"No. Never. I don't know what came over me," Eliza said. "But I feel fine now. I'm sure I can get home."

"Try standing, and then sit down here." Dr. Pugh guided her into a chair. "I'll be right back. I need to inform my wife I'll be with her in a moment, and I'll bring you a glass of water."

"I have water right here, Doctor." An elderly woman, about Grandma Edith's age, with somber, intelligent eyes that didn't match the brightness of her demeanor, sat next to Eliza.

How do I know her? Eliza worked to revive her brain, seeing only disjointed fragments of the present moment. Finally, the scene around her clicked into place. "Mrs. Perkins, thank you," said Eliza. She took the offered glass with both hands as Mrs. Perkins leaned in and touched Eliza's shoulder. Eliza continued, "I enjoyed your presentation so much."

"Well, given your current state, I won't make any jokes—though I could. You seemed to be the youngest person here. Are you a university student?"

"I'm a freshman at St. Catherine's. I've been looking forward to your talk for weeks. We don't have many classes in labor relations—none, actually. I hope I can find more coursework in women's studies somehow."

"If you are serious about that path, you'll find your way. You know who I am; what is your name?"

"I'm Eliza Malone," she said and offered her hand to Mrs. Perkins. "It's an honor to meet you."

Mrs. Perkins took Eliza's hand in both of hers and shook it warmly. Eliza noticed a thin layer of makeup on dark circles under the older woman's eyes, and she recognized in this close-up moment, the shadows of weariness kept at bay. "I am sure you are a bright young woman, Eliza Malone. We'll need you to stay well and do good work."

"Sorry to interrupt," said Dr. Pugh. He took Eliza's pulse and listened to her heart with the stethoscope he'd taken from his medical satchel. A moment later he added, "I think you're well enough to go home, Miss Malone. You may want to call on your doctor for a follow-up."

AT HOME, MOTHER WAS PREPARING dinner and, judging by the light classical music emanating through the closed door upstairs, Fa was in his library office. Hearing the familiar passage as she climbed the foyer stairs, passing by Mother's small collection of Malone family portraits, a sharp pang of nostalgia surfaced. She yearned again for the home life before Shannon's illness, but the music and images from the past only confirmed that the home she craved had somehow evaporated, leaving only a shell of mementos and daily household habits behind.

"Mother?" Eliza called out as she returned, refreshed and intent on presenting a sunnier outlook.

"Hello, Eliza. How was the lecture? Did you arrive on time after all?"

"Yes, Mrs. Perkins was wonderful. Inspiring, actually." Eliza answered. She leaned against the kitchen table and watched Mother peel the last of the lima beans she'd blanched earlier in the day. "Do you need help with dinner?"

"No, dear. But I'd like you to put the clean sheets on the beds—yours, ours and Edmund's. He'll be staying here tonight, I think. Grandma and Grandpa are coming for dinner."

"Mother, I fainted at the lecture today."

Nell turned off the tap and faced her abruptly. Eliza realized she'd shocked her. She scrutinized Eliza from head to toe and said at the same time, "Eliza, what? Are you ill? Do you have symptoms?"

"No, Mother. I mean, I don't think so. I don't have a cough or a sore throat, though I feel tired today. I stood too quickly and fainted."

Eliza had a foreboding sense that she'd opened some sort of hidden box that would not be closed easily. "I'm sure it's nothing, Mother. I just wanted you to know. A very kind doctor helped me, and I even met Mrs. Perkins in person."

"Eliza, this is nothing to trifle with. I'll make an appointment for you to see Dr. Johnston on Monday. Now, tell me exactly what happened, and then I want you to go upstairs and rest. You do look flushed." She added, "Don't worry about the bed sheets, I'll do them. Dinner's at six."

FOR ELIZA, A TRIP TO Dr. Johnston's office without Shannon felt strange and uncomfortable. Disquiet from a source she couldn't identify frightened her, and when frightened, she usually found strength in managing Shannon who was almost always nearby.

Dr. Johnston emerged from behind the waiting room door and beckoned them to follow. "Come in, ladies," he said cheerfully.

"It's a pleasure to see you both. How is Shannon doing this week, Nell?"

"She's doing well. It'll be two weeks tomorrow since the surgery, and when I saw her yesterday she was taking Communion, so that's a good sign."

"Hmm. And what can I do for you, Eliza? Everything all right?"

"She fainted on Saturday morning at a lecture. The physician who attended her thought it would be good for her to have a more thorough check-up," Mother interceded.

"Aha. You've started college, eh, Eliza? Just turned eighteen and already one foot out of the door. How do you feel about that, Nell? Ready for an empty nest?" He chattered through a series of routine procedures and finished by leaning back against his sink. "Everything appears to be in order, young lady." He looked at Eliza over his glasses resting low on the bridge of his nose. "Could you tell me any other symptoms? Sore throat? Coughing? Swollen glands? Sore muscles?"

Eliza shook her head. His examination of her throat, chest, and glands with his clammy hands and cold metal instruments had put her body on high alert, each touch an attack. Forcing herself calm, she admonished herself and considered apologizing for taking Dr. Johnston's time as though fainting were an irrelevant anecdote. "No, I feel quite fine. I'm sorry; I'm a little tired is all."

"When did you last menstruate?" he asked.

"I," Eliza blushed, "I haven't thought about it."

"Was it normal?"

"Yes. It always is." she said, looking down at the polished flooring and then over to Mother.

Dr. Johnston was silent as he looked from Eliza to Nell. If he had intended to ask another question, he thought better of it, saying instead, "I'm going to take some blood for analysis as well as another sputum sample, just in case. TB doesn't always present in the lungs first, though it normally does. We can't be too careful."

He poked his head out to the hallway and called for a nurse. "Let's get some samples. You should rest, Eliza, and let me know if anything changes. I'll phone you by Friday." He cocked his head and looked at Mother. "It doesn't seem to be anything too serious; I don't want you to worry."

"I'D LIKE TO STOP AT the chapel for Confession, as long as we're right here, Eliza," Mother said after their visit to the doctor. "I wasn't able to go last week or the week before."

Eliza looked at the elegant Chapel of St. Thomas Aquinas, pale in the winter sunlight and surrounded by pristine snow, and felt comforted. She couldn't remember the last time she'd done this with Mother, who usually attended her Catholic duties during the many hours she volunteered at or around the chapel. For years now, her mother had expected the girls to maintain their own Confessional obligations.

"Forgive me, Father, for I have sinned. It's been seven weeks since my last confession." At these words, Eliza clasped a hand to her lips and tried to stifle an unexpected sob. She locked her jaw, reprimanding herself, but she felt defeated by a combination of nausea and tearfulness that rippled through her. For a moment, she felt an equally strong urge to laugh. Where was this coming from? It was ridiculous. *Stop now*, she demanded of herself.

After a small eternity of seconds, she heard the priest respond with the query of her sins. Her Confessor was Father Christopher, the Indian priest who'd been with the parish for the last six months and was near the end of his stay. *My God*, Eliza thought, *this isn't fair*. His Indian accent, which Eliza had loved and had righteously defended when Shannon had poked fun, now struck her as ridiculously pronounced. Again, she wanted to laugh out loud. Was he doing this on purpose? Was she? Of course not, she told herself.

"How have you sinned, my child?" she heard him say again.

Eliza snapped back to attention, regained her composure and said, "I have sinned by ..." She couldn't find the words because she was confused by what sin it was that had been festering in her. She had a vision of Patrick Whitaker so close and real that she felt his black eyes boring into hers, and then another of her own contorted face in the kitchen mirror. She cried out more loudly than she intended, "I have sinned by an omission of truth to my parents, Father." She hesitated, considering something else before adding, "That's all." To her surprise, the two words seemed to diminish the crazed emotions she'd felt a moment ago. Exhausted, though not much relieved, she received from Father Christopher her penance.

11

FEBRUARY 1947

Nell found no satisfaction in cleaning a kitchen floor while standing on two feet with a stick in her hands. She had no use for mops. Not today. Not ever. A good, swift sweep with the broom followed by getting on one's knees with a bucket of hot ammonia water and a scrub rag was the way to do it. Nell let her methodical strokes transport her mind to a sheltered place where she could reason without constraint.

She knew in the days following their visit to Dr. Johnston that Eliza might well be pregnant, though, for the life of her, she couldn't find a way to make sense of it. Her mind shifted between flames of anger, disbelief, and grief. Best to wait until it was confirmed, she thought. She sighed, knowing she couldn't un-see what she now saw clear as day. Like a lock clicking open one cylinder at a time, Nell had noted one sign after another: the fainting episode, Eliza's flushed cheeks, her exhaustion and fluctuating appetite in recent days. She had also observed without much doubt that Eliza herself had no idea of her own condition.

In the hours before dawn that morning, Nell had lain awake, trying to consider the possible scenarios, but instead she'd felt panic. Now, backing up across the kitchen floor, she felt anger close to rage rise in her chest and course down to her hands and knees as she scrubbed. Rage toward whom, though? Eliza? Indeed, some of that. How could Eliza—especially Eliza—have allowed it? How could she and David be so irresponsible? It was, at the very least, sinful, not to mention thoughtless and naive. Was there something, someone else, at whom to direct the hurt she was feeling? Herself? Cecil? God?

"Nell," Cecil said. He stood at the base of the kitchen stairs with his satchel in hand, his hair still moist from the wet comb he used each morning.

She startled, and her gaze shot up to where he stood. "My goodness, Cecil. Must you shout?"

"Didn't raise my voice, dear. I wanted to get an early start today. I'll take my breakfast at the refectory." He sat in one of the kitchen chairs behind her and put a hand on her cheek as she continued to kneel, a wet rag held in her fist.

"Of course, Ceece. I'm sorry, I didn't mean to snap."

"It's all right, Mrs. Malone, I know." It was Cecil's way to refer to Nell formally sometimes, and Nell felt comforted by it. "Is everything all right? What's on your mind to get you scrubbing so early?"

"I don't know; the solid earth beneath me is turning into mud. I'm so worried for Shannon; the nurses say she's losing weight, has no appetite … and now this …" she said absently and returned to scrubbing—idle hands not a choice she gave herself.

"Now what, Nell?" Cecil asked.

"No, dear. Just … now this. She's so exhausted, I mean."

"Will Father Eggers be able to give her the blessing of the ashes on Wednesday, Nell? Maybe the four of us—Eliza and Edmund, too—can drive together and have it at the hospital."

"Why don't you stop by the chapel and ask, Cecil? I'd like us to talk with Father Eggers separate from the children. Could you try to arrange it with him?"

The grandfather clock chimed five o'clock. Nell had been cleaning for two hours. She wanted Cecil to leave, so she could fall back into step with her thoughts. She couldn't bear the gravity of the verdict bearing down in her mind, but she couldn't avoid it either. She was already immersed in thought when Cecil pulled the front door shut behind him, and the solitude of the early morning enveloped her again.

NELL FELT SICK. SHE COULDN'T chase from her mind the grim imprint of uncertainty she'd feared as a girl, when her father would leave for days, providing no food, no money, no words for her and the twins. She'd spent the early years of her marriage and the year after Baby Theodore's death beating back this feeling of dread. She thought she'd dispelled it, but recently she'd felt that dread again, black and threatening, tearing at the safe edges of self and family. It narrowed her vision and forced her to admit she was almost certainly making choices today she would regret.

"Eliza, I'm going to be direct," Nell said when they sat across from one another at the kitchen table, each awaiting a cup of too-hot tea. "Were you and David intimate?" As Nell spoke, the clock chimed one o'clock in the foyer.

Her daughter's face flushed to the pink-red hue of a fading

ember. Eliza sat back heavily in her chair and looked away from Nell as if she'd heard her name called from beyond the kitchen door. Her mixed reaction of confusion and something else—shame ... no, it was more like disbelief—almost persuaded Nell to change course. For a moment, she saw her daughter as a child who'd been tricked for the first time, upset when she sensed she (or more likely, her sister) had been wronged by an adult. Nell felt the urge to wrap the little girl Eliza in her arms and hold her as she'd done the day they buried Baby Theodore. But the young lady she saw in front of her forced an emotional gulf between them.

Nell stayed calm in her chair and repeated the question. "Eliza, please answer me. Have you and David—?"

"I haven't seen him since December." Eliza's voice came out rushed and wavering.

Nell didn't move; her lips stayed tight, and she looked piercingly at Eliza.

"No! We did nothing of the sort—nothing." Eliza wrung the napkin in her hand, looked down, and bit her bottom lip.

Nell thought better of reprimanding her for it and kept her gaze steady, instead.

Eliza lifted her chin and looked at Nell. "I don't understand why you're asking, Mother. Why that?" She cocked her head and glanced down again before adding, "David is a good person."

"Eliza, Dr. Johnston called from the infirmary today. They know what's wrong with you. Why you fainted. Why you feel so tired." Nell saw her way now. It was a course of action for better or worse that she knew she could muster. Any other would be too difficult. "You are pregnant, Eliza. If you want to tell me how this came about, now is the time. If not, we shall not speak of how it happened again."

Nell imagined she knew Eliza's thoughts. Her good, loving daughter, whose weakness was a tendency toward self-righteousness, would bear her burden more or less without the support of her mother.

"Mother, I promise, David and I never did anything other than kiss."

Eliza's conviction surprised Nell.

"Is Dr. Johnston sure? That I'm ..." Eliza, for whom linguistic precision was an art form, stumbled and gave way.

"Yes, Eliza. He, we are sure. Is there anything else to tell me, then?" Nell hoped her voice had softened, but from Eliza's look of despair, perhaps it had not.

Who is she? How could I have missed this transformation? She watched Eliza, fist at her chin, gazing down at the table and studying it intently as though struggling to see algorithms with the answer to life's mysteries inscribed in the yellow Formica. Eliza was, for the moment, a stranger to Nell—not yet an adult, but not a child either.

Eliza bit and released her lower lip once more and, looking past her, said, "No, Mother, there is nothing." She paused as if lost in a thought before returning attention to Nell. "Are you going to talk with David's mother? Please don't." She looked down at her hands. "Please."

Nell felt the sands shifting beneath her again. "I saw David's mother, Dorothy, at the pharmacy on Saturday. She confided that their nephew, Patrick, committed suicide in January. He suffered more than they knew. His poor mother. Dorothy said she hasn't been the same since he first disappeared overseas—and now this. What is the sense in being a hero after all?" Nell made the sign of the cross, giving a silent prayer of thanks that it wasn't Edmund.

Eliza's fingers clutched her teacup, and her shoulders pulled back as she heard the news. Again, she turned her head away. When Eliza placed her hand on her chest and closed her eyes, holding them shut as if in prayer, Nell hoped she would confess.

"It's too much," Nell said softly, "too much for all of us." But others have worse paths, she thought, imagining the grief of Patrick Whitaker and his kin. For a moment, she and Eliza sat across the table from one another, the seed of separation having been sown—until Nell could no longer bear it.

"Eliza, I urge you to speak with David, but it's your choice. You've made your bed, and now you must lie in it. As an unmarried, pregnant woman, you cannot continue to live here beyond a certain point. We'll need to look into other arrangements. Maybe Duluth with Fa's second cousins; maybe here at Watermelon Hill. And you'll need to defer fall semester at St. Catherine's." Nell stood quickly as if some higher power had commanded it. "Don't think for a moment I don't love you. I do, and your father does, just as we love Shannon and Edmund. But this? It's simply too much. I cannot bear it."

~⌒

"Nell, what are you telling me? She doesn't know what happened to her? That's absurd." Cecil sat on the edge of the bed fully dressed except for his socks and shoes. His hands gripped the edge of the mattress, his knuckles whitened and the tips of his long fingers flexed and sunk into the bedding. His tone of voice, soft and wavering with emotion, came as no surprise to Nell, who'd lived with him for twenty-odd years. "It's absurd," he said again in a whisper.

"Cecil, we'll have to accept it. I don't have it in me to demand details, nor to draw David's family into this. She may speak with him, and if they choose to marry, so be it. But until then, the Whitakers will be left to draw their own conclusions whenever they discover what has happened to Eliza. For now, all we can do is pray for her and make sure she's well-attended at the maternity home when the day comes."

"I don't know what to do, Nell. I don't know what to say to her.

What should I say? First Shannon, now this? Why? Why this?" Cecil wept—a steady stream of tears and biting of his lower lip that mirrored Eliza's habit.

An impatience rose in Nell, which she forced away, but not before speaking her mind, "She'll find her own way, Ceece. She'll be fine."

"She can finish out the semester at St. Kate's, can't she? Then she can start again next year."

"There's no putting it off. It is what it is. I am not in favor of having her attend classes beyond a certain point. And as for living here ..."

"Nell, you don't mean to say you don't want her here."

"She cannot stay here beyond a certain point, Cecil. Have you thought about how it would be perceived at St. Thomas? By the Board? President Flynn? Have you thought about Edmund? It's a risk for her even to continue at St. Catherine's." Exasperation with Cecil's naiveté hit Nell. "She may be able to remain at school and maybe here through the semester. It depends on how well she's able to conceal the pregnancy. We'll see." She saw a flicker of relief and said, "But as for me, I wish she could be sent away now. I cannot bear to see it happening in front of me."

"That's cruel, Nell," Cecil said softly. "And I don't believe you mean it," he added as he stood and left the room.

The following morning, Nell stopped next to Eliza's bedroom door, her arms heavy with a stack of clean sheets. She set the neatly folded pile on the hallway table and paused, as she often did, to look at the pastoral oil painting above the walnut console. Such a blessed childhood Grandma Edith had had: painting lessons, piano teachers, dance schools, and genteel, doting parents who protected and nurtured their young. Nell saw it all in the muted blue, brown, and green tints her gifted mother-in-law had used in her palette decades ago.

She wondered how much of Cecil's quiet manner was inherited from his mother—or perhaps unwittingly nurtured from the invisible threads of her family secrets. There must be hidden strands of betrayal or neglect or terrible loss such as the private memories Nell carried. Did Edith's family bear secrets transcribed to Cecil and then to Edmund or Eliza or Shannon in ways unseen?

An unwanted thought of Eliza's pregnancy surfaced, and Nell pulled back from it so vigorously that the stack of linens toppled and fell to the floor. She had an uncomfortable feeling she was being watched; she looked into Eliza's room, half expecting to see her daughter there.

Eliza had changed her bedsheets, as she always did on Tuesday mornings, and the room was tidy—tidier than ever, since Shannon's illness. Nell hesitated before entering, as if something in the room were askew and needed her attention. She felt an urge to be there, to lie down on Eliza's bed and rest her over-worked mind. Instead, she caught sight of the partly opened drawer of her daughter's writing desk. As Nell went to close it, she saw a letter inside that had been folded, then unfolded, so it lay not quite flat in the otherwise empty drawer. It was written on the stationery inscribed with their names that Grandma Edith had given each girl for Christmas.

March 1st, 1947

Dearest Shannon;

I want to be the one to tell you—although it will certainly come as such a shock to you that I am afraid to do so. Please understand that although I didn't want or ask for this, I will be all right, and when you get better, we will all be fine and together again. If I could tell you in person, I would, but I don't know for certain when I will be able to talk alone with you.

I am pregnant. Mother and Fa say I must go to the Catholic Maternity Home for unwed mothers in a few months' time until the baby is born. There it is. Dr. Johnston confirmed it. Tonight, after dinner, when Mother and I had finished dishes in the kitchen and Fa was listening to GI Jive on the radio, Mother told me to join him, and then she asked him to turn it off, so we could 'discuss the matter.' I didn't think I could manage it without you, Shannon—did you feel it?

Of course, there wasn't any discussion at all. Mother was the only one who spoke. She went to the stairwell and called upstairs for Ed to come down. She really did yell, Shannon. He was so startled he flew out of his room and leaped down the stairs. If I hadn't been so scared and well, just scared, I might have laughed. Ed would have laughed too, but he saw Mother's stony face, and instead he looked at me as if he hoped I'd send him an explanation through silent magic.

Did I tell you he has been so much happier since Christmas? I'm sure I did. I think it's because Olivia O'Rourke has come back from Northwestern—and I don't think I told you that.

I'm stalling because I don't want to recall what happened next; I'm afraid to write it because it will make it truer than I can bear. But I promised to tell you everything—at least everything I can tell. Mother looked right past me and demanded to know if he knew.

Edmund's mouth opened and closed twice like a guppy's, but this time, I didn't want to laugh at all. He looked so confused. He shifted his weight and asked me, "Know what? Is it Shannon?"

"*Eliza is with child; she is pregnant.*" She hesitated with the word 'child', and then emphasized the word 'pregnant'—as if she needed to correct her reference to the human being part of it. Stern voice again. "*I am telling you now, if you breathe a word of her condition to anyone, and most notably, to anyone at St. Thomas or in the Whitaker family, there will be a high price to pay.*" Her eyes drilled into him, and he could not look away for a moment, but then I saw him steal a glance at Fa for support.

Fa was staring down at his hands resting on his knees as if doing so would keep his legs from disappearing. The silence that followed was a relief, at least for me. Mother was determined (why are you not here with me, Shannon? I can hardly bear it), but all I could think about was, how? How can I do what she is asking? I can't bear to be alone in such a place without you, Shannon—without Mother or Ed or Fa. I think I'd go crazy.

It is all I can do to write what's here—I know it's unfair. I know I should ask all the questions about how you are doing, Shannon. How did you feel today? Is it difficult to breathe, or is it getting better like you said it would? I am crying now, Shannon—I can't help myself. I feel such shame. Part of me wants to burst into a thousand particles of dust. At least the pain would go away. Please write soon, even if just a little. Mother says I can visit you only once more.

Love forever,
Eliza

P.S. Shannon, please do not ask me about David. It is not his fault. You must never ask, Shannon. NEVER.

Nell wondered if Eliza had purposely left the letter for her to discover. She considered the double tragedy: one daughter confronting death, the other bearing unwanted life. For a moment, she felt the presence of her younger self on the night she'd stolen away, leaving her father and both siblings forever. Nell sat at Eliza's dresser, seeing for the first time a pair of veins crossing from wrist to fingers, swollen, uneven, miniature rivulets flowing under papery-thin skin, one on the back of each hand. She thought of her grandmother, then imagined the child Nellie and the child Eliza sitting on the bed between Jessie and Abel, all four somber, staring at Nell and silently cursing her, holding her responsible for all that had happened. Tears welled uncontrolled.

For a moment, she allowed the spirits of her grandmother and her mother to comfort her—even as she felt the spirit of her younger daughter slipping away. She took a sharp breath and put the letter back in the drawer, taking care to place it as it had been, then she stepped out of the room with the door wide open just as she'd found it.

12

MARCH 1947

Eliza shifted her weight in an attempt to battle a ripple of nausea for the second time today. She looked out the car window, hoping for a sight that might distract her for the remaining two miles to the hospital. In her matter-of-fact briskness, Mother had called it morning sickness, an obvious misnomer as far as Eliza was concerned. Again, a churning wave of rejection pushed high in her stomach causing her back to tighten and her throat to constrict.

Fa stopped the car at a four-way intersection. Eliza saw a little girl sitting on the grass with a toy sheep on a tether, while an older man, perhaps her grandfather, worked in a garden. She smiled and remembered her adoration of Grandpa Theo as a little girl. Had he and Grandma Edith been told yet? Mother had been silent about it since that night of reckoning, and Eliza couldn't bear to ask; she didn't know how far word had or would spread within or beyond the family.

A moment later, her stomach calmed, she saw a fading war poster painted on the side of a red brick building. Her thoughts narrowed to a particular episode, a crystal-clear memory from when she'd been fourteen years old and had sat close to Grandpa Theo on the leather couch in his dark-paneled library, her head leaning on his shoulder. She'd remained silent, observant, and felt almost invisible as he grimly conversed with Fa after radio announcers reported a news alert that US Air Force pilots had dropped the second atom bomb on Nagasaki just hours before.

"Well, son, I disagree," Grandpa had said. "It's my view *if you're going through hell*—and we no doubt are in Japan—*you'd better keep going*. To quote Sir Churchill, I believe. No other way out, Cecil, no other way."

Although she'd known very little about the war, young Eliza Malone had been certain that Japan must be the most hellish place on earth.

Now, going through her own agony, she knew her only way through would be to keep moving, distracting her mind from dark places, and to act as best she could as if very little in her life had changed. But at times, like right here in the car with Mother, Fa, Ed, and Father Eggers, pretending was difficult. The tumultuous machination of her body and her efforts to hide her fear from those around her were constant reminders of her new reality.

Ed looked at her, concerned. She realized she was both grimacing and holding her breath as nausea crested and subsided. She attempted a reassuring smile to which he responded by placing his hand on hers and squeezing lightly.

He leaned over and whispered, "Hold on, 'Lyza, we've almost arrived."

Ed's kindness helped, but her fear only deepened that nothing, not even visiting Shannon, would release her from the battle she waged to accept her condition and forget the unspeakable event that had created it.

"Ceece, how old were we when we first won the Summer's End Regatta? Twelve or thirteen?" asked Father Eggers, who sat in the front passenger seat of the 1935 Woody wagon Grandpa Theo had presented to the family with much pomp and circumstance twelve years ago. Father Eggers, a jovial man, turned his head to Fa and projected his voice so Mother, Eliza and Ed sitting awkwardly silent in the back seat would hear.

"Thirteen, I believe," Fa said. "I miss those days. I don't even know if they still run that race."

"Those rarified Excelsior families wouldn't let it die, would they, Edmund? You should know—I hear you're close with the O'Rourke family these days, young man—by way of lovely Olivia." Father Eggers took his gold pocket-watch from its niche beneath his cassock, checked the hour, and dug at his waist to put it back. He ran his finger along the inside of the stiff white collar as if it choked him, which made Eliza see him for a moment as the rowdy, athletic college boy he'd likely been. "Eliza, how do you find St. Catherine's, dear? Challenging enough?"

"Yes, Father Eggers." She considered saying more about the lack of coursework in socio-political affairs to which she was currently drawn, but she didn't trust herself with small talk these days. Maybe it was something else, too: a dulling of her ability— or more honestly her desire—to charm adults with engaging conversation and intelligent insights. Her mind had been under siege for the past ten days, and she felt unable to pry her thoughts away from the inevitability that she'd have to postpone her education, which was the only happy part of her present life.

Even more frightening, no one but she—and Shannon, once she heard the news—seemed to care.

"Do you know what you'd like to major in? Not finding a husband, I hope. You're too smart for that. You'd best graduate first, then start hanging around St. Thomas again."

"Father Eggers," Mother interrupted him, "Cecil and I hoped we could have a cup of coffee with you after you give the blessing of the ashes. I've called ahead to the hospital to arrange to use the chapel office. There is a personal matter we'd like to discuss."

"Of course, Nell. I'm going to the men's ward as well, so let's meet in the chapel at, say, eleven o'clock?"

"Thank you, Father," Mother said.

Eliza winced. Dual visions flashed before her of life without Shannon, and of a life cut off from her family's embrace. She couldn't fix Shannon's illness, but she knew her own dismal circumstances made her family's suffering all the more difficult. Imagining the discussion between her parents and Father Eggers caused a painful stab of loneliness and intolerable shame—new emotional territories—that began to cleave her self-image into two parts: Eliza from before—confident, optimistic, safe—and Eliza from now on—frightened and, for the most part, alone.

～◯

The low winter sun poured through the cloudless sky into the TB ward from the oversized windows, so that the walls appeared to be the pale-green color of raw milk. As usual, cracked open windows left the room too cold for Eliza to remove her wool coat. Shannon was propped up in bed wearing an indigo-blue shawl bound in front with a white abalone-shell pin, a gift from Grandmother Edith. Eliza thought Shannon looked lovely; her thin cheeks and loosely pulled-back hair reminded her of a renaissance depiction of St. Joan of Arc before her self-transformation into a young warrior. The shawl's blue yarn called out Shannon's eyes, and they appeared darker, more bejeweled than Eliza remembered. Mother, Fa, and Ed stood, while Eliza sat next to the bed, took hold of Shannon's hand, and held it firmly. Father Eggers, donned in his purple Lenten vestments, muttered brief Latin prayers, then took his blackened thumb from the silver urn and pressed it onto each sister's forehead, making a small cross before turning to the others. He walked through the room, giving the blessing to more patients and nurses, who held their rosaries and wore their head veils as indication of their Catholic faith.

For some time after Father Eggers left for the men's ward, the Malone family sat together around Shannon's bed while Ed regaled them with his stories of campus life. His roommate James Morgan, an affable kid he'd known since childhood, had an odd habit of stashing sausage and crackers under his bed, just to pull them out, eat them in the middle of the night and complain the next day that they'd gone missing. Only when James discovered crumbs in his sheets did he discover his old friend was a sleepwalker. If he didn't prepare a stash under his bed, both feared he would wander outside, fully asleep, searching for food.

Ed settled into his audience. Like Grandpa Theo, he managed to own the moment for the collective benefit of avoiding uneasy situations. It occurred to Eliza that academic excellence, good behavior, and righteousness might have been her chosen way, but where had it gotten her after all? Ed's path—one of least resistance and good nature—served him enviably well.

"It's the first time the five of us have been together since I was admitted," Shannon said, her face glowing. "And it's been over five months. Can you imagine? What a treat."

Eliza watched Mother, who smiled a brief, stern smile as she reached to stroke Shannon's hair and fix it as if it were slightly unkempt. She patted her cheek. "Dear girl, I'm so sorry for all of this. You'll keep getting stronger, Shannon. You will, won't you?

Are you eating all of your meals?"

Father Eggers returned to Shannon's bedside and said goodbye to Ed, Shannon, and Eliza. "Shall we go downstairs, then? Nell, Ceece? I have more time than I thought. It's only ten-thirty. Fewer Catholics in the men's ward, for some reason—or fewer who'll admit to it, at least."

When they'd gone, Ed and Eliza remained at Shannon's bedside, neither using the white face masks to cover their mouth and noses. Ed told another story of a new buddy Robby Berg getting stuck in the garbage chute of a downtown apartment building after a late night party off campus. Eliza noticed his expressive eyes as he led to the climax of the story, and she wondered whether it wasn't he himself who'd gotten stuck. For a moment, she forgot her own predicament and returned to the more comfortable role of the righteous sister who had no inclination to approve of his rowdy behavior.

"It sounds as if Robby got his just desserts, Ed," she said with a stern smile, no doubt looking much like her mother's.

"SHANNON, I'VE WRITTEN YOU A letter," Eliza said when just the two of them shared Shannon's small space among the other patients in the ward.

"I'm so sorry I haven't sent more letters home, 'Lyza," she said, unresponsive to the caution in Eliza's tone. "I don't know why not; I'm sick of embroidery and reading. I'm not a good letter writer. Not like you. I'll do better."

"It's all right. I want you to read this one while I'm here."

"Honestly? 'Lyza, why don't we just talk, and I'll read it later. Have you made up with David? I do hope so. We never have a chance like this; you've only ever been here four times, not that I blame you, with all my damned surgery."

"Please, Shannon, please stop cursing and read it. We'll talk afterward." Eliza's exasperation seemed to sober Shannon. Her sister unfolded the letter and held it with both hands, her forearms resting on her blanketed legs. Eliza watched the color in her sister's cheeks rise. Shannon's eyes widened, and she blinked heavily, but she remained silent until she finished.

Dumbstruck and searching Eliza's face in disbelief, she finally said, "No. No! This cannot be. Eliza, no!" She paused. Her voice grew hushed and quivered, "I know you said 'never ask', *but I've got to*. You must tell me. Aren't you afraid? Why doesn't David know?"

Eliza shook her head and struggled to speak. "No, Shannon, David had nothing …" She faltered and held her breath, pursing her lips, and biting down on her lower one until it hurt. Yes, of course she was afraid, and telling Shannon would lessen its rawness, her bewilderment—wouldn't it? Shannon was the one person in the world she was sure she could trust. She could tell her what happened that horrible night. At least some of it. She shoved from her mind a nagging protestation that it was Shannon, fighting for her own life here, she was protecting by keeping her secret in the first place. She suddenly yearned to expose the crazed, violent attack here and now, if only for a few seconds of relief from the loneliness and shame she'd lived with ever since. "Shannon, I …" she began but hesitated when Shannon's eyes brightened as she looked toward the entrance of the ward.

"Harvey! What a surprise!" she said. "I had no idea we'd see you today."

He came close to Eliza and put his arm around her shoulder, hugging her tightly before reaching down to take Shannon's hand after she placed the letter in the nightstand drawer and closed it.

"Harvey, it's good to see you." Relieved by the interruption, Eliza put the moment she'd dreaded behind her. Harvey was earnest, smart, and always self-deprecating. He was different from other boys—uncomplicated and trustworthy. It was good of him to come.

Shannon managed a quick, pleading glance her way, a wordless request to continue later where she'd left off.

Eliza knew it wouldn't happen, not today, not ever.

～◯

By late April Eliza was well into her second term, and her skirts pinched around her waist, though she'd lost weight everywhere else. The bed rest and pills Dr. Johnston had prescribed did little to relieve the morning sickness wracking her body for several unpredictable hours a day. Morning and evening headaches now compounded her misery, and although she often fell asleep exhausted by nine thirty, anxiety attacks often awakened her in the middle of the night. They frightened her, leaving her feeling both monstrous and meek—and worst of all, unwilling to close her eyes for fear of something unseen; but they were not matters she discussed with Mother or anyone else. Nor did she want to share the recent appearance of several patches of red bumps that turned into sores if she scratched them. She found she neither could nor wanted to have such intimate discussions with Mother about any part of this disaster.

Only once or twice did she allow herself to wonder how she would be, feel, think when the moment came, and each time she did, an internal burst of rage interrupted the vision and forced her to retrain her thoughts. Her anger flared with images of both Mother and Fa. Now her only salvations were her correspondence with Shannon, who'd begun to write decent—though short— letters, and, for the time being, immersion in her classes, her coursework, and her exam preparation. Even when sick, she could will herself to sit through classes no matter how horrible she felt— she'd missed just a handful of lectures so far. Mrs. Perkins, though she'd met her only once, was often on her mind. Eliza imagined the fulfillment of a career in government or law, the excitement of advising presidents or writing meaningful books on important subjects, subjects other than cookbooks and fiction. But just as her imaginings grew, so did her doubt that any such possibilities existed for her now.

Spring had arrived early, and the air was warm enough for Eliza's bedroom window to be open. On a Friday afternoon, she looked up from her final draft entitled The Migration of Labor from the American South to the Northwest Territories after the Civil War and noticed patches of lily-of-the-valley surrounding Ed's chicken coop. The beauty of their delicate-white bells surrounded by vibrant-green fronds shooting from winter-beaten grass brought a wave of melancholy. Such inexplicable attacks of raw emotion often overcame her. She didn't bother to wipe her tears, rather, sighing, she dried her pen, capped her ink, and retreated to her bed, where she curled up fully dressed with the letter she'd received today from Shannon via Ed.

April 25th, 1947

Dear E,

I have good news from Dr. Johnston, which I think M has not shared yet. My lungs are almost clear. While I do have to undergo the U removal, Dr. J says it is almost certain—after I recover from the final surgery—I'll be able to return home.

The saddest part, dear E., is it won't be until late June at the earliest, and M insists you will be gone then. So, I guess in a very big way, my news is not so very good. I am feeling stronger every day and am beginning to imagine what it will be like not to be here. I know from my experience you will do fine once you get comfortable there. It will take you less time than it took me because you are so confident and strong and positive.

We have a new 'renter' this week—remember, that is the term we old hands give to the new girls when they first arrive. Sheila Foxx is her name; isn't it exotic, with two x's? She's a wisp of a woman—quite dear, and, Eliza, she is pregnant too. The nurses all whisper the baby might not survive since her body is so enfeebled. It makes me think about you, dear E. I wish I knew better what and how you felt. I wish I knew what you were about to tell me when Harvey came to visit. I try to understand what it will mean to me to not be able to have children; yet you are struggling to survive what is a trauma for you. Or is it, E? Do you ever think of what it might be like to be a mother to your baby? We could at least dream about her (or him!), couldn't we? Please forgive me, I am so confused about the future; I want nothing more than for it to be simple, but it promises not to be.

Love,
Shannon

Eliza worried Shannon was too cavalier regarding her upcoming surgery. Mother and Fa avoided discussing it, which Eliza took as an ominous sign—one she could not afford to dwell on. As for the rest of the letter, Eliza tried to ignore the last three sentences. The suggestion Shannon made was repellant; the sooner this situation was behind her, the better. Shannon might as well have been writing in Greek, though Eliza did agree that nothing about their future looked simple. At least she finally stopped mentioning David as Eliza had begged her to do months ago.

David had left her alone for months, but in recent weeks he'd telephoned several times. She heard Mother explain that she was at the library, but, yes, she would give the message to Eliza. Each time she noted a crisp edge in Mother's voice that she was certain poor David must have heard as well. How terribly confused he must be. She felt sorry for him, though not in a way compelling her to act, and his calls went unreturned. The happiness she'd shared with David was removed from her current reality not once, but twice and then some. He wasn't responsible for casting her into this new world any more than she was, but whether he knew it or not, he was part of it, and he had his role to play. He should get her out of his head and move on.

Later in the day, Eliza began a letter to Mrs. Perkins, unclear as to what her message was, but urgently hoping to make the connection Mrs. Perkins seemed to invite when they'd met under such strange circumstances.

The telephone rang and interrupted her thoughts. Eliza hesitated to answer it. If David called she could simply hang up, rude as that would be. In a strange way, however, she urgently wanted to tempt fate—to hear his voice again, to hear for herself that he still cared. Nothing was straight in her mind, probably a trick of her hormonal condition.

"Hello, Malone residence," she said into the receiver after the fifth ring.

"Thank goodness you answered the phone, Eliza," Mother said in a controlled clip. "Grandpa Theo has suffered a small stroke today. I'm with Grandma Edith and will be taking her to the hospital as soon as the ambulance leaves. Is Fa home?"

"No, he's not; but Mother, he won't die, will he?"

"It was, as I said, a small stroke. They'll know more once they get him stabilized, I'm sure. You'll need to go to campus and tell your father to meet us at Milner Hospital as soon as he can."

Eliza hung the phone on its cradle on the kitchen wall and fell into the chair beside it. She felt the light in the room dim about her as the fear of losing him on top of everything else that was wrong took root. No, it couldn't be. A wave of exhaustion came over her as it often did this time of day, and as much as she wanted to lie down and fall asleep, she gathered her light wool cape around her shoulders and began the short walk to Fa's office.

April 28th, 1947

Dear Mrs. Perkins,

I am uncertain whether you remember the incident, but your kind support when I fainted in the front row after your speech at University of Minnesota meant so very much to me. I have felt compelled ever since to write to you—both in appreciation and also to express my admiration of your life's work.

I have never met a woman as accomplished as you. Since we met, I have researched and read everything available about your accomplishments as Secretary of Labor, and about your political and social welfare writings since then. I hope you can understand, perhaps from some experience in your own youth, my excitement at the prospect of building a meaningful career and intellectual life, such as yours.

As you may recall, the doctor who attended me suggested that I follow up with our family physician, which I did. I have told no one the truth—but for some reason, I feel that I may do so in greatest confidentiality, writing to you. I was violently attacked, raped, and drugged by a soldier—a local War hero, a POW, and the much-admired cousin of my suitor. It happened in our family's own kitchen—I was home alone while my parents tended my dear sister who is hospitalized for tuberculosis.

I want nothing more than to complete the steps I must complete—and to leave Minnesota. I am not so much an intuitive person, rather a rational one—yet, I sense I am safe disclosing to you. If you have advice as to steps I might take to best pursue an academic path as bold and enriching as possible, please let me know. My yearning to escape here is not just in response to the shame of my current condition—it is from an ember of self-knowledge that was lit when I heard you speak, and that I am determined to enflame.

Please send any future correspondence to the Catholic Home for Unwed Mothers, St. Paul, Minnesota, where I will be from early June through October.

Kind Regards,
Elizabeth Malone

THE FOLLOWING FRIDAY—NOTABLE FOR HER gratitude that she'd, for once, wakened not feeling nauseous and dizzy with vertigo—the call came from Watermelon Hill. Her "bed" would be available as of May twentieth. She had less than two weeks to face the depressing task of talking with her professors and arranging to finish the semester from her new residence. Whether her instructors knew of her condition, she could not guess, but she did, in fact, care. Lately, she'd become uncharacteristically concerned about how others perceived her. She couldn't ignore the glances of acquaintances floating down to her midriff and lingering there for a long second before looking quickly away. She noticed the extra foot of space some people now gave her when she was in their circle of conversation. Maybe she was too sensitive, but Jody Remminger could hardly speak to her without blushing and speaking in a voice too loud for normal conversation. Though not enough to make firm conclusions, the accumulation of incidents made her feel uncomfortably self-conscious, and the idea of finishing out the term elsewhere was not as horrible as it had first seemed.

At home, Eliza tried to maintain a routine, but every day brought new discomforts, and each of these brought a deeper sense of despair. Daily, she battled hot flashes, hunger and nausea, inexplicable itches on her arms and legs, and worst, an irrational weepiness that struck without warning, causing her to bury her head in her hands. Her bedroom was meticulous; anything reminding her of the Whitaker boys had been long-since thrown away, including the white angora sweater from David. She'd considered for a moment giving it to Shannon, but quickly realized that even that was impossible. Thoughts and nightmares of her attacker had faded away, replaced by constant reminders of her unwanted condition.

Mother regularly asked how she felt, and Fa found opportunities to kiss her forehead or cheek or to give her a careful hug. But she couldn't embrace their attempts because she didn't trust their actions as sincere. Imagined or not, she sensed unspoken judgment from both parents. Or maybe they simply couldn't cope with the burdens at hand. Grandpa Theo had been released but was restricted to bed rest for at least a month, and his daily needs overwhelmed Grandma Edith so that Mother spent as much time at the lake house as at the hospital.

Shannon awaited her next surgery—the worst one, by far— to remove her uterus, and only God knew the outcome of that. Either way, Eliza felt abandoned and shamefully needy all at once.

The letter she'd sent to Mrs. Perkins went unanswered, but she didn't regret sending it. The memory of their brief meeting uplifted Eliza like a spirit messenger sent from her future self, assuring her that from these ashes she could create the life that was rightfully hers.

HER FIRST DAYS AT WATERMELON Hill seemed easy enough. Eliza
had prepared for weeks, as if readying for a midterm exam in a
class she'd rather not have to take but was determined to complete
with a certain degree of perfection. She composed herself and
made the best possible impression on the nuns and staff—these
were, after all, the adult-pleasing skills that came to her naturally
and which, in recent months, she'd learned to moderate to her
best advantage. But through some sense of survival or perhaps
through an intuition to protect her self-image from further
damage, she kept a marked distance from the other girls—though
at mealtime they could not be escaped.

For the time being, she had to herself small personal quarters
furnished with two single beds, two plain dressers, and a large
wardrobe on the second-floor dormitory section of the building.
That luxury would change soon, as she'd been told when she
first arrived here, only six miles from home. Never more than a
few weeks passed with an unfilled bed at the Catholic Home for
Unwed Mothers, and on June fifteenth Eliza's roommate, Glenda,
arrived.

"Really pleased to meet you ... what did you say your name
was again?" Glenda said while looking down at her midsection
and sitting on Eliza's bed. Before Eliza could respond, she asked,
"Do you think I could have this bed? I sleep on my right side,
mostly, and I'd be facing this hideous wall if I have to sleep over
there. And it's right in front of the door. Horrible, really."

Eliza didn't know how to respond to the second question, so
she chose to answer only the first. "Eliza. My name is Eliza." She
felt an old familiar surge of fair play and said, "I'm sorry you don't
like your bed, Glenda. We can trade off, two weeks each. That's

reasonable."

"All right, but you've already had two weeks, so it's my turn, isn't that right?" Glenda asked as she inspected her fingernails and chipped away at the remaining polish.

"No, that's not right. You may have the bed I'm currently using in two weeks, as long as you promise to abide by switching every two weeks thereafter," Eliza said evenly.

"Fine. No need to snap your cap, Mrs. Grundy."

Eliza decided to forego being affronted, and instead asked, "Who is Mrs. Grundy? I've never heard the name."

"I don't really know. Ma is a Londoner; she called me that when I was being a little pest. Mostly when I thought I knew everything. So, there you have it."

Glenda was several years younger, and upon first impression not someone Eliza felt compelled to befriend. Of course, she felt the same way about almost everyone these days—not a fact she was proud of. How badly she missed Shannon. She sighed and took the four steps from bed to door before saying, "I'm going to the library for a spell. If you'd like, I'll take you to the dining room at six and introduce you to the other girls."

"Dandy." Glenda sat on Eliza's bed with her legs crossed, leaning back toward the wall.

As she walked down the hall to the library, Eliza wondered with a bit of dread whether Glenda's excessive use of slang was a hallmark of her personality or a reasonable response to managing first-day jitters.

The question was answered shortly after she returned to her room at five-fifteen and found Glenda not there. She changed her blouse, put on a light sweater, and waited five more minutes before going to dinner. From a distance as she approached the double doors, she heard a high, boisterous laugh in the center of the dining room.

"I'm the sixth of eight girls and the second one to get knocked up," Eliza heard the already recognizable voice of her roommate. "Ma says better me than her—she started at seventeen and hasn't yet stopped putting buns in the oven. She gave birth to number eight a month ago. We all hoped for a baby boy for once, but no dice. Slam bam, thank you ma'am; it's a girl."

"It's a horrible term, 'knocked up.' Where did you hear that?" said Babs Wilber, who sat across from Glenda.

Eliza felt grateful that Babs had beaten her to the reprimand.

"Come on, girls. It's the truth, anyway—getting in a fix is as old as the hills. But I won't say it if you don't care for it." Glenda leaned in and smiled slyly at Babs, who looked at Glenda as if she had two heads and broccoli for ears.

"Hi-de-ho, roommate." Glenda swung her whole body around and greeted Eliza. "Sorry to jump the gun, Mrs. Grundy. I was eager to meet the girls. Will you join us?"

After she'd eaten, Eliza excused herself early from the dinner table, one of five round tops spread out in the large dining room, and returned to the dormitory to retrieve her books. Thank God for the little library, she thought, half-wishing she could bring her bed in there. In the course of one brief dinner, her remaining four months had grown longer than she thought she could possibly bear.

A cream-colored envelope rested on her pillow, and she at first thought it might be a note from Glenda, either apologizing or claiming the bed for good. She couldn't think where or from whom it might be since it was larger than the stationary envelopes she and Shannon used. A printed return address on the front of the envelope made it look official, yet only upon closer inspection did Eliza see the crest of Cornell University pressed into the back flap. She sat down on her bed and felt an urge to tear it open right then and there. How could she have forgotten, even temporarily, about the letter she'd been anticipating for weeks?

Once in the library she picked the most remote of the few desks to set down her stack of books. She used her silver-plated letter opener with EWM imprinted on the handle to slice open the top of the envelope. In those few seconds, eagerness plummeted to doubt and then self-recrimination. How could she presume Mrs. Perkins, the first female Secretary ever in the US government, would have anything to offer her? And how embarrassing that she'd shared so much with a virtual stranger in a complex, painful moment of both despair and hope.

June 5th, 1947, Ithaca, NY

Dear Miss Malone,

I was most pleasantly surprised to receive your letter several weeks ago. I had begun to think our odd encounter was simply no more than that. I apologize as well for my delay in corresponding. While I have not been traveling or speaking publicly since my engagement at U of M, I have been deeply occupied with planning for the newly established Department of Industrial and Labor Relations here at Cornell. I mention this both as an apology and as a matter of certain interest to you, given the contents of your letter to me and your apparent curiosity in Labor Relations.

As you requested, I will have mailed this letter to the Catholic Home for Unwed Mothers. I was greatly moved and disturbed to read of the attack you endured at the hands of a traumatized soldier, God rest his soul, and of the difficult choices you have made since then. My own beloved college roommate was violently abused 30 years ago by her husband's father, also a distinguished war veteran, and I have no shame in telling you she took her life shortly thereafter, being unable to live with the strain and undeserved misery it brought upon her.

*Many women, or people in general I suppose, are fated
to endure such horrors, while others of us are blessed with
only common ailments and concerns.*

*I would very much like to remain in regular contact
with you and to further consider your question regarding
admission to Cornell University beginning in the winter
session of 1948. Please send me a ten-page writing
sample from a current course, as well as your high school
transcripts, if possible (if not possible, please summarize
your high school credentials). This will be a fine place to
start.*

Kindest regards,
Mrs. Frances Perkins

Eliza closed her eyes tightly and made fists so she would not
grab the letter and possibly destroy its perfection. She felt at
once elated and shocked. She gasped and made a girlish giggle
followed by unstoppable tears. But this was not one of her many
irrational moments of weepiness. The letter contained everything
she imagined she needed to escape a dim future here in St. Paul.
She envisioned a fresh start—a life like the one she'd imagined for
herself a year ago after the August storm—a way to close the door
on the staggering pain and all the daily reminders she'd secretly
endured.

Would Mother and Fa let her go? Surely not. She'd be stuck
here in the purgatory of St. Paul, her excitement about St. Kate's
ruined by daily reminders threatening to arouse the terror she'd
worked so hard to bury. Mother had blamed her. Fa had been
silent. Shannon was maddening in her talk about babies. They
had all in one way or another failed her. She would be expected
to return to her old, confident self. *How?*

Thinking of home, her bedroom, Fa's library, the kitchen, her throat constricted, followed by familiar nausea and a desperate longing for another lost life. Tears came, and she didn't try to stop them. She was no longer *that* person—the person Shannon relied upon for strength, the person Mother and Fa called upon for reason and intelligence. She had little sense anymore as to who she was at all. If she were ever to discover herself—the Eliza she yearned to be—she would have to start by leaving. Everything and everyone. Even Shannon. She wiped her tears away and looked again at the letter. Slowly relaxing her fingers, she pulled air into her lungs to calm herself and felt a strange kick—a small, angry punch at the base of her heart.

13

JUNE 1947

The ring on Nell's finger had grown loose in the months since Shannon's diagnosis. She glanced at it before offering her hand to Cecil, hoping her touch would calm his nerves—and hers. Shannon would wake soon, and weeks of uncertain recovery from her third and riskiest surgery would begin. The doctors had warned that Shannon was weak, yet they had no choice but to operate. The uterus was infected. Spreading to other organs was a possibility. Without the surgery, Shannon would die.

They looked somberly at each other and then at Shannon, who lay unconscious on a gurney delivered to the recovery room minutes ago. It would be some time before the drugs wore off.

Nell wished she'd not forgotten her knitting. Cecil gripped her hand; his foot stopped tapping, and he used his thumb to twist the ring on her finger so the gems faced up before placing her palm on his knee. He leaned over and gently pecked her cheek. Nell stared down at the ring, not wanting Cecil to sense the depth of her fear at losing another child.

She recalled their wedding night when Cecil had patted the spot beside him on the white cotton sheets of the four-poster bed. "Let me tell you about your new ring, Nellie Malone," he'd started in with the Irish brogue that mimicked his father's more than he probably knew.

Nell had smiled. She loved Cecil for many reasons, not least among them his surprising ability to spin a yarn, surprising, she thought, for a quiet man so drawn to books and contemplation.

"Nell, honestly, it's not such a good story, but I want you to know," Cecil had said, and Nell remembered all of these years later that he'd dropped his Irish lilt.

"On the night of my eighteenth birthday, Pops took me out to the bar for some cups. His lips loosened, and he got boastful and ugly. It changed the way I've seen him ever since, though for the love of my mother I try not to show it."

"Keep on, Ceece," Nell had said. She'd closed her eyes, but whether Cecil could see it or not, she listened as if by hearing her husband's story, she could graft his family onto her own insufferable past and absorb a new one in its place.

"He was a junior police officer in Chicago. They sent him off to pursue a young runner who'd been given some goods to deliver. He said it was a heist between rival gangs," Cecil said. "The poor kid was likely no older than he was, maybe twenty. He caught up with him. Beat him unconscious. He found a pouch of diamonds, took a handful, and left the lad there to die or be killed."

"Is that what he told you, Cecil?"

"Yes, Nell, blind to the sin in it. Pops held onto the diamonds and left Chicago for home a year later. He sent his brother Paddy to New York to sell the jewels, all but a few. And the two of them used the money years later to start Malone Steelworks. Pops kept the biggest gem and had it set with rubies to give to Mother on the day I was born."

"I shouldn't wear it, Cecil. Perhaps it'll bother you too much."

"No, Nell. Ma knows nothing of it. She met Pops years after he'd returned home and started the business. Now the company's worth a fortune," Cecil said. "Ma loves that ring. She loves you too, Nell. It'd break her heart for you not to wear it."

"It must feel strange for you." Nell had looked at the ring and twisted it around her finger, feeling the cool jewels on her fingertips for the first time. Closing the door on the past would've been the better way for Cecil's father. Why had Theo spoken of it so many years later, risking his son's affection? Nell had secrets she would never willingly share, not even with her husband. Much less so, her children. "But, Cecil, he's been a good father to you, right? That must count for something," she'd finally said.

The ring turned again under the weight of the jewels, and Nell, looking at Shannon's still features, closed her fist, clenching tightly enough to feel the large diamond cutting into the flesh of her palm.

~⬭

SHANNON'S EYES WOULD NOT OPEN, no matter how hard she willed it; her lids felt heavy with drugs, and she found the harsh light seeping through unbearable. She shaded them with a hand she could barely identify as her own, and managed to open them just a sliver to take in the white walls of the recovery room. She forced a smile that might have appeared as a wince to Mother and Fa, who sat beside her narrow metal bed, awaiting her return to consciousness as they had each time in the past seven months.

Morphine muddled her thoughts. To ward off the overwhelming sleepiness, she tried to remember why she was there. She'd had another surgery since December, and Dr. Paul had assured her this one to remove her uterus would almost certainly be her last. Considering she was now eight ribs short of normal, and breathing—if one could call it that—with a functioning lung half its original size, she felt lucky to be alive. Even without moving, she felt wickedly sore, as if her flesh and bones had been steamrolled, and despite struggling to do so, she couldn't keep the intense drowsiness at bay. Again, she trained her thoughts on the reason for her surgery, hoping the mental exercise would defeat the overwhelming urge to sleep.

After the meeting with Dr. Paul last week, Mother had explained again in her abridged clip, which didn't invite conversation, that she'd never be able to conceive children, but without the uterus removal, the remaining tubercular bacteria could not be eradicated. Shannon had never been good at dealing with bad news—especially without Eliza's help—and the lifelong consequence of this final surgery, now complete, was so terrifyingly large and hollow and dark that even counting her whites did not comfort her; she forced it away into the deepest corners of her mind.

In the minutes before surgery, before the anesthesia drowsed her, she'd pictured Eliza in her mind. How could she possibly be managing at home alone so much of the time these last few weeks? Given her pregnancy she could no longer visit the TB ward, so Shannon was left to worry, with no ability to comfort Eliza through what was surely a frightening experience. For the first time Shannon felt the protective urge an older sister was supposed to have for her younger sibling. With Eliza, it'd always been the other way around. Alongside her worry for Eliza, a new seed of concern was sown: was the baby, Eliza's baby, safe and healthy in her sister's womb?

"Shannon, my girl. We're here," Fa said.

Mother rose from her chair and reached over the metal side of the gurney to stroke her cheek.

Shannon took Mother's hand, squeezed it weakly, and tried to speak. She wanted to ask Mother whether Eliza was all right and whether the baby had been born, but she knew somehow it wasn't the right question, and as her mind fought to remember why, she fell back asleep.

THREE WEEKS AFTER SURGERY IN early June, Shannon was well enough to sit in a wheelchair and be taken outside to the courtyard garden off the first floor of the hospital.

"You needn't continue making excuses for her, Harvey," Shannon said of their mutual friend Gloria who once again had cancelled her visit. "There are plenty of people who've been afraid to visit—friends and family alike. I haven't seen my Aunt Janie or Uncle Jonathan once, though my cousin Michael's come a few times with Ed."

Harvey nodded in silent understanding. He left the bench where he'd been sitting across from Shannon's wheelchair and continued his course, leading her around the sidewalk.

"Harvey, do you know I've gotten wiser since September? All these days and nights with a bunch of women twice my age; we've solved all the world's problems many times over." She paused but didn't give Harvey a chance to speak. "You're a good friend. I know Eliza feels the same way. I think you should talk with her more. She's so smart about things. As for me, I can't imagine life without you, so you mustn't go too far away. One thing I've learned is that you never know what life will dish out, so you better hold on to what's—or I should say who's—good. And you're the best, so I'm not letting go. I don't care if you're a Martian or a Zulu warrior."

"Well, I'm not quite an alien, but how about a guy who doesn't feel quite the way I'm supposed to? It's hard, Shannon, with my Pop. I want to study law, but all he can say is I should become a priest. He's got it all figured out."

"You? A priest? I take it you're still Catholic, then?"

"Sure, why not? Truth be told, I do it to honor Ma. She worked so hard to become a good Catholic. And you?"

"Hell, yes," Shannon retorted. "Though my idea of it all—being a 'good' Catholic, I mean—has changed somehow. In here."

"Right now, I can't wait to get you out so the three of us can enjoy the summer—maybe do the church bazaar routine to properly bring you back to the flock. Do you think you'll be out in time for the State Fair?" Harvey asked.

"More like the Winter Carnival if I don't watch myself," Shannon replied. "I'd better get back inside; I tire so quickly, and I don't want to press my luck. I'm aiming for Independence Day. In time to help Eliza."

14

OCTOBER 1947

Shannon had been home since late July. The transition was ongoing and difficult. She was unsure whether she was unaccustomed to sleeping at home without Eliza or sleeping at home at all. Eleven months in the TB ward had brought her far away from the comfort of her childhood bedroom, and although at first its familiarity had elated her, the room closed in around her now. It was the last place she wanted to be. Most mornings she struggled to leave bed. Solitude overcame her when she first woke up and looked around, seeing only the set of dolls looking back. Eliza, who was due to give birth any day now, was at this moment closer to the TB ward than home. The Catholic Home for Unwed Mothers—Shannon hated the local nickname of Watermelon Hill—was three blocks from Milner Hospital.

The phone rang. Mother answered it, and it quickly became clear to Shannon that Dr. Johnston had called to say that Eliza was in labor.

"I want to see Eliza, Mother. Just for a minute or two. I've got to," Shannon said as soon as Mother had said goodbye and hung up the receiver. She hoped her desperation, causing her eyes to sting and her cheeks to flush, might be overlooked. Mother would have to allow it when she came to understand how much Shannon needed to see Eliza. But she doubted she'd approve of her yearning to see the baby, the new soul she'd dreamed about night after night—of holding it in her arms and feeling a surge of maternal love as if it were *her* child and not just a dream.

"Why?" Mother asked, walking in measured strides across the linoleum floor. The newly repaired heels of her canvas shoes clock, click, clocked, managing to create an air of intimidation. Despite months of anxiety and sleepless nights, Mother was still a presence, whose eyes—blue and unremarkable like Shannon's— could pierce her children's thoughts, and the power of her gaze now shook Shannon's wavering certainty. "Why must you?" she repeated evenhandedly—almost, but not quite, kindly.

Shannon looked down, found a morsel of resolve and lifted her chin. She met Mother's gaze with her own and tried to borrow the saintly face Eliza had mastered years ago. "Please, Mother, you must know why. I have to see her today, so she knows I'm with her."

~◯

THE THREE MALONES DROVE ALONGSIDE campus toward the hospital in the center of town. Wet, drab leaves hung on the dark branches of the giant king crimson maples lining the streets.

Shannon felt the car sway as wind gusts shook the ancient trees' remaining seedlings from their hold. She watched them fall, floating down through the low, gray sky in front of the car, a silent army of capricious whirligigs. Fa, had he been able to enjoy the moment as he once had, would have told Shannon again that the trees could both switch their sexuality on demand from year to year, and hold thousands more seedlings when they chose to be female. Shannon tried to concentrate on this miracle as Fa drove on, eyes trained on the road, seemingly unaware of anything around him, while Mother, in the passenger seat, knit a scarf with brisk pulls and jabs.

"Weather's changing," Fa said.

"Certainly is," Mother replied, without looking up from her knitting. With no more words between them, Mother occasionally glanced up, pursed her lips together, then looked down again. At a stop sign Fa looked to Mother and placed his right hand on her knee before returning his attention back to the road.

After twenty-three years of marriage, moments of mutual silence were probably not rare. Silence was the least of their concerns, Shannon thought, and she occupied the long moments in the backseat of the aging Chrysler Woody by gently closing her eyelids and trying to imagine a thousand lavender balloons tied to her wrists by broad satin ribbon, lifting her into the heavens. She'd discovered after the first of her four surgeries that if she slowly squeezed and relaxed her eyelids several times, the orbs within felt little, like the seeds of an apple, and she could disconnect her senses from the nasty smells and unnatural coolness of the ward. She could then imagine herself floating, weightless, into a calm, blue sky with wisps of translucent clouds. Since returning home to a life without Eliza, she'd sometimes populated this celestial world with vague images from her dreams where she, Eliza and Eliza's baby lived together in Princess Irene's castle, a place as safe and magical as heaven on earth.

She had no trouble imagining heaven or a God who, since her drug-induced recoveries, she'd experienced as a euphoric, all-loving presence rather than the stern-faced, white-bearded grandfather of her catechism. As she and her parents continued their approach to the hospital, she tried once again to invoke that holy presence. "Please," she prayed, "give me a sign, Heavenly Father. I know you spared my life for a purpose."

"Shannon?" her mother spoke as if from the depths of the clouded sky.

"Yes?" she replied, returning to reality. She opened her eyes and sat up straight, relieved to see Fa pulling into the hospital driveway.

"Dr. Johnston said Eliza's labor has started, and it could take a very long time or none at all."

In the kitchen that morning, Shannon had overheard Mother relaying to Fa that Eliza had a worrisome fever, but no one had shared any such information with her.

"I think it's best if I go into Eliza's room first to see if your visit is appropriate. You must wear a cotton mask—between her fever and your recovery, you shouldn't be near each other at all. But you may go in for five minutes or so, and then I'd like you to take the bus home." All of this was said in a clipped, absent-minded tone while Mother gathered her knitting and donned her hat and gloves. "Don't you agree, Ceece?" Mother asked, looking again into her hand mirror for several long seconds as if to archive this strange moment as an artifact from the "time before."

They arrived at the delivery room to find that Eliza had not slept for two nights and was close to delirium. Her eyes appeared glassy, and her puffy lids sagged. It would've terrified Shannon to see her like that in the past, but after her many surgeries and months of infirmity, she was not as concerned with Eliza's impaired consciousness as with the difficulty it brought to their communication. The few words she uttered dropped from her lips like lead weights, and her low, gravelly voice worried Shannon.

A brusque, middle-aged nurse with no eyebrows and a waxy upper lip administered the drug Scopolamine and said, as she left the room, that it would induce a "twilight sleep." *How obnoxiously lovely they try to make it sound.*

Mother kept her word and allowed her to be in the room alone with Eliza. Eliza gripped Shannon's hand and looked at the wall in front of her, seemingly unable for a moment to turn her head. Shannon fought off a desire to flee from the memory of the antiseptic smells and intruding hospital lights imprinted on her mind from months in the TB ward. She worried about Eliza and, even more, about how the unwelcoming strangeness of the room would soon feel to her sister's unborn child.

"Remember, Eliza, how I'd dance for you on my bed when we were little? You'd beg me to stop, but you couldn't stop laughing. You worried Mother would hear and come to scold us ... so afraid she'd be angry." Shannon hesitated, angry with herself for becoming emotional. "It doesn't matter, Eliza. Mother and Fa, Ed, we all love you. I've missed you so terribly." She leaned into the gurney and whispered, unsure whether Eliza could hear her, "And I love the baby, Eliza, even if you can't. You've always been ..." she hesitated because the word was so inelegant, but it was the right word. "You're strong. You know you are. We'll all be home soon; you, me ..." her list stalled as Eliza stumbled through her drowsiness to speak.

"I don't want it, Shannon. Don't say you love—I don't want ... I hate—" Eliza made a feeble effort to shake her head as her words of rejection trailed off.

Shannon saw Eliza's eyes close as the drugs took effect. She stroked Eliza's flushed cheek and said quietly, "Eliza, don't say that. You don't mean it."

Fa sat in the waiting room, engrossed in a manuscript for a new children's fantasy book to be published by a British colleague from Oxford. Shannon moved his leather satchel off the chair next to him and sat down. She put her hand on his knee, feeling the heavily starched crease of his khaki trousers and hoped not to startle him out of his deep concentration.

"It's quite good, if not a bit heavy-handed, a good-versus-evil allegory with a lion and a witch," he said, closing the book around his forefinger holding the page he'd left. "Eliza would especially like it, I think."

"I'm going to walk part way home, then take the bus," Shannon said. "Mother thought it would be a good idea; I can get some exercise."

His eyes, so often distracted or introspective, met hers, and he smiled with a slight upward jerk of his head. Shannon knew this response from her father well—the most minimal of physical gestures, but filled with an odd sort of empathy, perhaps, in this case, an unconscious acknowledgment of her true intentions.

MOTHER CAME INTO SHANNON'S BEDROOM in the late evening still wearing the tan lambskin gloves and matching cashmere cape she'd worn to the hospital. Thick strands of auburn and gray hair had loosened from her once-tidy bun, and her unpainted lips formed a somber line. She sat down at the very edge of the dressing table stool and peered out the window into the darkness, then she looked down at her gloved hands, clasped and pressed to one side of her legs.

"Eliza needs rest, but she'll recover and be home in a few days. It was a difficult delivery, Shannon," she said, her tone changing from concerned to matter-of-fact. "The baby took on a fever tonight." After a pause, she added, "There was nothing anyone could do ..."

Mother got up and stood in the doorway, wanting or needing

to say more, Shannon thought, but she kept silent and turned to leave. Perplexed, she watched as her mother walked out of the room. She resisted an urgent desire to run after her, to grab her by the hands and explain she was wrong. Instead, she sat in the middle of her bed, knees to her chest, shutting out the possibility of hearing more, knowing she would regret a confrontation. Whatever Mother was about to say was wrong. She had no doubt. Shannon had seen the baby with her own eyes on the other side of the glass windows separating the hospital hallway from the nursery—the dimple-chinned newborn was Eliza's child—beautiful, alive and most definitely a Malone.

PART TWO

15

JANUARY 1948

I believe you're the girl I'm supposed to meet, Miss Malone."

The young woman, perky and slight, had flaxen hair that glistened like corn silk cut in a page-boy style parted on the left and tucked neatly behind each ear. Her brown eyes, speckled with amber and shaped like teardrops on a paisley print, reached toward her temples—an appealing feature on an otherwise plain face. Her porcelain skin had a natural pink blush on her cheeks, which Eliza would soon come to recognize as a sign of her constant energy. Knee-tapping, finger-strumming, whistling; Beryl was always in motion.

An orientation luncheon took place in the Cornell University

Union Commons Ballroom at the beginning of each semester, an opportunity for newly arrived students to meet their roommates and to register for campus activities. Only a few dozen young men and women attended the January mid-year gathering, making the oversized space feel impersonal. The room, elegant and old, reminded Eliza of home. Within minutes, both new and returning students had found their assigned roommates.

"Please, call me Eliza. And you are?" she asked of the young woman who'd approached her. An unexpected memory of her first encounter with Glenda in the stark, sad room at Watermelon Hill grazed her thoughts and was quickly dismissed. Eliza had trained her mind to repel any reference to the horrible incident, the horrible year thereafter, and to the horrible final hours at Milner Hospital. Upon glancing in a mirror, she'd occasionally catch herself face-to-face with the girl fresh out of high school, the Eliza from before, who in a distant past had seen the world and its people as a series of delightful opportunities. But she always quickly dismissed that impression and the sinister memories accompanying it.

"I'm Beryl ... Beryl Jameson." The young woman stretched out a soft, cherubic hand. Eliza noted the warmth of the girl's fair skin, her perfectly manicured fingers, her classic friendship ring, a thin silver band with a modest radiant-cut emerald stone. The vigor of her handshake startled Eliza and she pulled back as her new roommate continued. "My first roommate Helen quit with one semester left to get married or some silly thing, so here I am, in the market for a new one. I went to her wedding over the holidays in Philadelphia; lovely," she stopped, and then added, "though a bit much. Helen's mother, well, let's just say she has something to prove." Eliza struggled to remain attentive until Beryl interrupted herself.

"... but, my, you do remind me of that unfortunate woman, Elizabeth something-or-other; I thought so the moment you walked through the door. Has anyone ever told you? I'm sure they must have. I saw her photo in the Boston Herald before the awful discovery, and I tell you, Miss Malone, you are the spit and image of her. Short! That was her surname. As long as you don't open your mouth, because her teeth were terrible wrecks." She paused long enough to assess Eliza's reaction—one of concentrated bewilderment. "Well, I see your teeth are fine … You mean you don't know who she was? Well, I'll be … Hah!"

"The name sounds familiar, but no, I don't. Where's she from? Boston?" Eliza remained polite, though her thoughts had already begun to turn away from Miss Jameson. She lingered briefly on the name of Elizabeth Short, vaguely resonant in her mind, but she was neither able nor interested enough to recall.

"Was she indeed! Well, I'm not going to be the one to tell you. You'll never want to room with me, then, dear."

Well, why, then, did you say it in the first place…dear? Eliza thought, exasperated as she might have been with Shannon, with people who couldn't edit themselves. Now, she supposed it was her place to continue the dialogue. What kind of introduction was this? And bother, when would she be able to leave this event? In the week since she'd arrived, she'd spent more than a few hours every day in the cozy nooks of the library. Her admiration for well-organized books was so profound she sometimes wondered if she weren't meant to be a librarian, as her grandmother had once been. In some ways Eliza knew more about her Grandma Edith, an accomplished artist, gardener, and lover of stories, than about her own mother, Nell.

"In any case, I think you're actually much more beautiful than she was, Eliza. You're clearly of a much better upbringing. Her father built mini-golf courses, of all the crazy things. They say she ran off to California for a life of sin. But my, the poor gal. Come on, let's lunch, and then I'll introduce you to the others from our corner of Dickson Hall dorm."

The orientation luncheon ended, and Eliza admitted to herself that she found Beryl charming—quirky and alarmingly exuberant, but well-mannered and, so far, respectful of her privacy. They might get along fine. For the first time in weeks, since she'd left her sister in St. Paul with her outright lie that they'd see each other soon in the lobby of the Plaza Hotel in New York City, Eliza relaxed, savoring the absolute rightness of where she'd landed. Memories of St. Paul and her family had settled into an untended corner of her mind. She was in Ithaca, New York, and she was precisely where she wanted to be.

My God, how horrible, Eliza thought that first night in their shared dorm room, as the moment passed from consciousness to the unconsciousness of sleep, in those seconds when dismissed thoughts of the passing day fall into their rightful places, *I do remember Elizabeth Short.*

16

MARCH 1948

Shannon looked at her reflection in the dressing mirror to check her lipstick. She puckered and tilted her head, trying to imagine another version of herself in another version of her life—one where Eliza was home, urging her to hurry or choosing an outfit for her, or assuring her the waves in her hair looked fine in the back, but her part down the middle needed a fix. She heard the door downstairs click open and close with Mother's signature firmness and looked out the front window to see her walking away from the house with her regular urgent gait, her appearance even more regal than usual from this birds-eye perspective. She wondered, was Eliza becoming more like

Mother? Would she return one day and be another version of Nell Malone?

She glanced at the mirror again and considered that the pink plaid skirt—her longtime favorite—was a poor match with the cream sweater. Eliza would never have let her leave the house in this. She cursed at her reflection, knowing the outfit wasn't quite right, but she had no idea what to do. Eliza and Mother shared a magical knack for pulling a look together with a simple scarf, a strand of pearls, or an unusual pair of shoes. A refined style was part of the same charm her sister had with people, or so Shannon used to think. Would she never stop thinking of Eliza every time she had a moment of self-doubt? How maddening to have gone from inseparable sister to a forgotten one. The sad quiet in the house made her want to scream.

Eliza had disappeared from her life the day before she and Betty boarded the train at Grand Central Station to return to the Twin Cities via Chicago after their well-planned, nearly perfect trip together to the east coast. The adventure they'd imagined in the months of quarantine at Milner Hospital had been all of the grand experience she'd hoped for. Her parents would've never let her go but for the fact that Betty was already thirty years old and had an aunt and uncle living in the Connecticut suburbs. Maybe they'd also believed, as Shannon had, that Eliza, who'd left weeks before, would return to her senses and come home once she saw her sister again.

A bulging envelope had been delivered to their Central Park hotel by a courier while they toured the city on a Friday afternoon. In it was a devastatingly sparse letter from Eliza informing them she would not be coming into the city for the weekend before their return trip home. Worse, she requested Shannon not contact her again.

I hope you can understand, Shannon, I need time. I will be in touch when I am ready. Love, Eliza.

She read the message again, neither terse nor fraught, neither rude nor kind, but neutral and to the point, and not at all in the spirit of the Eliza she knew. Not even the endearment of Shann or Lyza. It was as if the writer had been drained of her persona, any familial intimacy siphoned off and discarded. "Well," she said, turning away and looking down at the envelope, "We can't expect Eliza. Something has come up. She sends her regrets."

"I'm sorry to hear it." Concerned, Betty stopped reading the newspaper she'd brought to the room. "Are you all right? You so looked forward to seeing her."

But Shannon barely heard her. Along with the sparsely worded note was a velvet box Mother had thrust upon Eliza, upset and anxious, the night before she left home, the night she and Eliza had a shattering argument, the night that seemed to change everything.

Shannon opened its hinged lid, already knowing its content: Mother's brilliant wedding ring, the one Grandpa Theo had designed for Grandma Edith almost fifty years ago. Two days after returning from the hospital where she'd given birth, Eliza had come to Shannon's room, the center of their universe during childhood, her face red and blotched, hands clenched into fists.

Shannon had rushed to her sister and embraced her, quietening Eliza's trembling. "What happened, 'Lyza?" she'd whispered.

"Nothing, Shann. I'll be fine," Eliza had said, her eyes downcast. "Mother gave me this. That's all."

Shannon had led her to the corner of her bed, removed Mother's wedding ring from the velvet box, and touched the three gems she'd never been invited to touch before, then she'd returned it to its case and gently pressed it into her sister's palm. "'Lyza, I know what Mother says happened, but what if your baby ..."

Eliza had jerked back and jumped to her feet, the ring box falling to the floor, and Shannon, for a second, saw her sister as someone else, a stranger whose angry face looked like a terrible image in a circus mirror-house. "Shannon! Don't say it. Don't you dare. You cannot even think it. You don't know what you're saying, or what you think you want."

Her sister had raised her fist and opened her palm, and Shannon, confused, had waited for Eliza to slap her. When she didn't, Shannon picked up the box and reached to return it. For an instant, their eyes met, and she thought Eliza would crumble into her arms. But instead, her sister turned away, spitting words in a cold voice Shannon didn't recognize:

"Why are you such a child? You're a stupid, spoiled dolt! You don't think beyond your own nose." She turned back to Shannon, her eyes and cheeks aflame with rage. Her unsteady voice lowered to a hiss, "I swear to God, Shannon, I swear, right now I hate you." And then she was gone, leaving Shannon alone, speechless and terrified that something essential existing between them had suddenly vanished.

The next day, Eliza had left for the lake house. Grandpa Theo was ill, cycling between pneumonia and apparent recovery, then infection again. Shannon, unable to visit because of her own compromised health, imagined that Eliza was burying herself in the daily work of tending to him and helping Grandmother Edith. That was how her sister would naturally cope with pain.

By late November reports had come from the lake house that Grandpa Theo couldn't talk for more than a few minutes each day; wheezing and coughing would stop him mid-sentence, and his frustration would mount until Grandma Edith or Eliza sat beside him, stroking his cheek to soothe him. Grandpa, whose largesse and flamboyancy had made him seem immortal to Shannon, died a quiet death in early December. Without mention to Shannon, or so much as a note or letter, Eliza had already transferred her one full semester of credits from St. Kate's to Cornell University on the other side of the country.

Three months had passed since Eliza had left Minnesota. If

she'd truly gone, Shannon prayed she knew she always had a way back home. Grandpa Theo and Eliza had shared a special bond since the day Eliza was born, and Shannon suspected that Grandpa Theo had known what Eliza was planning and had interceded with Mother and Fa to let her go. She dearly hoped so.

The suspicion that lingered, the suspicion with visceral, nourishing roots in the center of her being, was the suspicion— or perhaps the premonition—that the baby, Eliza's birth child, the kindred soul whose spirit had reached through the hospital window and touched Shannon's spirit—whose human life God chose to spare—was somehow close by and needed her. How she would find the baby, when, and to what purpose, Shannon trusted God to reveal.

17

MAY 1948

Shannon relied on her friends Harvey and Betty to keep her busy. While St. Kate's had been put on hold, she had enough activities during the short winter days: volunteer work for the church, CYO dances, excursions downtown to see the new, six-level Dayton's department store, not to mention the regular physical check-ups to monitor her long-term recovery. Ed was a rare visitor at home. He spent most weekdays on campus and his weekends at the O'Rourke lake house with Olivia, now his fiancée. The hours thinking about Eliza and their argument, a far worse exchange than ever before, cutting and desperate and with an air of bitter finality, had worn away at Shannon, giving her an edge of melancholy buried deep within.

In the evenings, after somber dinners with Mother and Fa, after helping with dishes and reading in the library, after, or sometimes during, her nightly prayers, Shannon replayed the memory of her afternoon at the hospital when Eliza had given birth. The unforgettable image of Eliza's baby in the nursery hospital came to her. She closed her eyes and revisited each detail of the moment when the nurse brought to the large picture window the perfectly beautiful newborn whose crib tag read "Baby Girl." Sometimes, before sleep came, the thought formed a dream in which the ebullient nurse holding the newborn baby with her mother's dimpled chin, became Eliza. The window between them disappeared and Shannon, now an older woman and larger than young Eliza, embraced them both—mother and child.

~⌾

"HARVEY, HOW LONG DID YOU say we'd stay here at the church when you checked in this morning?" Betty asked as she re-organized the remaining selection of tea towels, napkins, and pillow cases—all items they'd embroidered while quarantined at Milner Hospital.

Shannon sat down next to her at the table they'd set up for the Spring Bazaar in the basement of St. Rose of Lima Church in Roseville and realized most of the day was gone.

"I told the ladies upstairs we'd stay another hour," Harvey replied. "Wait for the afternoon rush to end. Hope that's all right with you two; I'm taking Pops to the minor league game tonight. First of the season."

"It's fine," Shannon said. "I'd like to get home in time for dinner. Want to join me, Betty? Mother and Fa would love to see you again."

Betty didn't respond; she was smiling at someone behind

Shannon. "Look at that adorable baby, Shannon," she cooed. "My, how old is that precious little girl? Those ringlets—have you ever seen anything so darling?"

Shannon turned. The child's mother, a beautiful, immaculately dressed woman closer in age to Betty than Shannon, stood in front of the table where the three of them sat. She held her infant in her arms while her companion, probably her husband, stood by with a pram.

Shannon gripped the edge of the wooden tabletop with both hands and sprang to her feet. The paper cup in front of her tipped and threatened to spill water on the display of embroidered linens. "Oh! She's …" She could only speak one word, her voice just a murmur: "Eliza." After regaining her composure, she asked, "May I ask her name?"

"Miriam; my little darling." With a gloved hand, the woman removed the baby's fingers from her cheek and gave her a bounce. "She's being a fussy little girl, so I thought I'd give her a bird's eye view."

When Betty asked when the child would turn one, the woman shot a queer, pleading look to her husband. Shannon watched a silent exchange pass between them—a mysterious, private moment similar to occasional furtive glances she'd seen between Mother and Fa.

"We don't celebrate—an old Scottish superstition," he said, "but the Feast of St. Mirin—September fifteenth is her special day."

"Could I hold her?" Shannon asked, weighing the man's vague response to Betty's question and, at the same time, unsure of what she would or could say next to keep them close. "Just for a moment?"

"Well, yes; I suppose that would be nice while I look at the linens you have here. What a grand way to raise money. And how good of you to be volunteering. Are you St. Rose parishioners?"

"No," Harvey replied. "We're from St. Thomas of Aquinas, but we don't mind helping out, even if it is in a basement. We're hosting a joint CYO dance in a few weeks. Trying to raise money for it."

For Shannon, time stopped and conversation evaporated as she held the baby. The memory of standing in the waiting room of the nursery at the hospital last October flooded her. Eliza's baby in the hospital had the light-gray eyes of a newborn, like Baby Theodore's. The baby she now held, whose heartbeat she could feel and whose milky-sweet breath fell on her own cheek, was undoubtedly Eliza's child, her niece, Ed's niece, Nell and Fa's grandchild. She recognized every detail in her face as a facsimile of the face she'd seen behind the nursery glass: the exquisite shape of her eyes, now silvery-blue with no shade of newborn gray, and the broadness of her chin, with a dimple set in the center—a physical trait of both Fa and Grandpa Theo, not to mention Eliza.

Unaware of anything around her, she sat down with Eliza's baby in her lap, studying and smiling at her. God had finally delivered; here was the reason for her survival of four torturous surgeries and eleven months as an invalid. He had returned Eliza's baby to her, and this time, for all three of them, she would never let go.

"Look at that smile," the woman said. "You have a way with her, dear."

"Thank you, ma'am." Shannon resisted looking away from the baby for even an instant as she spoke; she had one finger wrapped in a curl falling from the baby's crown of thick, auburn hair. "I've taken care of babies before ... if you ever need help ..."

"Well, indeed I may. What is your name?"

"Shannon Malone, ma'am. I'm twenty. I mean I'll soon be twenty years old," she said, stumbling through the words.

"I'll be looking for someone weekly on Thursdays; it's my golf day at Como Park and I would like to get back to it now that

Miriam is settled into a routine. In the winter, there'll be bridge club and other events, no doubt."

"I can do that. And I can provide references. May I ask where you live?"

"We're right here in Roseville. And where do you live, dear?" She asked this not while looking at Shannon but while comparing the stitch-work of two donated sets of children's pillowcases embroidered by Shannon in her months of infirmity.

"It's not far; we live near St. Thomas, it's no problem at all to get here," Shannon said quickly.

"It might be a little too far," the woman looked sideways at Shannon and then to the baby. "I don't think so. We'd prefer a neighborhood girl. Don't you agree, Allan?" The woman looked over to her husband, who had moved several yards away and was talking baseball with Harvey. He lifted his head in pleasant acknowledgment. "Yes, too far, Ginny." Then he looked beyond his wife and said to Shannon, "But why don't you give us your telephone number, just the same?"

The next morning, Shannon cursed herself. How could she not have gotten their telephone number or even the couple's last name before they left the church basement? *How dimwitted can I possibly be?* She was, as Eliza had called her, a dolt. She'd held Miriam, Eliza's baby, on her very own lap; she'd been mesmerized, attuned to the baby's sweet-vanilla smell, the tiny-ness of her fleshy, pink fingers, the silvery-rimmed blue of her eyes, so everything, everyone else had melted away in the church that day.

～◯

IN THE FOLLOWING WEEKS, SHANNON could think of little else; she replayed the perfect moments of baby Miriam sitting on her lap, connected through every sense, and felt the clear edges of her own self begin to fade away, replaced by a wishful dream to be with her again. Her appetite and energy diminished; she missed meals, went to bed early, and slept late into the morning. Mother was convinced she was emotionally fraught but had no idea why. She'd been out of school for two full years, and Nell and Fa both expected her to begin thinking about classes at St. Kate's in September. Her sudden lethargy was, they told her, illness, avoidance, or both.

"Shannon, you have an appointment tomorrow at nine o'clock to see Dr. Johnston for a physical," Mother said when Shannon came down to the kitchen one day in early June and several weeks after the bazaar at St. Rose of Lima. "Perhaps he can clear up the mystery of your recent malaise."

Shannon didn't protest. A visit to Dr. Johnston wouldn't be so horrible. Somehow, after her year in quarantine and another year thereafter in outpatient recovery, Shannon found most everything about doctors and nurses—their bland-white uniforms, sterile utensils, gentle mannerisms, and even their probing questions—familiar and strangely comforting.

"I can make my way alone, Mother; no need for you to be there." She glanced at Mother. "I'm old enough to go alone to the doctor's office, don't you think?"

"Yes, in fact you are, Shannon, quite old enough." Mother continued searching in the cupboard for the baking powder. "I have to organize these cupboards. Maybe you can help me. I have no idea how they get so messy." She emptied out the cupboard, one box, tin or bottle at a time, and set each one on the counter. Shannon soaked a rag in hot water and wrung it dry before handing it to Mother, who continued, "See Dr. Johnston and let us know what he says. I'm sure he'll want to take some tests. I've already spoken to him about your symptoms." She scrubbed the empty shelves and returned the many items back to their rightful places.

"By the way, Shann, a woman named Mrs. Ross called for

you this morning. You told her you could care for her child next Thursday?"

18

April 1950

Eliza attended the eight o'clock Sunday morning Mass at Immaculate Conception Church in the college town of Ithaca, New York. Aside from the comfort of familiar rituals, the weekly opportunity to remove herself from the room she'd shared with Beryl Jameson for the past four semesters and from the chattering halls of the women's dormitory was essential to her equilibrium.

"Surge, et accipe puerum et matrem ejus, et fuge in Egyptum...." The priest, whose name she couldn't recall, read from scripture in monotone booming Latin. The series of vowel-laden syllables crashed and receded like waves into the well-amplified corners

of the church while Eliza let her head sink, both in prayer and distraction from it. Eliza's fluency in Latin did not lead her to greater spiritual focus; instead, she held onto an image of the boy and his mother—*puerum et matrem*—and through a litany of thoughts, she wandered down a random and unspiritual path:

Mother must have struggled with her concern for me in the summer of 1947 when Shannon was so sick, but why has she failed to find me since? To bring me home and never let me leave? And why did Eliza not judge Fa with the same sense of failing, even now? It was Mother's rejection that struck Eliza's core, depositing a jagged-edged mound of anxiety in the blackest corners of her consciousness. She stayed fixed, kneeling in the pew even after others stood to repeat the communal prayer. Two years after leaving St. Paul and the familiarity of St. Thomas Aquinas Chapel, Ithaca had become her home. How distant her past life and her own mother and father seemed to her now.

Eliza returned to the oak kneeler after Communion. While listening to the closing hymn of the Mass, she lifted her head to see a ray of mid-morning sun burst through the stained glass portrayal of the Virgin Mary and Child. She recalled again the horrible fate of Elizabeth Short, a young, independent Bostonian who'd gone to Hollywood to find her future and instead had been brutally murdered, drained of her blood, cut in half, and left in a ditch. Eliza remembered reading the story in the newspaper the very day she'd gone to the U of M library and had seen the poster for Mrs. Frances Perkins' lecture. She didn't know whether or not she bore a strong resemblance to Miss Short, but ever since the night after Beryl had made her offhand comment, Eliza had harbored some type of strange affinity with the ill-fated actress who probably knew the man who then tortured and murdered her.

"There but for the grace of God go I," she murmured, urgently making the sign of the cross from her forehead to her chest as the nameless priest passed by in his exit processional.

Eliza used her hand for shade against the bright sunlight as she approached the one open door of the church portico. She recovered her vision slowly as she stepped out to the cloudless day. She thought she recognized the outline of two figures standing together near the curb, looking to the entrance behind her. When her eyesight fully adjusted, the sun-darkened shapes came into focus, and Eliza didn't hide her surprise.

"David? Harvey? What in God's name …?" One step beyond the entrance to the church she tripped over a slight rise in the red brick paving and fell into David's left shoulder. He reached to catch her, but she pulled back, brushing her skirt, and asked again, "And what are you two doing here? I don't understand …"

Both men laughed nervously. Eliza glared at Harvey. She couldn't bring herself to look at David. Even in the slight brush against his arm, she couldn't deny the surge of attraction, the same she'd felt when he first kissed her years ago.

"Come on now, Eliza, you must be happy to see us." Harvey dropped the grin and became earnest. "I thought you'd be about ready for another visit. David here was kind enough to join me this time. He's doing a tour of eastern universities. Right, David?"

Harvey had visited Eliza twice in Ithaca. The first time, just weeks after she arrived, he preceded Shannon and Betty, who'd taken the train to New York to fulfill their dream concocted while quarantined for months. As a junior, Harvey had transferred to NYU with hopes of going on to study law, a choice that surprised many who'd considered him to be nothing more than a fun-loving, "not quite normal" fellow. But Eliza hadn't been surprised; she'd always appreciated the more thoughtful, serious side of Harvey, his search for knowledge, for accomplishment, for proving his worth to his widowed father. She'd tentatively welcomed his company when he came because, although hard to admit, she yearned for a small piece of home. It was with Harvey that Eliza had first attended Sunday morning Mass at Immaculate Conception the week after New Year, 1948.

"Swell to see you, Eliza," David said, looking at her as if she were a goddess who'd come down to earth through a mere church door. He sounded eager, seemingly oblivious to her discomfort. He stepped forward close enough to embrace her, although, of course, he didn't. Eliza wasn't sure where to look, so she focused on two children holding their father's hands in the grass strip near the street. He added, "I know we're unannounced, but would you be able to join us for lunch? We're only here until tomorrow, isn't that right, Harvey?"

Eliza's mind tangled into a knot of confusion. She had to speak if only to keep herself from running back into the church. *As if that would solve anything.* "Harvey, David, how lovely to see both of you; what a surprise. I appreciate the invitation, but ..." She took her gloves from her gray linen clutch that matched her pillbox hat and put them on, clasping them at the wrists with attention. She looked at them as if she'd briefly forgotten (although she hadn't) that they awaited the remaining fragment, "... but I'm engaged for lunch today with my advisor."

She looked at Harvey and smiled involuntarily, her heart shuddering at his goodwill, the familiar, earnest conviction in his eyes. She knew he'd do anything for a friend—especially this one: David Whitaker, the same boy who'd confronted playground bullies for Harvey in grade school, the same boy with whom he'd lived for months after his mother was killed in a tragic accident, the same young man he'd nurtured through a broken heart in 1947.

She glanced at David and hoped she could handle the encounter—it'd been more than two years, after all. "David, it's good to see you. You look so well." She knew her words sounded kind enough, but her desire to get through the moment as quickly as possible was not. "I trust your parents and Jan are fine?"

"Yes, thank you," David said with a visible look of relief that Eliza had finally spoken to him. "Eliza, if not lunch, please join us for dinner—it would mean the world to me. To both of us. Right, Harvey?"

What could she do? David had not been the one who attacked her, though looking at him now, two years later, made the vision of his terrifying cousin Patrick materialize, a sinister eruption from a dormant peak. Poor David—he'd never been anything but a gentleman, her first love, even. How he must have hurt when she shut him out of her life. And weeks later, the suicide; how had he endured? How had she?

"That would be fine," she said, fussing with the clasp on her clutch. "It will be nice to catch up on old times, I suppose. Why don't you come at six—I'm in Dickson Hall. I won't have much time, you understand, classwork and all." She realized as she spoke that she'd known since those days when David phoned the house weekly that this day might come. But how could she have prepared herself to handle it?

Harvey looked at her oddly as if trying to solve a puzzle, and said, "We'll be by to get you at six. You choose the spot."

"Swell!" David's face beamed as if he'd won a gold ribbon prize at the Minnesota Fair.

A disturbing thought surprised Eliza; was she unduly encouraging David? Worse, had she in some way encouraged Patrick? She wanted to deny she'd been aware of his odd attentions; but had she invited them? She chased the thought from her mind, back into the dark corner from which it had emerged, frightening and unwanted.

$\sim$

"WONDERFUL TO SEE YOU, MISS MALONE." Mrs. Perkins greeted Eliza with her usual vigor as she held open the door of the main entrance to her home several blocks from the campus. "I've just returned home from church myself. Make yourself comfortable on the verandah." She pulled two pins from her petite, veiled hat and placed it on the desk in the large foyer. She continued talking as she looked through several envelopes and turned away from Eliza toward her office behind the stairwell. "I should complete the letter I've been wrestling with all morning, if you don't mind. To the current Labor Secretary. I don't know what he's trying to get away with. He and his miserable cronies think they can stymie me with name-calling—lunatic, lesbian, little woman—I've heard them all. The insults goad me on." She laughed. "In any case, I'll be with you in a few moments. My young friend, Stanley, may join us, by the way."

Eliza followed Jemmie, Mrs. Perkins' young housemaid no older than she, to the verandah. Strange how three people today had claimed that it was wonderful to see her. *Do they honestly mean it? David ... who could he possibly see? The Eliza from before? Has time changed the way I'm seen? Does Mrs. Perkins see the woman David sees?* Eliza never allowed her thoughts to dwell on the blackness shoved into a dark corner of her being, but the encounter with Harvey and David raised a curtain in her mind. Lunch with Mrs. Perkins, who saw her the way she wanted to be seen, was one event that could claim her full attention.

"Eliza, dear, how is your semester shaping up?" Mrs. Perkins sat across from her at the small round table and smiled, switching to a less formal tone.

"Fine, thank you. I'm auditing the Labor Law course you suggested. I'm thinking about doing my thesis on *The Rise of Women in Manufacturing in the Postwar Auto Industry* when I take it for credit next fall."

"That sounds right. We should have some very fresh national data available for you to analyze by then. Will you be staying in Ithaca again this summer?"

"Almost certainly. Beryl has asked me to join her family on the coast, but I think I'd rather work."

"I'm sure the Jameson family would be delighted to have you—and they have a lovely cottage in Kennebunkport—but I'm hoping you might consider my less plush, more academically interesting opportunity," Mrs. Perkins said. "The Department of Industrial and Labor Studies is expanding. We need at least two additional administrative staff this summer to prepare the new curricula documents and such. It'd be a great deal of paperwork, but also a bit of time for research. Would you be interested? The pay is, of course, minimum wage."

Eliza smiled at the hint of pride in Mrs. Perkins' tone—unemployment insurance, financial assistance for the handicapped, the new federal social security program, minimum wage law—her formidable hand was at work in all of them. She returned Eliza's smile with a curt nod and continued, "We do have a stipend for housing available, though. Similar to last summer ... enough to find a room in a shared house."

"Mrs. Perkins, Dr. Katterman has arrived." Jemmie interrupted them and awaited her employer's response.

"Yes, Jemmie, please show him in," Mrs. Perkins said.

"So glad to see you, Frances. Very sorry for being late," the man said as he took the hand Mrs. Perkins offered and clasped it momentarily between his own. He removed his light suit coat and handed it to Jemmie, who stood close by, before seating himself at the table.

"Stanley, I'd like to introduce you to a rising star at Cornell, Miss Eliza Malone. You two have much in common; Eliza is quite fascinated with Labor Studies. She's my new protégé; I don't mind admitting ... since you chose to finally leave Cornell."

"Charmed to meet you, Miss Malone," he said.

"Likewise, Dr. Katterman." Eliza was struck by the impression that he wasn't charmed at all; he'd barely reacted to the introduction.

"But please call me Eliza."

"Yes, if you'll call me Stanley."

Eliza nodded, but wasn't sure she wanted to address this older man—he was at least thirty years old—by his first name. No taller than Eliza, he had a nondescript, serious face, memorable only for a groomed, flint-gray pencil mustache shades lighter than his partial crown of cropped and thinning hair. She was most taken by his deep-set, heavily lashed eyelids, which appeared admonishing when he looked at her. When he turned to Mrs. Perkins, however, his entire being softened and his eyes danced with enthusiasm.

"Frances, it's so kind of you to invite me; it's been too long. In fact, may I share with you a piece of legislation I'm preparing for the governor on maritime unions' health benefits? I don't want to bore Miss Malone, but—"

Eliza interrupted him: "Not at all. Mrs. Perkins is right to say I'm interested in all facets of labor, especially in women's issues. I'd very much appreciate the chance to listen."

By the time lunch ended, Eliza felt exhilarated, though she'd said hardly a word in the hour of dialogue between their hostess and Dr. Katterman. The exchange was like listening to a light Mozart concerto with Dr. Katterman as the lone clarinet earnestly stating his case, while Mrs. Perkins rebutted with her superior intellect and decades of experience, not to mention a decidedly maternal, no-nonsense inclination toward compassionate governance.

As a finale, Mrs. Perkins paused and threw back her head. "All right, Stanley, you win. If the governor wants to confront decades of maritime law in order to embrace the shoremen, so be it. Your arguments are quite sound, though I have warned you about the unintended consequences."

"Thank you, Frances; I'll do what I can to acknowledge your concerns, valid as they are. The governor is sending me and my deputy to the west coast for a month or so to audit California and Washington legislation, so this is a farewell luncheon, for now."

During her walk back to campus, Eliza considered her debt to her mentor and wondered if Mrs. Perkins could ever know the full extent of the misery from which she'd rescued Eliza. She would have to face David and Harvey tonight, but after bearing witness to an afternoon of provocative, intellectual intercourse between two such powerhouses, Eliza felt sure she'd not only survive the evening but also would push on to develop the full potential of her own intellect with confidence that not only she but also Mrs. Perkins believed she was capable of great things.

~⃝

AT A MINUTE PAST SIX, Eliza emerged from Clara Dickson Hall to find Harvey sitting on a bench and David standing nervously in front of him. She carried a clutch purse and an umbrella, insurance against the bank of dark clouds she'd noticed on her walk back to campus after lunch.

"It's just right, Eliza. I'm a big fan of Italian food," Harvey said later as he held the door open for her and David at Il Padrino Restaurant in town. He'd chatted all the way from the dormitory, and Eliza admitted to herself that she found his presence pleasantly comforting.

The dining room felt cozy and inviting; she'd never cared for loud, chaotic restaurants such as the ones Grandpa Theo had favored. Audrey Larson, a girl she knew and liked, worked nights as a waitress, and Eliza wanted as many points of contact with her new, happy life as possible in order to survive the evening.

"Yes," David said, "Good choice, Eliza. We have a new spot in St. Paul right near the pharmacy, Forno di Pisa." He glanced at her, face beaming as if eager to see if Eliza was at all interested in what he was saying.

She nodded politely and smiled at him. "So, what did you say brings you two to Ithaca?" she asked, distracting herself with the straw in her Coca-Cola. "It's a long way from home."

"Well, David wrote me and mentioned he wanted to come to the East Coast to look at schools, isn't that right?" Harvey started, looking at David to continue.

"I took last year off from school to work at the pharmacy full time and figure things out. But maybe I'd like to get my doctorate in medicine. If I do go back, I'd have two more years to get my undergraduate. Dad wants me to stay in St. Paul, but I've heard great things from Harvey about the East Coast schools. And of course ..." David looked at Eliza and blushed. "Eliza, it's so wonderful to see you again. You look great. I'm envious Harvey's had the chance to visit."

"It's nice to see you too, David," Eliza said coolly, not quite sure if she meant it or not. Looking toward the exit, she caught a glimpse of Audrey, who was putting a relish tray and rolls on the table of six nearby. She gave her a quick wave and a smile and was grateful when her friend reciprocated from across the room.

Shelves with dusty wine bottles cased in woven reeds hung alongside poorly framed Italian landscapes and oversized photos of the Cornell campus on the restaurant walls. *Home, Ithaca is home*; she gathered the photos into her sight and inwardly repeated the short mantra several times.

"How is NYU, Harvey?" she asked. "Are you going to the Twin Cities for summer break?"

"Great and yes," he responded to both questions and laughed. "I got a tuition scholarship all right, but I'll need to work all summer to save enough for living expenses for next year. It's not cheap out here, is it?" He sighed. "Pops isn't too keen on me being gone. He made it pure hell when I went back home for the holidays. He and my uncle fighting all the time and both ganging up to give me grief when they're done yelling at each other. I'm so glad to not be there."

"I visited with your sister when I was back for Christmas,

though," Harvey said, holding back a little as if to see if Eliza would respond. When she didn't, he continued, "I told her I might have the chance to see you. She's found a job as a nanny for a family in Roseville; been doing it over a year now, maybe even two, and she says she might try some nursing classes one of these days. But Shannon, a nurse? I'll believe it when I see it. She's not a hundred percent herself, if you know what I mean. Not the same energy as before the surgeries." Harvey stopped and looked at Eliza. "Have you spoken with her?"

Her eyebrows arched against her will. "No, Harvey, I haven't," she said too abruptly to seem casual. "I'm sure we'll talk when the time is right. Excuse me; I'm going to go wash my hands."

Eliza gripped the sides of the sink in the ladies' washroom to stop her hands from shaking. The mirror reflected the frightened eyes of a seventeen-year-old girl cast in her womanly face. Suddenly the kitchen floor was underneath her and she couldn't breathe; all in an instant, she felt his first painful thrust, the cold prick of Patrick's knife, the deadliness of his strange gaze. She closed her eyes and steadied herself, imagining she was carved from stone. But she couldn't stop an unrelenting flow of tears.

It came to her then that her anger with Shannon was not about her fantasies to keep the baby. It was that Eliza could not bear to face her. She couldn't claim to be the righteous confidante Shannon had trusted, no longer the strong and protective sister Shannon had always needed. No longer that Eliza. That girl was gone, perhaps forever—and this one, the woman sitting here cast in stone, was damaged, uncertain; this one was struggling to stay ahead of her demons. Eliza wiped tears from her cheeks and opened her eyes. She sat in the absent attendant's chair, forced another look in the mirror, and held her own stare, methodically packing away each fragment of her mind's emotional tornado. She reapplied her lipstick, took another fierce, demanding look at herself—as if threatening the seventeen-year-old girl into submission—and returned to the table with Harvey and David. She would be fine.

"Eliza, I'd like to walk you home to your dorm, if it's all right with you," David said, his voice wavering. "Harvey'll walk back to our lodgings, won't you, Harvey? It's not too far."

Harvey nodded and raised an eyebrow, looking at Eliza with an expression she could read only as a friendly, well-intended challenge. Being alone with David Whitaker was an obligation they both knew she'd avoided for over three years.

They left the restaurant and stepped into a cool April night. A young woman needed something extra, a light shawl or cardigan, to stay comfortable after sunset in these weeks before mosquitos and June bugs. It suited Eliza fine that they walked silently for a while. She chose an image and a conversation from earlier in the day, of Mrs. Perkins and Stanley, to replay in her mind, so she could escape the awkwardness of the time alone with David.

"Stanley, are you telling me you're willing to compromise the governor's relationship with Washington D.C. simply to align him with the most narrow-minded faction of the maritime union? And how will you manage to convince his constituency that it's the right track? Have you budgeted for the public relations cost?"

"Frances," Stanley had replied, "you've spun my words from gold to hay yet again."

Eliza had recently discovered the propagandist, Edward Bernays, well-known for developing a near science around molding public opinion. He coined his work "Public Relations," and here Mrs. Perkins used Dr. Katterman's dilemma as a current example of that very idea. She could spend days pondering connections between all she was learning. The discourse invigorated and challenged her in the safe territory of the intellect far away from the murky emotions of the heart.

"Eliza, can we sit here for a moment?" David led her to a bench on the side of the path.

Had he been asking her questions during the two blocks they had already walked? She hoped not. They stopped and sat on a bench close to the suspension bridge across Fall Creek. Eliza held steady, wondering if David knew of its legend: that if a young woman accepted a kiss from a suitor while crossing it, a lifetime of happiness awaited them; if she rejected him, the bridge would fall.

"I know it looks crazy. But I had to see you. When you stopped speaking to me, well, my life went blank. I mean, life went on, but I couldn't focus on anything. And then Patrick—" His voice faltered, and he cocked his head as if recalling a fond memory that turned dark before fading. "For the past two years … I couldn't get you out of my mind. And I know you …well, I knew you … enough to feel certain you wouldn't be so cruel unless you had darned good reasons …" David spoke as if exhausted by his own words.

Eliza looked at him and interrupted, "David, I know—"

"No, Eliza. You've got to let me finish," he persisted. "Please look at me." He took her hands in his. She gazed at his fine, long fingers before tilting her head upward. "I look at you and I feel there must be something. Some hope for us. You are as beautiful as ever to me—as important to me as that first kiss, the night of the storm. I can be here, in New York, maybe not at Cornell, but close by. Could you consider giving us another chance, Eliza?" A tear fell onto one cheek and then onto the other; he wiped them away with a sweep of his upper arm, startling Eliza. He looked down at her hands and took them to hold in his.

But Eliza was not herself. Her throat had constricted, and she felt dizzy; she imagined he—no, not David, but Patrick— her attacker was hiding nearby. She mustered all of her wits and looked at him, biting her bottom lip before speaking and trying to force rational words rather than the bile she felt rising within:

"David, I'm glad you came here. It's good you did. We needed to see one another, I suppose. I know you think we were in love …" and for a moment she faltered because she recognized she had loved David, too—as a young girl loves, with all the innocent vibrancy of her being. She had loved him the night she was raped. The euphoria she'd felt with David was forever eclipsed by the brutality of Patrick's attack. His hand on her breast, the stench of his breath. She knew she could never separate that night's poisoned mix. The emotions were forever intermingled. "… but I wasn't in love with you. I …" Eliza wasn't sure what to say; no matter what she chose, they would be words to push David as far away as she could.

"I did hear some things people said, Eliza. But they didn't make any sense to me. Anything you did, I can forgive …" He persisted, but it was clear from the look on Eliza's face that he'd crossed some line with these words. "What I mean is, it doesn't matter who you were with, or what mistakes happened. I don't care. I never stopped loving you."

With that, her world darkened. "It's in the past, now. I'm with someone here, at Cornell; we're … together. I'm sorry if you came all the way here to see me. If you'd known, perhaps you would've decided not to come." She saw he was incredulous. "I would've told you I'm spoken for … This is my home now."

After a quiet moment, David leaned over and kissed Eliza on the cheek. She watched him inhale and exhale deeply through his nose, before smiling ruefully. "Goodbye then, Eliza," he said quietly. He released his grip from her hand and stood, looking away from her and into the distance.

"Goodbye, David," she said, although so feebly she wasn't sure he heard it. "I can walk myself back from here."

Grateful Beryl wasn't yet back in their dormitory room, Eliza prepared herself for an early night and put the card in the door she and Beryl had devised to indicate one or the other was sleeping. She crawled into bed exhausted.

Sleep did not come as quickly as she'd hoped. Anxious thoughts of Patrick mixed with memories of David refused to fade: the excitement of his kiss, the warmth of his voice and coolness of his hand when they'd lingered in the shop's doorway; pounding on the door, sour breath, his mouth forced onto hers. Confused images passed into dreams, and she and Shannon stood together, lost on the elaborate stage they'd created for their summer play for Fa's birthday. They looked about, confused by their whereabouts as if this stage were a life-sized kingdom covering the entire land around Grandpa Theo's home and extending well beyond and below it into frightening caves—dark, cold, dripping with icy moisture—they'd never known existed. Eliza was to be the princess and Shannon was already angry with her for insisting that she be the grandmother. Eliza fixed this, as she always did, by telling Shannon she could be the princess with her ... Eliza would be both of them ... Eliza would be both Shannon and herself ... but Shannon needed to be the magical grandmother, too, or no one would be able to save the princess.

While she was explaining this to Shannon as if it made perfect sense, Eliza felt the goblin king, who was Patrick, sneaking up on them from the dark, steep sides of the cave where they stood. Patrick looked exactly like the real goblin king from the description in the book—short and stocky with large, filthy, hairy feet and bulbous warts on his face and body. His blackened teeth stank of rotting peat and burning coal. But she knew it was Patrick because he carried a very real knife, and he was angry at her, angry enough to kill her.

When she saw the knife, she became petrified and couldn't move. She wanted to run; she knew David would be the coal miner's son if she told him to, but she had to find him first. The coal miner's son would save the princess. Even though she'd rejected him, as she had rejected David. She needed to tell David to follow the invisible thread of the magical grandmother's ring.

Eliza looked down at her hand and saw that she wasn't wearing the ring. The steel band had gone and that meant she'd be killed. She'd given the ring to Shannon. Why had she done that? When? She couldn't remember, and she couldn't move her legs to find Shannon to ask her. She remembered she was, for now at least, both herself and Shannon. She knew Patrick, the goblin king, wanted to cut her in half. He wanted to separate them. He wanted to kill her. But which half was Shannon, and which half was Eliza? And why could she not move? She had to get away. She had to find David. But what if David were both himself and Patrick? She alone had to protect Shannon, who was a baby. How could Shannon be a baby, if she played the part of the older sister and the magical grandmother?

She looked down and discovered she was indeed cut in half. She was the head and chest; Shannon was the torso, hips, and legs. She laughed because it made no sense at all, like poor Alice in Wonderland. This is not how the play was supposed to happen. But Patrick came to her and put his hand over her mouth and put his mouth to her ear and told her to stop crying. She wasn't crying, was she? She was laughing. Shannon was crying, wailing like an infant. Eliza heard the infant wail from inside her chest. She heard Shannon's voice, but the cry was coming from Eliza, and it was the wailing of an infant.

Why had she told Shannon she could be the princess? It was too dangerous. She'd led baby Shannon to her death. Her mother would be angry. They would all be distraught, as they were when Baby Theo died. They would despise her, never forgive her for what she'd done. And she would have to leave the family. The baby's death was her fault, and now both were dead and in some kind of afterlife—some frightening afterlife with the goblin king who was Patrick. And she was Elizabeth Short, who must have been a bad woman. And there was no escape. Patrick the terrifying goblin king was holding her arms, pushing his sweaty, coal-stained hideous face close to hers, and she saw he was David, not Patrick.

"Eliza!" he cried in the voice of a woman.

Eliza bolted upright, finally freeing her legs from their inertia and gasped. She screamed, "No! No! It's not a stage!" and opened her eyes to see Beryl, who was holding her tightly by the arms.

"My God, Eliza!" She looked into Eliza's wild, frightened face and whispered firmly, "Are you awake, now?"

19

JUNE 1950

Two and a half years had passed since Shannon had met the Ross family at St. Rose of Lima Church Bazaar. She'd arrived every Thursday afternoon since—and for the past year on Monday, Tuesday, and Wednesday mornings as well—at the ranch-style home in the suburb of Roseville. On this day, a crew of men worked in the front yard removing an old elm tree Mrs. Ross insisted was too large. A similar tree in the back yard had been chopped to a mere stump and made into the centerpiece of a round flowerbed. Shannon thought it reflected an odd relationship with nature.

"Hello? It's me, Shannon," she announced as she entered the

house through the unlocked door. "Hello?"

"We're back here, Shannon," Mrs. Ross called from the master bedroom near the end of the hallway. She waited until Shannon was within earshot before continuing, "Little Missy is being quite naughty this morning; she's already gotten a paddling, and I've told her to stay in her room until you arrived. I expected you earlier. I'll be unforgivably late for my tee time…"

Shannon stayed at the bedroom door, watching as Mrs. Ross finished applying lipstick. She then found a safety pin in her drawer to mark a stain on a nearby garment, and continued, "I won't be surprised if the ladies … ouch!" she gasped as the safety pin missed its cache and pricked her finger.

Shannon, who felt little affection for her employer, suppressed satisfaction at the needle's work and inwardly rebuked Mrs. Ross. Even the thought of a spanking disturbed her when it came to Miriam, the little girl she'd cared for at every opportunity. If Virginia Ross were the older sister of a friend or a neighbor, Shannon might like her just fine, but the woman's imperious attitude toward her, combined with her lack of what Shannon considered to be appropriate maternal instincts, drove her mad.

"May I check on her, then, Mrs. Ross?" she asked.

"Of course. She's been quiet in there for at least fifteen minutes," Mrs. Ross said as she gazed into her mirror with an absentminded look of critical admiration that Shannon couldn't imagine replicating.

"You haven't forgotten about watching Miriam Saturday at the club, have you?"

"No, I haven't forgotten." Shannon stepped back from the master bedroom door and opened the one across the hall, struck with the same sense of anticipation and fullness she always had in the seconds before seeing the child. She spotted Miriam, clutching the red blanket Shannon had crocheted, asleep on the floor, her head on the belly of her old stuffed rabbit, as if they'd whispered each other to sleep.

Shannon heard the front door close. She gave another short and critical consideration of Mrs. Ross, the type of woman who would leave without saying goodbye to her own child. Shannon got down on the floor next to Miriam and leaned on her elbow. She observed the rise and fall of the child's chest with each breath and was overcome with emotion as she recalled again the first time she'd held her, a seven-month-old baby, in the church hall.

Miriam slept with her head resting on Fat Bunny's soft, bulging middle while Shannon stayed next to her on the floor, dozing in and out of sleep herself. When she felt the touch of Miriam's fingers on her lips—how she loved that—she sat up, smoothed her gray wool skirt and leaned back against the bookshelf behind her. Miriam, now three and a half, climbed into her lap with her red blanket.

"Story, Shann?" she asked sleepily.

"Yes, my little one, but then we must get your dress ready for Saturday. Will you be my helper?" Shannon laughed as Miriam snuggled herself into Shannon like a bug burrowing into a pillow.

At five thirty, Shannon heard Mr. Ross's car in the driveway and watched from the living room as he stepped out to open the garage door. Although years younger, he seemed to her a bit like Fa—a befuddled and gentle giant. A square chin and hazel eyes, deep set and protected with dark, thick eyelashes, made him look either perpetually content or weary, depending on the circumstance. Like Fa, he was tall and fit, but instead of disappearing into books, he retreated to his mechanical hobbies. The garage housed one car in the middle and a variety of electronic or motorized projects in tidy workstations along the walls.

On this afternoon, he sat down at the kitchen table and lifted Miriam onto his lap. "Thank you, Miss Malone," he said as he reached into his suit jacket's interior pocket to retrieve his wallet. He found two dollar bills and folded them in half before handing them to her. "In fact, thank you very much," he added, cocking his head and looking at her as if rather amused.

He gave Miriam his wallet and let her find its rightful pocket. Managing the challenge well, the toddler giggled and clapped both hands on his cheek so he muddled his words as he continued, "Ginny tells me you'll be helping out on Saturday at the club while we golf in the couple's tournament. Much appreciated, Miss Malone. You're a true faodail. Scottish to say, we're lucky to have you."

~~~

SHANNON ENTERED THE HOUSE AN hour later without a sound, hoping not to encounter her mother, who was undoubtedly in the kitchen. The Malone household was a somber place, permanently dulled by the multiple traumas of 1947. Almost four years later, life had not returned to normal, and Shannon doubted it ever would. What would normal mean with Eliza gone? With Ed married and working in Duluth, keeping their summer home on Lake Minnetonka, happily burying himself in work at Malone Steelworks as Grandpa Theo had done? Shannon had wanted very much to like Olivia O'Rourke, hoping her sister-in-law might in some way compensate for the loss of Eliza, but by now she knew it was futile. Olivia treated Shannon like a flighty child.

Mother was, at least, pleased by Ed's success, although Shannon had a difficult time understanding why. She wasn't a greedy woman, nor was she overly impressed with the wealth surrounding her, but Shannon sensed the further entrenchment of the Malone family into the deepest waters of affluent society of the Twin Cities somehow comforted her.

None of this mattered much to Shannon, at least not since the Rosses had taken her on as Miriam's nanny. God had spared her from the worst of tuberculosis and had given her a calling, a path she couldn't quite predict, but one she trusted absolutely.

October 11th, 1950

Dear Eliza,

Sometimes (like today), my heart feels so full of love for Miriam I think I'll burst. I am completely grateful for and trusting of God's plan and pray you'll someday feel the happiness I feel when she's with me. I pray for you as well, not knowing what you're doing or even where you are, or most importantly, how your life is, dear sister.

Today, we played the loveliest game. It's one we've played many times, now that she knows hide and seek. I take off Mother's ring (I don't wear it because it would hurt Mother immensely to know I have it, not you ...) and I tie a ball of thin silver yarn to it. I count to twenty very loudly as I make a twisted path from her bedroom, down the hallway, finally to the living room, leaving little raisins along the way. When I'm ready, she puts the ring on her thumb and gathers up the yarn around chair legs and under beds and under rugs until she finds me and saves me from the horrible goblin king, who is really Fat Bunny, the (overly!) stuffed rabbit I gave her for her first Christmas three years ago. I started to read The Princess and the Goblin to her, but in fact, I think she is too young; it's terribly frightening in parts. I hadn't remembered ... had you?

When she found me crouched behind the sofa in the master bedroom she crawled onto the armrest and looked down at me, then spoke to the Fat Bunny goblin king very seriously, as if the creature himself stood before us:

"You can have the ring, you bad goblin, but you mustn't hurt Shannon, goblin king, because she needs to

take care of me for a very long time. Now go away."

Eliza, I can hardly explain it. I see she is cared for and loved by the Rosses (although as I've written before, I am not fond of Mrs.), and I know she is not mine, although sometimes I think I will go mad hiding the truth in plain sight, as I do, that she is ours—a Malone, as much as you or me. I suppose it's even strange, but I'm completely certain that my presence in her life is God's Will. And I'm so utterly grateful because I honestly don't know what my life would be without her. I felt it from the moment I saw her in the nursery on the day she was born. And we will stay together until you come home. I know this to be true. Somehow.

Love,
Shannon.

20

December 1950

hoose, Lyza; either the dance tonight and take no breaks tomorrow or have an easy day tomorrow and no dance tonight. Eliza gave the ultimatum to her shoes, one of which was particularly stubborn in the heel as she bent over, pulling at her brass shoe horn until her foot slipped into place. "It's not vanity," she mused as she checked the repaired soles of her favorite shoes—golden-brown, patent-leather pumps with a chocolate-suede bow and matching piping. "I'm simply a perfectionist."

A perfectionist indeed, as was Stanley, she thought. Of course, she liked to think she towered above him intellectually, never mind the inch or two of superiority these shoes would give. His intellect, though, was his greatest pride, and she'd learned that to challenge him directly was never worth it. Not to mention that it undermined the wonderful and contentious dialogues they enjoyed on an endless range of topics. Eliza hadn't been attracted by his sharply trained mind as much as by his patient, methodical sense of order that she'd observed upon their first meeting. An organized mind, she believed, was the most fundamental tool of propriety and success. Everything in its own place, in its own time. As much as she'd tried to teach Shannon her creed of an orderly life, it was the opposite of her sister's chaotic approach to almost everything.

Throughout their childhood, the only items Shannon had properly organized were her odd compulsions, like counting whites and lining up her Dionne dolls, her ceramic Seven Dwarfs, her stuffed bears, all according to size and putting them under the beds, instead of playing with them. How it used to make Eliza's heart pound to return to their shared room and find her sister's clothes, clean or soiled, scattered about the beds, or her schoolwork bunched together in a senseless pile of papers.

Ed had been a mystery to her, especially difficult to recall after four years away from home. It surprised her that she couldn't remember whether or not he'd been an organized child. The few times she'd gone into his room, well, it looked clean enough, but it was likely Mother's doing. Shannon used to call him a mama's boy, to which Eliza would respond that she was being spiteful. She smiled; Ed did have his chickens and pigeons organized, and the stray dogs and any number of wounded animals showing up by his side. Occasionally, a melancholy thought about home would unexpectedly wash over her, like a wave of vertigo.

"Are you coming, Eliza?" asked Beryl, who must have stood in the doorway observing Eliza for at least a little while.

"Why? Is Stanley downstairs? I'll be down in a moment, Beryl. I haven't decided, though …"

"Hogwash, Eliza. Have you looked in the mirror? You've got your best party dress on; you're all made up, looking beautiful, I might add. Like—"

"Don't say it, Beryl. I don't care who I look like. I just want to look like me," Eliza said curtly. "And, yes, I suppose I am going. Even if you are being pushy."

"Hmm. Grouchy, I see. Shall I tell Stanley you'll be down or not? Chas and I are heading over now, but if you want us to wait, we can all go together. Your choice."

Eliza regretted the deflated look Beryl gave her. "I'm sorry, Beryl. I promised myself I'd finish my thesis before break ended. You look sweet, too, old girl. Just like Doris Day."

Aside from her flaxen hair, Beryl didn't look like Doris Day at all, but her disposition was equally sunny. Eliza remembered the terrible nightmare almost two years ago when she'd woken up screaming and shaking in Beryl's arms. She'd spoken to Eliza as you would a child, stroking her hair, holding her hand, listening to her horrible descriptions. Eliza had told her everything about the nightmare her mind had conjured up that night, except the real identities represented by the two menacing goblin creatures, and Beryl had never asked.

~⌒

"DO YOU THINK WE COULD sneak out and take a walk?" Stanley asked after their first cocktail of the evening. "I have something I'd like to share with you."

"I'm not so sure about walking on the sidewalk, Stanley; it is snowing, you know," Eliza replied.

"True enough, darling." He looked down at her feet. "And it would be a shame to damage those heels. I do want to talk with you tonight, though. And more than sweet nothings on the dance floor. Don't go home without me, all right?" He turned and smiled at the man with two cameras slung across his chest, who stood just feet away waiting for the right shot. "Cheers!" he said, catching the man's attention. He raised his glass to Eliza with one hand, put his other arm around her waist, and pulled her close. The photographer snapped a shot.

Afterward, Eliza asked, "How'd you know the photographer was there? I could have sworn you had your back turned to him."

"Sixth sense, I suppose; I hope you'll get used to it," he said. "Come on, I want to introduce you to Mr. Capp. He's Governor Lodge's second cousin and is pegged to be named the New York State Commissioner of Labor—my boss's boss, so to speak. Frances held—"

"Yes, I know. Mrs. Perkins was appointed to the position when it was first created in 1929 by then Governor Franklin Roosevelt." Eliza completed his sentence.

"I dislike it when you do that," Stanley said with a beguiling smile. "But I suppose you dislike it equally as much when I state what is, to you, the obvious."

"Perfectly summarized, Stanley," Eliza said, smiling back.

An hour passed, and she lost Stanley to someone she didn't recognize. She sat with her legs crossed on one of two dozen wooden folding chairs lined up against the back wall of the dance hall and surveyed the room.

Beryl was dancing a holiday waltz with her longtime suitor, Chas Mellon. Everyone thought they would marry soon and live in Boston, close to both of their old-moneyed, prominent families, surrounded by a mountain of old-moneyed, prominent friends, and live a rarified life. Beryl might convince her father to let her practice her degree in nursing, rather than dance her way through life as a Boston socialite, but life would be filled with months on the coast, equestrian weekends, and sumptuous parties on manicured lawns. It wasn't envy Eliza felt at their excessive privilege; after all, her own family came from substantial wealth, even if of the more understated, Midwestern variety. If anything, she felt comfortable in her acquaintance with the Jameson family. Stanley, son of Jewish New York immigrant merchants, came from a different background, but with a similar distance to the epicenter of the aristocratic East Coast universe—a qualified similarity that they both understood.

"Eliza, there you are, darling, a million miles away." Stanley sat down next to her and stretched both legs straight as far as he could. He slouched low in the chair, loosely turning his head toward her, and she thought he'd had one drink too many. "I've something I am dying to ask you, but I don't feel now is the time. I'm sorry to admit I can't hold my whiskey, as you know," he sighed with his eyes closed. "And Mr. Capp wanted to bend my ear over one—or was it two …? Could we plan a walk in the morning?"

In the eight months Stanley had courted Eliza, she'd not seen him drunk or even tipsy. She'd only seen him in complete command of himself: body, mind and even, for the most part, heart. His current state of drunkenness was mild, and although some people might have found it charming, Eliza did not; upon smelling a whiff of stale whiskey on his breath, she reeled back, vaguely repulsed, but not enough so to complain.

"Stanley, I'm going to get a ride home with Beryl and Chas; they're leaving in ten minutes. If you'd like to join us, fine. If not, I'll see you in the morning, after I attend Mass. We can take a walk downtown—if you're feeling up to it, that is."

Stanley nodded and straightened up. "I'll go with you, I think. It's quite late, and I'd like nothing more than to sleep as soon and as long as possible," he said. "I'm not oblivious to your tone, Eliza; I'm sure I'll feel quite fine in the morning." He finished with a delighted smirk. "I hope in the morning you'll say a special prayer for me, the agnostic Jew from Brooklyn who can't hold his gin. Or was it whiskey?"

ELIZA'S FINAL WINTER SEMESTER WAS a whirlwind of academic successes, honors, and social activity. Taking a combination of undergraduate and graduate courses inspired her more than she could've imagined possible, and both her professors and deans noted her output. Beryl moved back to Boston, and Eliza moved off-campus to student housing with a group of women she'd known for several years.

In May, Eliza graduated at the top of her class with an undergraduate degree in labor relations and a flotilla of credits toward her master's degree.

"I'd like you to consider immediately embarking upon your doctorate," Mrs. Perkins said a week later at their quarterly luncheon. "There's no time like the present, and if you return home, you may allow yourself to be diverted into lesser endeavors."

"I hardly think I'll go back to St. Paul, Mrs. Perkins," she replied. "I haven't been back for four years. I hadn't yet considered a Ph.D. Is it possible without a master's degree first?"

"After reviewing your transcripts, I'd say you're on your way to an M.A. already. And, yes, it is possible to go straight to a doctorate degree, with a strong portfolio of papers and a letter of recommendation from your advisor, or, in some cases such as this one, me," she said. "The question I have is what field of research would you pursue?"

"I hadn't thought too much about it, but I will." Eliza didn't mention that Stanley, Mrs. Perkins' older, mustached protégé had asked for her hand in marriage—not once, but two times since the Holiday Dance. She couldn't be sure how Mrs. Perkins, a devout Episcopalian, would react, although Eliza imagined it was what their shared mentor had in mind all along. Today wasn't the time to bring it up even if she'd wanted to, since Eliza hadn't yet decided about Stanley's proposal. The invitation to apply for a Ph.D., on the other hand, was the type of challenge she'd readily embrace. She had much to think about.

"Mr. Jameson has invited me to Boston for the summer to help Beryl manage her wedding plans. I'm sure you've heard they're planning an early October ceremony. Her father thinks she needs someone around to keep her focused on the goal, although I think she'll be fine," Eliza added. "I must admit this last semester exhausted me. I'm as ready for a holiday as I've ever been, although I'm not quite sure how I'll survive one this long."

"And what about Stanley?" Mrs. Perkins asked. "If you don't mind me asking, is he in the picture?" She smiled and looked intently over her glasses at Eliza. "Although I don't hear much from you, dear, I hear plenty from him. My, he is smitten; I've never seen him quite like this"—she paused—"for quite this long. I was beginning to wonder if he had it in him."

"I'm sure Stanley will make it to Boston plenty of times this summer. He's not a fan of Mr. Jameson's politics, or religion for that matter, but we all get along well enough."

"Not exactly what I meant, but I won't pry. Especially since I'd rather have you consider your doctorate than immersing yourself in some romantic affair that could take your mind off your work." Mrs. Perkins looked down at her plate so Eliza wasn't sure whether she was being sincere or ironic.

Eliza had assumed from the beginning that she'd pursue academics as far as she possibly could, preferably here at Cornell. Her beloved library, the mellow wooded hills, dramatic bridges cast between dense-green ravines, and even the town of Ithaca were her home, either through force of will or genuine suitability, and it was fine with her to remain. Her relationship with Mrs. Perkins had been one of great inspiration, along the lines, Eliza imagined, the great mentors of history must have had with their students.

Regarding Stanley, she had no idea today or likely tomorrow, what to think. Consideration of marriage came paired with an inexplicable, unpleasant foreboding. She didn't undervalue that Stanley Katterman professed to love her for all the right reasons. Rarely did he refer to her physical beauty, unlike any other young suitor she'd encountered, and never had she felt the need to hide behind feelings of intellectual superiority, as she had with the few other men she'd dated at Cornell. Instead, he claimed he was in love with her mind—equal to his, he also claimed—her righteous spirit, and her desire to make something of her life.

"Why don't you ever speak of your family, Eliza?" Stanley had asked one evening six months into their courtship. She knew the matter perplexed him. She supposed he must think it something terrible, that she'd not speak of them, even individually— Shannon, Mother, Fa, Ed.

"It's not that I don't think about my family," she'd replied. "I made a choice to be here, and the way for me to be here, to succeed here, without falling apart is to start fresh. If I reminisce, it'll be difficult to concentrate on my studies. I'm sure I'll go back one day. Just not now. I need more time here."

"More time for what? Why don't you go home at least for summer, like other students? They'd surely be happy to see you. Or did something happen with your mother?"

"With my mother? My goodness, no; and please stop asking, Stanley. It is what it is and I'm fine with it," she said, forming a smile negated by her arched brow and pursed lips. "And when the time is right, I'll go back."

~⟃

THE WEEK AFTER GRADUATION, ELIZA went to Boston without giving Stanley an answer to his proposal, although she promised she'd have one by the first week of August. For the first time in her life, she was uncertain of the correct path. Time and a different environment, she hoped, would provide clarity.

Beryl came out to the guesthouse as soon as she learned of Eliza's arrival. "Father is more excited than anyone that you're here." She handed Eliza one of two tall glasses with long silver spoons hollowed in the stem for sipping and interrupted herself, a habit of Beryl's Eliza had grown used to. "Have some lemonade; it's baking outside. Awfully early in the year for such heat." She took a sip before continuing, "I'm pleased, too, of course; but who knew a tired old banker could perk up like he has? I hope his enthusiasm doesn't intimidate you."

"Not at all, Beryl. He's quite a charming gentleman. From what I've seen, enthusiasm looks to be a family trait. I would've liked to have known your mother as well."

"I can hardly remember her. Now when I think of Maman, images of Aunt Flo barrel right in and take over. As she generally does whenever she sees the chance." She sighed, "Nobody's life is perfect, I suppose." She sat down on the small white-wicker rocking chair, smiled and murmured, "I do remember this darling old thing; funny, I'd forgotten about it all of these years, and yet it's been right here, and I can all of a sudden remember the very day I got it from Maman. It was a gift to make me feel better after falling from Father's carriage and breaking my ankle." She laughed and looked at Eliza, who was sitting on the edge of the bed. "I couldn't play outside for forever afterward, so I played nurse with my dolls. That must have been when I first wanted to become one. A nurse, I mean; not a doll, of course."

Eliza looked at Beryl, who rocked in the child's chair with its hand-carved finials of crouched rabbits and runners stenciled with lavender and ivy, and laughed. "Well, you look like an oversized doll sitting there; I'm sure Chas would like seeing you as you are just now. Is he in town?"

"Yes, since we've got seven engagement parties to go to in the next eight weeks, he'd better stick close. His mother and father are hosting the first. I hope you know it's the duty of a Maid of Honor to attend each and every one."

"You didn't mention Maid of Honor, Beryl," Eliza said. "Why on earth would you ask me when you're surrounded by friends and relatives you've had since childhood?" Eliza wasn't pleased with getting trapped into a social calendar. Beryl was so much like Shannon. Neither had any guile, although Beryl sometimes acted—as was the case now—from a place of profound entitlement. Shannon, she realized, acted more from naive simplicity even when tuberculosis and multiple surgeries threatened her life. Had Eliza scorned her simplicity as she'd written the perfunctory note to Shannon cancelling their rendezvous in New York four years ago, or did she simply dismiss the hurt her letter must have caused? Eliza didn't want to think about Shannon now.

"Eliza, please don't be angry! I meant it as a grand surprise. I thought you'd be pleased, except maybe for the endless engagement parties. I know you're younger than me, but somehow I think of you as my older sister. Well, sort of, anyway. And I need your help so desperately with getting it all right."

A moment passed, and Eliza said, "In fact, I should be honored. I'm sorry, Shann. I mean Beryl. My, I haven't done that for quite a while, have I? Sometimes you remind me so much of her. More than ever now, in fact." Eliza leaned over and reached for Beryl's hands with both of hers. "I am honored. Truly. Although seven engagement parties is extraordinary. Is it always this extravagant when a Boston debutante gets married?"

"Two of the parties are in New York, actually, and one is in Kennebunkport. I don't suppose you have to attend those." Beryl looked at Eliza with eyes as big as saucers and a sheepish grin. "Unless you want to, of course."

"We'll see," she said as she stood and brushed her pale-blue seersucker dress, then took off her ivory cardigan and hung it in the large wardrobe. "For now, help me unpack, would you?"

"I could, or you could let Mary do it and we could go have lunch. I'm half starved." Beryl looked at Eliza. "Oh, all right; I'll help you. And then we can return to the house together."

Eliza fit easily into the Jameson household and into the elite Boston society to which they belonged. Although she wasn't quite sure why, everyone embraced her as a member of the Jameson family, with the exception of Beryl's maternal Aunt Florence, who'd moved in with the family when Beryl's mother Constance suffered a terrible cancer and died twelve years ago. Aunt Florence, or Miss Watson as Eliza was instructed to call her, didn't engage in outward displays of disapproval, but Eliza sensed her hospitality, at least for now, was little more than common civility.

~⌐

"I THINK I'LL STAY HERE," Eliza said when Beryl informed her of the family plan for a week-long trip to Kennebunkport after Independence Day, leading up to the engagement party at a beachfront estate. "I'd like to go to Cambridge and finish some research. Stanley is coming to town on Monday; he wouldn't be too happy if I'd skipped town." She wasn't sure whether Beryl thought of Stanley as a suitable match for her; she was a Protestant blueblood. Could she imagine such a pair?

But Beryl responded with a knowing wink and took Eliza by the arm. "Come on, then, at least you can help me pull together my accessories for the fish bake and dance tomorrow night at the Walkers'. You're absolutely gifted at it," she said. "If you're not coming to Kennebunkport, I'll leave it to you to explain yourself to Chas. He relies on you to survive the circuit."

Eliza found Longuejour Mansion quiet and even a little dull after Beryl and her father left, but she enjoyed her solitude in the garden. She often walked from her guest quarters, the original carriage house that'd been converted to living space by the Jameson family during the Great Depression, and followed a pebbled footpath around the south end of the main house. The rose gardens in the front of the mansion centered the landscape, dominating both sides of the brick driveway. They stretched from the large, fieldstone porch to the public road that hid behind the ten-foot-high hedge.

Each side of the garden was built from the center out with flower beds of various elliptical sizes. Undulating paths cut through the gardens, like rays pulsing unevenly from two suns. In the center of each side stood a statuette—an art deco interpretation of Apollo on the east, and on the west a similar one of Artemis. One morning while the sun dried grounds moist from midnight thunderstorms, Eliza sat on a bench facing Apollo and noticed that she could barely see the top of Artemis above the flowers—now in full bloom—her defiant head and bow and arrow cocking upward to the sky.

She returned to her walk and almost stumbled over Miss Watson, who was on her knees pruning a bed of cream-colored rose bushes so quietly that, aside from minimal motions with a hand clipper, she could've been meditating. Eliza caught herself, not sure whether to stop to greet her or continue walking. "Good morning, Miss Watson."

"Good day, Miss Malone," she replied without looking up. "Indeed, it is a lovely one, is it not?" She turned and wiped her gloves on her smock. "Do you like to garden?"

Her question surprised Eliza—she hadn't had a dialogue alone with Miss Watson in the three weeks since she'd arrived. "Yes, I do. My grandmother had a splendid garden in Wayzata. Our native species are similar to yours, though not so many colorful hydrangeas. Roses, though, were her favorite."

"Were?" Miss Watson asked.

"Well, are, I'm sure. She was widowed in forty-seven, but she lives at home and has a wonderful lawn and garden overlooking Lake Minnetonka," Eliza said.

In a strange way, it seemed Grandpa Theo had died just weeks ago—his funeral, when she'd said goodbye and prayed for him, was her last intact memory of home. Without visits from Harvey over the past three and a half years, she'd have learned nothing of her family. She'd told herself she needed time away; time to dispel the fear and heal; time to find and rescue the real Eliza—the one she wanted to be. But visualizing Grandma Edith's garden, she wondered if her exile wasn't a form of continual self-loathing. What must the world, especially this old Chestnut Hill world, think of her self-inflicted removal from her own people? She hardly knew what to think of it herself.

"Hmm," the older woman murmured. With little effort, she stood and turned to Eliza. "Did you happen to notice the damage in the bed of Peace roses behind you?"

"No, not really. I'd imagine the less beautiful bushes have already had their day," Eliza replied. "Or the blossoms eaten by deer?"

"Look here, there isn't a single petal left, although the foliage, you'll see, appears quite fine. And over here," she turned to the bed she was attending, "these flowers are spectacularly healthy and with care will last for a month." Miss Watson kept on as Eliza went back to inspect the bushes in question. "Do you recall last week we had a summer storm and it hailed for ten minutes straight, just before lunch? The buds on those Peace bushes came weeks early—not quite in full bloom, but opening—and for that, they suffered. The ice pelted off their petals like so many scraps of pink tissue paper. The others were protected. By their immaturity, one might say."

"Miss Watson, I'd very much like to help you in the garden if you have tasks for me to do. I have a bit of schoolwork, preparing my application for next fall, but I have plenty of time and would love to get my hands in the dirt. I'm afraid all of this socializing isn't my cup of tea."

"I'll see to it we find some dirty jobs for you," Miss Watson said with what Eliza felt sure was a smile. "Certainly more agreeable than the interminable engagement parties you've signed on for." She removed her gloves and tucked them into her work-basket. "In the meantime, I'm going to the city for shopping and a luncheon today. If you'd like a ride to Cambridge, you're welcome to join me. We'll have the car pulled around at ten."

"Yes," Eliza said, thinking Miss Watson had read her mind. "I'd like both of those things, actually. Thank you."

Eliza watched Miss Watson walk away, almost as if they'd never spoken. From the back, tall and broad-shouldered with a thick, tightly pinned bun of hair, she looked like Mother. She also bore similarity to Mother in her stern demeanor. In Eliza's childhood, her mother's emotions had seemed impenetrable, but now Eliza imagined that the protective walls Nell had erected contained a deep well of suffering—perhaps tragic or traumatic memories she'd never shared.

Only a few times in the past years at Cornell had she thought about Mother, and when she had, the thoughts fled, cut short by an ache she refused to dwell on, as if starving it of attention might make it vanish. Now, as Miss Watson disappeared around a bend in the path, Eliza was struck by an unexpected and powerful yearning. The memory of Mother was in front of her, just as she'd been on that terrible afternoon:

Nell, sitting on the edge of the bed she shared with Fa, thrusting the velvet ring box at her, looking at Eliza, at first beseechingly as if she couldn't find the right words. She'd looked down and paused before looking at Eliza again, her face cleared of either confusion or doubt. "I cannot condone what happened, Eliza, you know that. And although we'll miss you, I accept that you're leaving." Mother had hesitated, as if perhaps those weren't the words she expected or even wanted to say. Her voice became husky and her words quickened. "I want you to have this; to remind you, so you don't let go, as I did. As I knew I had to."

She'd waited for her mother to explain further, for her voice to turn tender, for her arms to open, but, instead, Mother went quiet, her face tense, her lips drawn, her eyes distant, as if Eliza had vanished. "Goodbye, Mother," she'd whispered, feeling small and unsure in a way she never had before. She'd turned away, clutching the box until its edge cut into her palm, then closed the bedroom door behind her.

From the time she read Mrs. Perkins' first encouraging letter in the library at Watermelon Hill until the day she packed her bags for Ithaca, Eliza had not doubted her decision to leave, but the memory of her mother's cool words and hollow gesture resurfaced and stung; her eyes watered, and her breath left her.

Standing alone in the gardens of the Longuejour Estate, she realized it was not Mother she saw in Mrs. Watson's profile but herself. She remembered how she'd felt, pretending not to notice his tears as she'd turned away from Fa, who'd driven her to the bus station. She wondered what her mother had meant when she'd said she'd once let go. She thought of her own letting go—of the horrible truth she could never allow herself to fully recall, a well-guarded secret kept from everyone. Everyone, and most importantly, from her carefully groomed and future self.

~⨀

ELIZA HAD BEEN TO CAMBRIDGE several times in the past three weeks—first with Beryl and her father, and then alone. A library's demand for human quiet revealed all sorts of comforting sounds and made her feel secure like nowhere else on earth: the rolling of book carts; the opening of large, old doors into capacious, book-lined rooms; the quiet thud of low-heeled shoes crossing waxed floors; the dinging of a single bell indicating a request for help. She looked around today, calmed by a handful of glowing-yellow desk lights marking the occupied tables, like ship beacons in a safe port.

She'd avoided the matter of Stanley's proposal since her arrival in Massachusetts. This was partly justified, given the change in her daily life brought on by the onslaught of activities around Beryl's engagement. The parties she'd unwittingly signed on for were only the beginning. She was also expected to shop for gowns with Beryl, help choose gift registry items, dictate thank you notes—and write them, if Beryl had gotten her way—and be a sounding board for Beryl's ever-changing moods around the whole affair.

She closed her notebook and turned off the electric lamp at her desk in the back corner on the second floor of the library. She'd finished both the preliminary documentation for her Ph.D. application and a formal letter to her mentor Mrs. Perkins asking her to write a letter of recommendation. Feeling invigorated, she pushed back a strand of loose hair from her forehead and checked her watch. She had four hours left before Miss Watson's driver would return to retrieve her.

Cambridge—Harvard Library included—was more museum than reality, with forest-green lamp posts guiding earnest intellectuals and summer tourists between bookstores and red-brick and mortar academic halls, all well-tended despite being two centuries old. Eliza wanted to see more of the real Boston, where ordinary people lived and worked. She'd read accounts of the New England Home for Little Wanderers in Boston's north end, where the orphan trains of the late 1800's carried thousands of homeless city children, many victims of the Civil War, westward to new families. The orphanage had since moved to the south side, close to the neighborhoods of Quincy and Jamaica Plain. There, immigrants from far away countries joined together in tightly-knit communities, working at exhausting, sometimes risky jobs to provide opportunities for their children. She took the city map from her purse and planned a simple route to the south side of town.

A hefty man likely in his mid-thirties sat across from her on the streetcar and held his boy on his lap so father and son faced each other. The man, swarthy and muscular, had deep-set brown eyes and pronounced cheekbones. He wore clean but frayed work pants, coarse suspenders, and a dark, short-sleeved shirt. Handsome, Eliza concluded, trustworthy, a good-hearted family man like Fa. She watched as they played a wordless game, the father making dramatic expressions and the child mimicking him: happy, tired, frightened, sad, surprised, angry. That the boy looked so much like his father made it all the more entertaining. Eliza tried to watch discreetly, but when the boy mimicked angry, she couldn't help herself and put her hand to her mouth to stifle a laugh.

She'd not noticed the short, stout woman sitting to their right who wore a plain-cotton dress and a patterned scarf tied under her chin, despite the summer's day heat. Now she looked up from her embroidery ring, and her face brightened. She brushed the palm of her reddened hand first on her son's, then her husband's cheeks and spoke quietly in a language Eliza guessed was Russian or Ukrainian. Both father and son smiled back at her, looking like different-sized versions of the same person. The man turned the boy around on his lap, so he faced outward, and placed his hand on his wife's knee.

When they got off the streetcar in Jamaica Plain, across from the Sacred Heart Ukrainian Catholic Parish, Eliza decided to follow. She stayed well behind as they walked several blocks to a row of tenement buildings on Washington Street, in a neighborhood where the few shops, including a fresh produce stand, had signs in languages Eliza didn't recognize. The heavily cracked sidewalks had been swept clean, and dozens of people gathered outside, standing in doorways, sitting on chairs along the sidewalks, ambling in arm-linked pairs. Their building's stairwell was cracked and broken, one railing was bent to the ground, and plain cotton curtains hung limp behind opened windows. The contrast to Chestnut Hill was dramatic.

Eliza wanted to spend as much time wandering these streets as she could in the remaining days of summer. Beryl might be interested in joining her once, but probably not twice. The bigger question was Stanley: was it the kind of adventure he would like? Would marriage to him bring her companionship in the worlds she hoped to discover or would she lack the courage to ever find out?

Weeks later, when Stanley brought Eliza out for an evening in Boston, she felt sure of her answer. After the symphony, he led her across the street to a restaurant they'd visited earlier in the summer.

"Yes, Stanley," she said when he asked her for the third time with the same earnest delivery as before, "I'll marry you."

Stanley took her hands in his and gazed at them. He then kissed her lips gently before pulling back a little and smiling "We'll make a great team, darling; you're ... so good." He hesitated, and Eliza pictured Shannon, who'd always insisted on Eliza's goodness as an irrefutable fact, like the sword in Merlin's stone.

Eliza doubted if Shannon still believed in the purity of Eliza's moral character. How could she, after what Eliza had said and done? Eliza told herself she was better off without the burden of her sister's idolization.

Stanley continued, "You're so good for me. You make me better than I am."

Eliza's lower lip disappeared for a second before she forced an unintentionally glib smile. "I hope you'll return the favor, Stanley." She considered the many times Shannon made the same remark.

In those days, the idea of improving others with her goodness pleased her. Now, she wasn't so sure.

By evening's end, she couldn't shake the thought that she'd have to work hard to make a good wife, as the concept wasn't as clear to her as good student or good daughter. She was thankful Stanley knew her well enough to know Eliza-the-wife would still need to be accepted as his intellectual equal—and an ambitious one, at that—in order to be happy. Of course, he knew that.

21

OCTOBER 1951

When Shannon arrived on Friday afternoon to help with Mr. and Mrs. Ross's anniversary party, she found the back door to the kitchen locked. The October day was another one in a string of beautiful autumn days—cool and bright with high, bleached clouds that gave no humidity to the air. Shannon inhaled the spiced bitterness of the fallen maple leaves crowding the lawn in reddish-brown mounds, ready to be removed before guests arrived.

Virginia Ross stood in the kitchen, instructing the bartender and waitress she'd hired for the evening. Although she wore a plain-cotton dress, her hair was coiffed in a Sophia Loren-style loose bun and her nails manicured and polished a deep red to match her pendant earrings. She looked stunning, even before dressing in her new Indian-chiffon cocktail dress, crimson with gold-thread inlay, which Shannon had hemmed for her last week. Mrs. Ross's confidence in her own beauty made Shannon feel plain, almost invisible, as she waited to catch her employer's attention from the other side of the glass-paned door. The bartender saw her and opened the door to let her in before taking a tray of cold hors d'oeuvres to the living room. Mrs. Ross sat down to write out place cards for the dining room table, while Shannon removed her coat and hung it in the pantry.

"You're finally here, Shannon; I broke the bud vase in the bathroom. Sweep it again, would you? Make sure the broken pieces are gathered," she said, writing carefully and not looking up. "You know where the broom is, don't you?"

Shannon nodded. "Yes, I do." She took a short breath, forcing back a wave of anxiety before asking, "Mrs. Ross? Could I take Miriam to the Harvest Festival at Lakeside Parish two weeks from Sunday and bring her to my grandmother's for the night?" She'd been anticipating for weeks the possibility of taking Miriam to the church festival near the lake house she and Eliza had loved as little girls.

"How sweet of you. Can we talk about it later? Maybe after the party tonight?" she said, still not looking at Shannon while she organized the stack of completed place cards on a blotter. "I don't think I've mentioned yet that Mr. Ross has taken a new position in Edinburgh. Can you believe it? Part of a professional exchange between 3M and the UK. We're leaving in a little over a month. Mid-November, it looks like, and I'm sure we'll be saying our goodbyes on those last Sundays. But we'll see if we can't work it out for you to take her. It might actually help; we'll be so busy." She finished speaking and walked away from Shannon, who forced one foot to follow the other in an effort not to cry out or possibly, she thought, even faint.

Mrs. Ross looked at Shannon. "Don't worry, dear, we'll pay you for a month of work and give you a shining recommendation. It's only fair, after all. You've been an absolute charm with Miriam—and it's been how long? Three years, isn't it?"

Three years and five months, to the day, Shannon thought, with a feeble nod of acknowledgment.

Mrs. Ross went on, "We've already arranged to rent the house out since we may well come back in a year or two. Mr. Ross is from Scotland, of course, so who knows, maybe we'll stay." She turned and faced Shannon. "Come now, you look as if someone died. Don't be ridiculous. It'll be good for us. And good for Miriam to be close to more family; I'm sure you agree. She has only Mr. Ross and me here." Done with her explanation, she turned and left the kitchen.

MR. ROSS WAS READY TO take Shannon home at nine p.m., though half-a-dozen guests remained gathered around the coffee table, playing informal hands of poker. Shannon found her coat and bag in the pantry and watched Mrs. Ross wrinkle her nose with a smirk and giggle when Mr. Rink—the next-door neighbor, whose wife was bed-ridden—bent close, whispering into her ear.

In the car, Mr. Ross asked her about her plans for school and suggested that since they were leaving, she might have more time to pursue her nursing diploma. Shannon didn't remember telling him she was taking classes at Milner Hospital. He must have noticed her books, or maybe one day she'd mentioned it in passing and forgotten.

"Mr. Ross," she asked, "do you think you'll return? You know, after your project in England."

"Thankfully, it's Scotland we're headed for, not England, Miss

Malone. I wouldn't mind staying for quite a while, to be honest," he replied. "My mother's outside Edinburgh. She's in bad health … not too many of us around anymore, other than my cousin and his family. She's a lovely old gal. Lonely, though."

Shannon thought his Scottish accent had deepened, and it distracted her for a moment from the terrible pit festering in her stomach since her earlier words with Mrs. Ross. Perhaps their previous conversations included only a few niceties here and there, or maybe he was indulging in his native brogue now that he knew he'd return home. Shannon thought it beautiful, so beautiful she could hardly focus on the meaning of the lilting, melodious strings of strangely familiar syllables and words. She closed her eyes and imagined Miriam's first encounter with her Scottish grandmother. Her chest tightened when she remembered in another version of the story, Nell was the girl's rightful grandmother. Not exactly the kind, magical one in *The Princess and the Goblin*, but in another world, she thought, how Mother and Fa would love Miriam, their first grandchild.

She watched Mr. Ross's large, freckled hands gripping the steering wheel and thought about how very little one needed to turn it for a dramatic change in course.

"Miriam was excited about the game you've been playing," he said. "She told me you read her part of a story first, about a princess and a coal miner, and then you hide while she counts. She said she finds you by following raisins and a magic thread?"

"Yes; it's a story my father used to read us; I hope it didn't frighten her too much. I'd forgotten some of the gruesome descriptions. But it's quite lovely; a classic in English literature."

"Scottish, Shannon; Mr. MacDonald was Scottish. Or at the very least, British," Mr. Ross said, laughing. "I'd forgotten it altogether, though it was our family favorite, too. My mother kept both books, *The Princess and the Goblin* and *The Princess and Curdie,* right next to our Bible on the mantle above the fireplace.

She had a rich voice she'd amend for each character, and they'd all come alive in our sitting room many times on the long winter nights. You could almost see the goblins dancing about in the flames of our fireplace. My father as goblin king was far too realistic, so Mother wouldn't allow him to read. Good evenings, those were."

The house was dark when Mr. Ross pulled the car close to the curb. The full moon in a cloudless sky illuminated the outline of his tall, muscular frame as he walked around the car and opened her door. "Don't drop the enchanted thread, Shannon. Far too few of us see it anymore." He smiled wryly, perhaps even woefully, as he followed her to the door, turning around only after she'd let herself in.

Inside, nothing but the single light in the kitchen shone. Mother had left a note for Shannon on the kitchen table to remind her of the eleven o'clock morning Mass at St. Thomas's for the baptismal service of Jonathan, Olivia's new baby boy. No one had asked Shannon, but the celebration had been expanded to include a family luncheon at her brother's house across the bay from Grandmother Edith's home on Lake Minnetonka. Of course, the new baby, the first acknowledged grandchild, would be the center of everyone's attention.

Shannon didn't want to sleep, though she was tired from hours of work at the Ross's party. Thoughts of the Rosses—Miriam—leaving the country scared her as if she herself might cease to exist as well. Hadn't she almost ceased to exist after Eliza left? She reached for the book she'd been reading, *The Problem of Pain* by C.S. Lewis, but put it down again. Despite her exhaustion, she knew she'd not be able to sleep until she took her pen and stationery from her bedside drawer and wrote her sister another in a growing pile of unsent letters.

October 20th, 1951

Dear Eliza,

Devastating news. I'm sorry to begin my letter so brusquely, but you must know I feel my world has come to an abrupt halt—or maybe it's spinning so fast I can't get my footing. You might tell me I had it coming, that I shouldn't have done this in the first place or that I shouldn't have put so much trust in the Rosses. Of course, it's not their fault, exactly (although as you know, I have no love lost for Virginia.)

In less than a month, they're moving (permanently?) to England—or I guess it's Scotland. Mr. Ross has been given a role as lead engineer for a project between 3M and the British coal mining industry, or something like that. He told me in some detail tonight as he drove me home, but I could hardly listen. I don't care one bit why or where they're going; I could only think about living my life without you and, now, without Miriam. And what if they don't EVER come back? I know you think I've been foolish, but I knew the day I first saw Miriam in the hospital that He had spared my life for a greater purpose, to somehow bring us back together.

Today, when Mrs. Ross told me the news, I felt I would faint, but writing to you now is giving me comfort. Somehow, it will be made right, dear sister. For now, please hold for a moment all of my love for you, and know that someday we'll be close as sisters are supposed to be again—as close as before—as mother and aunt to this little girl. I know it sounds absurd, but I believe it's true.

As Dr. Lewis has said, "For you will certainly carry out God's purpose, howsoever you act, but it makes a difference to you whether you serve like Judas or like

John."

> *— C.S. Lewis, The Problem of Pain*

Love,
Shannon.

Shannon folded her letter in half, put it in a matching envelope, and wrote the date again on the back, as she'd done with the dozens of letters she'd written to Eliza since February 1948. She wrote *Eliza Malone, Ithaca, NY* on the front and placed it on top of all the many others, unsent and stashed in the drawer next to her bed. She picked up her book again, a gift from Fa in the days before her second surgery, and read a few, worn pages before falling asleep.

On Wednesday afternoon, when Shannon returned from her classes at Milner Hospital, she found a note from Mrs. Ross on the front porch. She'd be taking Miriam to Scotland two weeks early in order to settle into their new home well before the holidays, while Mr. Ross finished up business and the rental of the house. If Shannon would like, the note read, she could come to say goodbye to Miriam this Thursday and spend a few hours helping her pack boxes while Miriam napped. Beyond that point, her assistance with Miriam would no longer be needed.

22

OCTOBER 1951

Three months after Stanley's third proposal late in the summer of 1951, Eliza arrived at Penn Station on the morning train from Boston for their civil wedding at City Hall. While still a guest at Longuejour Mansion, she'd fulfilled her duties as Maid of Honor leading up to Beryl's September wedding, which the Boston Globe called "the nuptial event of the season." Stanley met her at the train with a small bouquet of pale-pink tea roses. Eliza hovered above him in heeled boots, and he embraced her awkwardly as her overnight bag caught between their uneven bodies. Both laughed. It wasn't the first time their attempt at an impromptu hug went sideways.

Eliza and Stanley enjoyed an early lunch at the Russian Tea Room near Central Park, as they'd done a dozen times before. The pearl brooch he gave her as a wedding gift was not, he told her, particularly valuable. It was a memento, carried here by family members who'd survived the Holocaust. He wanted her to have it. Eliza was touched.

"Our treasured objects have journeys of their own," he said, "and few more so than this one."

They exchanged vows in front of a silver-haired, lean, and kindly judge who reminded Eliza of David's father. She fought to keep images of Mr. Whitaker, as well as David, out of her mind as she promised herself to Stanley. They left the courthouse laughing at the middle-aged court recorder's high-pitched voice, made worse by his random and violent sneezes that paused the short ceremony—not once or twice, but three times. The autumn air was crisp and clear, seasonably cool, enough so that Eliza felt justified to put on her kid-leather gloves, newly monogrammed with EMK. After a late-afternoon walk through the park, Stanley took her to the Plaza Hotel.

"Shouldn't we at least tell Frances?" Stanley asked when they entered the elevator in the main lobby of the hotel, Eliza holding her bouquet and Stanley carrying her bag. "She'll be thrilled and not too pleased if she isn't among the first to know."

Despite appearances, Eliza had not overcome thoughts that the whole business—the courtship, the talk of their future together, their plans to share a home, maybe even have children—had been a sham, and now, after the civil ceremony, she found she didn't quite believe her own marriage to Stanley to be legitimate. It wasn't only the unexpected and unwelcomed ghosts of David and his father; she couldn't shake feelings of having been betrayed by the Church, feelings which, until now, she'd considered unimportant. In the time since her arrival at Cornell, she'd held on tightly to Catholic ritual, though she considered it to be indoctrination she simply never had the energy to intellectually dissolve. The Masses and holy days of the Roman Catholic Church provided her a convenient proxy for the family she'd walked away from, and the hours spent at weekly Mass gave a meditative respite from the nagging persistence to push herself ever harder at Cornell. At other times, though, especially around the winter holidays, she felt an uneasy defiance toward the Church, a seedling of murky rage that, if unearthed, might orphan her from religion forever.

As they'd awaited the judge, Stanley had taken Eliza's hand and squeezed it gently. She'd smiled nervously—she couldn't be marrying, could she? Even though she could be satisfying a social gateway, at least in a civic sense, what about God, the Church? Considering the Church's judgment made her bristle, but did God think her a fool? Or worse, did He see as clearly as she felt the unshakeable falseness of the path she was taking?

"I do think we should tell her, darling. Let's send her a telegram. Right away, in fact."

Eliza comforted herself by imagining a lunch with Mrs. Perkins as soon as she returned to Cornell. Her mentor would both chide her for keeping such plans secret and gloat at her success in matching her two favorite protégés. Her certain approval would serve to ease, if not replace, Eliza's doubt for now.

Eliza knew her emotions were raw on her wedding day as her menses had begun the day before. Despite the rollercoaster of insecurities and fatigue it always caused her, she was relieved. Had she willed it to arrive? She had no idea how she would talk about it with Stanley, but she also knew imaginings of her wedding night had begun, quite irrationally, to terrify her.

To Eliza's relief, telling Stanley about her bleeding was no cause for concern. When she mentioned her monthly cramps, he gave her a quick hug around the shoulders. "Not to worry, darling. We have plenty of time. Why don't you take a nap? And I'll go find you some tonic water." Stanley had already gone to the sink to splash water on his face and comb his hair. He toweled his face and continued in the same light tone as before, a tone that Eliza, increasingly irritable from her cramped organs, found to be cloyingly upbeat. "When I return, we can talk about dinner—and how about a movie in the Village? Maybe *Ivanhoe*, the film Marguerite Roberts worked on?"

Mrs. Roberts, the California screenwriter who, along with her communist husband, had refused to testify in front of the House Un-American Activities Committee, was currently blacklisted from Hollywood. Eliza and Stanley shared their disdain for the HUAC, chaired by Congressman John Wood, by all accounts a southern bigot. Social liberalism was one of the many similar, in some ways radical, points of view that Eliza and Stanley shared. Despite their alliances to democratic principles, both felt reaction to perceived communist threats had gone too far since the final chapters of World War II and distracted the legislature from more important work. This was not an opinion shared by everyone. To express it publicly was to run serious risks of being labeled a communist sympathizer.

"It's a wonderful idea, Stanley." Eliza was relieved and touched by her new husband's sensitivities to her temperament. She wavered between her true affection for him—sixty percent—and her doubt she could survive the inevitable intimacies of marriage—forty percent. The latter was completely irrational and weak, and she vigorously refused to believe she could not will success. Women everywhere and throughout time had managed to make marriage work. That her affection was on a more intellectual rather than emotional footing was something she chose to dismiss.

"Ivanhoe sounds just right. It's one of my father's favorite novels." She took off her shoes, silk stockings, and peach-colored linen jacket with elbow length sleeves that complemented the sleeveless white and peach linen dress. How she loved thoughtfully tailored clothing. She folded the jacket and dress over the wing-backed chair and lay down on the bed. Stanley emerged from the hallway closet with a light blanket to cover her.

"Someday you'll have to tell me properly about your family, the whole bit this time. Back in an hour, darling." He pecked her cheek and left the room whistling a tune.

She closed her eyes, but then opened them and, from her curled position on the right side of the bed, looked over every part of the elegant room that she could see without moving her head. She was tired, and as she closed her eyes again, she felt a tear forming in the corner of her eye. It tickled as it slid down the side of her nose, and she resented the need to lift her hand to rub the tear away. For the first time in years, she felt a desperate urge to be sixteen years old again, safe in her childhood world with Shannon, Ed, Mother, and Fa. It was as if she'd stopped running. Eliza felt uncertain and wondered how she'd gotten here to this moment with Stanley. Did other women on their wedding nights feel as unprepared and exposed?

That night after returning from the movie, a modern portrayal of Sir Walter Scott's famous twelfth-century love story, Eliza felt once again secure in her choice to marry Stanley. She imagined only he among all men could share her ambitions; only he could keep up with her intellect and curiosity. With him she could let sleeping dogs rest. Her secrets would fade, and she and Stanley would—as he'd promised so many times—travel the world, write articles and books together, support each other's professional pursuits, socialize with enlightened and stimulating people, and maybe someday have children. Yes, if she put the date far enough in the future, she could convince herself of that possibility. She felt new confidence as they shared a bed for the first time. Stanley held her closely in an embrace, then slowly released her and fell asleep with his palm resting on the fine silk of the night-shirt covering her warm, bare thigh.

PART THREE

23

November 1961

t didn't surprise Shannon that several of her nursing colleagues at Milner had suffered a childhood trauma. She thought a year stuck in a hospital bed must be similar to being a foot soldier in wartime. As much fear, pain, and boredom as it might involve, one becomes accustomed to it and begins to rely on the comradery and the communal suffering to find comfort in even the miserable routines of daily survival. A patient might admire her doctor and nurse as a corporal admires his lieutenant, or a student her favorite teacher. It was natural, she thought.

"Shannon, could you take my shift for Thanksgiving?" asked Jeanne, the youngest nurse on staff, whose mother had been one of Shannon's TB ward mates years ago. "We learned Jack's leaving for Saigon in January ..."

"Look no further, Jeanne." It was a handy excuse not to be at Ed's for Thanksgiving. Each year had been easier than the one preceding, but Shannon found it unpleasant to attend the holiday with Olivia's extended family at the Lake Minnetonka home. When the late November day was too cold to be outdoors, hours in the kitchen spent listening to Olivia and her two sisters spinning mean humor into thinly veiled provocations unnerved her. Olivia's passing remark on Alice's philandering husband flowed into Eunice's running commentary on her nephew's drippy nose; Alice's reddening cheeks revealed years of hurt and justified her pinching Olivia in response to being called "Fragile Al." Tensions would mount until late in the afternoon when their otherwise meek mother would bark "Enough!," sending the sisters to huddle in a corner whispering like schoolgirls. She could've managed it with Eliza, but alone she stayed quiet, cautiously aware that Olivia's sarcasm, in particular, could be redirected to her.

"Shannon," Jeanne said, "you're a dear; I'll make it up to you— maybe over Christmas?"

"No need—you'd be doing me a favor. I'm so sorry about Jack. How old is he now? Twenty-six?" Shannon leafed through a stack of patient files in front of her. It was 1961 and the world had changed since the Navy first took Ed to the South Pacific in 1943. People felt little sense of shared sacrifice in this new conflict, just fear and confusion as the government asked families to say goodbye to their boys for a war the country had recently entered in a region few had ever thought about before 1960.

"Jeanne, I am happy to work Thanksgiving. Especially for you." How she would love to be here in the nurses' station on the fourth floor of the new hospital building, surrounded by the comforting whites of the walls, the file cabinets, the nurse smocks, and the rolling metal carts. Mother would have something to say about her change in schedule, but even her judgment was less painful than an interminable afternoon with the O'Rourkes.

Shannon felt the hand of God at work in her life, although since the Ross's departure she had far less understanding of His plan. She sometimes cursed the seeming cruelty of God's method.

She looked at the wall calendar hanging above the desk in the nurse station. Tomorrow was Friday, November 10, 1961— Mother's birthday. Ten years had passed since the Ross's house in Roseville had been rented and they'd sailed from New York bound for Scotland.

Losing Miriam had pushed Shannon further from her parents, far from joy, and into a reclusive state that she'd grown comfortable with over the years. In the weeks after the Ross family's departure, and knowing nothing of Miriam, Nell and Cecil worried she was relapsing into illness, or that sadness at the loss of Eliza had resurfaced. They'd been alarmed when she dropped out of nursing school and upset when she told them she'd found a small apartment at Horton Park, halfway between Roseville and Milner Hospital. Only when she promised to enroll in nursing classes again did Fa arrange access to the monthly stipend Grandpa had provided for each of his grandchildren.

She felt them watching her, fretting about her, as her life became smaller. She wished they'd let her be. Not that she thought her parents were wrong; she, herself, felt diminished, sad, maybe even traumatized by the combination of events and physical scars life had delivered. But despite all of that, she was grateful to be alive. She felt both humble and strong in a way only those who've survived have a right to claim. The sobriety of beating back death had made her resilient to everyday loneliness even as her friends moved on. Harvey, who'd spent six years traveling back and forth between university and home, was settled in New York as a young, ambitious lawyer. Shannon had been a bride's maid to Betty, who'd married Bud and moved to a town near Chicago. Last year's Christmas card demonstrated in full color two children and a third on the way; Betty promised to name this one Shannon, whether boy or girl.

Her new world was simple: shifts at the hospital, weekly lunches with Mother, a modest return to painting, and volunteering at her new parish. She narrowed her daily experience to essentials. She knew her neighbors—but in the shallow, pleasant way she knew the checker at the grocery store or the man who repaired her shoes. She often confused the loss of Miriam with the loss of Eliza. In her mind, they were one and the same.

But loneliness felt very different from emptiness. Emptiness came from the unresolved heartache of loss, and that was what she feared most. To hold onto herself, to ward off her fears and build a connection to reality, she compelled herself to take notice of everything around her—animals, birds, human voice, colors. She consoled herself with painting—watercolors, oils, charcoals— wanting to create something real and concrete from any morsel of beauty, as if she were the same little girl who'd sat on the tree stump decades ago, afraid of not existing and forcing back tears by counting her whites.

At the end of her shift, as Shannon collected her belongings to leave, a man with "Jax Auto Body" embroidered on the sleeve of his clean but tattered jacket approached the nurses' station. He had a mess of curly dark hair; grease spotted his faded blue dungarees, and his calloused hands revealed fingernails embedded with dark stains.

"Excuse me, my wife was brought in by a neighbor lady. I was at work, see. She's about to have a baby—our first," he said, nervous excitement pitching his words.

Jeanne nodded, ready to recite oft-repeated directions to the maternity ward, but Shannon felt compelled to intercede. "I'll show you the way, if you'd like—" A vague recollection she'd felt upon hearing his voice caught up with her, and she reflexively touched her blouse where it covered the old scar across her shoulder and chest. She smiled at him, noticing that he smelled more of cigarettes than of cinnamon and chocolate.

The fellow half-smiled back, as though perplexed by the recognition that Shannon didn't think to hide. "Excuse me, ma'am—do I know you?" he asked.

"No! I don't suppose so." She felt her cheeks redden. "You just … I think you remind me of someone …"

Their eyes met and lingered briefly before she touched his elbow to lead him to the maternity ward—the same place Eliza had given birth to Miriam. It occurred to Shannon that she'd held onto her encounter on the chapel steps with the chocolate-cinnamon boy for fifteen years as though it were an incomplete painting kept safe in a closet. Hideous scars, infertility, the painful loss of Eliza, followed by the loss of Miriam—these were the obstacles that had destroyed Shannon's rightful path—the path she'd first dreamt about when she met this boy, now a man. She'd cared for the memory as she'd cared for her collection of dolls—as if by keeping it untouched on a high shelf it could last forever. Had he held onto it for any time at all?

24

November 1961

Nell reached around the back of the table to the right of the altar where the gifts of wine and bread were placed at the beginning of Mass. She wore rubber gloves, as was her habit, having been chastised by germs far too many times in the past thirty years. She pulled at a piece of chewing gum stuck into the far corner and smiled; the culprit could've been Ed, twenty-five years ago.

After decades of Thursday afternoons dusting each pew and sweeping each of the fifteen corners of St. Thomas Aquinas Chapel, she appreciated her private rituals. Nell was seen as a devout Catholic, but she knew she wasn't a true Christian. She was an imposter, who with each passing year felt more alienated from the idea of a loving, guiding Father. The very word Father made her shudder. God might exist, but He was fearsome and as unpredictable and wrathful as her own human father had been. God the Father was not to be trusted, but to be cautiously respected and, at times, to be bargained with. The fewer words the better, so devotion to daily chores was the currency she invested in, instead of daily prayer.

She sat for a moment in the front pew. The church was quiet. She looked up to the remodeled cornice and read the newly scripted passage set against the pewter paint in white block letters that ran close to the ceiling: "You shall be able to discern the will of God ..." She closed her eyes. The act of breathing had changed for her, and after weeks of denial, she sat back and allowed herself to consider why.

Cecil had noticed it first in the early hours of the morning some weeks ago. He'd whispered hoarsely to her, "Nell, you awake?"

"No, I wasn't yet, Ceece. But I am now. What time is it? Must be early."

"It's not quite five. It's just ... your breathing sounds heavy. Were you having a bad dream?"

She couldn't remember Cecil ever asking her this question, and it struck her that indeed she'd been in the midst of a violent dream: the low and memorable gray-green clouds of a picnic celebration from many years ago were being pulled down to earth one by one through the force of Nell's will. When she discovered this power, she wanted to show the girls and Edmund, as if it were a parlor trick. She lay flat on her back on the cool, moist grass in between four blankets, like the bulls-eye in a green, earthbound target. She concentrated her thoughts, deepened her inhalations, and the clouds began to stack and drop. But they wouldn't be as benevolent nor as controlled in their descent as she commanded. They thudded down and layered themselves like molasses on her chest with such malice that she became confused and breathing became laborious.

Shame at her pride for toying with an untested power overcame her, but she couldn't cry or speak because the suffocating moistness of the clouds immersed her from head to toe. All she could think about was her next breath. One by one her family left her except for Cecil, who was calling for her, unsure of where she'd gone.

"Yes, I was dreaming. And thank you for waking me, as it was very unpleasant." Nell lay still for a minute more and felt the pressure remaining on her chest. She took quick inventory of other symptoms—no fever, no aches except in her chest, no congestion—and with some relief, left her bed to begin another day.

Although its intensity faded, the heaviness did not leave her. She recalled no more violent dreams, but it became commonplace to awaken with a start in an effort to free her chest from some weighty oppression.

"Nellie," Cecil would say before he crossed the bedroom to begin his daily ablution and prayers. "You don't sound right this morning. Won't you please visit Dr. Johnston? I hate to keep on at you ... but if not me, who?"

"I will, Cecil," she'd said on three occasions. "I keep forgetting. That's what I should see Dr. Johnston for ... my miserable memory."

"Here, then," Cecil had said this third time, "I'll write it on a piece of paper and leave it on the kitchen table where you can't miss it." He then came over to the bedside and pulled up the dressing-table bench to sit beside her. He put his cool hand on her cheek and gazed at her for a moment. "I love you so." His eyes welled in the way that had often made Nell angry in the past.

His liberal access to certain emotions sometimes unnerved her, and she often responded with a gruff dismissal. But today, because it caught her by surprise in a moment of half-sleep or perhaps because they rarely spoke with such intimacy anymore, she embraced what he offered and took his hand in both of hers. She thanked God for at least this: that she could, thirty years on, recognize and not destroy the unquestioning acceptance, and even more, the love Cecil had sustained for her. How she was able to accept this gift after all she'd suffered was a mystery to her. It was her only foothold into some kind of true spiritual faith.

"I …" Nell stopped after this single word. She tried again: "I will call, Ceece. I want to tell you …" She wasn't practiced in putting feelings into words, even after all of these years, but she closed her eyes and continued, "I'm to blame she left us. And I'm sorry, so sorry …" Nell turned her face away from Cecil and sank it deep into the pillow, but she continued to squeeze his hand as if healing energy might flow from his palm.

"Nell, that's not true. I don't feel that way. It happened. And God knows why it did. Please don't, Nell," he choked out the words. "I need you."

"But, Cecil, it's done. It's between us. You say you don't feel that way, but we both know. Whether you blame me or not, I pushed her away, and we let her go. We let her suffer alone. And, somehow, she took Shannon with her. You must know what I mean. They're both gone from us. And now, we're almost gone from each other. Don't you feel that? We have Edmund, yes, we do … and his boys, of course. But they're not really ours, are they? They're Olivia's, and she'll not let me forget it." Nell stopped and stifled her words with her hand.

This seemed too much for Cecil—indeed it was more words with more emotion than Nell had put together on the subject of their children or their life since Baby Theodore had died. He put his head in his hands and faced away from her. "Jesus, Mary, and Joseph … Jesus, Mary and …" He faced Nell again, put his hand to her cheek and kissed her forehead. As he left the bedroom, he turned and said, "Nell, my love, you said you'd call Dr. Johnston today. And it's first Thursday, you'll have lunch with Shannon, isn't that right?"

The branch Cecil had offered was enough for Nell. She rose from bed, barely recognizing the fraught woman she left behind in the bed linen. The sun wasn't yet up, but she could tell from the stillness around the slightly opened window that the weather had not changed and today would be much like yesterday.

She'd called Dr. Johnston this morning before coming to clean the chapel and had made an appointment to see him next week.

Now, with her eyes closed and her back pressed hard against the right angle of the pew, she felt an unexpected relief in her chest. She swiveled on the seat, lifted her feet onto the pew, then lowered her back and head, and stretched out, following a thought brought on by an old memory. Yes, it relieved the discomfort of pressure to recline on a hard bench. As she lay there in meditation, the church around her disappeared. As if having been handed a photograph, she saw her mother helped out of bed by her father in an episode of rare sobriety so she could lie on the hard, earthen floor that he'd leveled and swept and covered with a roped rug. Ma's waning body, light as cotton balls, rested with feet flat on the rug where, with knees pulled up, her legs formed a small tent with the thin blanket that covered her. Nell recalled the urge she'd had to climb under the triangle of blanket and retreat to a magical, peaceful dimension where she would find her real mother, the one who didn't cough and moan and sleep.

Nell didn't know what disease her mother had suffered from. She only knew it was her heart that gave out one day as she slept on the nearby cot where she'd given birth to Nell years before, and her shallow, tortured breaths grew less as little Nellie stood steps away, preparing a simple broth on the blackened wood stove.

Nell fell asleep on the pew, and as far as she knew, it might be a sin, but when she awoke, it was with a knowledge that made such sins unimportant. How well she could now recall Ma's restless slumbers that had paid no mind to hour of day or night. Whatever name might have been given to her mother's illness would be the name Dr. Johnston would give to hers, she was certain. How far it had gone for her and how similar the fate, well, that was another matter.

~⊘

Shannon was late. Nell waited, sitting at the kitchen table, her mind absent from her body. Discomfort shadowed the surface of her skin, and she wished she could remain alone today. Not that she wished to wallow, but what she most wished to do was to clean the chapel again, to scrub the pews, the altar, and a dozen holy corners down on her hands and her knees, without gloves this time, to tempt God—no, to beg him—to be more merciful with His blows to her than this.

She fingered the gray and pink handle of her teacup, the one that matched none of the others in her kitchen, the one she'd sipped from almost every day of her married life.

"I have a few mementos for yea, darling girl," her grandmother had said in the days before her father took her and the twins away from Oklahoma. "Not so practical, I suppose, but I want ya to remember me, even if it's jist an old Irish teacup."

Tears—hard, fast, and angry—came to Nellie then. It was the last time she'd cried until decades later at the death of Baby Theodore. Grandma had helped her wrap the china cup, a single piece from the remains of a once-full set, and the garnet rosary in a faded linen towel. "I have the matching rosary, wedding gifts to Charles and me from my grandmother," she told Nell. "Come, now; give me a smile and pack those salted tears away."

The prayer beads had been placed in Nell's jewelry drawer years ago, like a delicate anchor-chain securing the branches of her new family to the misshapen roots of her past. The porcelain teacup, though, had been part of her daily life from the day Nell's tragic father pulled her away from the only home she'd known. A stealthy presence from her hidden past, the single teacup with the red Gorham stamp was displayed in broad daylight, but its origin was never questioned by Cecil or her children. In a house full of cups and books and dozens of belongings that had marked both comfort and plenty, it was one of many ordinary things.

Nell felt Grandma today, and even her mother, as if they stood on each side of her. More than a memory, it was a kinship, as if the two women were infusing her and warming her chilled bones through the tea she sipped alone in her kitchen of thirty-six years.

The grandfather clock's single chime of the quarter hour masked the sound of Shannon's entrance through the front door. "Hello, Mother? Where are you?" Nell heard Shannon's voice, too lilting and youthful for a woman in her thirties.

"I'm in the kitchen, dear."

Shannon removed her coat and hung it on the hooks next to the mirror by the screen door. She came over to kiss Nell on the cheek and hesitated. "Sorry, I'm late … Mother, what's wrong?"

"Just tired. I cleaned today; I think the fumes from the new ammonia made me a little nauseous. But I'm fine."

"Well, Happy almost Birthday, Mother," Shannon said, patting an envelope she'd set on the table. "Does Fa have something nice planned for you? I know we'll have Sunday at Ed's, but somehow I'm afraid it'll be more about the kids and cake than about you."

"Thank you, Shannon. I'm sure you're right about that. Edmund will do his best."

"Well, I don't understand either of them. It's as if she wants nothing to do with me unless Ed forces her. And he doesn't seem willing to do that very often."

"Babies do strange things to some women. I wouldn't have thought it when they married," Nell said.

"No sense to dwell on it. I've also brought some bulbs for us to plant for your birthday if you'd like—irises from Harvey's sister."

"Shannon, will you ever learn about gardening? It's too late to plant bulbs now. I'll put them in a brown bag until next spring; we'll see if they survive." Nell smiled and patted her oldest daughter's arm. "Then you can paint them for me, perhaps. How you and Eliza could be so different, I don't know." Nell knew it was an odd thing to say. She'd not spoken about Eliza for months, years even, and yet there it was, her daughter's name rolling out onto the table as if they'd both seen her this morning.

"Have you been thinking about Eliza, Mother?" Shannon asked.

"Well, I'm thinking of plenty today, I suppose, including her." Nell imagined a shaking in her voice. "I have a plate of sandwiches ready in the icebox."

She moved slowly from the table to the refrigerator, still referred to as an icebox out of habit and stubbornness. She was aware of her movement as if her body had separated into two equal parts, one the observer and the other the observed. She wasn't sure which of the two bodies she inhabited until she looked back and confirmed the teacup on the table with no one in the chair beside it. The same oddity had happened once before, several weeks ago. She and Cecil had walked to campus despite the frigid early October morning. When they'd arrived at church, Nell felt the change in temperature from outside to inside, as if she'd put her head in the oven. Cecil caught her as she blacked out, and the fainting spell passed, but for the duration of the walk to their seat in the pew, she felt her body was in two places at once.

"I think of Eliza, Mother. I miss her so terribly sometimes. Here it is, the sixties, and I have no idea how she feels about it all."

"Feels about all what?" Nell asked.

"Everything. I read *Sex and The Single Girl*, for example. Betty sent it to me along with instructions for Catholic-approved birth control. I'm thirty-three years old, and it makes me feel ancient."

"Why do you read it, then? Why not stick with real literature?" Nell had heard about the book Shannon referred to, but she wasn't going to admit to it. She disapproved of the notion that women should liberate their desires from the shelter society—and the Church—provided. All well and good until an unwanted pregnancy happened. Isn't that how she'd lost Eliza? No, she knew that wasn't fair. Even now, she found it easier to tell herself lies, although the truth was inescapable. She'd have to make it right with Eliza, to finally tell her what she knew to be the truth of that horrible year.

"I sometimes write letters to her, Mother," Shannon said as she refreshed Nell's tea with the water remaining in the kettle.

Nell took her spoon, stirred, and poured a bit of the hot liquid onto the saucer, then poured it back into the cup.

"You'd scold us if we used a saucer that way," Shannon said. "But I see now it was you who taught us to do it in the first place."

Nell smiled. "True, I'd say. I simply didn't want you to do it in public, dear…So, what do you write to Eliza?" Nell knew the girls had written each other letters during the horrible year but hadn't considered that it continued now.

"So many things, Mother." Shannon hesitated. "But I don't mail them. I'm not sure why not."

Nell felt an odd relief and wondered why they were having this conversation now after all these years. Thirteen years ago, Eliza had run away to Cornell with the blessing of no one except her grandpa, who Nell suspected to have provided her tuition, along with his generous allowance to each of the children. *Yes, run away, as I did when I was even younger.* Nell had not known then how painful it would be to lose Eliza, especially in this way. Had she known, what would she have done differently?

"Has she ever written to you?" Nell asked.

"No." Shannon brought her napkin to her lips, wiped each

corner, and set it down while gazing at Nell. She pursed her lips, closed her eyes and inhaled, then smiled and opened her eyes again—a habit Nell had seen her develop in the difficult days of her illness. "No."

"It's time for me to write to her, Shannon. It's time for her to come home."

"I wonder what it would be like. To see her again. I sometimes imagine she and I are together, here in the house, but it doesn't last. I fear she'd leave as soon as she'd come." Shannon and Nell kept silent for a moment, and then Shannon said, "Harvey sees her sometimes."

"Is that so?" Nell considered demanding a reason for being kept unaware, but fatigue kept her from it. "I had no idea." She felt her heart race again, and a lump rose in her throat for reasons she couldn't name. Maybe it was fear that whatever Harvey knew of Eliza wasn't good, or even worse, perhaps Eliza had spoken of her disdain for Nell. "What does he know of her?"

"Not much. He says she's doing well at Cornell, quite the intellectual—no surprise. She's been mentored by Frances Perkins for years and ..."

This is what it was. Eliza had found in Mrs. Perkins a better, more intellectually suited, forgiving mother figure, one Nell could never compete with on any front. "What else?"

"Are you sure you want to hear it, Mother?" Shannon asked. "It's not that there's much more to tell."

"Shannon, I want to know. When was the last time Harvey saw her?"

"I think it was a while ago."

"And what else?" Nell asked.

"She married a fellow student ... well, maybe not a student. I think he's a graduate. His name is Stanley something. He's from a Jewish family in New York."

Nell saw Shannon eyeing her for signs of anger or agitation, but there was none, just a deep sigh of loss and resignation.

"And according to Harvey, they've been living in two places for years: Stanley in New York City, Eliza in Ithaca." She eyed Nell again. "When I last spoke with Harvey, he told me she'd been appointed Assistant Dean of Labor Studies." Shannon smiled at Nell. "Can you believe it? I always knew she'd be in charge of something other than me." Shannon tried to laugh, but her voice wavered.

"How is it we've never spoken of her?" Nell asked, staring out the window to the backyard, where Edmund's chicken coop lay in a dilapidated pile of rotting wood and wire, surrounded by lake-shaped patches of dirty snow. "I'll write her soon. What was I thinking?"

Nell wasn't certain whether she'd spoken these last words aloud or not. As soon as their luncheon was over, she would write to Eliza, and, unlike Shannon, she would mail the letter.

~◦

NELL HAD NOT ACQUIRED BEAUTIFUL penmanship as her children had done through their years at Catholic schools. She wrote carefully, the letters fat and loopy, although the words came to her quickly like streams of water falling and mixing into murky pools of her life's memory, and she felt a panicked urgency to get them recorded.

November 9th, 1961

Dear Eliza,

Today a veil was lifted from my eyes, my daughter. I hope you might find a path to forgive me and to return home, if not for good, at least so I may look upon you and hold your hands in mine, and demonstrate that my love for you never changed and never faltered, especially then.

I hear from Shannon that you are a successful academic, as we knew you could be. I was in the chapel today and noticed as if for the first time, the writing along the cornice where the wall meets the ceiling: Romans 2:12 ~

'Do not be conformed to this world, but be transformed by the renewal of your mind, that by testing you may discern what is the will of God, what is good and acceptable and perfect.'

I will tell you, Eliza, I am not much of a Catholic after all, although I find shelter in much of the Church's offerings. It is God I cannot help but mistrust, and when we suffered that second horrible year, I felt He had pushed me too far. I wanted, more than anything, to back up, to return to the years before the War, before Baby Theo even, in which we felt whole and happy and, most of all, safe.

I couldn't see that, at least in part, it was my rigidity that drove you away; but it wasn't anger with you that made me so, it was fear—a paralysis stilling my heart in between beats, a force extracting any courage I might have had to be otherwise. If I could have loved you better when you needed me…. At first, I told myself you could take care of yourself—especially while Shannon struggled through surgeries. But my failure to understand you were just a child, and my difficulty in reaching you in the days leading to and after childbirth, these were because I knew your pain so clearly, I felt it as if it were my own, and it terrified me—so much that I could do nothing but try to feign anger, and then to let you go. Thank God for Grandpa Theo and Grandma Edith; they understood you, your need to leave, I think.

I couldn't find my way to help you, even after I was told about Patrick's letter. He confessed in devastating detail what he did to you. The Whitakers (him included, may God rest his soul) had suffered so much and knew we had, too. For years, his parents told no one; they felt it would be better to let sleeping dogs lie. In time, Patrick's mother was overwhelmed by a need to tell me the truth, to explain the depths of her son's suffering, to ask for forgiveness, as if I, equally as guilty, could somehow grant it on your behalf. She came to visit me three years ago. I suppose she hoped I would tell you, and that it would change something. But what could it change? We had lost you.

How could your father and I not have seen this? How could we not find you and bring you back long before now?

If only you knew of my childhood, Eliza, maybe you could understand and forgive me. Forgive me for letting you go; forgive me for my lies of omission in the days after your difficult labor. My story is too much to tell you here in a letter; I had believed all of these years that you—your life—would be better off to have left as I did when I was not yet sixteen.

But I was wrong. I beg you to return home so I might be with you again, my grown daughter, and so I might share with you the makings of my life, which I've never had the courage to tell. I see now, today, that despite my suspicions of God, I can and do discern "… what is good and acceptable and perfect." A mother's undying love— as my mother had for me, and as I have for you and all of my children.

Love,
Mother

The post office would be open for another hour. Nell had no stamps but now that the letter was written she didn't want to wait and lose courage. As she refreshed her face powder and lipstick in the bathroom behind the stairwell in the kitchen, she remembered tomorrow was her birthday. Fifty-five years old—nineteen years older than her mother had been when she'd died, days after giving birth to the twins.

By the time Nell left the house, the winter air had grown bitter cold, and low clouds sat like shallow pools of ink overhead. Nell didn't mind the long Minnesota winters, or the dark skies, though this afternoon's sharp wind took her breath away. She slowed her pace and gathered the folds of her fine-wool coat close.

She held like an evensong, the click-clicking noises her low-heeled shoes made on the cold cement and felt uneven gusts pushing at her back, nudging her, urging her toward a place she felt but couldn't yet see. She remembered the winds of Oklahoma, never as cold but equally constant, equally unforgiving. Her grandmother and mother walked with her now and lifted away the chill, delivering the long-awaited ablution for the weighty secrets held by a little girl. The envelope addressed to Eliza slipped from her hand and fluttered with the wind, and as she watched it, she collapsed, unable to breathe. Grandma and Ma softened the landing of her body on the street, yards in front of her destination. A light, warm and soothing, familiar and welcoming, overcame her, and she wondered, just then, how Shannon or Eliza would die, and whether she would be there for them.

25

NOVEMBER 1961

The bedroom closets of their Ithaca flat had seemed too small at first, but now Stanley's side, previously overflowing with suits, shirts, shoes, and ties, seemed cavernous. Only the fragrance of the cedar-wood paneling and a handful of outdated garments remained: the few ties strewn over a metal bar, like tired soldiers separated from their regiment; three pairs of trousers folded crisply in a short stack, and a lone tweed vest—the last icons of Stanley, and the last of her failed marriage. Eliza removed three hangers hung with slacks, each a different shade of brown, and wondered where they'd come from in the first place. The thought of him in brown anything seemed smile-worthy—even today. She packed everything into boxes for Stanley to keep or not. She'd take them to New York over the weekend and say goodbye once and for all.

She'd last slept beside him in their Upper West Side apartment on their seventh anniversary in May of fifty-nine. Years earlier, she'd trained her mind to go elsewhere, anywhere, while making her body available to Stanley—a neutral zone in a war-torn country. Yet even that wasn't enough. Eliza ran her fingers down the ridged silk of a tie before rolling it into a neat coil and putting it next to the others in the box.

"Hah," she said to herself with a trace of mirth. "Seven-year itch, indeed."

November rain fell hard and fast, and its rhythm on the bedroom windows put her in a sort of trance. She finished removing her husband's items from his closet and tallboy dresser. A drawer full of socks surprised her—the twenty or so pairs remaining could last any man for years, even a clotheshorse like Stanley. She imagined he had a drawer of similar socks in the New York apartment, where he'd retreated from their marriage, slowly at first, and now fully over the past eight years.

Eliza placed the socks into the last of the boxes she'd prepared. From another drawer, she removed a boxed pair of garnet cufflinks, a gift she'd chosen for Stanley at Henri Bendel on West 57th Street in New York two days after their wedding. They'd both been drawn to the rectangular shape made of four gems set in silver. Afterward, while walking from one end of Central Park to the other, they'd talked about their plans. Their main residence would be Eliza's new apartment in Ithaca for the next two years while she got her Ph.D. They agreed it would make sense for her to move to New York City thereafter should Stanley still hold the position as the governor's labor deputy, posted in the city's financial district. In the meantime, Stanley would maintain a smaller, one bedroom on the Upper West Side, without roommates, where Eliza would visit on special weekends.

The cufflinks, however, became a painful reminder for Eliza almost from the day she'd given them to Stanley as her wedding gift. They symbolized all she'd hoped for in a marriage but couldn't find her way to have.

They'd been expensive, and he'd been genuinely surprised. She even surprised herself, given her typical thriftiness. That night in the honeymoon suite of the Plaza Hotel, Stanley held her again, his arm wrapped around her waist. They whispered their thoughts and hopes until both fell asleep.

The following morning, Sunday, Eliza packed her belongings while Stanley packed his. They were so similar in so many ways—none more so than in their sense of personal organization and attention to detail. One would think they'd been raised in the same home, given their patterns of cleaning, storing, and caring for their belongings. Stanley finished first and called a bellboy to attend to their luggage.

"I've invited the inner circle to meet us tonight for a final celebratory cocktail, Eliza. Is that all right?" Stanley's inner circle included two roommates and two brothers, the only four people privy to their new marriage.

The six of them, Eliza the lone woman, gathered on red leather benches in a dark booth at Harry's Bar, where Stanley and his friends were regulars. Dozens of aging photos of famous Irish literary figures collected greasy dust on the walls, and a fiddler sang Irish ballads. His plaintive melodies and nostalgic lyrics tugged at Eliza's earlier, light mood as midnight approached. The first two cocktails hit Eliza like a wave, dousing her energy and fogging her mind so that she hesitantly accepted a third from Stanley's pushy roommate, Ernst.

"This one and you'll sleep like a baby, Eliza," Ernst said. "It's called B&B, sweet but potent—like you." He rubbed the back of her head, and his hand sneaked down past the nape of her neck in an overly intimate, irksome gesture. Eliza felt too slowed to respond. "You won't even hear us get home."

She didn't doubt it. The apartment Stanley shared with the two men was large, with his bedroom and bathroom more like a separate suite, while two smaller rooms and a bathroom occupied the opposite side of the living area. It was precisely that sense of privacy that had allowed Eliza to consider staying there, married or not.

"Darling, shall we stay here for one more?" Eliza heard her husband say.

She'd finished the sweet cocktail, admitting it was delicious, although she'd begun to feel a little out of body. "Home for me, I think. Would you walk me to your front door, Stanley? I'll be fine on my own after that."

"Of course, darling; I'll even tuck you in." Stanley was well into his cups already; Eliza figured he'd drunk at least two cocktails for every one of hers. He helped her up with a clumsy movement, and she was surprised when her knees buckled and the walls seemed to sway as she stood.

The evening air was crisp and the street quiet as midnight approached. Distant sirens made the uptown city block seem tranquil, though a man could be heard berating his wife or girlfriend in an apartment far above street level, and two cats fought for scraps in an alley. Eliza could think only of getting into bed with her novel and falling asleep. Stanley had said nothing about marital duties since she'd mentioned her cycle on Friday night—of course she knew sex was inevitable. In the four years since the attack, she'd avoided all physical advances and had put off men as soon as they expressed interest in dating—such had been her mistrust. Stanley had waited for Eliza, eventually satisfying himself with hugs and long, sometimes chaotic kisses that grew from light to fervently intense. She'd grown to accept his physical desire and to cut off any sign of sexual stirrings in herself. As long as the pre-marital boundary was clear, she'd indulge her fiancé's expectations; they both knew the rules of the game.

Stanley tucked her in. With a strange look of concern on his brow, he asked, "How are you, darling? Do you feel all right?"

She'd responded with a murmur and then, overwhelmed with drowsiness, nodded off. The book she'd hoped to read fell from her hands unopened, and somehow the light next to the bed was extinguished.

It could have been twenty minutes or two hours later, but Eliza, asleep on her back, was suddenly conscious of an odd tingling throughout her body. She realized Stanley lay next to her, naked, with three fingers buried between her legs. Her vagina was warm and moist, her swollen vulva enveloped his fingers and pulled them in. Stanley was whispering to her as if she'd been involved in the intimacy for more than a second.

Before she could speak, he murmured in her ear, "I thought you'd appreciate being relaxed, darling; I hope you don't mind. Your luscious black box doesn't mind, does it, pussy-cat? ... Are you still bleeding, my love?"

She did feel desire—a desire unlike any she'd ever had before. Far more sexual than the attraction she'd felt for David years ago. Her body felt as if years of blocking nature had failed and a dam restraining an ocean of sexual desire had burst. Placid, half-asleep, and groggy from drinks at the bar, she didn't open her eyes. His hard cock pressed into her thigh, and she knew Stanley's head was somehow above hers. She opened her eyes to complete darkness, and once again felt a surge of warmth spread from her vagina into her loins. She turned her head to find Stanley's, and the unexpected odor of his boozed and smoky breath overcame her. A burst of panic and fear erupted, erasing any feelings of desire or safety. She felt the tip of his nose on hers and saw only the insane and outraged eyes of a rapist.

"No!" The word came out as an ugly, bellowing sob, and

everything went black.

Eliza woke up on the bathroom floor, covered with a blanket, a pillow under her head. The note on Stanley's dressing table was scrawled on a single sheet of his stationary: "Eliza—I don't know what happened last night, but I think we can agree it went sideways. I'll try to be back by ten, darling, to take you to the station. If not, you'll have to call a taxi. I'll do my best."

They didn't see each other until the following Saturday in Boston when Stanley and Chas arrived at Longuejour Mansion to bring Beryl and Eliza to the engagement party hosted by Mrs. Adams and her twin daughters.

The events of Sunday night left Eliza feeling like a different person, though Beryl—always effervescent and with perpetual enthusiasm for her social life—seemed oblivious to the change. Thus, fresh and painful as they were, Eliza found it easy to cordon off her disastrous marital experience into a dark corner in her chapel of memories.

Stanley made no mention of Sunday night until a week later when he called on her at the Jameson's, where she still occupied the guest house.

Eliza held his hand as they walked on the garden paths. Stanley turned toward her so their knees touched on the bench in front of Artemis. "Eliza, I want to believe it was a reaction to the drinks. I know you don't like booze, but if there's something more, you should tell me, darling."

Eliza had not expected such candidness, although she supposed she should have. Stanley was the most precisely straightforward person she knew.

He continued, "I love you, but you must admit, you are uncomfortable around, well, around physical affection. I may have been misguided, but I thought if you could relax a bit, you would enjoy what I could make you feel."

Stanley's olive branch could put all the shame, panic and

incoherent fury of her rejection behind them. But would it be any different next time? Eliza's reaction to Stanley's advances had been extreme. Although she'd not known before that the terrifying night still resided in her, she knew it now and feared again that she'd never be able to overcome it.

"We can take it slowly," Stanley said. "I promise, no more of Ernst's trick drinks. That was a stupid idea."

Eliza's heart flickered. A thought was born in that moment, a premonition that the days of her marriage—despite her true affection for Stanley and her equally genuine desire, even yearning, for love—were probably numbered. She would never want another pregnancy, much less children, and she doubted whether she'd ever get beyond her trauma to enjoy intimate relations with Stanley or any man. That she'd always been more in love with academic achievement than the prospect of hearth and home was a dark blessing. The opportunities that unfolded for her at Cornell became her salvation.

For the first few years of marriage, she made efforts to fool Stanley into thinking that she was who he thought her to be, even if it meant she was often on the verge of emotional terror. Perhaps predictably, now eight years later, their union was fully shambled. Fourteen months—two anniversaries—had passed since she'd seen him. She'd heard from Harvey about Stanley's plans to remarry. Good for him, she'd thought. And for her, a small relief.

She put the cufflinks back in the box with a note: *Stanley—like my treasured brooch, may the story of this gift live on in your care, Warmest Wishes—E.* She nestled it into a box of trousers and ties and searched for packing tape.

The doorbell rang, making her jump.

A Western Telegram messenger stood at the door. He gave a short bow. "Mrs. Katterman?" he asked with a slight inflection, then handed her an envelope.

Dear E Mother passed away yesterday Great shock to all Pls phone home or Eds so we may arrange for your return Planning Tuesday Do not have your phone Eds Dudley 8 5294.

After reading it twice, she picked up the phone to call Fa, and then placed it back in its cradle. Going back wasn't an option. Not yet.

26

November 1961

Shannon felt Nell looking over her shoulder as she and Fa planned the funeral service. Memories of her own fears and thoughts of death in the days after her many surgeries came to her before she fell asleep and confused her—was it she who'd died or Mother? She imagined herself wearing Mother's elegant coat and her practical shoes, falling to the street as strangers in cars witnessed her clutching her hand to her tightened chest and staggering to regain her footing. Headlights in the November darkness might have made her fall seem theatrical to the passengers in nearby cars. Shannon recalled her own painful breathing and the strange, potent dreams as she struggled to emerge from anesthesia. She remembered it was Mother, not she, who'd died. Another sharp pang of loss and loneliness brought her from the brink of sleep into an anxious wakefulness that didn't leave her until morning.

Shannon and Fa sat side by side in his library upstairs. Fingers trembling, he searched for a certain passage for his prayers at Mother's funeral Mass. He fumbled through pages of his small and sturdy Latin Bible. His hands calmed as he moved the woven silk thread to mark his place. "I don't know how to be here without Nell," he said, frowning, his attention still on the Bible's cover.

Shannon blinked as he uttered her mother's Christian name. She felt excluded from the intimacy of his loss and wished he'd said "Mother" instead.

Fa stared across the room as if it were an ocean. "You know Dr. Lewis, Jack, and I correspond. Years now. His wife died two years ago. Unexpected, too. He's invited me to Oxford many times. Maybe I'll take a sabbatical soon and go. Not forever. A few months. I'd like to see him. To meet him face to face."

"Really, Fa? You'd do that?" She gripped his arm gently. An image of the Malone home dark and uninhabited swept over her like cold, dry fingers, pulling her from safety. "If you leave, the house will be empty," she said almost to herself, imagining Eliza's sadness upon returning to an abandoned home.

"I suppose it's the fancy of a lonely man, Shannon." He paused as if reading her mind, then answered her question: "No, probably not."

A thought darkened her mind while Fa wrote a note to himself for the service and tucked it in the Bible. *Am I meant to move home, then?*

Mother's church service took place the following Monday at St. Thomas Aquinas Chapel. Shannon sat in the front pew with Fa to her right, Ed to her left. Olivia and their two boys sat in the next row back. Ed had been unclear about Eliza. He'd sent her a telegram Friday morning and offered Shannon nothing more about it since. Had Mother written to Eliza, as she said she would? No letter was found the day she died, but who knew? Maybe she'd mailed it, or perhaps someone had found it near her and had posted it, as a Good Samaritan might do. Maybe it was in the street, disintegrated to the color and texture of the dirty snow that clung to crevices between street and sidewalk. Mother must have written Eliza—she wouldn't say such a thing without carrying through. But, of course, Shannon could never really know.

Shannon received Holy Communion, then returned to her seat, afraid to look at the closed casket covered with a white cloth that rested on the first of three broad steps leading to the altar. Before turning to sit, she skimmed one side of the church to the other, surprised to see so many familiar faces.

Dr. and Mrs. Johnston sat at the far edge of a pew in the back of the church. Behind them, a man she didn't recognize bowed his head as he whispered something to the young woman beside him.

Shannon ran her fingers along the pew's dark-stained wood and imagined Nell's methodical, circular motions on this very spot. She wondered whether anyone thought of the ammonia and wax Nell had administered to the floors, benches, and banisters of the church on the day she'd died. Her mother's spirit would remain cast in the wax of these planks and floorboards for a very long time. Maybe forever.

Later in the day in Nell's kitchen, Shannon spooned yellow deviled-egg paste from a bowl back into the white half-spheres before arranging them on one of Mother's plates and sprinkling them with paprika. Shannon thought she heard church bells somewhere outside.

Olivia strode in, leaned on the doorframe and said, "Shannon, a gentleman's outside. He said he's a friend of yours. He wanted to wait to see you before coming in." She gave a brief cheerful smile and tapped her temple with a forefinger. "A little strange, I think."

"It must be Harvey. You remember him, don't you, Olivia?" Shannon frowned, dreading her path through the sitting room, where a dozen guests remained. It wasn't like Harvey—besides he knew almost everyone. She stood and straightened her skirt, then wiped at a morsel of egg on her blouse, watching as it fell to the ground.

Olivia's response was lost on Shannon. She frowned, observing from the kitchen doorway while the grandfather clock rang its short half hour refrain. Fa stood close to Grandma Edith, who presided affectionately over two well-behaved great-grandsons clutching at her roomy black dress in a muted game of tag. He looked about as guests approached to offer condolences, and Shannon wondered whether Fa had truly grasped that Nell Malone was no longer here.

She turned back to Olivia, who said before she could speak, "As I said, Shannon, he preferred not to come in. He's on the porch."

I should be better at this, Shannon thought; what other woman her age failed at social graces as profoundly as she? Mother would be furious if she knew the lengths Shannon had gone to in the last two hours to avoid almost everyone who wasn't family.

She opened the front door, ready to scold her friend for not coming in directly, but the man from the back of the church stood by the porch swing, not Harvey. In an instant, the man in the pew clicked with the man who stood before her. Mr. Ross. She looked about for the young girl from church who, Shannon thought, must be Miriam.

Mr. Ross took off his hat and extended his hand. "Miss Malone, pardon my uninvited presence, but I wanted to express my condolences in person. I am so sorry for your loss." The man's Scottish accent, deepened by ten years in his home country, surprised her.

Shannon wasn't sure what Mr. Ross had said as she struggled to piece together what she thought she was experiencing. She knew she should speak, but her mind was blank.

"I hope you don't think it rude we attended the service, but I very much wanted to. And Miriam didn't want to be left alone … You remember Miriam? She's waiting for me in the car. She … well, I suppose she's a bit shy. I hope you don't think her rude."

"By no means, Mr. Ross. It's just that … well, thank you for coming. Won't you come in?"

"I don't want to impose, nor leave Miriam for long; I saw the notice of your mother's service in the paper yesterday and thought we might—" He interrupted himself. "We've been back for only three weeks, you see."

Although his hair had lightened with gray and two deep lines etched the space between his thick eyebrows, Mr. Ross looked much as he had ten years ago. She felt they stood closer in age than before—almost as contemporaries. She wanted to hear his voice again.

He continued to speak, "… and so, I hoped there was a way to get in touch, to let you know, as a courtesy, you see, that we'd returned. I had no idea how to reach you, and as I've said, wanted as well to pay my respects." Mr. Ross, she realized, fumbled to find the right words.

"Mr. Ross, you have no idea how wonderful it is to see you," Shannon managed to say. "And Mrs. Ross? How is she?"

Mr. Ross raised his eyebrows and looked at Shannon with pleading in his gaze. "Mrs. Ross, regrettably, did not return with us." He pursed his lips and tipped his head down and up, and Shannon worried that he planned to leave, but instead he said, "You meant so much to Miriam when she was a wee child."

Miriam, whose absence she'd mourned like a death, now sat in a car within view of the porch.

"I'd like to invite you for tea, Miss Malone. Not that I expect you to do anything; but could I seek your advice? We've been gone for quite a while, you might understand."

Shannon realized she'd been staring in the direction of the street. She returned her attention to Mr. Ross and found him attractive in a manner unobserved by her years ago. He obviously expected a reply, but whatever she'd heard him say a few seconds ago was gone again.

"Excuse me, could you repeat that, Mr. Ross? I'm sorry; I'm so surprised to see you."

"I should leave you to your guests, Miss Malone." Mr. Ross touched her elbow lightly and glanced toward the door. "I hope it wasn't improper to have come today. I thought it would be … I thought Miriam would like to see you again and perhaps you'd also like to see her."

He put his hat back on his head and extended his hand to Shannon once again. "Miss Malone, I do hope you'll join us for tea. Would it be possible? Soon?"

"Yes. It would be …" Shannon didn't know what she wanted to say. She knew such an encounter would be many things—joyful, essential, a sign from God.

"Next Saturday, then?" Mr. Ross asked. "Of course, Miriam would join us."

When she returned to the kitchen, Ed gave her a playful hug around the shoulder. "Who was the gentleman, Shannon? 'Liv said you had a mystery guest."

"Just an old friend, Ed. Someone I used to work for." She returned to the plate of deviled eggs and smiled.

Hours later, after settling in her childhood bedroom, she wandered into Eliza's room and found a box of letters from David. She looked at each of the dozen or so envelopes surrounded by a handful of loose photos and considered opening one. She could practically hear Eliza's reprimand for even thinking about it, but surely she could figure some way to justify a peek at a single letter.

With the prospect of reuniting with Miriam, Shannon once again longed to discover a clue as to why Eliza had broken up with David. Why if—as she'd insisted to Shannon—her pregnancy had nothing to do with him? She held the top letter for a long moment before putting it aside and fingering through the photos instead, choosing one in particular to study, a photo of Eliza and David the day after the storm when a series of small twisters had ripped through town in August 1946.

David had come to the house to help remove debris from the yard and street. He thought of any excuse back then to be in Eliza's presence, even if it meant physical labor. She dropped the photo back into the cherrywood box, closed the lid, and went to the top of the stairs, expecting to see Fa reading in the sitting room late into the night, as he always had. She saw the glow of his lamp and bid him good night.

"Goodnight, Shannon, dear. Thank you for staying."

Instead of returning to her bedroom, she walked down the hall to her parents' suite, which ran the length of the north-facing side of the house. To the east, a partial wall and an arched entryway separated a sunroom from the large bedroom. She sat at Mother's small desk where she'd kept her correspondence and the family's important documents.

Everything in the room was as it had always been. The wastebasket under the oak desk was empty but for a crumpled sheet of Mother's stationery, pale blue with a faint watermark.

November 9th, 1961

Dear Eliza,

Today, I have been graced with understanding. I hope you forgive me. I hope you will come home, if not for good, at least so I may see you one more time and show you my love for you has never changed.

I hear from Shannon you are a successful academic, as we knew you could be. I visited the chapel today. New scripture's been placed along the cornice where the wall meets the ceiling. It is from Romans 2:12:

'Do not be conformed to this world, but be transformed by the renewal of your mind, that by testing you may discern what is the will of God, what is good and acceptable and perfect.'

Shannon was certain Mother had written a clean, completed version of the letter she'd begun with this page. She wondered whether Nell had been going to the post office or returning home when she collapsed to the ground. Eliza would receive the letter too late for reconciliation, but perhaps Mother's plea for forgiveness—her last maternal act—would move Eliza to finally return home.

27

November 1964

The large, rectangular window above the sink reflected the ceiling lights so that Shannon and Miriam couldn't see the snow falling outside except for the largest flakes. Though only four thirty in the afternoon, darkness had fallen, and several new inches had accumulated on top of two feet of snow from past weeks. Shannon took another carrot from her small pile and peeled it. She hadn't thought about how the storm would affect her bus ride home; maybe Mr. Ross would drive her as he'd done so many times.

The kitchen, like the house, was contemporary with sleek-white countertops. Spacious, open rooms ran into one another, sharing light and windows to the outside—the opposite of the dark-cherry and mahogany interior, heavy with wallpaper, wainscoting, and drapery, of her childhood home.

"Shannon?" Miriam leaned back from her homework at the dining room table and spoke her name like a question. At sixteen years old, the girl was coltish in her adolescent development; all legs and arms, she ranked tallest in her class at the Catholic high school for girls. Outwardly, her height and classic features, so like Eliza's, masked a simplicity that'd stayed with Miriam since their return from Scotland two years ago. Though as smart and pretty as Eliza had been, Miriam's shyness kept her from being at ease in the world around her. Politeness and empathy were natural traits, but trust in friends, teachers, anyone other than Allan and Shannon, came hard and slow. Given the erratic behavior of Virginia Ross, Shannon could well imagine why.

Shannon came from the kitchen to sit with her. Miriam closed her school books and rested a cheek on crossed arms. "What was your favorite class in high school?"

Stubbs the cat, named for his almost-but-not-quite missing tail, stretched in the corner. He ambled over and jumped onto the chair nearest Miriam, which was pulled back from the oblong, Danish-teak dining table.

"When I was your age, I suppose it was art. Or literature." Shannon reconsidered. "I suppose it was always both literature and art." A memory came and went of Fa, sitting on the edge of the overstuffed high-back chair in the paneled library at the lake house on dark winter afternoons such as this, animated as he read aloud to her and Eliza from Edith Nesbit's tale *The Magic City*. Fa had had the endearing skill of matching the season and even the time of day with perfect books, passages, and illustrations.

"How did you feel about biology? And math?" Miriam carried an accent from her years in Scotland. "You're a nurse, after all. You must have needed lots of science."

"True; I was all right in the sciences. Eliza excelled—she won a prize in the eighth grade for her fish-egg experiment. She was better at everything. It made it difficult to know what I was good at." She'd never put it quite like that before, but she knew it was true. She'd hardly understood the point of school until they'd moved Eliza up to be in the second grade with her. With Eliza nearby, she'd felt calm and much more confident about school, catechism, sports, and many other aspects of childhood, too.

"I do wish I had a sibling, although maybe not in the same grade." Miriam came into the kitchen and hovered near Shannon, who returned to find a baking dish for the washed and peeled vegetables. She wiped her hands on her apron; despite its protection, she'd managed to spot melted butter on her sleeve.

"Were you envious of her? Was she very pretty, too?"

"I wasn't ever envious—not at all. More ... proud, I'd say." To talk about Eliza in the past tense, especially with Miriam, felt wrong and uncomfortable. She reminded herself that Eliza was alive and well. She put down the pan of meatloaf she'd taken from the oven. "I was a little envious of her relationship with Grandpa Theo. She was his favorite. I think I can admit that now ... And, yes, Eliza was, is, very, very beautiful. But most of all she was smart and good."

This was the part Shannon couldn't understand, would never understand. Eliza was the smartest and most morally correct person she knew. Her sister's strength of purpose had grounded her, and, by association, Shannon from her earliest memories. But then she disappeared from Shannon's life, as if there'd never been stability or practicality—or the Eliza she thought she knew—at all.

"Did you play with her?" Miriam asked. "Or did she treat you badly because you weren't as smart?"

"Oh my, how much we played. All three of us." Shannon joined Miriam at the table, compelled by her sudden interest. A rush of childhood memories filled her mind. "We and our brother Ed, and our cousins, even some neighbors, used to make theater performances of the stories Fa read. Huge productions. They'd take days and days to prepare." Shannon envisioned the stage, the hand-painted backdrop with finishing touches from Grandma Edith. "On rainy summer days, Eliza and I would play make-believe under the covers of our grandparents' enormous bed. When the sun came out, we'd visit animals—pigs, horses, and sheep at the farm across the street. I once rode a sheep through the pathway in Grandpa's strawberry garden on a double dare from Ed and got in terrible trouble. He was so naughty. And he loved getting me in trouble. It drove Eliza mad. 'Mother will smack your behind, if she catches you, Ed,' she'd say. But I was an easy target. I was easily charmed by his adventures."

"Did you always know you wanted to be a nurse?" Miriam awaited Shannon's reply with genuine interest, absentmindedly biting the tip of her pencil, her long, thin legs crossed under the table.

"No," Shannon replied. "That came about when I was in the hospital with tuberculosis. The nurses were angels, mostly. They made a scary world less so."

"I like the idea of making the world less scary. It's noble," Miriam said. "Today was Career Day. The big ones for girls were secretary, nurse, or teacher. But Sister Annette said we shouldn't pay any attention to that. She says women can do anything men can do. It makes sense, don't you think?"

"Of course I do," Shannon said. "Eliza went off and got her Ph.D., and now she's a college professor. My friend Harvey tells me she gives speeches in Washington, D.C., and that she even met President Kennedy back in 1960. Can you imagine?" Shannon reached for her purse, which hung from a hook near the kitchen door, and found her wallet. "I don't think I've shown you this photo … I almost forgot I had it."

She opened the clasp and removed a well-protected photograph of two young women sitting with their legs outstretched on a large Hudson Bay blanket with a cribbage set between them. They looked surprised as if the photographer had taken them off guard, making them laugh just as he clicked the button. Shannon recalled Ed hovering above them, fussing with Grandpa Theo's new camera. The resulting photo was the first in real color she remembered ever seeing. "Can you tell which girl I am?"

"Of course I can." Miriam laughed. "You're both so beautiful—but Eliza looks so glamorous. Do you think she's still stylish?"

Shannon nodded. In the photo, it was difficult to see that Eliza was five foot nine inches, the same height as Mother. The white dress she wore had deep-blue polka dots the size of half dollars, and a wide headband, deep blue with much smaller white dots, pulled back her hair. She clasped her white-framed sunglasses and poised them at her forehead to block the sun as she faced her photographer while Shannon laughed beside her.

Certainly Eliza had not changed. Shannon remembered the weeks and years after she'd left for Ithaca when Shannon struggled to maintain the sense of fashion Eliza always tried to teach her. After she left, Shannon had studied her sister's outfits—grateful so many had been left at home, even after she'd requested a trunk be sent to Ithaca.

When the Ross family left for Scotland, Shannon fell into a period of anxiousness and compulsivity that had made getting out of bed a challenge—forget about style. For months, she'd imagined traveling to Scotland on her own, so she could be close to Miriam. She'd begun a letter to Virginia, but by the very act of writing, a variety of anxieties had surfaced—airports, strangers, strange places, maps, strange foods, disease—and she knew she'd never make it. The day she'd returned from New York, especially after the disappointment of Eliza's letter, had been a huge relief for Shannon. She wasn't the adventuress she'd hoped to be.

"Mother is stylish, too—but kind of different. More modern, maybe …" Miriam mused. "But do you talk with her?"

"You mean Eliza? Not anymore; I write her birthday cards and …" Shannon paused. "I … write her letters." She put the photograph back in its wallet-sleeve and returned to the sink. "What kind of jobs sounded interesting today? You're great at math; how about a mathematician? You could sit in a castle tower every day, mastering long, exciting calculations no one has ever done before."

Miriam shrugged but laughed, too. "No way, Shannon. Part of me wants to be a stewardess because it sounds glamorous, and I'd get to travel the world and go back to Scotland for a visit … But, maybe a lawyer? In Scotland, so many mothers were widows … And almost everyone was poor. Grandmamma hated to spend even a shilling. So different from life here."

Shannon wondered how Virginia had adjusted to the tiny hamlet outside Edinburgh in those early years. If Shannon had mustered the courage to go, would Virginia have welcomed her? Would they all be there, now? Would Virginia have left Allan? What happened to her? Asking questions never felt right— besides, Shannon wasn't sure she wanted to know the answers.

Three years had passed since Mr. Ross asked Shannon to help him manage the house. In the months after Nell's funeral, she visited once a week. As time passed, Shannon found reason to be at the house most afternoons when Miriam returned from school. Mr. Ross had beamed with appreciation when she finally asked to formalize the daily assistance. She attached herself to every moment with Miriam with the same fervor she had with Eliza as a child. But unlike Eliza, Miriam likely didn't know the extent of her affection. Shannon's reticence wasn't because she didn't want Miriam to know she loved her. Rather it came from the terror of losing her again, as if expressing her love in words might jinx this miraculous arrangement.

"If I had a sister, I'd be her best friend, too," Miriam said, "but I'd want to be the smart and good one." Then interrupting her own thought, she said, "I wish you could come to my teacher conferences with Daddy. It's not that I want you to pretend to be my mom, or anything, but he's so awkward."

Shannon smiled at the thought of attending Miriam's teacher conferences with Allan Ross. She'd written out her shopping list earlier in the day, each item proof she was a legitimate part of this home, caring for these two people as if they were, in the most meaningful way, her family. The unconventionality of it didn't bother her, at least not anymore. Odd as it was, for now it fit just fine into her vision that God did have a plan to bring her, Miriam, and Eliza together. And while she was mystified as to how that plan would be unveiled and cautious about its undoing, she interpreted her current sense of well-being as proof of its existence. Any lists she now created had practical, household purposes—not the purpose of managing her anxieties like counting whites or listing the names of her dolls had been ever since she could remember.

Butter, milk, and eggs for cookies she'd bake tomorrow—all white, incidentally—waxed paper to wrap Miriam's sandwiches for school before she left this evening, picture nails for the walls, new grout for the bathroom, and then the list of errands she'd run tomorrow on her day off from the hospital. Her work as a nurse had been reduced over the past three years to two days a week. She kept these shifts as insurance, in case she lost Miriam again.

Every Monday after dinner, Shannon and Mr. Ross washed dishes, then sat together at the dining room table and reviewed the week ahead. In the first weeks of this arrangement three years ago, Shannon had offered that she'd do whatever she could to support Mr. Ross—trips to the dry cleaner, wardrobe repairs, arranging for plumbers, electricians, handymen—anything short of housecleaning, for which different arrangements had been made.

It was mid-April, close to the end of Miriam's senior year of high school, when Miriam said, "You'll never guess what, Shannon. Mother's coming back." She dropped her books on the dining room table, ran to her room, and came back with the photograph she kept by her bedside of Virginia and herself crouched down in a field of tulips. "We took this in Holland when I was seven. We traveled there together with her friend." Miriam paused, and Shannon watched as she searched her memory. "I think maybe he was her cousin. Daddy had to stay in Edinburgh and work, but Mummy and I had such a grand time, though I only got to stay with her for two days. I can't wait to see how she looks."

Miriam followed Shannon into the kitchen, chattering uncharacteristically for the thoughtful teenager she'd become: "Daddy says I shouldn't get too excited, because who knows how long she'll stay. But I want to show her my school, and I want her to meet my friend Alison, and to take us shopping, and to the American movies. She missed American movies so much in Scotland … Have you met my mum, Shannon?" She laughed. "Of course, you have; you took care of me before we moved. Maybe the three of us could have a girl's afternoon at Dayton's?"

At dinner Miriam told Shannon and Mr. Ross each of the items on her list for Virginia.

"Miriam, why don't you go and finish your homework?" Mr. Ross said. "I'm sure Shannon will be here for another hour or so. Isn't that right, Shannon? In fact, if you complete your work, darling, we can take her home together, so she doesn't have to take the bus. It's one storm after another, lately. I, for one, cannot wait for May. April showers are not meant to be snowflakes."

"I don't know what to expect," he told Shannon when Miriam had left the room. "She arrives tomorrow. I'll get her from the airport at midday. She says she doesn't know how long she'll stay. I don't have the heart to tell Miriam, that it's not …" Mr. Ross sighed and rubbed his brow. "She says she wants to see Miriam, but I don't know if it's the right thing. Maybe she'll change her mind if she sees her—maybe she'll want to stay. And if she does, I don't even know if I should allow it. It's been three years. But does what I want even matter? She's her mother. In Scotland she'd disappear for weeks at a time, come back, and be a different person for days—distant, cool … happy maybe, but not with us. Miriam always gave her a fresh start, time after time, and now, again."

Shannon wanted to ask him if he loved Virginia, but she couldn't. This little bit was the most he'd ever shared with her. They never spoke of the reasons for her absence. His face was taut, his hands clenched together. He looked years older. He must be tortured by the thought of hurting Miriam again, she thought. His concerns for his own heart probably paled in comparison. The relationships of the Ross family, despite her role, remained as mysterious as they'd been years ago.

"Is she emotionally stable?" This question arose and escaped before she'd thought it through, and she began to revise it, "I mean, do you think—"

Mr. Ross interrupted her: "It's a fair question, Shannon, don't worry. I've wondered that myself. She grew secretive about five years into Scotland. She'd be fine one moment and gone the next, with some interludes of either anger or euphoria …" His voice trailed off. "I don't imagine it's easy for her. You understand. I can't judge her too harshly …"

Shannon didn't understand. Virginia was a selfish, lost creature, a middle-aged monster of a woman who had no idea about the harm she'd already inflicted. Shannon couldn't bear the thought of Miriam's disappointment if, or when, Virginia would leave again. She wished Mr. Ross could be either angry or decisive—or both. Why couldn't he say no to her visit?

He took his handkerchief from the pocket of his sweater, wiped his brow and refolded it, intent upon restoring its symmetry. "All that ever mattered to me, well, ever since … the most important thing is to have Miriam close to me and safe. I cannot judge Virginia," he said again. "She is who she is. I'd rather she finds her happiness if …" Mr. Ross looked at Shannon and their eyes locked in an unexpected moment of intimacy around an unspoken but shared suffering. He stood and abandoned the sentence. "I'll go and get Miriam … We should get you home."

April 14th, 1965

Dear Eliza,

Once again, I'm lost. I have been with Miriam and Mr. Ross for three and a half years now. Special days, months, years of loving her again and watching her grow into the dear girl that she is. So beautiful. She has your sense of style, your intelligence, I think, your eagerness for knowledge, your candor. Not to say it has been easy for her. I've told you how sad she was for a year when they returned. She was shy and insecure … she struggled to make friends … but now she's happy. I am, as I should be, like an auntie to her.… She makes me think of you constantly. Do you remember the letter I wrote about her first experience with Debate Club? She's nobody's fool.…

Eliza, Virginia is back. Mr. Ross told me she's coming home tomorrow, and I know I should hope nothing more dearly than that she would embrace Miriam as her daughter in the way she so deserves—and needs! But I'm sure it will not happen. And in fact, while it is what I should hope, it is not what I DO hope. I hope she doesn't show up tomorrow. I hope she evaporates.

I pray Miriam wakes up tomorrow not even remembering the name 'Virginia.' It doesn't feel very

Christian of me, but I cannot help how I feel. She can only do more damage.

Mr. Ross predicts she'll be gone within a month. Long enough to remind Miriam she's motherless. I don't say this to make you feel guilty, Eliza. It's the truth, and all I can do is stand by to remind her she is so dearly loved. She is a Malone. She is as much part of us as of the Rosses. Eliza, you would feel the same.

I have no business being there while Virginia is back. I am to be invisible again. When they left years ago, I thought I wouldn't recover. I thought I'd never see Miriam again. And I've always believed she'd lead me back to you—or you back to me. Eliza, could you please, please, come home?

Love,
Shannon

The letter, like the others before, confused as much as comforted her. She knew it would be added to her pile of unposted letters to Eliza. She knew she wouldn't send any of them that she kept bound with a ribbon in her drawer. But she knew she had to write them. It was her way of keeping the secret she'd created without falling apart.

28

April 1965

The day dawned overcast and cool, early spring but late in the semester at Cornell. Students in faded jeans and untucked shirts sat on the steps of Day Hall Administration building, while others picketed in a protest—the exact issue unknown to Eliza—in a circle in front. She'd been summoned to the offices of President Malott, and with the meeting finished, she walked through campus toward her office, as light and exhilarated as she'd felt on her first day at St. Kate's as a freshman girl.

He'd spent no time on idle chatter. Instead, he'd gestured for Eliza to sit in a high-back leather chair in front of his desk. Before speaking, he used both hands to straighten his tie and push his horn-rimmed glasses high on his ruddy, hooked nose in a ritual Eliza had witnessed many times before.

"Dr. Katterman, I know you're aware of the changes to the Industrial and Labor Relations Department. Your exceptional work as Associate Dean has not gone unnoticed." He paused and lifted his eyebrows as if to validate his words. Double-tapping his forefinger to the desktop, he continued, "I'll cut to the chase. The Board of Trustees has tasked me with initiating a new program called simply 'Women's Studies.' We would like you to develop that program: scope, curriculum, faculty placement and development, student outreach, library ... all of it." He paused to scrutinize Eliza's reaction.

Eliza couldn't help but notice his halting style, evident when he spoke publicly and even more so one on one. She didn't allow it to distract from her growing excitement.

"We count on you to develop something extraordinary—a curriculum in line with Cornell's tradition of 'reaching beyond the times without fear of judgment.'" His reference from the nineteenth-century writings of Cornell's founder Andrew Dickson White in *A History of the Warfare of Science with Theology in Christendom* was common knowledge to Eliza and her colleagues. As the first president of Cornell University, White shared publicly his dedication to a new kind of university, one not beholden to any particular theological or religious thought. Although it had been successful from the beginning, the idea of a secular university disassociated from a religious institution was considered heretical to some of his contemporary critics.

Andrew White was just as visionary in his understanding of equal rights across both race and gender. Eliza hadn't known this when she'd first arrived at Cornell as a student, but his progressive example drew her close to her alma mater when she first discovered it. How proud he would be of his legacy, she thought.

"I expect quarterly updates. The program should begin in the fall of 1966, and we should be able to offer a full degree by 1968. And a masters soon thereafter. If all goes well, I daresay you'll become Cornell's first Dean of Women's Studies."

When Eliza reached her office, she stepped inside, closed the door, and leaned her back against it. She'd not seen this coming. She knew the Board of Trustees had been considering a program dedicated to Women's Studies. Naturally she'd hoped to be involved. But this was a bigger vote of confidence than she could've imagined. Eliza turned to her bookshelves near the window and looked at three large red Cornell binders with her final drafts of the trio of publications written to complete her Ph.D.:

A Study of Women in Union Leadership.

A Study of Immigrant Women in the Northeast Fisheries and Related Industries.

A Study of Negro Women in the Farming Sector of Southern Coastal States and the Great Depression.

Tucked between the set of binders and a collection of Cornell magazines, she kept her only photograph of Nell and Cecil. The oval frame was dated, overly-ornate compared to the simple modern frames that came to mind as she studied it now. She touched the glass gingerly as though discovering it for the first time. The photo had been taken after Fa's promotion to Dean of English Literature. Mother stood behind him in his office on campus. She wore a fashionable day dress with a short-sleeved jacket and mid-length white gloves. A small, feathered hat was stylishly perched (Mother, like Frances Perkins, loved hats), and her clutch purse was slung on her left forearm. Her right hand rested on Fa's left shoulder, and she looked down at him with the slightest look of amusement. Fa stared straight into the camera, his face placid and maybe a little triumphant.

How playful and impromptu the photograph seemed— something she'd never noticed before. It occurred to her now that they actually loved one another.

She felt a stab of yearning to share with Fa the news she'd received today. Instead of chasing the urge away, she held onto the bittersweet pang and observed it as it faded, holding the gaze of the man, her father, in the photo. And, now, Mother was gone. How did Fa manage the long days and weeks? Was he involved in research and writing? He was sixty-five years old—twenty years younger than Frances Perkins.

Frances had lived three lives in the last two decades, and she was active and loved—and relevant. Presidents and intellectuals, students and cab drivers celebrated and honored her. Eliza wasn't even sure whether or not Fa still held an office on campus. She hoped so. She'd spent hours in his office as a child dutifully reading her own stories while he worked on his various projects. They didn't often speak, both buried in their books, but she'd sensed that Fa understood her love of knowledge. She knew he would, despite everything, be proud of her today.

Eliza put the photograph back in its place. She knew better than to dwell. As much as she wanted to share this news with Shannon and Fa, even Ed, it would never be as easy as that. If she reached out now, she'd have to explain why she'd walked away and never looked back, but how could they understand? She imagined each of them—but most hurtfully, Shannon—might very well reject who Eliza had become. Someday she might be strong enough to bear it. But not yet.

~⊙

"FRANCES, ARE YOU HERE?" ELIZA poked her head in the front door of her mentor's home where they'd met for lunch regularly since Eliza arrived on campus in 1948. She looked forward to sharing news of her new post. Frances had a cool wisdom about life and people—she had dealt with the chronic depressions of both her husband Paul and her daughter for decades. Since Paul's death thirteen years ago, she'd lived alone, maintaining her involvement with government affairs while guest lecturing at Cornell, where she also had a weighty reputation with the school leadership. Though her matchmaking with Stanley had failed, Frances continued to mentor her, treating her almost as a daughter.

Two like-minded women from different generations, their personal lives had similar ebbs and flows. Both had religious upbringings—Frances, Episcopalian; Eliza, Roman Catholic—yet neither woman felt confined by her spirituality. Religion's potential as a foundation for social justice inspired both of them. Frances had included Eliza in her wide circle of friends, and they had grown even closer after the marital split. She was sure Frances maintained her relationship with Stanley as well; their failed marriage was not something she'd ever hold against either one of them. And although they never spoke of it, no one other than Frances knew of the attack in the kitchen that altered the course of Eliza's life.

She approached Jemmie, who sat by the telephone desk beyond the foyer. Something wasn't right. She couldn't remember ever seeing her so motionless, and for a moment, Eliza thought she might be asleep.

"Jemmie, is Mrs. Perkins home?" Eliza said, touching her forearm. Jemmie looked at her, about to speak, but Eliza continued, "I didn't hear from her about lunch today; I know she's been in New York this week.... Is she still gone?"

"She died this morning. She had a stroke in New York while on retreat at All Saints. Sometime in the night. They took her to a hospital, but she was ... close to gone. She must not have suffered too much, they said ..." Jemmie swept her fingers underneath her eyes and wiped at the tears, trying to smile. "No one—man or woman—held a candle to her, wouldn't you say, Eliza?"

Eliza felt a crushing need for more details but forced away the urge to press Jemmie. She sat down and took her hand. The two women stayed silent for a moment, the sharp ticking of the hallway clock seeming irreverent to Eliza.

So much of her life in Ithaca had evolved from her relationship with Frances. Perhaps to forge a connection to home, Eliza had arranged for Harvey and Mrs. Perkins to meet several years ago after she'd given a speech at the New York Bar Association on changes to New York's Progressive Labor Law resulting from the Triangle Shirtwaist Factory fire of 1933. Eliza remembered Frances' first impression:

"Your Midwestern boys are the best types, Eliza. Straightforward and honest. Those are the two words that came to mind when I met your friend Harvey. And I'm sure life's not always been easy for him. Keeps his private life private—sadly the only way for these dear, young men. I'm sure I'll see more of Harvey Bligh, as he is an excellent ballet companion. Did you know the New York Ballet is now his client?"

~⊙

HARVEY CAME TO ITHACA ON Tuesday for Frances's memorial service at the Interfaith Church at Anabel Taylor Hall. The evening of the service, Harvey and Eliza dined together at the same restaurant they'd first visited in 1950 when he'd come with David. Harvey had aged well—the baby fat that had persisted on his cheeks and waistline into his mid-twenties was gone. He was lean and fit, and the tailored silk suit he wore was likely from Bergdorf Goodman's, along with his wing-tipped shoes and mother-of-pearl cufflinks. Still a Midwestern boy on the inside, on the outside he was all New York City. Even his well-manicured hands, sculpted and strong, inspired trust and, overall, Eliza considered he was one of the most handsome men she knew. Frances had been right; Harvey's moral compass had always been steadfast despite the challenges he'd undoubtedly faced along the way.

"Will future generations appreciate, or recognize at all, what Frances did for this country?" Eliza mused. She pushed a few olives around her plate, aware that she wasn't at all hungry. She'd ordered a Manhattan and wondered whether it, too, would go unfinished. "She did more in the last ten years of her life than most of us will ever accomplish."

"True," Harvey said. "But more importantly, she nurtured fulfilling relationships with those around her. I met her grandson today—very nice kid. Poised, thoughtful.... We don't get to see many children these days, do we, Eliza?" His eyes narrowed and bore down upon her.

Eliza returned his stare and folded her arms. "Are you trying to say something, Harvey? Please, don't beat around the bush."

When Eliza had announced she'd eloped with Stanley Katterman, Harvey had dropped his occasional attempts to persuade Eliza to repair her ties to both David and Shannon. He was a friend, but she'd not tolerate judgment from him or anyone else.

A bachelor, who preferred the company of men, Harvey had plenty of doting women in his social circle. But Eliza and Harvey's friendship was cut from a different cloth. Each far from home, Eliza believed that both shared an unspoken need for mutual acceptance. For years she'd supported his subculture lifestyle, and he'd eventually honored not only her seemingly inexplicable split with Stanley but also her break from family and community back home.

"Did I mention I've received a new post? I think Frances had something to do with it ..." Eliza said, filling in quickly when Harvey hesitated to respond.

"No, Princess of the Changed Subject, you hadn't told me. But please do." Harvey twirled the ice cubes in his drink with the straw.

"I've been asked to create a new program called Women's Studies. It'll be under the broader Industrial and Labor Relations Department, at least to begin with."

"Congratulations." Harvey leaned back and crossed his arms. "Eliza, I'm happy for you. The challenge suits you, and I know you'll do an incredible job."

"But ..." she let the word trail, watching him from across the table, suspecting he might unleash something wicked and potent.

"But Eliza, it's time you come to terms with your life, don't you think? Here you are, thirty-six years old, unmarried, no family, and spending all of your time holed up in Cornell Libraries." He delivered his thoughts as if establishing a well-planned legal position in front of a jury. Factually correct and dripping with earnest delivery.

"Not true," Eliza rebutted. "I spend plenty of time in New York City and Boston, and until now, in Frances' office. Harvey, don't start. I don't think I can take your clucking right now."

"Clucking? Eliza, that's insulting. I care about you. I'm fairly certain I'm one of a remaining handful who genuinely does. Did you know Stanley and Barbara had their second child?"

She didn't know, and hearing it surprised her, although she was determined not to show it. She retorted, "Who are you to talk about family and children and spouses? You haven't so much as tried to have a relationship with a woman suitable for marriage."

"You know perfectly well I'm homophile, Eliza. I have tried 'suitable women', and it is a mistake to go that route, no matter how much I'd like it to be otherwise. Not having the chance for a family of my own is my biggest albatross. I'd give my eyeteeth to be able to. Great. Now you've gotten me to say 'albatross' and 'eyeteeth' back to back." He took a drag on his cigarette and stared at it, while tapping it on the edge of the ashtray and blowing smoke upward, away from the table. "It's not meant to be for me or for many others. You, on the other hand, you intentionally deny yourself the possibility. I don't know why. But I can see how devastating your avoidance will eventually be for you."

Eliza scoffed. "You see no such thing, you ass. Why don't you go pick on Shannon? From what you've told me, she's little more than a too-skinny, reclusive nanny. She was the one who wanted oodles of babies. Not me."

"Yes, and she's the one who can't have even one. But I think Shannon is doing fine. She is a late bloomer, yes, but I think she's found her place."

"What do you mean, she can't have one?" A knot of dread hit Eliza between the ribs. "What does that mean?"

"Are you saying you didn't know she couldn't have children?" Harvey looked incredulous. "I guess she never told you. She never told me either … it was your mother who did…. She was so worried about Shannon after you left."

Eliza sat back in her chair and searched through her clutch purse. She said nothing as she took out a silver-plated case, opened it, took out a cigarette and put it to her lips, both hands trembling. Harvey was quick with his lighter, flicking it twice before the tobacco caught. "I did know. Yes, I knew," she said in a near whisper.

"Don't worry, Eliza. She's all right. She may have even found love. Too early to say. It's complicated. By the way, I saw her last week when I was home. She asked me to deliver this letter. She said she's not sure how to get mail to you. I'll admit, she's a bit flighty when it comes to the modern world. It's as if part of her, a very charming and guileless part, hasn't matured past sixteen."

Eliza crossed her legs and turned away from Harvey. She removed her glasses and ran her fingers through her thick, wavy hair before she put them back in place. The waiter, a young, pimply college student whom Eliza didn't recognize, came to the table and took their order. She then gave Harvey a triumphant smile, knowing the subject of her shortcomings had been successfully interrupted. It gave her time to think about what he'd said.

How could she have blocked out memory of Shannon's infertility? Of course she knew—Mother had told her the day they'd received the blessing of St. Blaise. But was she in love? With whom? She looked around at the other women in the restaurant, some she knew well. Shannon would, of course, look like a woman approaching forty, as she did. A few gray hairs, a changing neckline, hints of wrinkles like the wispy lines around her own lips. *God, I don't know her anymore, do I? And now she's sent a letter.*

"Eliza, I'm not saying you should have or should ever get married again, have babies, and all of that. I am saying that whatever it was that got in your way in 1947 needs to be addressed. By you. Soon." He finished by raising his eyebrows and returning to his cocktail.

"You have no place, Harvey, telling me what to do. I've never looked back for reasons of my own. I haven't needed to. Thanks in large part to Frances, but also thanks to a great deal of hard work and focus, I have a fulfilling professional life—and a perfectly agreeable private one. And I intend for it to be even more fulfilling and remarkable. This new post is yet another door opened through which I plan to walk. One of the great lessons I learned from Frances: Walk through the door. It's half the battle. No time to reflect on past wounds."

"I wish you luck, Eliza. I do. But no one gets away with burying the unpleasant past. Whatever it is, it'll not go unresolved." He softened his tone, leaned across the table, and put his hand on top of hers in a motion she'd have considered impertinent from any other man. He looked at her unflinchingly with his intelligent gray eyes, and she could imagine how devastatingly convincing he might be in front of a jury. He kept his hand on hers, and continued, "I know you aspire to be as good as Frances, as well you should. You want to make a difference in the world, and you, more than anyone I know, have the brains and the will to do so. But you will not succeed until you face your demons. Other people may give you your space … Shannon, David, me, your father … But in the end, it'll not be enough. You'll not be your best self until you come to terms." He ended by smiling, his eyes serious, and Eliza could imagine a mesmerized courtroom. "There, I've said my piece. You can change the subject now and I won't protest. But if you ever need an ear, darling, mine is yours."

"Thank you, Harvey. After that earful, I think I have all the ear I need for now." She removed her hand from under his and attempted a self-satisfied chuckle, but it came out like a little snort. *Damn him, how dare he give me this lecture today, of all days?* Eliza, like everyone she knew, admired Frances as nearly a saint. And Eliza had the privileged relationship with her of a protégé and a friend. This made her feel as if she were, by association, saintly as well. Frances had had that effect on people. She made them feel better about themselves than they actually were. But in her heart, Eliza knew very well that the black core of unspent emotion that Harvey had alluded to kept her from true greatness, true compassion of the level Frances had achieved. And Frances, the only person who knew Eliza's past, had probably known her limitations as well.

She walked through campus, feeling Shannon's letter in the pocket of her slacks. Eliza hadn't spoken with or seen Shannon since the last days of 1947. The only news of her had come from Harvey, infrequent and sparse.

As much as she may have wanted to, she couldn't take the next steps. Her final words to Shannon came out knotted with accusation and painful emotion, too toxic to unwind. She'd called Fa before Mother's service to explain that she couldn't come home. She'd felt she could handle his mellow, slow voice. When he answered, she expected him to be shocked, but he wasn't. It had been as if he was waiting to hear from her, and the conversation had been intimate and bittersweet. They spoke of Mother, of Fa's loneliness, of Eliza's accomplishments, and Fa's second published textbook. When Eliza asked about Shannon, Fa remained silent and lost the thread of conversation.

Had she ever wanted to get on a plane and fly back through the years to 1946, it was after the call with Fa. Even so, her fear of what she'd need to face in order to reconcile had been reason enough to let the urge pass.

She came to the suspension bridge over Fall River where she and David had last seen each other. The day years back when he'd arrived in Ithaca with Harvey, unannounced. Where he'd kissed her and she'd lied to him. She'd told him she was in love with someone else. How shameful. How could she have done such a thing? She leaned on the railing of the bridge. She wanted to take Shannon's letter out of her pocket and read it, but she couldn't find the courage to do it. She couldn't. But what if the letter somehow provided her a way home? She never considered Shannon capable of saving her. Eliza was the one who'd always done that. Shannon relied on her. Shannon had been frightened of life without Eliza, but today Harvey had told her Shannon was fine.

Eliza closed her eyes and, gripping the railing with both hands, pulled her body close. It had rained in Ithaca, and, although mid-May, the air was warm and muggy, more akin to late August. She felt David next to her as if she were seventeen again. They'd stood together at the railing in the park after the summer storm had wreaked havoc through the neighborhood; they'd looked down at the swollen and turbid flow, carrying branches of all sizes downriver. She'd felt lightness that evening in the storm's aftermath.

She relived the moment. He'd leaned over and kissed her, and the sound of rushing water below became part of the vivid memory. She could smell the wet, fresh pungency of the evening air. She felt the stubble on David's chin on her fingertips, and his stomach muscles tighten where she'd placed her hand as he tilted her head with his thumb and forefinger. She felt the light pressure of his lips and remembered their cool touch turning soft and warm. She remembered the sweet fragrance of orange peel. She opened her eyes, half expecting him to be standing next to her now. It'd been her first real kiss.

Never before or since had Eliza felt so elated, so enamored, not just with David, but with life itself. Never in the years since she'd left St. Paul had she allowed herself to revisit that evening, that happiness of first love. It had always been attached to Patrick. She banned the memory of David's first kiss and the sweet youthful feelings accompanying it. And if honesty mattered, she'd admit she'd been running away from the vulnerability of that moment ever since.

Eliza crossed the bridge and sat on the same bench where, years later, she and David had come together in awkward silence. What else had she told him that night? She couldn't remember. Now, her legs felt weak. Her mind usurped all her physical energy to keep the terrible memory of her attacker at bay—despite logic, Patrick's ghost lurked nearby, and it frightened her. She yearned to replace the fear once and for all with a happy memory of David. An image from their stroll on the night of the August storm. She wanted to stop running, to find and protect that emotion—pure and simple first love—though she knew it was nothing but an old memory, like the dead stump of a once-noble tree, with no roots or branches to carry it into the present.

Early evening on a Tuesday, few people would be walking over the bridge. The last thing she wanted while regaining her composure was to see someone she knew, but she felt unable or unwilling to walk, as if her legs would malfunction and take her around in circles. She felt Shannon's envelope between her fingers. The St. Paul address was embossed on the back in a pale blue, elegant font. Shannon had crossed out the address and written her new one—somewhere in the town of Roseville, near the hospital where she worked, Eliza supposed. Eliza laughed unevenly to herself. Maybe it was nothing more than a late holiday card.

Mother, Ed's wife Olivia, even Shannon had sent her Christmas and birthday cards every year. No message. Always signed, "Love."…. *How absurd.* Whenever she received them, she felt like some kind of wild, dangerous animal…. *Caution, don't feed the lioness, she may attack.*

But perhaps it contained something more, this Harvey-couriered letter from Shannon. Uncertain as to what it might convey, Eliza inhaled deeply and allowed herself a kernel of inexplicable hope.

She read the letter once and crumpled it between her hands. Whatever she'd expected, it wasn't this. Shannon had written as if she were asking a favor of a distant acquaintance. It began with a few vague niceties, ending with "… and of course, I hope you are well …" The middle paragraph was short and to the point. She asked whether Eliza would consider writing a letter of recommendation to her admissions department for favorable consideration of her charge, Miriam Ross. The young woman, a high school junior, would graduate with honors from high school and thought she wanted to pursue studies in Social Work. Funny, Eliza most certainly remembered that the family Shannon had worked for had moved to Scotland. Hadn't Harvey told her that Shannon had considered moving there herself? He'd been concerned she was too attached and had told Eliza that he'd advised her against it. Harvey had moved to New York City not long afterward and began several years of sleepless commitment as a junior partner at a prestigious law firm. She realized now that for those first years, she'd heard almost nothing more about Shannon. Eliza had been so caught up in her own world of the Jamesons, her ill-fated relationship with Stanley, and her heady ascent in the world of Industrial and Labor Relations at both

Cornell and in Washington, D.C., that she'd barely noticed the years slip by.

Maybe these Rosses were a different family altogether. She was sure Harvey must have told her some things, things she hadn't remembered. Shannon's life, for all Eliza could tell, must be small and sad. Yes, she knew she'd become a nurse. Shannon had shown her the scars from her surgeries in the days before their disagreement. Their ... estrangement. She'd tried at the time to make light of Shannon's scars, but they'd shocked her. Shannon had never been vain, but Eliza understood how difficult it would be for any woman to accept them. Harvey had told her that Shannon's left shoulder drooped now, and her collarbone protruded from where the ribs had been removed, giving the appearance that it was permanently broken. Who was the person he thought might have gotten beyond Shannon's barriers? A familiar, protective instinct for Shannon materialized, mixed this time with a surge of something else: envy.

Eliza suppressed the ugly emotion, one of the seven sins, and considered all that Shannon had suffered during her illness and thereafter. At least her own scars hid from sight, invisible, packed away and under her control with no eyes upon them—not even her own.

Her mood lightened briefly as she recalled Shannon, fingers pressed into her temples, insisting she could read Eliza's mind like a child mentalist if given enough silence and concentration. It had been Shannon's way of prying into Eliza's emotions—futile attempts to get her to admit thoughts she had no intention of sharing.

As often happened when Eliza thought of Shannon, her mind skipped to the day she met Beryl and was initially exasperated by her silliness. Her roommate shared some of her sister's signature traits—flightiness and a habit of blurting things out top among them. Neediness, too.

God, when had she become so judgmental of these two who'd shown her nothing but goodness and acceptance? Even worse, perhaps she'd replaced Shannon in her heart with a worldlier, privileged version in Beryl—a version who didn't insist on unearthing her secrets as Shannon undoubtedly would. But where was Beryl now? Consumed with her life as mother and wife? Busy with exclusive country-club cocktail parties and Kennebunkport sailing trips, New York summer camps, and private nannies? Eliza hadn't seen her for three years. The last time she'd spent the weekend at Beryl and Chas's home on the Maine coast, Eliza had felt like a fifth wheel, struggling to appear interested in her best friend's mundane life, privileged as it was.

Her cheeks flushed hot with disappointment at Shannon's letter. She'd been cruel to Shannon that afternoon in their childhood bedroom. But why couldn't Shannon see through Eliza's anger that day and recognize it for what it was? Desperation. Fear. Loss. Why had Shannon let go of her? Shannon, who'd been doted on through her year of tuberculosis like a martyred saint. Couldn't she see the unfairness? The shame Eliza had endured when Mother and Fa sent her away like an unworthy slut? And for that matter, why hadn't David tried harder? Oh God, she wasn't making sense. She couldn't have pushed him or Shannon any further away without breaking the laws of gravity. Regret, brought on by Harvey's lecturing, had gotten under her skin.

Eliza considered throwing Shannon's letter in the river along with the memory of Harvey's diatribe, but the spirit of Frances was not far from her mind. Of course, she would do as Shannon asked—it was nothing, really. Shannon had included the young girl's writing sample and transcripts, which was all she needed. Of course, the girl would be accepted at Cornell—anything Eliza could contribute would be superfluous. And Eliza would, of course, meet with her. If she passed muster, perhaps there could even be something more—a connection to Shannon that Eliza's heart yearned for, though she couldn't outwardly acknowledge it. She felt herself raising a familiar wall of indifference—those feelings ran too close to the edge of the goblin king's cave.

29

OCTOBER 1965

"Now, this one here ... is River Tummel," Allan leaned on his side with the length of his warm body close to Shannon's, tracing with his forefinger the six-inch scar trailing from her kidney across her abdomen. "It's such an interesting river—much like its name ... tumultuous, deep, and dangerously rapid in places."

Shannon, captivated by Allan's lilting voice, felt she was floating as his fingers made their way across her various disfigurements: keloid scars that after eighteen years remained puffy and red—stubborn reminders of her body's aggressive effort to heal its skin.

"And this, the River ... ohh-ho-ho, I could never forget the name of this one."

She shuddered with pleasure as he placed his palm on the shorter blemish that ran from her shoulder to her right breast and let his hand pass between and around it to where the second scar ended. He put his head down close to hers, let his lips brush her cheek where it met her ear, and whispered, "This is the River Beauty, which needs no further description."

As Allan continued to describe her body as if it were a topographical map of Scotland, she allowed herself the unexpected, electrifying pleasure of his touch. It was late October, a month since the flowers—pale-yellow mums with white tea roses and sprigs of baby's breath—had been delivered with the note: *My dearest Shannon, I hope you don't think me old-fashioned, but unless you direct me otherwise, I intend to court you—and to continue to do so until you are mine, and me, yours. In deepest admiration, Allan.'*

Tonight was the first time they'd found his bedroom with intentions other than searching for some misplaced item—a lost sock, a can of moth spray, a spare quarter for the bus.

Shannon inhaled through her nostrils into her chest and felt the familiar limitation of her diminished lungs. But she felt deeply relaxed. Her reduced lung capacity was the last thing on her mind. She'd been shy and hesitant as she removed her blouse, exposing to Allan her botched body, worried he would recoil, or laugh, or worse, pretend the scars didn't exist. Instead, he took off his own shirt, and without losing eye contact, gently grasped both her arms above the wrists, caressing them with his fingertips. He turned to sit on the edge of the bed and asked her if she'd lie down with him. As she did, she left an entire life behind. A veil of shame and physical grief she couldn't have described moments before fell from her, a prickly shroud of emotions separating from her skin and slipping off under its own feathery weight. She imagined herself as a new person, a newborn woman, coming into the world for the first time.

A vision of Virginia Ross floated in and out of her mind like a single frame in a family slide show. After Virginia's return in April, she'd mailed Shannon a note dismissing her as caregiver to Miriam. To ward off the void she knew so well, Shannon had taken extra shifts at the hospital, visited Fa weekly, and enrolled in an oil-painting class. She covered white canvases from corner to corner with bold, geometric shapes layered one upon the other, until she could see nothing but her own vision of symmetry, and finished her work with a thin, meticulously applied whitewash. Whites, even a thin layer, calmed her. Shannon's anxieties resurged in a series of waves, first insignificant and then overwhelmingly big. Without her easel, she felt these fearful surges might have killed her. She couldn't take buses, or tolerate even the smallest stain or untidiness. The sound of rain and wind grew in her mind until she imagined it as little flames, burning her ears from the inside.

In early August, Miriam called to tell her she'd been accepted at Cornell University, the school Shannon had suggested in any number of different ways ever since her return from Scotland. She asked if Shannon could come for dinner before she left, to say goodbye. Before Shannon could ask about her mother, Miriam said, "I'm sure Daddy told you, Mummy's gone again. She left weeks ago."

"I'm sorry, Miriam," Shannon had said, glancing at a photo she kept by the desk of the child as a toddler. "How are you?"

"Fine. She's a bitch, anyway. She was awful to Daddy." A few seconds of silence followed, then, "Good riddance."

Shannon had arrived at the Rosses for dinner the Saturday following Miriam's unexpected call. In the months since April, the girl had changed. Teenagers evolve, Shannon thought, but this? Miriam wore heavy eye makeup, her nails bitten short and painted. She'd cut her bangs so they fell uneven and high on her forehead. Shannon remained quiet and braced herself for Miriam's words, thinking they might be those of an angry young woman. How grateful she was to be wrong! Miriam had leaned in and smiled; she told Shannon about her plans to attend Cornell, the name of her roommate, her ideas for classes. Cornell!

"Daddy was a pushover," she said to Shannon later as they washed dishes together. "He was pitiful. I overheard them arguing—her mostly, at least it was her voice I heard. He's so meek and quiet. I hate that." Miriam stopped washing. She ran her wet hands across a towel and leaned against the counter facing Shannon. "Mummy, or, I should say, Virginia, said she couldn't do it again … Whatever *it* is." Shannon saw Miriam's expression change from defiance to hurt. "I suppose she meant me."

"Miriam, that's not true. She didn't mean you. And do you think it's fair to judge your father? It would break his heart to hear you talk about him so disrespectfully."

"What about my heart, Shannon? What have I, me …? What have I done to deserve her hate?"

"I'm sure she doesn't hate you, Miriam. It sounds like she hates herself."

"That doesn't even make sense. Her life is more adventurous than anyone I've ever met. You should've heard her. She's fine without us. In fact, that's exactly what she said to him."

Two weeks later, in the lifetime before the flowers and the handwritten note and the rivers of Scotland, sitting in the passenger seat of Mr. Ross's old, clover-green Ford Galaxy, Shannon had looked to her lap and imagined her mother's hands—the same sculpted dorsum with slender veins and bones just under the surface of translucent skin. Her hands, like Nell's, had very little excess flesh. Nell's hands had always been occupied with purposeful motion—except in church, where Shannon recalled that her Mother was impenetrable, deep in meditation, not at all part of a communal religious ceremony. When her eyes were supposed to be closed, Shannon would often squint instead, staring at Nell's hands clasped in prayer. Her mother appeared entranced—her slackened jaw and her hands pressed together, held erect and pointed toward heaven with her forehead touching her crossed thumbs. Not like Fa, who tucked his chin into his chest and held his hands together low over the back of the pew as if crushing rocks in his palms.

"So, there she goes," Mr. Ross said, "off to college."

They were alone, not for the first time, but it seemed to Shannon, something had shifted to make this time different. Together, they watched the bus carrying Miriam off to college pull away from the station. Mr. Ross reached for the radio dial, eventually settling on a station playing a piano sonata. Shannon guessed Beethoven, though she wouldn't have put money on it.

She and Eliza had taken piano lessons as children, but only Eliza had the discipline to continue throughout high school. Shannon wondered if she'd played at Watermelon Hill. How often these days she thought about the adult Eliza. With Miriam on her way to Cornell, was Shannon finally pushing fate in a direction that would reunite them all? She closed her eyes and, for a moment, relived a memory of Eliza playing piano, while she sat in her wheelchair in the first months of her long, frightening quarantine eighteen years ago. She tried to imagine Eliza now, tried to picture her receiving the letter she sent via Harvey many months ago, yet couldn't conjure up Eliza as anything but a seventeen-year-old girl.

The memory of Eliza in the hospital bed, feverish and incoherent, had forced itself upon Shannon in the lonely first months of her absence. But over time, through meditation similar to prayer, she managed to preserve an image of Eliza that endured and strengthened her. Like a pixie spying from a perch in a nearby tree, she'd often relive the childhood scene when she and her sister relaxed on the Hudson Bay blanket, chatting at the picnic before the storm, just days before Shannon's collapse.

In Ed's snapshot from that day, and forever in her mind's eye, Eliza remained young, confident, beautiful. Though no longer her actual protectress, the memory of Eliza still lived.

"I believe Miriam will do well, Mr. Ross." Looking again to her lap, Shannon took care in choosing her words. The music faded into pianissimo.

He sighed before responding, "Indeed. And life will go on in the tundra …"

She smiled. In the course of the last several years, Shannon had often heard Mr. Ross's dry wit find its way to the surface.

"It's time you called me by my Christian name, Shannon," he said. "I'll give you three guesses."

"Of course I know your name." Shannon turned to face him. "Allan. Right?" She rubbed the nape of her neck and added with a shy laugh, "Though it may take me a while to remember since I've called you Mr. Ross for quite a long while now."

Shannon realized as she spoke that she had no good reason to remember his name now that Miriam had left for college. Living alone, Mr. Ross hardly needed a housekeeper. He didn't seem the type who would seek a bachelor's social life. She imagined him spending hours in his garage, bent over his metal work tables, tinkering with tools and various Heathkit electronic sets.

"Shannon, please join me for dinner on occasion, would you?" Traffic was light and Mr. Ross looked straight ahead, both hands on the steering wheel.

She looked at him and paused, taking in his profile and seeing him as Allan for the first time. "Yes, I will. I'd like that, Allan."

"Will you make a habit of it? Is once a week too much? Perhaps on Thursdays?"

"Yes." Shannon's cheeks warmed. "I mean, yes, it would be nice to make a habit of it. And I'm not sure if once a week would be too much. But, no, I can't do Thursdays because I've taken a shift at the hospital for now, and I've enrolled in a class on human anatomy. I need to ... I ought to keep busy."

"I know you'll miss her." He rubbed his chin and gave his cheek a light slap. "Maybe we can miss her together from time to time."

"How about Saturdays, then?" Shannon said.

"It's Saturday today. No time like the present. Would you join me for dinner? I think a restaurant is in order, if not in celebration, then at least to mark a momentous occasion. My little girl is off to college ..."

She'd seen him smile from the corner of her eye, but only as she'd said, "Yes."

He'd parked the car in front of her apartment. "Shannon Malone, I want to thank you. Somehow, you've always been here, waiting for her, for us ..."

Shannon had nodded and smiled, silently saying a prayer of gratitude.

Now, lying on Allan's bed, although early in the evening, she felt herself drifting off to sleep. Allan murmured his words, and the palm of his hand, now warm from its travels along the contours of her torso, lay flat against her skin and made slow circles on her abdomen. Warmth spread from her belly button to her thighs, an unexpected, prolonged thrill. Her moistened inner thighs awakened, full of desire. Where she'd dozed seconds ago, she was now attentive to new, thrilling pleasures that aroused her body in unimagined places.

She turned to Allan, whose lips had not left where her cheek met her ear. She couldn't speak. Instead, she gave a slight moan; her earlobe and the tiny knob of fleshy cartilage above it had become a divining rod of near ecstasy that he licked and kissed in precise measures, occasionally whispering single words in a husky Scottish lilt—*soft, want, lick*—that made her back arch and her vagina tingle. Three confident fingers traveled into her crevice, and within no time, a burst of physical pleasure she'd never dreamed possible washed over her. She embraced the waves of bliss flooding from her breasts to her thighs. Allan came onto and into her, a graceful motion between lovers in the small, perfect world he and she had created.

"SHANNON, WILL YOU MARRY ME?" Allan asked, when they awoke together the next morning.

Was it as simple as that? Nothing was wrong. Everything was right. With a simple touch, the scars that had repulsed her became a totem of his intimacy, and he'd sealed her destiny to stay close to Miriam. Moreover, she loved Allan. In part, she loved him because they shared Miriam, but was there anything wrong in that? Wasn't that much of the reason for love between two grown people—the shared devotion to their children? Shannon imagined she had more thinking to do on the subject of Allan and Miriam and how her secret might affect their life together, but for now she was content to believe this was part of God's plan. In some happy way this turn of events, she was sure, would somehow bring Eliza and Miriam home together.

30

OCTOBER 1965

Three fat stacks of correspondence and a deck of phone messages awaited Eliza when she returned to her office after a month of traveling. Her assistant, an eager, red-haired, post-graduate student named Jonathan, waited impatiently for her like a racehorse pacing about the starting gate.

"Lots to do, Professor." He stood and tapped his foot in front of her desk, his eyebrows alternately arching and furrowing, lips pursing and puckering. "You need to review and sign off on these and just review these." He touched each pile as he described it. "I put the super important items—the draft of the president's report on new projects, the old program budget you need to update

ASAP … those kinds of things, in this." He slapped the palm of his hand on the manila envelope and smiled as if he'd won a prize. "You have a board meeting to attend on Friday morning, and the president's chief of staff—that would be the real president … Johnson—invited you to the White House for a dinner to memorialize Madam Perkins. Next month, but he wanted a yes or no now."

He looked at his watch. "And … in about twenty minutes, you have a meeting with a freshman student from Minnesota, a Miss Miriam Ross. She's called three times since September, says she's a family friend and you expected to hear from her. I finally made the appointment, thinking you'd want to get it out of the way. Or I could cancel when she arrives."

Eliza's face reddened. She couldn't imagine she'd forgotten to tell Jonathan to schedule an appointment with Miss Ross when the young woman inevitably reached out. Yet more and more of these non-essential tasks slipped her mind lately. "Of course, it's all right, Jonathan. Thank you. Please show her in when she arrives."

"And this is today's mail. Just arrived—do you want me to prep it?"

"No, I'd rather you start transcribing my notes from Berkeley and Northwestern candidate reviews." Eliza handed him her notebook in exchange for the correspondence. She thumbed through the stack and pulled out the letter she'd been waiting for: A young Oxford Brit who'd finished his Ph.D. at Harvard and was now at Kent State. He excelled in Industrial and Labor research and was considered to be a gifted lecturer. She'd made him an offer for one of her lead professor positions. Surely, he'd be interested. When Jonathan left the room, she opened the envelope. The note, on personal letterhead, was brief and to the point. Professor Jarbell was passing on the opportunity. Eliza sighed. This was the third letter of regret for the same position, and she needed to secure these posts by end of January at the very latest. Four months from now. What if she failed to secure the talent for the four positions she was expected to fill? Were her colleagues around the country unconvinced she could lead an innovative program such as the one she was designing?

"Hello?" A tall, lanky girl with uneven bangs and too much blush on her cheeks stood at her door. "Your assistant was on the phone. He said I should knock."

Eliza stared blankly at the girl before remembering the scheduled appointment. She wasn't sure what she'd expected, but the young hippie in front of her was not it. She wore bell-bottom jeans that dragged on the ground around her flat, brown sandals. A flowing halter-top with an indigo-blue macramé shawl covered her delicate, pale shoulders. No bra. Her thick, dark hair was plaited in a braid that landed near the top of her shoulders, adding to her look of frailty despite her generous height. She wore dark, oversized sunglasses that Eliza despised.

"Miss Ross. Miriam, right? Please come in." She motioned to one of the chairs in front of her desk before she sat down. Oh, how she wished for solitude in her office right now. "Can I get you some tea? Water?"

"No, but thanks," Miriam said. She looked around the office as if surprised to be here.

Eliza expected her to say something more, but she didn't. She thought she identified the scent of herbal cigarettes or perfume, meant to disguise whatever else might've been recently smoked. Miriam completed her appraisal of the office from her seat, then gazed at Eliza, nervously pursing and biting her lips. Eliza wondered whether the girl had any awareness of the habit.

"Perhaps you could take off your glasses so I can see your eyes," Eliza said, trying to keep her tone light and friendly. When had talking to freshmen become so challenging?

"Of course, sorry; it's just, I ..." She removed her glasses, revealing red puffiness around otherwise pretty eyes. "I think the grasses here are an irritant," she explained. "It never happened at home, but …" She shrugged.

"Miss Ross, please tell me how your classes are going. What are you enjoying? What do you find challenging?"

The young girl raised her eyebrows as if pleasantly surprised by the question. "I think I find the anti-war and civil rights movements the most interesting part of Cornell. I knew protests happened on college campuses, but I didn't know what that meant. I can't imagine it's only happening at Cornell, right? We were sheltered back home, I guess. I've joined the Students and Teachers Against Vietnam Coalition. Are you a member?"

Eliza sighed, refrained from rolling her eyes and pulled her chair closer to her desk. She rearranged the folders her assistant had delivered from one stack into two. She didn't find this girl interesting. Nor could she imagine what Shannon had been thinking by encouraging her to attend Cornell. Surely, she could attend an adequate school closer to home. She glanced down at the letter in front of her and shook her head. If not the Kent professor, who else might she recruit for the program? Time was running out. Pursing her lips, she returned her focus with as little outward reluctance as she could muster to Miss Ross.

"No, I am not, although I have always been opposed to sending troops to Vietnam." She paused and pursed her lips. "You know, you can protest and march without paying tuition, Miss Ross. While this campus and others are important centers for free speech, we are primarily a place where young people strive to broaden and deepen their knowledge through classic means of acquisition—lectures, tests, research, and dissertation. I'm sure that's what your father and mother had in mind when they sent you here."

Miriam arched her eyebrows and then furrowed them. She looked ready to retort, but stood to leave instead. She smiled primly, her eyes set and even scolding. "Thank you for ushering my application through, Dr. Katterman; it was very kind of you. As Shannon always said, you really are very beautiful." She looked around the room again. "And really smart, I guess."

"Miss Ross, I didn't need to do anything unusual; you're qualified to be here as a student. Cornell is a very special university, at least to me. As I said, protesting has its place, but if you court trouble, I'll not be the one to help you out of it."

"I don't intend to *court trouble*," Miriam curtly repeated the two words, lifted her head like royalty, and looked beyond Eliza to something on her bookshelves.

Eliza grimaced, recognizing the habit she herself had of scanning and assessing other people's literary collections as a shortcut to forming an opinion about their character.

"I don't want to keep you, Miss Ross," Eliza said, her voice bristling involuntarily. "If you'd like, we can touch base every month or so in case you need anything. Please call Jonathan to make appointments. I have advisory hours for students on Thursday and Friday mornings."

Miriam put her sunglasses back on. Before she turned to leave, she looked at Eliza, as if surveying a sculpture, and said, "You're not at all like Shannon, are you?"

Upon hearing Shannon's name, Eliza fought an urge to beg Miriam to stay. She wanted to tell her everything about Shannon: how Grandpa Theo so aptly named her an Irish pixie when she was ten; how her outfits never matched until Eliza fixed them; how she loved to draw brightly-colored bugs and flowers; how she hated Mother's cauliflower dishes, and how she made Eliza laugh so hard she would cry. How had Shannon described her to Miriam? She'd forgotten—actually forgotten—that Miriam might know Shannon better than anyone. But she knew she couldn't do such a thing. She was an assistant dean, and this girl was a first-semester freshman. She had no business being casual with Eliza. Frances Perkins did not invite casual when they first began their monthly luncheons, and Eliza had been grateful. Her mentor had been regal in her authority, and Eliza had revered her. She would've never behaved with the impertinence this girl had shown in five short minutes.

"Goodbye, Miss Ross. Please let me know if I can assist you with anything this first term." She softened enough to assuage the faint voice of Shannon's reproach in her mind: "I know freshman year can be challenging—especially for young women." Eliza looked down at her three orderly stacks and picked up the folder with urgent items, intending to end the meeting on her terms.

"Not as challenging as this little get-together has been," Miriam responded coolly under her breath, but loud enough for Eliza to hear. "Thank you again, Dr. Katterman."

Eliza stood by the window and watched Miriam leave the building. An upperclassman whose chaotic hair and ridiculously long Fu Manchu mustache Eliza recognized as belonging to a well-known student activist known for crossing the line to rabble-rousing strode up to Miriam. He kissed her and slung his arm around her shoulders, then led her to the nearby tent where students canvassed volunteers to picket the local Army recruitment offices. For a moment, Eliza imagined the girl in the courtyard to be Shannon and an ancient urge to mother her sister surfaced and took her breath away.

Eliza phoned Jonathan, whose small office adjoined hers. "Please make a note to reach out to Miss Ross every six weeks or so. Offer her a meeting with me, and make sure I know if she's coming." Eliza's first impression of Miss Ross wasn't good. This would be a chore. In her mind she heard Shannon's voice say, *And whose fault was that, Eliza? The girl's, or yours?*

31

NOVEMBER 1965

n the weeks following Allan's proposal, Shannon's thoughts naturally wandered to the many details of a wedding. Where should it be? When? Spring or earlier? *Earlier—she didn't much like the idea of living in sin.* Was she too old for a big wedding and reception? *Yes, thankfully.* Did she care if it couldn't be a church wedding? *Not really.* For her, the very thought of a Catholic wedding ceremony troubled her, just as the thought of marriage had been previously inconceivable. She'd trained her life so intently on Miriam and on surviving the earlier losses of both Eliza and Miriam that if any man had shown interest, she'd been unaware. A twisted spine, puffy red scars and a missing uterus combined with increasingly introverted habits and quirky self-sufficiency all served as useful shields against any possible advances.

Of course, Allan had been different from the beginning. He had an inside track and worked his way beyond her wounds to the essence of Shannon without her ever suspecting it. In her memory of the early days before Scotland, he was only an occasional presence, a minor, though charming, character in the story. She remembered him as someone who loved Miriam as she did, but who mostly appeared as she prepared to leave, both too distracted by the routines of daily life to notice each other. But since reappearing at Mother's funeral four years ago, he'd staked a claim on Shannon she wasn't even aware of. Until one day, there he was—hers.

Her own wedding was not something she'd ever dreamt about. Allan would be divorced. Did that matter? *No, it did not.* She'd been concerned about Virginia since she'd disappeared with no forwarding address, but last week Virginia had finally telephoned, indicating her plans to return to Scotland and eventually move to Spain with the man she referred to as her "cousin." She also provided an address for legal separation documents.

Now Shannon's living room overflowed with boxes stacked against the wall. Her bedroom closet had been packed and ready to go for two weeks, except for a few nurse's uniforms. To leave here felt right. Even if it was little by little—even if it created chaos in her otherwise orderly routine, because home was where Allan was.

Miriam planned to return from Cornell for the holidays. Shannon had sent letters, weekly at first and then monthly, and Miriam had called twice. The first time she'd been over the moon about her Comparative Religions professor. "What a free thinker, Shannon! He calls us 'comrades,'" she'd said, giggling.

The second time, she'd been in tears over her roommate. The young woman from upstate New York had falsely implicated

Miriam in a cheating affair that ended in the young woman's dismissal. She'd written Shannon a single letter in October including a photograph of herself among a group of protestors who'd staged a sit-in at Cornell's student union. In that letter, she mentioned her "interesting but brief" visit with Professor Katterman. *And yes, her sister was still glamorous.*

"Shannon, where are you?" Allan called to her from the front door.

"Back here, darling; packing a few items. It's so much easier doing it a little at a time."

"Miriam called today," he said as he joined her. "She'll be home Saturday. No finals next week. I told her we could use the extra days to go shopping for a little car. Nothing fancy—maybe a few years old. Something she can take back and forth to Ithaca. What do you think? Or is it impractical, given the snow storms?"

"Could you drive out with her?"

"Spectacular idea! I could meet the mysterious Eliza."

Shannon sat down. She hadn't expected that. Of course, he should meet Eliza. But would he know, somehow, once he met her, the truth about Miriam? Would Allan see Miriam in Eliza? It struck her that so far neither Miriam nor Eliza seemed to notice markers so obvious to her—the way both cocked their heads to the left and narrowed their similarly beautiful eyes, the identical dimple in each woman's chin, the shared ability to argue any point without being overbearing. "Maybe you should buy yourself a new car, instead," she suggested. "You've been eyeing the new Mustangs."

"A brand new car is not in the cards, I'm afraid," he said.

Shannon squeezed his hand, a pulse of tenderness passing between them. She knew he'd provided Virginia with much of their savings, and, predictably, the remainder of his money left with her when she finally disappeared.

"We'll be saving at least three hundred dollars per month by moving in together," Shannon said, "and I have a little nest egg. Why don't you teach me to drive, and we can buy a new Mustang together?" Shannon surprised herself with this idea. Learning to drive had always been out of the question for her—terrifying and unnecessary.

"You're a fine Irish lassie, Shannon Malone," Allan said, twirling her into his chest. "I'll get back on my feet soon, and we'll be fine."

SHANNON'S WOOLEN WINTER COAT, RAIN jacket, boots, gloves, hats and scarves hung in Allan's front hall closet. On Saturday morning, she moved them all to Allan's bedroom closet to make room for Miriam's outerwear and waited for their return from the bus station.

"How could you, Shannon?" Miriam didn't say this, but Shannon knew her well enough to guess her thoughts when she opened the door to greet her and saw the hurtful look Miriam shot at her. The girl's overnight bag was slung over her shoulder, and her knee-length wool coat hung open. Not waiting for her father, Miriam tilted her head away and walked toward the bedroom hallway without a word to Shannon.

"That didn't go very well," Allan said as he followed his daughter inside. He had a suitcase in each hand and kicked the front door closed with his foot, then took off his boots and shook them. "The place was a zoo."

Shannon put her hands on his cheeks, letting her warmth transfer to his cool skin. "Dear, I'm sorry."

"When I saw her come off the bus, I couldn't believe it was her. She's so thin; I didn't recognize her until she was five feet away from me. She hugged me and said she didn't feel well. The trip gave her motion sickness."

Shannon followed him to the living room; they sat close together on the sofa, Allan with his long legs stretched out, his stockinged feet crossed at the ankles. Shannon had the urge to get down on her knees and rub them.

"She didn't respond to anything I said with much more than a grunt. It got so uncomfortable; finally, she caved and told me about a few of her exams. Then about her new roommate. They get along. At that point, I thought it was as good a time as any to tell her about us."

"But it sounds like maybe it wasn't …" Shannon said.

"I don't think any time would have been good." Allan put his arm around her shoulder, leaned into her, and kissed her on her temple. She blushed. "I explained to her that in September I asked to court you. I explained that after she left, I realized that aside from her, you were the one person in my life who mattered to me and that it was the most natural thing in the world for both of us. When she didn't respond, I continued saying that by now we are more or less living together and that I hope to marry you as soon as the divorce is final."

Shannon remembered the day Miriam told her about the argument she'd overheard between her parents. It'd happened early one morning in the days before her mother had left for good. "At least I didn't hear the D word, Shannon," Miriam had said. "I guess I shouldn't care since I'm almost an adult. It would be awful if she never came back. I think Daddy loves her—we both know she's crazy, but still. I think I … well, of course, I care; she is my mother! I think when she works things through once and for all, she'll be back. She kind of said as much when she took me shopping. She said, 'Shortcake, over the holidays I'll take you to Chicago and we can have a grand time. Just like Paris.'"

Allan took his arm back and rubbed his chin with both hands, his bushy eyebrows furrowed. He ran fingers through his thick, graying hair and continued to recount their dialogue, "When I said the word 'divorce,' Miriam cried out and turned toward the window so I couldn't see her face at all. I pulled off into a parking lot and tried to get her to talk, but all she said was that you and I have betrayed her and Virginia. No one told her about the divorce, she said. I thought it was abundantly clear when Virginia left, but who knows…. It's clear she'd hoped—"

"I suppose it's natural," Shannon interjected, "for a girl, a young woman, to want her parents to be together forever." Shannon tried to imagine how different childhood would've been if Fa and Mother hadn't been together. From the beginning of time they came as a unit, like an element on the Periodic Table. What if they'd not been together when she went through tuberculosis? They were the constancy that had kept her going. Different parts of a single entity. Virginia and Allan had never seemed like one unit made of two parts, at least not to Shannon; but it could be that children always see their parents that way, even when it's not clear to the rest of the world.

"I thought, though, she'd be happy—not only for us, but for herself," Allan continued. "She adores you—you've been as much a mother to her for years now. I hope you don't take it personally, darling. She'll come around."

"Allan," Shannon turned to face him, "my feelings for Miriam … are nothing short of … I mean, I know I'm not her real mother, but I know who her real mother is." She paused, correcting course away from a complicated issue. "Since I first set eyes on her, nothing she, or anyone, could say or do would ever change my devotion to her."

She didn't add that the years after their sudden departure when the child was a toddler felt bleak and empty—months of feeling invisible and wounded, followed by years of daily struggle not to fall into an abyss of loneliness. She hadn't missed Virginia or even Allan. By then she didn't think daily about Eliza either. Her secret yearning for Miriam, her own child in a sense, had molded

Shannon into the person she was now—an odd blend of quirks, self-deprecation, and deep compassion that only people who've suffered great loss can claim.

"Maybe I should stay at my apartment for the next few days. You and Miriam need time. She's home for more than a month before the new semester begins." Shannon couldn't bear to think of what would happen if Miriam didn't, as Allan suggested, come around. If that happened, it would've been best if Miriam had never left St. Paul. Shannon knew her influence led Miriam to choose Cornell, all in the hopes that somehow it would bring Eliza—Eliza and Miriam—home. What if by accepting Allan's love she'd lost Miriam for good?

~⊙

WINTER DAYS WERE AT THEIR shortest and a clouded sky hid the moon and stars, making the early evening sky pitch black. Lost in thought about Miriam, Shannon scrubbed her dinner dishes as if they were surgical devices from the operating room. She nearly broke one when the phone rang and startled her. She hoped it would be Allan. Instead, Olivia was calling to invite her to a holiday dinner.

"We're taking the children to London for Christmas, Shann; so … hoping we can get the Malones together two weeks from Sunday instead. We leave on the twenty-second to spend a few days with my sister's family before Christmas at the country house. London's too wet this time of year, she says. Does that Sunday work for you?"

"Yes, and I'll be bringing a friend, Olivia—I hope that's all right. It might be two guests, actually." Shannon surprised herself. Was she ready to do this? Were Allan and Miriam ready?

"It's a simple family dinner, Shannon … Edith, Fa, the kids. Any other time, of course, you'd be welcome to—"

"Olivia, I've something to tell you. I'm engaged to be married. His name is Allan Ross. I've known him for many years. I'd like to bring him and—"

"Well, congratulations, Shannon. Is he a doctor from your hospital? This is big news—worthy of celebration. When were you going to tell us? Maybe you planned to elope?" Shannon thought she was joking, but Olivia didn't laugh. "Why don't you tell your brother the news?"

The line went quiet for many seconds, and Shannon frowned, imagining Olivia making a face of utter shock as she passed the receiver to her husband.

"Hello? Allan? I mean, Ed; I'm marrying a man named Allan. His daughter, Miriam, is eighteen years old, home from college." She stopped, giving time for a response that didn't come. "She's attending Cornell."

"Remarkable. What a coincidence." Ed sounded dumbfounded. "Has she met Eliza?" Was he more shocked by her engagement or by the fact that Miriam may have met Eliza? Was it such a surprise that Shannon might find love?

Shannon went back to Allan's a full week after Miriam's return for the holidays. On her bus ride, she wondered what she'd say to Miriam if she happened to be home and awake. When Allan met her for lunch yesterday, he'd explained that Miriam slept until noon almost every day. The two of them had dinner together on Saturday night, but Allan said the silence was thicker than the overcooked split pea soup. Shannon smiled, thinking about the many dinners the three of them had shared over the past years, and it occurred to her that while she considered herself shy, she'd often been the one to initiate conversation between the three of them.

If after a week at home, Miriam had not yet opened up to Allan, would she be ready to talk with Shannon? Surely she'd be able to reconcile her anguish about Virginia with her trust in Shannon? In the past, Miriam had sought Shannon's opinion about such things—especially Virginia, whose relationship with Miriam was layered and complex. She understood how intertwined Miriam's sense of self-worth, her stability, even her happiness was with the image she held of Virginia. Her sense of how Virginia loved her—her need to define it, unconventional and unproven as it sometimes was—created an even deeper emotional canyon for Miriam. Shannon saw it all, and it broke her heart.

She fumbled for her key to Allan's house and let herself in through the front door. The house was as she'd left it days ago, yet it seemed an eternity since Allan had driven her home in agreement that some space would be good.

She took off her boots and walked quietly down the hall toward the bedrooms. If Miriam was awake it wasn't evident now. *Let the girl sleep,* she thought. Shannon decided she'd gather the few things she needed from Allan's bedroom closet, clean the kitchen, and would only then *maybe* knock gently on Miriam's door before leaving.

As if spotting a friend in a crowd of strangers, Shannon looked from the bedroom doorway to the framed photo on the dresser of herself and Allan at the State Fair. She smiled. It sat next to another, a photograph of his mother taken decades ago before he was even born. Her eyes, intelligent and soft, looked beyond the camera as if she could see into the future—*perhaps to today.*

The State Fair photograph in which she and Allan held a large plastic ring, ready to toss together toward the field of cola bottles, had been taken by a man Shannon guessed to be at least sixty years old. He'd moved with the briskness of a magician, staging the two of them, telling Allan to hold her tight around the shoulder and directing Shannon to smile toward the camera, all delivered with an efficiency Shannon found very funny. She'd laughed heartily while looking at Allan and looping her arm around his waist so their hips overlapped. The older man had taken the picture, and Allan's money—a dollar fifty, exact change, please. He'd written Allan's name and address on an envelope similar to the collection envelopes at church and told him it would be mailed in ten days. He'd ripped off a portion of the envelope seal with a number on it and handed it to Shannon, holding it out to her with both hands as if it were sacred.

"You hold onto this, sweetheart," he'd said, looking at her squarely, and Shannon noticed for the first time his crystalline-blue eyes ringed with gray, so similar to Eliza's that seeing them caused her to gasp. He spoke to her with such gravity that she wondered if maybe God had sent him, and if he was referring to her new love for Allan, not the receipt he'd just given her for the keepsake.

The photo had been taken three months ago in early September on their second date. The envelope arrived two weeks later, and Shannon had trouble recognizing herself. She looked older, more attractive than she considered herself to be—not so much in the manner of physical features or appearance, rather, more than just happiness. She saw in the photo a patina of mature femininity that she suspected had surfaced in her on the day Allan first held her. Her image in the photo reflected an aspect of womanhood that she realized she'd avoided ever since her third surgery. When she first saw it framed, and every time she'd looked at it since, she'd been both surprised and comforted that this new part of Shannon Malone had finally awakened for all to see—like a Monarch butterfly, fully separated from its damaged parchment.

She held the frame and looked more closely at how Allan looked at her. It was real, wasn't it? He beamed at her, his arm tight around her shoulder, his fingers lightly pressed into her fleshy forearm, his head held back as if happily assessing his good fortune—both with the ring toss and with the woman in his arms. She remembered feeling light as air—the Monarch floating around the fairgrounds, happy, energized, grateful for life. Grateful for Allan.

But what good was their love if it made Miriam unhappy?

Allan's teacup and plate from breakfast with a smear of butter and some toast crumbs lay on the counter next to the sink. He was either rushed or distracted this morning, Shannon thought, considering his typical tidiness. There was no evidence of Miriam in the kitchen, although a neat pile of books sat on the dining room table, and a pale-yellow, tie-dyed cloth bag hung on a chair back. She recalled dozens of afternoons when Miriam returned from school, first junior high, then high school, to fling her book bag on the same chair, sometimes scaring Stubbs the cat, causing him to flee. She'd sit at the table and remove everything piece by piece for three stacks—notebooks, homework, and things to read. Shannon brought her a snack, cottage cheese and canned pineapple, graham crackers, or toast with cinnamon sugar and apple slices. On those occasions they spoke of everything: classmates, teachers, the differences of life in Scotland and Minnesota. Sometimes Miriam spoke of Virginia, or, less often, of her mother and father as "they," referring to her parents as a single unit. *As it should've been.*

She sat at the table for a moment and looked at the stack of books. She hoped Miriam would not consider it an invasion of privacy—the books were out in plain sight, after all. She was almost afraid to see what literature Miriam had brought home, worried she'd become even more of a stranger to Shannon through her literary choices.

Twenty Years at Hull House by Jane Addams, *One Day in the Life of Ivan Denisovich* by Alexander Solzhenitsyn, and one she didn't recognize entitled *Clockwork Orange*. On the bottom of the pile sat the smallest book, a paperback with a bookmarker somewhere near the end. Shannon bent her head to read the spine. *Sex and the Single Girl.* Shannon supposed she'd been reading it on the train from Cornell. Hadn't that been the book Betty had given her the month before Mother died? The one she'd started but left at work hidden in a drawer before she'd even finished the first chapter?

"Shannon?" The sound of Miriam's sleepy voice startled her.

Shannon shut the book she'd been holding. Miriam stood, smiling sheepishly at the head of the narrow hallway leading to the bedrooms, wearing her slippers and an oversized cotton shirt that must've been intended for a man twice her size.

"Miriam! Good morning. I didn't hear you ... I hope my knocking about didn't wake you up."

"Hi. No, I set my alarm for noon, just in case." Miriam looked down at the floor around her and hesitated, as if unsure about crossing into the territory beyond the hallway. She focused on a tissue in her fingers and twisted it for a few seconds before continuing, "Have you read any of those?"

"This one." Shannon held up *Twenty Years at Hull House.* "Fa insisted Eliza and I both read it in the summer of 1946. I was reading that book when I fell sick." Shannon took a few steps around the table and stopped. She hoped Miriam would want to stay and talk.

"We read that one in Reformation History. I wanted to read it again," Miriam said, leaning against the wall where the hallway met the living room. "Jane Addams was so, oh, I don't know. So good." Shannon could see Miriam was tired. She appeared worn out, defeated, pale. She looked down at her hands again. "I wish I could be more like her."

"She's an excellent role model, Miriam. I remember thinking the very same thing when I read the book twenty years ago." She hoped her desperation wasn't evident in her voice. "Why don't you come have a cup of tea with me? I was going to leave soon, but I'd much rather stay and get caught up if you ..." Shannon remembered Miriam's outburst. "But if you're not ready, I understand."

Miriam didn't seem angry. She walked to the dining room and stopped at the far corner of the table. Leaning her weight against it, she sighed as if crossing the room had depleted her energy. "I'm sorry for the way I behaved, Shannon," she said, moving her head in a side-to-side motion so familiar to Shannon. "I guess I'm tired. I wasn't expecting any news from Daddy, you know? I wanted to see you. Really. But your news kind of shocked me." She hesitated. "It still does. I'm sorry, but it just does."

Shannon took a few steps and reached her arms out to hug Miriam, hoping she'd accept the embrace. In some ways she hardly recognized the girl—she looked pale and thin, and the despondent edge in her voice worried Shannon. Was it about her and Allan, or was there more going on that caused her to appear so wounded even as she accepted Shannon's embrace?

"You have no idea how much we've missed you here. How I've missed you." Shannon held Miriam in her arms for several seconds, then released her, gently clutching her forearms. She couldn't help but smile. Without forethought, she lifted a finger to Miriam's cheek and tucked an escaped length of her dark hair— same color, same texture as Eliza's—back behind her ear. "You have every right to be angry, Miriam," she whispered. Shannon wasn't sure what more to say—it wasn't easy to say things out loud. She wished she'd thought about this moment. She wished she'd written Miriam a letter or at least tried to.

"You mean about you and Daddy. Angry? I don't know. About that, or about Virginia, or ... I can't believe it's ... real." Her sentence trailed off. It was the second time Shannon had heard Miriam refer to her mother with her Christian name, and again it surprised her.

Shannon wanted to sit close to Miriam for hours and hear her talk about Cornell, about her classes and classmates, maybe even about Eliza. She didn't look forward to the conversation about her relationship with Allan, but she'd have to face it soon in order to get to the other side. How could she have put herself in this position? Everything seemed so clear when she and Allan were together. Not only the first day, but every day since. They'd both assumed that because it was so right for them, it would be right for Miriam. Had they been naive and selfish to overlook Miriam's inevitable hurt? And what now?

"Miriam, you must know you mean the world to me."

Miriam sighed and looked at Shannon with a shrug. Shannon sensed that she was thinking of something else, maybe something related, but different from and larger than Shannon's words. "Shannon, do you think Daddy loves her?"

"No, I don't. If I thought that, I wouldn't be here now."

"You wouldn't? I figured you'd always be here if you could. I always thought that was what you wanted. To be in our lives."

Shannon sat back. For the first time, she considered how she must appear to Miriam. She was the spinster nanny who latched onto their family—not once, but twice. Did Miriam think Shannon drove Virginia away in order to get to Allan? Or was she surprised her father could fall for a woman who was little more than a housemaid to him? It occurred to her that Miriam had always returned her love and affection from the very beginning— *as children do*, she supposed—but of course Miriam had no way to know why she was so important to Shannon. A child's affections were simply given.

"When I first started to care for you, Miriam, you were seven months old. I was young and so scared about what life might be— or not be—for me. Caring for you, although it was only a few hours a week at first, I knew was absolutely right. After months and months of illness, you were a godsend for me. I suppose you don't remember the time before going to Scotland, do you?"

"I do have a memory, or maybe it was a dream or a book I read, about a ball of silver thread and raisins that I followed through the house from my bedroom to the hallway and over there to the sofa. I'd climb on the sofa and tug the yarn, and you pulled back. And I'd tug again and the ring would sail over the top. And I'd look behind the couch and find you smiling at me, and you'd say something to me … something like, 'Princess, you found me.' And you let me wear the ring sometimes. Right? … Was it a dream? Do you remember playing that game?"

"No, not a dream. We did it over and over again until you would crawl over that sofa right there and fall asleep in my arms." Shannon pointed to the wall as if it were the same house. For a moment, it was as if thirteen years hadn't passed, as if she could turn and see three-year-old Miriam scamper over the back of the couch, covered in yarn, ring in hand.

Shannon glanced at Miriam, who was lost in thought. Her skin was normally pale, but now it appeared gaunt, and Shannon noticed, for the first time, some blotches of redness. Miriam pursed her lips, perhaps wording thoughts to herself before saying them aloud.

"Shannon, do you think Daddy would hate it if …" She inhaled deeply and put both palms down flat on the table. She crossed her arms and put her head down, looking at Shannon sideways, just has she'd done as a child, then she shook her head and closed her eyes as if to say "never mind."

"Remember how the three of us used to have dinner on Monday nights?" Shannon said. "Well, your father and I have been doing that again for a while now. We usually spend a lot of time talking about you. How about if we start there? Dinner tonight?"

"Maybe. I'm so tired. I'm going to rest for a while longer. My friend Denise—I met her at Cornell—she's coming around to get me in a few hours. I've got to"—She hesitated—"help her with a few things." She stood to leave, and Shannon did, too.

She yearned to hold Miriam again, though the opportunity passed quickly. "I'll bring you some tea."

Miriam shook her head, no, and Shannon watched her walk, shoulders hunched, to the bedroom hallway.

Finished with her tasks, Shannon surveyed the refrigerator and pantry to check items for dinner. She'd have to phone Allan with a shopping list. She knew the prospect of dinner for three would make him happy. But if Miriam backed out? Well, it just might happen.

From the kitchen window she watched two fat cardinals, the brightly colored red male and the dull-rust female, pace across the undulating blanket of fresh snow that had fallen across the backyard last night. Allan often sprinkled a handful of sunflower seeds on top of the snow near the base of the bird feeder to ensure the backyard occupants would provide birdsong in the winter. Now the two birds looked for the bounty, convinced it was buried nearby, a well-hidden truth from the past. The winter blue and cloudless sky and late morning sun reminded Shannon of another gentle creature, Fa, and countless winter days from her childhood.

THAT AFTERNOON SHE RETURNED TO Allan's ready to prepare a simple casserole of beef tips topped with carrots and boiled new potatoes—Miriam's favorite meal. She considered preparing it at home in her small apartment, but she preferred this kitchen where she'd cooked countless meals in the past. In this kitchen, she felt at peace with the odd life she'd created—this kitchen where she sometimes knew Nell watched her with the graceful acceptance of the dead; this kitchen where she felt closest to her spiritual calling.

Shannon wiped the countertop, remembering Mother's fastidious habit of boiling rags. Surely Nell-in-heaven accepted certain things she wouldn't have been capable of understanding during her lifetime—like why Shannon was unmarried and living in sin with a man more than ten years her senior. She assumed heavenly understanding on that matter, but wondered whether, even as a spirit, Nell-in-heaven would cast harsh judgment for the bigger secret she kept.

"What time will she be home?" Allan asked when Shannon explained that a friend from school had come for Miriam earlier in the day. "Was this person a woman? Did you meet her?"

"No, I wasn't here when she left. She mentioned a girlfriend from Cornell, but it could've been a young man, I suppose. Miriam and I did have a nice talk. I think we'll be all right—though it might take some time."

"She's barely said a word to me since dinner on Saturday. I don't understand," Allan said. "She doesn't seem angry—she seems exhausted." He finished pouring two scotch and waters and paused to peck Shannon's cheek with a kiss before returning the bottles to their cabinet.

"So, let's take it slowly." Shannon joined him on the couch, happy to enjoy another of the many new rituals of her life with Allan.

She'd set the dining room table for three. By quarter past seven Miriam hadn't returned.

"We can start without her, I suppose," Allan said. "I'm sorry, Shannon. She knows better."

"Allan, we agreed. Slowly. She didn't actually say she would be here ... it was a 'maybe.' We've been having dinner alone for months—one more won't hurt." She placed the casserole on the sideboard and left the dining room to retrieve the nearly forgotten bean salad from the refrigerator. A key turned in the lock of the front door. Miriam pushed it open and stomped snow off her feet in the entryway.

"Miriam, won't you join us?" Allan stood and pulled out a

chair for her. "Shannon's made one of your favorite dinners."

Miriam was already on her way down the hall to her room, still wearing her coat and boots. "No thanks."

"She's being rude." Allan wiped his mouth and put his napkin down. "I'm sorry. I don't know what's gotten into her." He pushed his chair back. "I'm going to talk—"

"Let her be, Allan." She put her hand on his. "You don't have to say anything. It's so much for her to process. Exams, Virginia, us."

"It's not that I'm angry, Shann. I'm concerned. Maybe she's drunk or even on drugs. Didn't she seem so? I barely recognize her. She's not just older—she seems to have lost her innocence.... Even with Virginia that survived. Is it gone?"

"I recognize her, Allan. She's the same girl. We have to take her on her own terms," Shannon said, then thought to herself: *Who was I to think I could be more of a mother to her than Virginia? Of course, she's confused ... she has no mother and three mothers, all at once.*

Allan finished clearing the table and came up behind Shannon in the kitchen as she washed dishes. He wrapped his arms around her waist and nuzzled her neck. She could feel him inhale deeply before his tongue teased her earlobe. It sent a thrill through her and yet revealed a seed of doubt. For the first time since she'd discovered the Rosses at the church bazaar, she questioned her place in their lives. How did any of this make sense? She knew she couldn't be with Allan without Miriam's acceptance. If she wasn't intended to be here for Miriam, why had God bothered to spare her life after depriving her of motherhood—the one thing she'd always wanted? Did selfishness drive her to find Miriam and put faith in some inexplicable destiny to bring Eliza home? Had she ever really wanted to share Miriam with Eliza? With Virginia?

She turned and hugged Allan, hesitating before pulling away. "I need to think about this. About what we're doing. To Miriam."

"Stop talking about me as if I'm a leper." Miriam surprised them both from the dining room, where she slouched on a chair pulled away from the table with her coat and boots on. Shannon watched as she became rigid and tall in the chair. "I want you both to know something. I'm going to say it once." She paused but then rushed her words: "I don't give a damn about your great love affair. As far as I'm concerned, you, Shannon, are a first-rate whore. And you, Daddy, are a cheater. Do what you want; live how you want. I'm leaving. I hate you both." She stood up, stumbling on a chair-leg as she hastened to leave.

The front door slammed; Stubbs fled down the hallway, and a current of icy air rushed in. Shannon and Allan stood close to one another, stunned and speechless, listening to a car pulling out of the driveway, too fast.

⁓

THEY HARDLY SPOKE WHILE ALLAN drove Shannon home. He walked her to her front door and stood close as she struggled to place the key in the darkened lock. *What an odd and frightening metaphor, she thought, her fingers shaking: keys and locks, inside and outside ... safety and danger.*

The door opened, and they tried to console each other one more time. "Shannon, we'll be all right, darling."

She nodded, unable to say more as she squeezed his gloved hands and brought them to her lips. "Goodnight, Allan."

Later that night, unable to sleep, Shannon took her stationery box from her nightstand drawer. Next to the tidy pile of letters to Eliza was the box with Mother's wedding ring; the one Eliza had sent to her New York hotel in 1948; the one she and Miriam had played make-believe with years ago; the one she'd recently considered as a wedding ring. She opened the box. Would Allan have agreed to the heirloom ring as their symbol of wedlock? She placed the ring on her finger—an imperfect, loose fit. She gazed into the gems, imagining their mysteries, imagining how Mother must have felt when Fa first proposed as she slipped the steel band with three large gems on her finger.

Was their marriage as simple as it had always seemed to Shannon? They all knew Mother had secrets. Why had Shannon never asked? Not in passing, but with deliberation—out of love and respect for ancestry, if nothing else? What if Nell had asked Shannon about her secrets, her sufferings—not just physical, but heartfelt, too? She and Nell had little in common—Eliza had Mother's character—but couldn't they have shared more? Helped each other carry forth in the deepest emotional waters of life? Shannon now knew she had been mistaken about many ideas she'd held over the years. About Eliza. About Mother. But most of all, ideas about Miriam.

THE HOWLS OF HEAVY WINDS woke her, and she rose to look out the window with the nervous energy of a trapped animal. Low clouds blanketed the darkened sky. Large, dense snowflakes whipped about in gales, swirling in tiny cyclones until they landed on the already white surfaces. Shannon's sleepy anxiety swirled around just as incoherently as the snow outside. Would Miriam forgive her? Would Allan, if Shannon left him? After last night, she wouldn't be surprised if Miriam didn't want to see her now or ever again.

Once more, in a swift moment, her life had been turned upside down. What Shannon thought was the perfect fruition of her attention to God's plan turned out to be her undoing. She'd assumed Miriam would embrace the notion of her relationship with Allan as the natural outcome of their history together. Instead she saw, too late, her error: her love for Allan had served to reinforce in Miriam's mind that she was the outsider, a bit player in her own, cobbled-together family.

By eight in the morning, the snowfall slowed and daylight began to filter through the scattering clouds. Two hours in the kitchen helped to release her anxieties. She finished preparing a lamb and cabbage casserole, and placed it in a sturdy bag for transport to Allan's.

Surprisingly, the snow hadn't accumulated, so buses ran on schedule, and Shannon arrived less than an hour later. The house was quiet. She moved noiselessly around the kitchen and planned to leave the dinner behind, put a note on Allan's dressing table and depart as quickly as she'd come. A door closed. From the end of the hallway she heard from behind the bathroom's closed door Miriam gasp for breath between sobs:

"God, oh God ..." Miriam stifled a moan and then cried out again.

"Miriam? Miriam, let me in."

"No, Shannon, please! I don't want you to see ... it hurts ... I'm sorry. I'm sorry ..."

Shannon opened the door. Miriam lay curled on the floor, clutching at her side, hands bloodied from a deep-red stain the size of a dinner plate on her nightgown. Cardboard boxes and plastic containers had tumbled out of the opened cabinet, and Shannon knew she must have been looking for pads.

"It hurts, Shannon; I'm scared. What's happening? I didn't take anything ... I couldn't. I couldn't do it." Blood dripped down both legs and smeared around her feet on the pale-blue tile.

Shannon guided Miriam to the edge of the bathtub. "You promise you didn't take anything? You didn't do anything to make this happen, Miriam? It's important; tell me."

Shannon had helped many young women at the hospital who'd tried to self-induce miscarriages—abortions—through any number of means. Some swallowed toxins or henna, others douched with turpentine, lye, or bleach, even Coca-Cola. The worst cases, women who lacerated their cervixes with coat hangers or knitting needles, often bled so heavily that all a nurse could do was give comfort as the life ran out of them, if they made it to the hospital at all.

"No, Shannon, I promise. I wanted to do it. I was going to douche with, you know, with something to ... you know ... but I was ... I couldn't do it. And this morning I woke with a terrible cramp, and there was already blood everywhere, and then a huge glob—" Miriam frowned and her face contorted as she nodded her chin toward the open toilet. She covered her head with her forearms and hands and sobbed. "Shannon, what's happening?"

Shannon took one of the blue hand towels from the cabinet and rolled it into a tube. She handed it to Miriam with a nod to her legs. "Use this and try to breathe deeply right now. Take off your nightgown. Let's get you in the shower. You'll be all right, sweetheart. You will." She put her hand on Miriam's forehead—no fever. Her skin was clammy and pale, but Shannon could see no signs of pre-eclampsia—too early in the pregnancy. "You're having a miscarriage. It's frightening and horrible, but you'll be all right."

She sat down next to Miriam, wrapped her arm around her, and held her close for several minutes, commanding calmness in herself so Miriam might feel it, trust it, and absorb it as well. "You will be all right, Miriam. You will; we will ... I promise." She hesitated and kissed Miriam's forehead, now noting the fever, present but not dangerous.

Shannon estimated the fetal mass floating in the toilet to be about three months along. She silently prayed in gratitude that nothing worse had happened. "Let's get you back into bed, Miriam. You need rest. It'll take a few days, maybe a week, for this to pass."

December 7th, 1965

Dear Eliza;

We have had a difficult time since Miriam's return. She is resting now, and I can only wonder how it all happened. Maybe you know something, or someone who is involved. Some young man at Cornell, I imagine.

Shannon was unsure how to continue.

… Instead, I'll tell you more about how Miriam came to Virginia and Allan. As is so often the case, people who appall us—those we judge most harshly—once we understand their circumstance are those who deserve our deepest compassion.

Last night while Miriam rested, recovering from the worst of her miscarriage (as I wrote before, it was terrible, painful—she clearly shares some of your genes in the challenges of pregnancy), I brought a cup of tea to where Allan worked in the garage studio.

"Shann," he said, "I want to tell you about Virginia. Why she's not here. Is that all right? I don't want to upset things, but I think you should know"

Of course, I NEEDED to know!

I'll summarize: Allan met Virginia while studying at the University of Pennsylvania in '37. He was here on scholarship money from his county in Scotland. Virginia was his roommate's cousin—he met them both the day he arrived. They fell in love, and when he was called back home for the War in '39, she decided to join him. Allan says her decision, and maybe even her affection (but I wonder if he mentions this for my sake ...), was a way to escape strict and judgmental parents. She lived like a shooting star then—brilliant to watch, impossible to pin down, he said. They returned to Edinburgh, moved in with his mother, who, as I've written, keeps the family farmhouse and mill on a bit of land. By the time Allan left for active duty on the continent (France, mostly), Virginia was pregnant. It wasn't the original idea—they planned to wait—but when it happened, they celebrated. Certainly, he and his mother did.

At this point, Eliza, Allan stopped what he was working on and lit a cigarette. He took a long drag, then placed it in the copper ashtray in front of him and exhaled slowly. I knew how hard this was for him, but I wanted to hear ...

"It was a difficult birth; the midwife said she wouldn't have another. But that was fine—after all, we had a little boy. Cutest little devil I'd ever seen. Ralston. We called him Rollie Ross. Thick brown, curly hair, like mine when I was a young lad. Into everything. Not that I saw him much, but Virginia wrote me letters filled with details of his every move. He'd turned two, and I'd only spent three weeks' time with them, such was my time overseas. I got permission for extended leave just days after his second birthday."

He took another long drag from his cigarette and put his hands on the edge of the metal table, pretending to assess where in his project he'd left off. He picked up the base of a circuit board, scrutinized it and set it down again. "But on the day before my leave began, my superior officer called me to his office with news from home: the boy had drowned."

Allan smashed his cigarette in the tray, leaned forward on his stool, and was quiet for a very long time.

"He got out of the house.... Who knows what Ginny or Mammy were doing. But they weren't accustomed to him moving around on his own. He'd gotten out of the house.... She—Virginia, that is—found his little body afloat in the stone well. It must have been minutes. Some fool had left the hinged lid on the well half open. In all of my years on the farm, I'd never heard of such a thing..."

He told me, Eliza, that they'd come to Minnesota to start over.

Sorry, I can't continue now...more later, dear Eliza,

Love,
Shannon.

32

December 1965

nstead of returning to Ithaca to repack for an extended trip, Eliza had the concierge at the Sherry Netherland Hotel in Manhattan book her a one-way ticket for a premium class PS Sleeper on the 20th Century Limited train from Grand Central Station to Chicago. Once there, she'd buy the connecting bus ticket to the Twin Cities. That plan would have to do.

All five major airlines were on strike after five months of failed negotiations, and Eliza had lost track of the snowstorms creating havoc across the Midwest for the last two weeks. She didn't want to risk driving anywhere, much less Minnesota. More than the possibility of bad weather, Eliza distrusted herself to drive home, given the news she'd received. Had winter conditions caused the accident or something else? Who had been driving? Where were the three of them going? Or were there four in the car?

A kindly-faced, elderly Pullman Porter with no hair other than a neat silver beard and mustache introduced himself as Isaiah. He took her by the elbow, led her down the famous red carpet emblazoned with gold-lettered TWENTIETH CENTURY LIMITED, and helped her board. A young, pretty train hostess handed her an elegant little bouquet of tea roses and gypsophila and a gift-wrapped bottle of perfume. As they walked to her compartment, the porter listed the amenities of the train: barber shop, secretarial services, a twenty-four-hour buffet car, two dining cars with cocktail bars, a medical suite in case of emergency. He asked Eliza if she had questions. Once at her compartment, he placed her single suitcase on a rack behind the narrow door of the worn, art-deco "roomette" and handed her the large satchel with her paperwork and reading material. She placed the strap of her clutch purse—tiny in comparison to her satchel—over the chair in front of the mirrored desk and tipped the porter a dollar. He bowed his head and, in a gravelly voice, wished her a pleasant journey as he left the room and closed the door.

Earlier in the morning as she'd entered Grand Central Station, Eliza had thought of Shannon who'd arrived and left from this very station eighteen years ago. Eliza had been here dozens of times, but today was different. Today the wall between her two lives, past and present, had begun to crumble, and she had no idea how to stop it.

She walked through five cars to the smoking-car lounge with her book, *The Rector of Justice* by Louis Auchincloss. She had little confidence that she'd be able to concentrate enough to care about a fictional hero as remote to her life as an Episcopal boarding school headmaster, but it was worth trying. She passed the last set of doors, overcome with a sense of dread that once she sat down, nothing could keep her from thinking again about the telegram she'd received last night.

Now it seemed ages ago that she'd returned to the Sherry Netherland Hotel after a heady and engaging day. As one of three appointed executive advisors to President Johnson's Equal Employment Opportunity Commission, Eliza had been asked to address a gathering of three hundred people from the recently formed National Organization for Women. President Johnson had called upon Eliza as a leading intellectual in the new field of Women's Labor Rights to help his administration grasp and respond to NOW's increasingly aggressive stance on the application of his 1964 Civil Rights Act to women's issues, such as labor and even abortion rights. There was talk of a lawsuit to force the government—namely the EEOC—to comply with its own government rules. Privately Eliza sympathized with NOW, which was led by Betty Friedan. She was confident they understood her support, but she had to moderate her public comments in a way that wouldn't reflect poorly on the president. At least not yet. These were exciting times in the world of equal rights for minorities and women. She'd returned to the hotel to freshen up after her speech—and before her scheduled meeting with Betty and NOW's chairwoman, Kay Clarenbach, to discuss their secret proposal that she resign as a presidential advisor to the EEOC.

She'd spotted the yellow Western Union envelope slipped under her hotel room door and her heart had lurched. Shannon! No, of course not; why did that thought force its way into her mind? Of course it wasn't Shannon. It was probably some pressing matter from Ithaca. Or could it be Fa? Why did her mind insist on telling her it was terrible news from home?

Eliza - Shannon Allan Ross and daughter all in bad car crash Sun night S & A in hospital stable for now Shann's back broken Call Dudley 8 5294 hospital nurse station Love Fa

Everything from the moment she'd read the telegram—a

rushed and frantic skim over the abbreviated words—until now, when she sat amongst strangers in the lounge car while the train sat delayed in Grand Central Station, faded into nothingness. Her eyes stung, and she couldn't control the tears as they trickled from her tightly shut lids. Certain that they made her look ridiculous, she dug her sunglasses out of her satchel nonetheless and wore them. She didn't want to be alone in the claustrophobic compartment, which she imagined would swallow her up like particles of dust if she returned there. Instead, she faced the large panoramic window of the luxurious car and waited until her anxiety subsided. She trusted the familiar ability to remove herself from emotion, patiently watch it take its course in her psyche, then dominate it again with rational thought and control. It would pass. She would make it so.

Eyes closed, she remembered Shannon years ago, quarantined for tuberculosis. Had she really been ten months at Milner Hospital? From the distance of time, she thought it remarkable Shannon had survived the experience: bed-ridden, sick, enduring surgery after surgery. At least at Watermelon Hill Eliza had been able to enjoy the outdoors and move about, although not gracefully and in a hideously floral maternity gown. She'd been able to complete her coursework without nurses and doctors poking her, medicating her … frightening her.

She hoped Ed had contacted Harvey. If not, she would send him word. Maybe he was home for the holidays as well, although she doubted it. Her last encounter with Harvey had been fine—a relief to both of them. They'd met for a Broadway show and dinner right around Thanksgiving. Neither mentioned their uncomfortable encounter seven months ago, in April, when he'd insinuated that her life was a mess.

He didn't show it, but Harvey had suffered through the years, evolving into the successful lawyer he was today while navigating the secretive culture of homosexuality in New York.

As compassionate as Eliza felt toward the people she studied—immigrants, minorities, impoverished women—she'd never tried to understand the challenges of his life. Why was that so hard for her? It was somehow related to Shannon, to their estrangement, to that terrifying night. It was all off-limits. Behind thick walls. Or it had been. In the front of her mind, fear was gathering strength like a rogue band of warriors storming their own castle. If she lost Shannon now, the fortress she'd built would crumble as well.

Eliza eyed the yellow envelope again and snatched it from her satchel. She tore the note out and reread it.

Eliza - Shannon Allan Ross and daughter all in bad car crash Sun night S & A in hospital A stable for now Shann's back broken Call Dudley 8 5294 hospital nurse station Love Fa

How could she have missed that? Her mind had tricked her. Fa was clear in his precise, grammatical way that Shannon was not stabilized. Only Allan was. She must be unconscious. Or worse. Maybe Shannon had already died? Eliza's body swayed, and her stomach lurched to nausea as the train swung a wide turn into a long, echoing tunnel.

Eliza paid her porter, Isaiah, to keep an eye on her luggage at the Chicago La Salle station. She rushed to the bank of pay phones near the ticket office and called Fa, praying he would answer.

"Fa, it's me. Eliza."

"She's unconscious, Eliza, unconscious for two days now ... But it's not a coma. Some of it's the morphine. For the pain. There is hope. The doctors think she has a good chance because she's young and her heart is strong. But her lungs ..." Fa whispered. "Are you coming home?"

"I'm in Chicago. I'll be there by tonight, Fa. Harvey's told me her apartment is near the hospital. I'd like to stay there."

"Miriam Ross can let you in, I'm sure. I'll try to call her. I've met the girl at Ed's; she's very kind, Eliza—you'll like her. If somehow the door is locked, come home. You can take my car to the hospital tomorrow morning. I don't drive much anymore."

"Yes, thanks." She hesitated. "Fa?"

"What, darling?"

"Fa, I'm sorry it took me so long …"

He interrupted, his voice close to a whisper: "No, Eliza—not now. Not now."

Silence hung on the line for several seconds. Bricks crumbled in her mind.

Eliza pulled the receiver away from her face and brought it to her chest, her mind reeling. Again, Fa was asking her to bury her needs in the shadow of Shannon's trauma. Again, pushed aside by Shannon's neediness. Confusion set in; *it's not Shannon who did this*. The unleashed pain carried bloated memories: Mother confronting her about sex with David; her own attacks on Shannon; her cold rejection of Stanley. The fierce urge to leave home came from an instinct to protect Shannon. Shannon needed the finite love of Fa and Mother more. There wasn't enough for Eliza. No, not that; it was that Eliza could survive without their love, yet she knew Shannon never would. She told herself this again and again while the phone's black receiver warmed against her face. She was the strong one.

"Eliza?" Fa spoke, and she returned the phone to her ear. "We'll get there, darling. We will. Eliza, I promise, we'll bring you home this time."

A small, unexpected sob escaped her. She pushed down the lever in the phone cradle, ending the call, and joined Isaiah, who stood patiently by the dolly with her suitcase and satchel atop.

A LARGE, BLUE-CERAMIC PLANTER ON the front doorstep topped with a crust of dirty snow around dead geranium plants made the entrance to Shannon's apartment feel bleak and abandoned. She simultaneously twisted the handle and knocked. The front door was unlocked. Clearly, the daughter—what was her name? *Damn, I've forgotten her name!*—must be here. When no one answered, she opened the door and stepped inside.

"Hello? Anyone here? Hello?" Had the door been left unlocked by mistake? Was this the right apartment? She stepped inside and scanned the room. A young woman came out of the kitchen, unaware of Eliza. She held a small, red transistor radio and wore a single earplug connected to the device by a thin, white cord. She glanced up and yelped when she saw Eliza.

"Sorry; did you knock?" she asked, a note of apology in her voice. She took the plug from her ear and set the device down. "I … we've met before. I'm not sure if you remember me." The young woman extended her left hand. A white plaster cast covered her right arm from elbow to wrist.

"Yes, of course, I remember our meeting, Miss Ross." Eliza offered her left hand to shake the girl's, but for the life of her, she couldn't remember her first name.

"Please call me Miriam, Professor Katterman."

Eliza nodded. "Thank you. I will." Perhaps the girl expected her to offer a similarly informal option, but she wasn't inclined to provide it. *Maybe later.* She remembered her brief interview with Miriam. *Had it been in early October?* They'd met in her office the day she'd returned from her extended research trip. *Yes; just ten weeks ago, though it seems ages since then.* She remembered her feelings, bordering on disgust, as the hippie activist embraced Miriam on the walkway and kissed her as if he owned her. Why had it bothered her so much to see that from her office window? After fifteen years on faculty, she was accustomed to the students' banal public behavior. What did she care how Miss Miriam Ross spent her free time?

"I have the kettle on. Would you like tea? Your father said you'd be arriving late tonight. I wasn't expecting you yet." Miriam bit the left side of her bottom lip and furrowed her brow." Shannon's nurse said she'd asked for a few books on Monday—I don't know if … well, now she's not …" She handed Eliza two books, *The Problem of Pain* and *Mere Christianity*, works by Fa's hero, Dr. Lewis, which Eliza had long since abandoned.

"Tea would be nice," Eliza said as she set down the books, pulled off her gloves, scarf, and gray camel-hair coat. She removed her boots and took a pair of wool socks from her satchel to wear in the apartment. Already she suffered from the lack of essentials. Hopefully Shannon had items she could use. She half-smiled, thinking that maybe she'd find some of her own somewhat-dated treasures in Shannon's closet. She was right to have come home, even if she wasn't alone, and even if Shannon still wasn't within her sight.

"Do you, um … want to know how it happened, Professor?" Miriam, her hair gathered loosely into a ponytail, came back to the living room with two cups. She put one on the coffee table, then curled into the loveseat by the miniature fireplace.

Eliza thought Miriam's tasteful, gray-flannel slacks and black sweater fit her beautifully and set off her rosy complexion. She couldn't recall why she'd pigeonholed the girl as a hippie when they'd first met almost three months ago. She noticed Miriam's effort to get comfortable, and, for the first time, saw the three-inch bandage on Miriam's neck and the series of bruises, camouflaged with light makeup, that trailed from above her left ear down to her jawline.

"I don't want a detailed account now. I just need to know … is Shannon conscious? Did you see her today?" Eliza wasn't being polite, but she wanted nothing more than to be left alone. Miriam's presence in the apartment unsettled her, though she couldn't imagine why. She tried again. "Why don't you summarize the accident, then I'll turn in. I'm exhausted. You understand, I'm sure."

"Shannon isn't conscious. Daddy is, although both his legs are broken and he bruised his rib cage—in case you wondered." Miriam cocked her head in what Eliza took to be ever-so-slight recrimination.

Eliza recoiled just as slightly; she'd never tolerate such a moral lashing in normal circumstances, much less from a young student.

"I'm sorry," Miriam said. "That was mean. Shannon's injuries were ..." Miriam took a deep breath. "They're more critical. Her spine's fractured and several ribs are broken; worst of all, she has a torn lung. They say it won't be ... easy for her." Miriam looked down into the cup she held between her hands. When she looked up, Eliza realized that she was struggling not to cry.

Eliza pursed her lips and bit down hard. The muscles in her jaw tightened, and she swallowed before speaking. "Briefly, what happened?"

Miriam glanced down again at her teacup and swirled the spoon slowly. She looked up, but not at Eliza. "We'd gone to your brother Ed's home at Lake Minnetonka for a holiday dinner. They planned to leave yesterday for London to be with Olivia's sister's family, so Christmas was moved up. Daddy had a whiskey to celebrate their announcement; he enjoys a good whiskey, but it sometimes gives him terrible headaches, so he asked me to drive home. And he's been encouraging me to, well, to drive the car."

Eliza leaned forward. She would ask no questions yet, but what and whose announcement? And why had a young girl been driving at night, instead of a grown man—and had she also been drinking? The phone on Shannon's desk rang, startling them both.

"Stay put, Miriam." Her intention was out of concern for the girl's injuries, although she knew it came out harshly. She tried to compensate as she walked to the desk, her hands clasped tightly in front of her chest. "Please, I'll answer. I'm closer."

"Hello? Yes, Fa, I've arrived safely.... Yes, I'm here with Miss

Ross, who'll be leaving in a little while. I'll take the bus to the hospital tomorrow. It's only three stops. Will I see you there? … Good, Fa. Good."

For the briefest moment, Eliza reflected that this was the third time she'd spoken with Fa in almost twenty years. His voice was so familiar, like a long-forgotten tune, and it gave her comfort she wasn't expecting. She hung up the phone and turned around to see Miriam close by, gathering her purse and Shannon's books from the desk.

"I suppose I'll see you tomorrow. I'm spending my days between Daddy's room and Shannon's room, both on the same floor at least." She picked up a date book from the coffee table and leafed through to the very end. "Though I have my own doctor's appointment tomorrow afternoon."

"Will your mother take you?" The question slipped out before she had a moment to think, though surely the girl's mother was somewhere about. Eliza struggled to put together the fragments she'd been given. Where, in fact, was Miriam's mother? Why was she not in the car, at Ed's party, or in the picture at all?

"No, that's not likely, Professor Katterman. I haven't seen my mother since last April."

Once alone in Shannon's apartment, Eliza unpacked her suitcase, wincing at the paltry selection of appropriate clothes. As she guessed, she found many of her old cashmere and wool sweaters, slacks and skirts stored in a cedar chest that must have come from Grandma Edith. She pulled out a dozen or so items, timeless in design and color, and stored them in the drawers of Shannon's lowboy dresser for easy access. She found enough stockings and undergarments to last at least a week and give her enough time to go downtown to shop for necessities. Good thing spring semester didn't start until January 26; Shannon should be home by then.

She unfolded the last old garment in the stack, a vibrant,

peacock-blue cardigan that she'd no doubt chosen decades ago to match her eyes. Something sharp pricked her finger. As the sweater fell to the ground, she saw the gold and enamel fraternity pin David had given her on their evening walk, hours after an unexpected summer storm had ripped through the neighborhood. Quickly, as though it might hold a curse, she removed the pin and buried it in the chest under neat piles of clothing and linens.

~⊘

ELIZA HAD FORGOTTEN HOW SUNNY mornings often accompanied the bitterest cold in a Minnesota winter. As she left Shannon's flat the next day, the icy air cut at her neck like a blade. She wrapped her wool scarf up as close to her eyes as she could without blinding herself and didn't remove it until she was deep inside the hallways at Milner Hospital.

Shannon was unconscious with a tube down her throat and a bandaged head and chest. One cheek was bruised and swollen. Aside from a few scratches, the other was unscathed. Eliza expected to see her sister's face exactly as she'd recorded it in her memory in the days before Shannon fell sick with tuberculosis. Instead, she had a look of peaceful resignation at odds with the way Eliza thought of Shannon; despite the wounds, her sister's face held an unnatural calm that frightened her.

A card rested on the belly of a stuffed bear on the cabinet next to the bed. She opened it to see it was from Donald Bligh, Harvey's father. He'd taped a telegram from Harvey inside:

Shann darling – praying for you Godspeed in recovery. You won't make me bust out the Red Lips, will you? Yes – I have them Love, H

~⊘

FOR THE NEXT THREE DAYS, Eliza woke early, took a walk in the cold winter sunshine, returned to make toast and tea for breakfast and went straight to the hospital, where she spent hours sitting in Shannon's room. To quell the constant knot of worry, she read aloud from several of the books on Shannon's nightstand while praying for her to regain consciousness. The rubber tube falling from Shannon's lips was a reminder that Shannon was still victim to tuberculosis, first discovered in her lungs twenty years ago. Shannon's life had likely been marked in a thousand ways by the burden of that terrible year, and Eliza, who as a child was convinced she was Shannon's protector, faced again the misery of her failings.

Several days after her arrival, in the late afternoon, she returned to her childhood home on the edge of St. Thomas campus. Muted music coming from Fa's library led her upstairs. He stood on Mother's step-stool and changed a lightbulb in the ceiling light. He was mostly as she remembered—tall and broad-shouldered—still sturdy but thinner in his chest and waist. Several deep lines etched his face; his skin seemed less supple, and his wavy hair, gray, and less thick.

"I've washed the globe as Nell would have me do," he said, smiling sadly as he stepped down. In the same movement, he reached over to lower the volume on a turntable that had replaced his beloved Victrola.

Before she knew it, Fa enveloped her in a tight, long embrace. Her head rested on the surface of his dark-blue woolen vest, and her breath carried inward the forgotten fragrances of his presence.

"You're home," he murmured into the top of her head. How had she survived for this long without Fa—his proportion to hers, unchanged—inviting her, urging her to be once again a girl, safe in the simpler world of her father's arms?

Fa, too, came to the hospital each day and stayed with Eliza for hours at a time. They talked quietly about Eliza's academic career, avoiding 1947 and the years Eliza had missed here at home. Fa, as she remembered, was charitable to a fault in his judgments even as he lacked the ability to confront suffering—hers, his own, or anyone's—and he took great joy in Eliza's many successes. Maybe this was as good as it would ever be: loved and accepted, but never reconciliation or accounting of the traumas of the past. Eliza couldn't imagine sharing with him the events that had driven her from home so long ago. Years of absence hung separately in a parallel zone—not forgotten but somehow invisible, at least for now.

Christmas decorations in hospital hallways and patient doors served as her only indication of the season. Ed, alone in his home on the lake, came to visit Shannon twice in the days since Eliza's return home. Though he offered for her to stay with him and Edith at the lake, Eliza remained at Shannon's apartment. She wanted to be close by. If she could have, she would've slept at the hospital, as Mother and Fa had done when Shannon had been upstairs in the TB ward years ago.

DECEMBER 25, TEMPERATURES HUNG ABOVE freezing, and rain showers washed away most of the glistening snow that had blanketed the city since her arrival. The ground had become muddy gray, and low clouds boxed the city in, forcing people to accept the loss of a White Christmas. After four days, the twenty-year-old memories followed a few steps behind her, like shadows not quite within her reach, but teasing and ever-present.

Shannon remained unconscious, though the attending doctor told Eliza there had been moments of lucidity in the late hours of the night before. He warned her that Shannon faced bigger hurdles in her recovery that had little to do with consciousness. A rib had shattered and tore her lung. The tear itself wasn't too serious, not quite a puncture; but the vestiges of old surgeries made her vulnerable. She didn't have enough capacity to fight back should infection occur.

Nurse Jeanne poked her head into the room. "Eliza, Shannon was awake for more than an hour last night. I heard her murmuring time after time, 'Jesus Mary and Joseph-.' Hard to understand with the tube, but she was wide awake and looking around. I think she was asking for you and her rosary. I didn't know she was so devout. We all think of her as a free spirit—or I should say, a reclusive free spirit. She's one of a kind." She winked at Eliza. "We love her."

"Thank you, Nurse. We can only hope." Eliza couldn't help but believe this meant Shannon knew she was here. "How is Mr. Ross doing?"

"He's doing much better. He'll be good to go in a couple of weeks. In a wheelchair, though. Maybe for a long time." She sighed. "Just when they'd found each other. It's all terrible. My shift is over, but I wanted you to know we didn't see her rosary anywhere in her belongings, so if you can find it ... I won't be back here until after New Year's Day. God bless you, dear. And here's to peace at home and abroad in 1967." She raised the medicine cup in her hand as if to toast Eliza before leaving. A simple reminder that despite what was happening in her singular world, life was going on everywhere else.

Eliza hoped she'd see more of Miriam at the hospital in the days following her arrival. She was hungry for more information but didn't know where or how to find it. *Who*, as Nurse Jeanne said, had *found each other*? Shannon and Mr. Ross? She didn't understand. They must have known each other for years while he was a married man. What had Shannon done? She was his employee. Not only that ... she was a nurse who'd spent years nannying a grown girl because Shannon didn't have a life of her own. This was the story Eliza had told herself for years whenever

Harvey mentioned Shannon. Truthfully, she preferred her own version because the pain of hearing about Shannon's real life—happy or not—was far too dangerous for Eliza.

She stopped in to see Mr. Ross each morning, but only once found Miriam in the room. Miriam visited Shannon daily as well, and each time Eliza sensed the girl's unease. Or perhaps it was Eliza, who, unable to patch the reality of their relationships together, felt uncomfortable. Ed and Fa told her that Shannon and Allan were to be married. They'd heard the news the night of the accident. Neither had met Allan before. The engagement was almost as new to them as it was to her.

Remarkable, Eliza thought, and sad. If Nell were alive, none of this would be a mystery at all; they'd know this man. If he wasn't suitable, they'd protect Shannon. Did he love Shannon or was he after something? Was it a marriage of convenience since his wife had apparently left him? Or had he left her? Throughout these years, Eliza had expected that her family remained as close-knit as they'd always been before that terrible year. But all signs indicated otherwise. The remaining Malone family had shrunk to little more than a set of individuals leading separate lives, intersecting only because of proximity and an increasingly distant, shared past.

The time spent with Miriam at the hospital didn't help to move her beyond the inexplicable discomfort she felt. Was it distrust? Intuition? She knew well enough it was unbecoming and perhaps unjustified, but she also imagined there could be a good reason to not trust Miriam or Allan. She simply hadn't figured it out yet. On her first visit with Allan, he'd startled her by clasping her hand in both of his and, almost involuntarily, pulling her close to him in the hospital bed.

"Sorry," he'd said, and she noticed his Scottish accent. "So very sorry." He'd surveyed his body from his propped-up position and chuckled dryly. "Nothing here drives like it used to. So, you are the famous Eliza. My, we have much to talk about when Shann and I get free from here. How is she today, Eliza? Have you been to see her?"

"Yes, of course. I've been with her all day. She's still unconscious." She'd wanted to scream at him to be dour, to not make light, to shed tears for both her and Shannon. To mourn for himself, his daughter, his daughter's absent mother. "I stopped by to introduce myself. I should get back to Shannon before visiting hours end. Do you need anything?"

"Oh, so many things," he'd said, more solemnly than Eliza expected, then he'd sighed and winced as if even that caused pain somewhere. "I'm not much of a praying man, but I do so daily with hopes the Good Lord hears me. I need Shannon more than I need my legs, my arms ... She's my heart, my life."

Eliza had stepped back unevenly, her heart not anticipating the unbecoming claws of regret and envy.

Later, when she stopped by Allan's room again, Miriam had gone, and he was asleep. Instead of leaving, she went in and stood near his bed. She looked at him, noted his slow, steady breathing and wondered whether the accident had added many years to his face. He looked as old as Fa—or at least how she remembered Fa before coming back home. It would make sense, she thought. Fa had been in his early forties when she left. He was sixty-something now. Allan was mature and handsome, even in the hospital bed with bandages on his face. She could understand why Shannon might trust a face such as his. But what about the man himself? Did he deserve Shannon's trust? He must have left his wife. That didn't sound trustworthy. Was he after Shannon's inheritance? Was he a philanderer? A womanizer? Miriam clearly didn't think so. But of course she wouldn't. She was his only child. Eliza remembered the girl telling her she'd not seen her mother since April. Allan stirred and his mouth fell open. Asleep, he turned his head so it faced Eliza. Eliza felt the intimacy of the moment like an invasion, and, of course, it was her own doing.

On Christmas afternoon, Eliza returned again to Fa's home in Merriam Park. The two walked side by side to the cemetery to visit Nell and Grandpa Theo's graves. She prayed for them both, then stifling an unexpected sob with fingertips to her lips, she searched in vain for another headstone, one for her newborn infant.

They had supper at home and attended evening Mass at the campus chapel. Later, Eliza returned to Shannon's apartment, sat on the side of the bed, and allowed her tired mind to wander. Visits home without Mother had left her with a cool edge of emptiness and nostalgia. It was as if a layer of translucent, ash-gray paint had sunk into every wall and surface—such was the absence of vibrancy that had once filled the rooms. At least the kitchen, which had grown in her memory into a cave-like room filled with sharp corners, cold-metal rods, and dark cupboards, was no longer scary but benign. If ghosts from her past lingered, they were no longer menacing, just sad.

Fa was happy enough, immersed in his books, his research, his writing. Was it anything more than a curse to find comfort in old literature written for children of another era? But then again, it was surely less damaging than her solitary version of escape.

As her thoughts wandered, she took in the details of Shannon's bedroom, with her neatly organized books, her easel, and the silly, old doll collection, most of which had come from Grandma Edith decades ago. A series of abstract paintings, each a different color theme—blue, red, orange, yellow—and each covered with a watery veneer of white tones, hung on the walls with little blank space between. Eliza found them complex and pleasing and wondered if Shannon had painted them.

She recognized the matching nightstands—they'd been part

of the set from one of Grandma Edith's guest rooms at the lake house. She opened the single drawer of the nightstand closest to her, surprised to find the rosary, twin to the one she'd buried in storage years ago, strewn on a pile of letters in light-pink envelopes and tied with a ribbon. Something stirred in her, stronger than a memory—an image pushing itself forward as if it were a photograph placed right in front of her eyes. Touching the sacred and familiar chain brought her back to the day she first walked the Stations of the Cross at the campus chapel, an adolescent girl preparing for Confirmation. A slow, deliberate path, observing fourteen carved reliefs of Jesus's progression from condemnation to burial, Mother and Fa had both joined her—a rare, precious moment of undivided attention; no Ed, no Shannon, only Eliza, twelve years old. Her exact thoughts as they stopped to pray at the fifth station: *I would have risked death, too, to help Jesus as he carried the cross. I would have understood His suffering, not as his needy disciples did, but as Veronica did when she offered her veil to wipe his brow.* Her capacity for wisdom, virtue and strength, she thought that day, would be limitless.

She set the letters down on top of the dresser, noticing that they consisted of two stacks. The first, a loosely bound set of the letters she'd written Shannon and those sent to her in return, all from the horrible months of 1946 and '47, the months of tuberculosis, pregnancy, despair. The other set, six inches thick and neatly bound, had each letter enclosed in one of the monogrammed envelopes Mother had given them as a Confirmation gift. The wide, white ribbon hung as if it had been untied often, partially blocking the address on the top letter.

More bricks, larger and darker, crumbled in her mind. She sat down again on the edge of the bed, first looking at each envelope, then putting it on the bed beside her. After a dozen, she fanned through the remaining stack, confirming that every single one bore the same inscription: *Eliza Malone, Ithaca, NY.*

The second packet included over a hundred letters written over the course of eighteen years. How Eliza used to argue with Shannon about her laziness when it came to correspondence, and yet it was Shannon who had diligently written, apparently year after year. Eliza now had in front of her an undelivered chronicle of lost years. She remembered her sorrow the day she'd read Shannon's letter requesting help with Miriam. Sorrow that Shannon had let go.

The first letter was dated February 4, 1948, several days after Eliza had sent Mother's diamond ring back to Shannon's hotel in New York with a brief, distant note. That was the day Eliza had sent word to Shannon that she wouldn't join her in New York City. The day she wrote her fragile, child-like sister that she wanted to be left alone. She needed time. She remembered it all. *I'll be in touch when I'm ready*—a firmly closed door. Those were the last words she'd written Shannon. She couldn't bear to start there.

She found a heavy sweater in Shannon's closet and took the stack of letters to the couch near the unlit fireplace where Miriam had sat the day Eliza had arrived. After removing each letter from its envelope, she unfolded it and set it to her right, face down as if she were preparing to review college term papers. She put the envelopes to her left, stacked precisely in the same order, although it hardly mattered. Outwardly calm, she fought both an urgent desire to know everything at once and an equally strong urge to put the letters back in the drawer, unread.

She picked up the third letter:

February 10th, 1948

Dear 'Lyza,
Happy Birthday, dear sister. The house is quiet; Fa is giving a big lecture on campus ... But we all remember

this is your day. Especially me.

I can't help but feel that each of us was jolted out of our very selves—Ed in the War, you with the pregnancy, me with TB—and now, although the house and rooms remain the same, the Malone family we knew and loved is gone, like a missing soldier. But today, Eliza, I can't stop thinking about you and your baby; I know if you'd seen her, as I did, you wouldn't be angry with me. Maybe you wouldn't agree, you would beg me to be rational, but I know you would understand.

Needing time to let the words sink in, she gathered a blanket around her, and, after a few moments, continued to read more of the letters describing Shannon's life.

March 21, 1948

… But Eliza, I have thought so much about you, and the worst for me is not knowing whether you left because Mother was angry and you wanted to escape, or because something horrible happened. I didn't think about it back then, but now I can't stop wondering if there was something else. It would be just like you to make a painful choice to protect someone else. David? Me?

Sometimes I daydream about finding your baby. I think about going to Catholic Services and tricking them into revealing the couple who've adopted her. All I want is to know her. It sounds crazy, but when the nurse brought her to the window that afternoon, I was sure God was present. Eliza, I'd been so close to death; I believed from that day on that He spared my life for a reason. I knew, and believe, He has a divine plan, and if I avail myself of it, His plan will bring her back to me—and somehow you

*as well. Why is it, Eliza, we are forced to give away our
babies before we even have a chance to consider another
option? Why is it this way? It seems tragic. At least to me,
today.*

Eliza relaxed her hands and sank deeper into the sofa; a curtain
of misunderstanding lifted, and she imagined Shannon as a young
woman with a scarred and infertile body. Eliza understood for the
first time how difficult it must have been for Shannon to witness
her own sister not only reject the pregnancy, but then relinquish
the infant as well. The closest possibility to a child of her own.
She prayed for the first time in twenty years it wasn't too late to
explain to Shannon in her own words why it had to be so.

April 28th, 1948

Dear Eliza!
   *I FOUND HER. Baby Miriam. Your baby, Miriam—
she is beautiful! I knew if I kept faith and constant, God
would show me ...*

Eliza stopped reading and put the letter down. She closed her
eyes. Questions, like a series of heavy doors opening into dark
caverns forced themselves to the front of her mind. Did Shannon
really discover her baby? Eliza knew this was impossible. Shannon's
grief, her own loss of motherhood, her irrational fixation ... *Was
Shannon unstable? Out of touch? How much does it matter now?*
Either way, Shannon had found a way to overcome the solitude
she'd always feared, and that Eliza had thrust upon her, knowing
full well her sister's fragility. Eliza's closely guarded walls came
crashing down. Shame melted into sorrow and rushed forth. Her
shoulders heaved and tears flowed in a torrent of tangled emotions
until she fell asleep.

She awoke close to dawn and continued reading all but the very last of the letters. Shannon's descriptions took her through Miriam's first years, through Shannon's depression when the Rosses left for Scotland and referenced her sanctuaries in nursing and painting during those years. Shannon described her shallowing relationship with Mother, Fa and Ed, until Mother's death in '61, and her deeper, more personal relationship with her faith, a hybrid of Catholicism, personal conviction, and a leaning to the non-denominational insistence of Dr. C.S. Lewis. Eliza was surprised to feel joy for her sister as she read about Shannon's reunion with Miriam, and again when she and Allan found love. The last one had been written only a week ago:

December 18th, 1965

Dearest Eliza,

I am sorry you will miss another Minnesota Christmas—although they have become bleak affairs for the Malone Family. Ed and Olivia will take the children to London again to stay with her sister's family (remember, they moved there in '56), Fa will stay at the lake with Grandma Edith. E and O will have a family 'holiday party' tonight, and E has warned us that Grandma Edith has an announcement to make. I have no idea what he's talking about, but somehow, it makes me nervous for her. He has developed a way of being a real know-it-all bully ... as I have explained in earlier accounts. I try to steer clear of his nonsense, and there are moments, like in the old days, when he is a fine brother ... only more serious than I ever thought possible. But what meddling could he and Olivia be up to? Does he want her to sell her house? Or move in with them? She is, as you can imagine, absolutely fine where she is at home, even if she is eighty and losing her hearing (but not, you can be sure, her eyesight! She still paints, and I sometimes go to the lake to join her in the old studio barn). Other than that, she is fit as a fiddle! (Please excuse the alliteration; I know you despise that! And excessive exclamations!! Ha!).

Eliza, you may notice I feel differently today. I cannot describe it except to say I am content. I feel "in my own skin" in a way I haven't for years. Since you left, I suppose. And even so much more. Miriam has recovered from the event I described in my last letter. We have grown closer than ever, even in the past week, and she is not only accepting of my engagement to Allan but also honestly happy for us. I think she didn't expect Allan and me to be as calm and accepting of her turmoil ... We asked her nothing of the details, except what she wanted to share. When it was over, really over (it took more than a week), she let us dote on her, and she also doted on us! She has recently learned to drive. We insist she chauffeur us everywhere. We already have enjoyed, amongst the three of us, the best holiday season I have had since childhood.

I believe, Eliza, you do want to come home; Harvey wrote me and says you will, someday ... and I am always hopeful. But I'm also accepting that perhaps God did not, after all, intend for me to be the agent of your return or your reconciliation with Miriam. I have put my life in the service of that effort. Willingly! I believed God spared me from death to bring you home, and to bring you and me together with Miriam. In truth, Miriam has been the child I could never bear, and she led me to the greatest happiness I could have imagined—one I fully believed was impossible for me. If anything, I do hope and pray you have found, or will find, a similar happiness. It is, I suppose, very much the same love Mother and Fa shared, or Grandpa Theo and Grandma Edith, though we might not have seen it for what it was back then. It makes me feel sad for Fa. I'll try to spend more time with him now that I'm leaving nursing for good (or at least, for now).

This may be the last letter, Eliza. As I look at this ridiculous pile of unmailed envelopes (at least I didn't put postage on—smile), I am tempted to destroy them. I want to let go of what I had long considered to be my life's purpose: to hang on to the invisible thread between us by holding on to Miriam, so I could somehow bring you home. I may have been mistaken all along. Or worse, I've failed. But even failures can have silver linings, isn't that right? I hope you'll understand.

Love always,
Shannon.

On her morning walk to Milner Hospital, Eliza stopped at St. Taddeus Church, where Shannon was a parishioner. She sat on a folding chair in the chilly vestibule, considering the irony of seeking comfort in the church. Looking back, she knew it was ageless Catholic dogma that had severed her from her family, her sister, her home. It was the unspoken mantle of shame reserved for an unwed, pregnant woman, regardless the reason. Compassion was parsed out in the shadows, within the sanctioned walls of places like Watermelon Hill, mostly by nuns who had no relatable experience. Or if they did, they hadn't shared it with her.

Eliza looked to the large, modern doors, pulled together with two fat locks to keep her from entering. What had the Church done to help her? The Bible was one thing—eventually, she'd returned to find comfort in a few of Jesus's parables, as she had in many childhood stories. *But the Catholic Church? The priests? Bishops? What good were they—the very ones who created the oppressive rules of secrecy and shame in the first place?* Yes, she took refuge in the rituals of Sunday Mass in Ithaca, but it had always felt, and did again now, like a Faustian bargain.

In painful isolation, she'd suffered the hidden and terrible damages of a war—a child wounded by the emotional trauma of a hero soldier—a devastating blow to her sense of self, her own humanity, which she had neither courted nor controlled. The Church had insisted a woman in this circumstance be pushed into the shadows, relinquish the child, and then be held accountable to an ordinary life. She couldn't even pray at her own baby's grave. Catholicism had made Eliza, her parents, her entire world complicit—everyone, it seemed, but Shannon—the path of secrecy, shame, and sacrifice was an unmarried woman's only choice. And so it was for Eliza—because Catholicism had been the world in which the Malone Family lived.

33

December 1965

Both as a patient and as a nurse, Shannon was no stranger to the challenges of a damaged body forced to lay on her back for days on end. Her back and limbs ached. She came back to consciousness at the pace of a snail, investing in fits of lucidity, only to feel the familiar discomforts of immobility and stiffness, nausea, and worst of all, anxious confusion.

Nurses monitored her hourly. At times, she could sense a colleague moving efficiently about her bed, checking pillows, the position of the endotracheal tube, fluid intake. The younger ones talked themselves through the five rights of medication: right patient, right drug, right dose, right route, and the right time.

Aside from wanting to heal her wounds, each nurse knew how much Shannon appreciated the precious value of a trained and steady hand. Caring for a fellow nurse was like homage paid to the universal grace of their calling.

Lenora came in at the beginning of the morning shift to check for hot spots on Shannon's backside where skin rubbed against fitted sheets forming abrasions. Left untreated, they became angry and dangerous bedsores. Shannon couldn't will her eyes open, but she recognized Lenora by her nasally Canadian accent and her way of calling her Miss Malone. "When will we get you up and out (*ah-ute!*), Miss Malone? You're missing all the fun— yet another snow storm's coming our way in the morning."

Shannon breathed in as deeply as she could before a knife-like pain stabbed her lung. "Christmas?" she whispered, fighting down a wave of nausea as the tube stroked her throat like a thick, itchy ribbon.

"Christmas, you say?" Lenora laughed and clapped her hands twice. "Finally, Shannon. I was hoping we could have a bit of a chat tonight. The ward is almost empty, and you know it gets sort of lonely on the night shift."

"Missed it?" Shannon fumbled the words, her speech thwarted by the tube. "Kissmas?"

"Yes, dear; it was yesterday, but don't you worry. I spoke with your beau down the hall and he said he would wait … You could have Christmas in July. The best news is that your lovely sister has been here every day, waiting for you." Lenora stood over Shannon and gently lifted her head a few inches so she could remove the pillow and replace it with a fresh one. "Not sure if she or anyone will make it tomorrow, though—it's a doozy coming. Worst of the winter, they say."

"Al'n?" Shannon squeezed her eyes shut. Her mind was clear, but word formation was a skill her mind wouldn't recognize. "Al'n's good?"

"He's doing so well, Shannon. Neither of you'll win medals for speed racing anytime soon, but he's getting strong for you. That's what he told me." Lenora had finished straightening Shannon's bed linens. She leaned into Shannon, squeezed her hand gently, and held it for a long moment while stroking a wisp of hair off her forehead with the palm of her other hand. "You can do it, Miss Malone. You can get strong again, eh?" She smiled. "For all of us? Get some rest, now. Doctor says the tube will come out tomorrow."

Shannon didn't want to fade back into sleep or unconsciousness. Allan was here. Eliza was here. Miriam was here. She had to stay awake, especially for Eliza. She had so much to tell her. She tried to concentrate on a single task, figuring out how many days she'd been in the hospital, but she couldn't do it. Every time she began counting from Sunday, the night of Ed's holiday dinner, her mind faltered, and she struggled to remember what she'd been figuring out in the first place.

It was a blessing she couldn't recall the accident, or any of the time in the car ride home. Thinking about Eliza, the years of anticipation, the memories of their last encounter, agitated her already disconnected thoughts. Instead, she pictured Allan. She imagined she was sitting at her easel next to Grandma Edith at the lake house with Allan posing in front of her like a professional artist's model. She studied every detail of his face, his jowl, his neck, shoulders, back, forearms. In a near dream-state, she reached out to touch his hand, to feel and memorize again every ligament and bone.

~⌒~

Lucidity returned, the tube was gone, and Eliza was there, reading aloud from *Windswept*, the very same book Eliza had given her in the TB Ward years ago, weeks before everything changed.

Eliza must have found it in her bedroom. Shannon had reread it in the days before Allan and Miriam returned from Scotland.

"I can't imagine us ever enjoying this novel, Shannon," Eliza said to her when Shannon opened her eyes. She brought the chair closer to the bedside and took her hand.

Shannon smiled when she saw Eliza bite the right side of her bottom lip—some things don't ever change.

"It's overly dramatic and poorly edited. Far too many characters."

"Please, read more for now…" Shannon whispered, barely recognizing her own voice. Shannon assumed that her sister felt the same lightness of body that she did—as if her innermost self recalled a lost way of being, a long-forgotten form, and was re-aligning itself back to its natural state. She imagined that through locked palms they both emanated a bright aura of light, like an endless blue sky, backlit by the sun. She remembered Eliza climbing into bed with her and holding her the day she left home for Milner Hospital, terrified of dying. Time passed and Eliza read, though Shannon had no idea for how long.

"… *By the time the spring darkness had fallen, Jan knew Anna's letter by heart. It was strange, he thought, as the stars came slowly out and the air grew cold, how one could never get oneself quite ready for sadness. One could know for months and years that sadness must come, and yet one was never ready for it when it came. All the good food a man could eat could not prepare his heart against its sickness. All the good thoughts one could think could not save one's mind from the pain which the very act of unasked for living made sure and certain* …" Eliza closed the book, leaned back, resting her head on the high back of the chair, and closed her eyes.

"Don't stop, Eliza," Shannon murmured, unsure if Eliza heard.

After a moment, Eliza opened her eyes and reached into the pocket of her cardigan, pulling out something that Shannon couldn't see.

"*Dearest Shannon,*" Eliza began, and Shannon knew it was a letter.

"*I have received your letters. You must know how grateful I am that you didn't destroy them. I'm overwhelmed with all that I've missed in your life. We'll spend days catching up, darling sister. I promise!*

"*But first I'll tell you, once and for all, the circumstances that led me to leave home in '48. To my self-exile ...*" Here, Eliza stopped reading. "Shannon, I don't know if I should ... if I even can ..."

"Yes, Eliza," Shannon whispered. She squeezed her sister's hand again.

Eliza put the letter down and closed her eyes. Shannon did the same.

"Shannon, please listen. I'm not sure ..." A calm silence followed. When Eliza spoke, her voice was low and quiet as if she were recalling a long-forgotten dream. "Just before New Year's Eve. I was alone in the house. I was in the kitchen. I saw the beam of a flashlight shine across the backyard and thought maybe it was Ed. But I heard my name and recognized the voice. I didn't know it when I went to the door, but he was drunk and forced his way into the kitchen. Not David, Shannon. He smelled sharp and horrible, alcohol mixed with sweat and dirt. I tried to get him to leave, but he was crazed. Nothing I said stopped him. He pulled me in and pinned my body against him as he leaned against the door. He put a knife to the side of my throat." Eliza's voice quickened, "He begged over and over, 'Forgive me, Eliza, please forgive me.' I was too terrified to speak, so I shook my head, no. No! I couldn't speak those words. I don't know why, Shannon, I don't know why I couldn't. Maybe I thought if I said yes, he would kill me. Or ... I don't know? Kill himself? I couldn't think straight, and then he pushed me to the floor, and with the knife at my neck, he pressed his mouth to mine so hard my lip bled. I could feel the hair on his jaw, stiff, sharp bits of wire tearing at my cheek. ... Shannon, I've never been honest with myself, with anyone, about … all of it. Never."

Eliza stopped. She leaned close to Shannon, took her hand in both of hers, and a moment passed. "It was Patrick. David's cousin." She hesitated and stifled a sob before continuing, "He held the knife again to my throat. I didn't move a muscle. His other hand was—" She stopped again. "On my breast. He tore to get under the sweater David had … I couldn't even close my eyes. He forced himself into me. His odor was rank and savage and stung my throat when I inhaled—I can still smell him now, Shannon. Here."

Shannon thought she'd finished, but Eliza continued, "I prayed to make it stop, and when it didn't I prayed to black out instead. When it ended, he let his weight fall on me; I thought he'd passed out, but then he moved. He pulled a damp cloth from a pocket and held it over my mouth. I welcomed it. How long I'd prayed for it. When I woke up, I was on the kitchen floor, and he was gone. Every day was like a battle. I tried to focus on school. At St. Kate's everything was good and right. But me, in me … everything was wrong."

Shannon gripped Eliza's hand tighter.

"I thought everything might be all right after I heard Mrs. Perkins speak at U of M. I thought I could excel at something important; I could be the old Eliza again if I narrowed my focus. But I couldn't. I forced his attack out of my mind, but the smells, my terror, my fear that it could happen again, they were everywhere at first. And not, of course … there was no escaping the pregnancy, the baby." Eliza sighed heavily and rubbed a spot above her eyebrow, covering her face with her hand. She rested her elbow on the bed railing.

Shannon opened her eyes and gripped Eliza's hand, imagining the aura of light growing dim.

"Watermelon Hill was hell. Only a few bright spots. None I can recount. I was confused and ashamed and lonely. I missed you at first, but it turned to resentment, and then even *you* angered me. Your expectations that I would want the … I tried not to blame you, but you acted so naive." Eliza went quiet. "And worst of all …"

Shannon opened her eyes and saw Eliza watching her.

"Shannon, I felt only hate for the baby." Eliza shook her head, and Shannon felt her sister's anguish as if it were her own. "I was constantly sick. My body was monstrous and ugly. When the day came and I was taken to the hospital, I waited for hours. I was feverish and scared. And so angry. I remember so little, although I think you were there for a moment, weren't you? That night, after my fever broke, an old nurse came in. She put my baby girl on my chest. 'You don't have to look at her, Miss Malone,' she said, 'but this infant has taken a fever. She may return to her Maker. I will be damned if I don't give her the warmth of at least one embrace from her mother.'

"Only a monster could say no. I wasn't expecting it. It engulfed me—she engulfed me. Of course I looked at her. I held her. I memorized her face. I touched her wisp of brown hair, stroked her small and perfect fingers." Shannon watched as Eliza—her eyes downcast—reached out as if to touch her baby's forehead. "And then her cheek, already hot with fever. I felt her heart beating, my chest to hers, Shannon. I don't remember what happened next, but I was changed. Despite everything, she was unforgettable, undeniable. She was mine. And I loved her."

Eliza straightened her back in an effort to regain composure, but instead gulped for air trying to force back sobs. She gripped Shannon's hand, careful even now not to hold it too tightly. A long moment passed.

"I named her, Shann. No one would ever, ever know, but I named her Thea; after Grandpa; after our baby brother," she whispered, her head still bowed, looking intently at her own hand, holding Shannon's on the bedside. "It was so faint, but she was breathing." Eliza seemed to be holding her breath as if breathing would revive the anguished moment even further. "I don't know how much time passed, but the same nurse returned. I suppose it couldn't have been more than five minutes, but Shann, holding her, I felt her as part of me, as more than me. But when the nurse looked at her, she gasped, 'God have mercy, child; she's …' But she didn't finish her thought; she took her from my arms and rushed her away. When she came back, she told me to never breathe a word of it. I wasn't sure what she meant, but it didn't matter. I knew I could never speak of that night.

"Three days later I went home, and Mother and I argued about my plan to attend Cornell. Before our fight, Shann, as I was leaving her, I asked if the baby had died. She told me what happened was for the best, that what happened was the will of God. So, it was true; my baby whom I'd hated for nine months and loved for one moment, was … you see, I killed her. How else could I explain it?"

Her sister's grip slackened. Shannon pictured an eighteen-year-old and frightened Eliza, who now, no longer alone, could let go of the last bricks in her crumbling fortress and bury her head in Shannon's injured chest.

Shannon stroked Eliza's hair and whispered, "But Eliza, what if the baby didn't die?" She felt Eliza's shoulders tighten and release as she emitted a long, quiet whimper, like that of an exhausted wounded animal. Shannon couldn't move her head, but shifted her eyes to the space behind Eliza's chair, where Miriam stood holding a bouquet of privet berries and holly, Mother's favorite, bound with a red plaid ribbon.

Epilogue

January 1966. Milner Hospital, Intensive Care Unit

n ancient memory comes to her: She is in the recovery room with Mother and Fa after her hysterectomy; the surgery that robbed her of motherhood, the one that left her close to God, close to death and far away from childhood. Though she wants to, she cannot open her eyes because the light is too bright. Painfully bright, as if she were facing the sun. From that long-ago place, she dreams of Princess Irene and Eliza. And the baby. The baby who would bring Eliza home.

Shannon's back is healing. Certain moves send sharp daggers into her spine and even stillness is accompanied by a dull, constant ache. A shard from a shattered rib has pierced her already diminished lung so breathing, too, is difficult. *It will get better soon*, she thinks; *I know how human pain operates.* Part of her, the part that observes, struggles to remember how long ago the morphine was administered.

Shannon yearns for Nell—not as her earthly mother, but as the spirit Shannon had come to love in a knowing, unchildish way, the way, maybe, Mother had always loved her, but had been unable to show.

Now, Shannon imagines herself upstairs in the solarium at Grandma Edith's house on Lake Minnetonka. She sees herself at the mahogany writing desk; the one Mother used every summer to write notes and letters to friends when the girls were children. She sees herself, and in doing so, becomes one with her hallucination.

From this perch in the large, sunlit room, she looks out the paneled bay windows to the lake. Dozens of small, fast-moving clouds in an endless blue sky reflect their perfect whiteness onto the serene, silvery water. The old dock has been repaired. She can see Ed's boys racing up and down its planks, trying to catch sun-ray fish with balls of bread cast on shiny metal hooks. Fa sits near the dock box he crafted with Grandpa Theo ages ago, occasionally looking up from his book. Grandma Edith works in her garden, digging holes for new rose bushes. Allan, her beloved Allan, sits nearby in his wheelchair, holding a rose bush, waiting for instructions and charming her grandmother with his Scottish wit. She is pleased to see his cane nearby. He will practice walking and recover as he should.

Two gentlemen walk alongside Eliza to the water's edge, and Shannon recognizes one as Harvey. Maybe the other is David Whitaker. She hopes so, but he's facing the lake and she can't be sure. She watches and wonders whether Eliza knows she's upstairs looking down. The sun impedes her vision, but when the man, not Harvey, embraces Eliza and kisses each of her cheeks and they throw their heads back in laughter, Shannon laughs too. The two men walk away from the shore, turn around, waving to Eliza. The man who could be David blows her a single long kiss as she turns away from them, laughing, smiling. Eliza takes Miriam by the hand and they walk to the dock. They pull the rowboat close to the edge and get in, one after the other, and row to the center of the bay in front of the house.

Shannon finds a key taped underneath Mother's desk, and unlocks and opens the center drawer of the writing desk. She takes out a crudely made wooden box with a hinged lid and inspects it. She smiles, pleased to find the contents. What if someone had found them and thrown them away?

The yellowed newspaper clipping is partially ripped in the middle where it had been folded over, probably decades ago. It is just as she'd first discovered it, months after Nell's death. The article is brief, just a few paragraphs, from the *Duluth Gazette, August 18, 1923, "Man, Two Children Perish in House Fire."* The man, new to Duluth, had been drunk and the twins, a boy and girl, motherless. Shannon knows now this was Nell's widowed father and her two young siblings. She removes the article, along with a handful of fragments from a broken teacup wrapped in a handkerchief, a garnet rosary, and a faded photograph in a felt frame of a hefty and ruddy-faced old woman with ankles and wrists thick as tree trunks. The woman in the photograph, Nell's grandma, whom Shannon had only heard her mother mention once, sits on a wicker rocking chair in front of a wooden house in a field with several large trees scattered about. She looks intelligent and kind—out of place in the dusty bleakness around her. Shannon places the three items in a cluster on the blotter of the writing table and turns her attention back to the lake.

She finds Grandpa Theo's binoculars on the low bench along the window so she can watch Eliza and Miriam as their boat floats aimlessly in the bay. She leans forward, watching as Eliza reaches into her pocket, her hand emerging with something, which she gives to Miriam. It must be the ring Fa gave to Mother on their wedding day, the ring Grandpa Theo gave to Grandma Edith when Fa was born. It's the ring Mother gave to Eliza the night before she left for good and which Eliza then sent back to Shannon in New York. But to Shannon, it's the ring she made magical with a spool of thread in the long afternoons with Miriam, when her niece was a small child.

"There you are, princess!" the child would squeal, clapping her hands, and gathering the silver thread bound to the magical ring, then throwing herself on Shannon as she crouched behind the sofa. "I rescued you again! My turn to be saved!"

Shannon cannot see Eliza or Miriam but knows they are both close by. She knows Nell is near. Shannon senses that many women who know her are gathering around her, and believes she knows their stories like she knows Eliza and Miriam's, and even Virginia's and Grandma Edith's. Like she knows her own. She mourns the truth she'd once been blind to but can no longer deny, for alongside Nell and Nell's young Ma, in the arms of Nell's grandma, is Eliza's newborn, the baby she named Thea, the baby who died at birth.

For a moment, her story angers her, a wasted life she created from her odd, stubborn faith, her foolish belief in a fairy tale. Mother steps forward and strokes her cheek. "Shannon, Baby Thea died that night. But don't fret, child. She is loved. She was always loved." Overwhelmed, Shannon wants to grasp her mother's hand, but she's too weak and can't. Instead, she memorizes each feature of Mother's peaceful face, so as to never forget. So as to give her courage for what she sees ahead.

Mother knows her thoughts and nods toward the window overlooking the yard. "But no, Shann, my dear child, it's not your time to join me. You mustn't leave Eliza. Nor Miriam. Nor Allan. This is what your love has brought." A glow of maternal pride, an affirmation Shannon never felt before, washes over her.

"Shannon, are you here?" She hears Eliza and imagines her sister ascending the grand staircase at the lake house. "Shannon, can you see me? Can you see Miriam?"

"I'm here, Eliza," Shannon says, "I'm right here in the sun room." The room becomes intensely white before the brilliance recedes. Shannon sees blurry forms of people gathered by her hospital bedside. She reaches out with both hands and two women each take one. She knows which hand is Eliza's and which one is Miriam's by the feel of their skin. She feels Grandpa Theo's ring on Miriam's finger and uses her thumb to touch the cool gems. Though she has barely enough breath to speak, Shannon knows that her sister is finally home and they will be together again. "Eliza, do you remember the story?"

"I remember, Shannon."

"I was the magical grandmother," she says, "and you were Princess Irene. Next time, I will be the Princess—" She laughs a small laugh that only she and Eliza can hear.

A Note from the Author

Did you enjoy my book?

If so, I would be very grateful if you could write a review and publish it at your point of purchase.

Your review, even a brief one, will help other readers to decide whether or not they will enjoy my work.

About Frances Perkins

Frances Perkins (1880 – 1965) was an American sociologist and workers-rights advocate who served as the U.S. Secretary of Labor from 1933 to 1945. As a loyal supporter of Franklin D. Roosevelt, she helped pull the labor movement into the New Deal coalition. Perkins played a key role in the cabinet by writing New Deal legislation, including minimum-wage laws. Her most important contribution, however, came in 1934 as chairwoman of the President's Committee on Economic Security (CES). She worked tirelessly for the U.S. adoption of social security, unemployment insurance, federal laws regulating child labor, and adoption of the federal minimum wage.

She remained in office for the entirety of Roosevelt's presidency, becoming not only the first woman appointed to the U.S. Cabinet, but the longest serving secretary in that position. She also became the first woman to enter the presidential line of succession.

Following her government service career and after the death of her husband, Perkins remained active as a teacher and lecturer at the New York State School of Industrial and Labor Relations at Cornell University until her death in 1965 at age 85.

For the purposes of this story, I have fictionalized various elements of Mrs. Perkins life, such as her lecture at University of Minnesota in 1947 at which Eliza first meets her, and the actual timing of her work at Cornell, which began in 1957. The date of her death, while approximately correct, is also inaccurate in this novel. Finally, for many years while at Cornell, she lived at the Telluride House, an intellectual community of students and faculty, primarily men.

Acknowledgments

I now understand why novels have acknowledgments, for it's been a journey marked by plenty of alone-ness, but also a near constant need for support – emotional reassurance, skillful critiquing, diplomatic listening as my story was written and unwritten, rewritten and better written—over what must seem to anyone involved, an interminable, self-torturing pathway.

Bruce, my husband, is a better editor than I deserve. Angie was first and fiercest in her conviction I would cross the finish-line, followed closely by Gayle. Eliza was steadfast in her honesty as only a fellow novelist can be. Kathy, Lori, Traci, Alice, Mary, Eraine, Dagmar (who-drove-to-Volunteer-Park-everyday-to-read!), Denise, Amy, Carly, Christine, Steve-each took on the task of beta reading at various, unsightly stages. Each lovingly provided suggestions, corrections, ideas that helped me bring it to a place where I am proud to say it is the story I want to tell. Most of all, they encouraged me. And for that, I am truly grateful. Molly Schulman's professional services delivered with immense heart and wisdom made my writing better, and Tahlia Newland can't be thanked enough for her final refinement, her on-going advice and her commitment to making *A Thread So Fine* as good as it can be. A final word of appreciation is due for Hugo House in Seattle and the many instructors who've taught me the art of the novel.

About the Author

Susan Welch grew up in Minnesota and Wisconsin with either her nose in a book or her toes in the water. Always a writer, Susan often attempts to solve her problems in third person, creating fictionalized versions of herself and the main characters in her life—mostly in her head, but sometimes on paper. Nearly a decade ago, in the days after discovering her own adoption story for the first time, she turned to her imagination to trick her reeling mind so she could get a good night's sleep. *A Thread So Fine* was born of those creative threads weaving into nocturnal dreams as she struggled to re-write the beginning of her own life story. Shannon and Eliza, Nell and Miriam are much loved fabrications, layered with truths and insights about her cherished mother, her brave birth mother, her beloved mother-in-law, her younger sister, and herself. Susan lives with her husband Bruce in Washington State.

CPSIA information can be obtained
at www.ICGtesting.com
Printed in the USA
LVHW110411271119
638407LV00001B/3/P

9 781733 848503